Grants Ferry

This is a work of fiction and as in all fiction
literary perceptions, observations, and created situations
are based on the author's experience.

References to any real persons, their actions,
beliefs, or behaviors are entirely products of
the author's imagination and have no basis in fact.

ISBN: 978-1477538319
ISBN: 10: 1477538313

Other Work by David Chase

A Peasant of West Brattleboro
Selections from his column in the *Brattleboro Reformer*

As Fair As You Were
A stageplay in three acts

Cover art: David Chase
Cover layout and design: Debra Wright

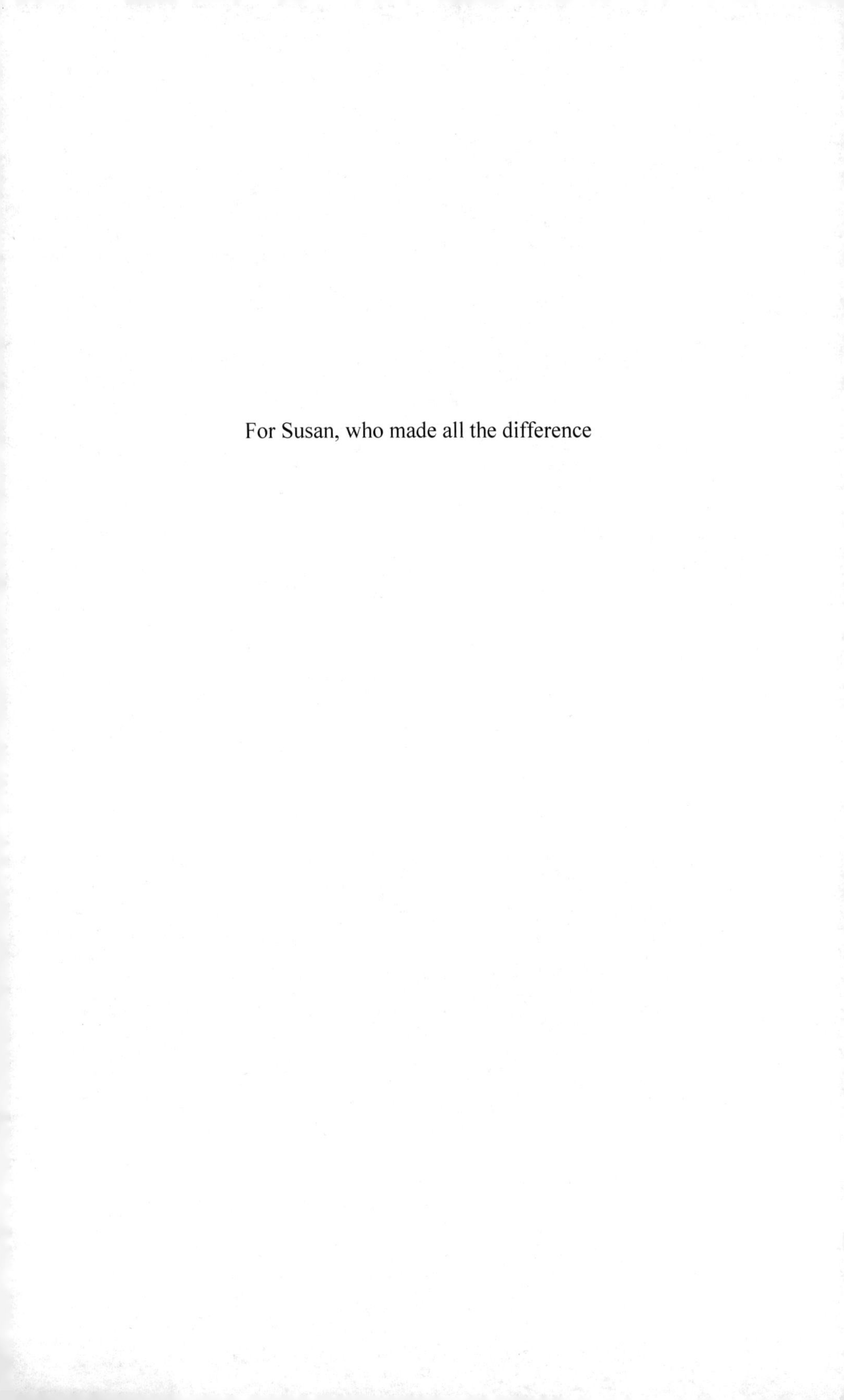

For Susan, who made all the difference

Chapter One

1998

It was a Thursday.

The downstairs clock chimed six and two big cats bounded up the stairs, into Fanny's bedroom, and onto her bed. One of them bit her toe.

"Stop that," she said, but her words were muddy. The cats clomped up the bed toward her head. "Oh, go away." Again the words were thick, as if wads of cotton were packed beside her tongue. She turned on the lamp and the light hurt her eyes. There were two images of her alarm clock. Each was clear but when she tried to bring the two together it made her dizzy. Fanny Forbes was many things but no one would ever suggest she was dizzy. Dizziness implied a lack of control and that was unacceptable.

She sat up and her stomach took a menacing turn. For the first time in years Fanny thought she might throw up. She lay back down, closed her eyes, and let the nausea pass. Her confusion and discomfort turned to fury. She was being kept from her schedule and nothing fired Fanny's determination more than being denied. She sat up again and opened her eyes. Without warning this time the vomit rose up and sprayed six feet. It landed on the cherished hand hooked rug her grandmother had made before Fanny was born and spattered beyond onto the cherry floor.

They were the most intense, wrenching spasms Fanny had ever experienced. She fell back on the bed, exhausted and confused, her eyes closed. Every muscle from her shoulders to her knees felt as if it had been stretched and torn loose. With her eyes closed, however, her head didn't spin and she could gather her wits. Perspiration ran off her forehead and her nightgown clung to her damp, clammy body. The bed was wet, too, from urine that escaped during the vomit attack.

She moaned, kept her eyes shut and worked to steady her breathing. She needed to make her eyes work together. That's what caused the dizziness. Perhaps if she used just one at a time… She held a hand over her left eye and cautiously opened the other. Her stomach didn't resist and she sat up again. The two cats were on the floor inspecting the vomit.

"Shoo! Get away!" Fanny waved her free arm at them but her voice had no strength and the cats ignored her. She knew she should clean up the vomit but if she left the cats alone she'd have less to do later, a thought that both surprised and disgusted her. She stood up with her hand over her left eye.

"Shoo! Shoo!" she said again but it was no use. Her eyes – she needed her eyes. She lowered her hand for a second but her stomach lurched and she quickly covered it again.

Her nightgown stuck to her skin and was cold against her legs. She had to get downstairs to the phone. People at church had been after her for years to put a second phone upstairs but she'd not wanted to spend the money. More than one phone in the house was not only unnecessary, but decadent. The concept of convenience was not familiar to Fanny, and besides, she was still furious with the phone company for converting to the dial system. With the old exchange she could just pick up the phone and have Olive Trombley ring up anyone she wanted. For a number of months after the conversion Fanny had tried without success to discount her phone bill since she was now required to do the dialing, a job she felt still belonged to the phone company.

She walked unsteadily into the hall. At the top of the stairs, without thinking, she uncovered her eye and reached for the handrail on the left side of the staircase. The dizziness came back at once. Her right foot went over the edge of the top step and landed hard on the next. She heard the crack as her ankle snapped but then she was tumbling end over end until she stopped in a twisted heap at the foot of the stairs.

*

Archie Whitaker stood at his kitchen window with a mug of coffee. He savored this quiet time before day began, a habit begun when his Uncle Henry lived with them. Henry was Archie's father's brother and he'd come after a medical discharge from the Army. Henry was a quiet man, often content to sit and stare at nothing for hours.

At night, though, Henry's nightmares brought screams that cut through the house like a buzz saw. Henry remembered none of it. He woke early, completely refreshed, and began the day with his coffee in the kitchen. He enjoyed Archie's company. Some days he liked to talk. Occasionally it made sense, other times it didn't, but Archie and Henry developed a particular bond during these early hours. When Archie came down one morning and found the kitchen still dark he knew at once that Henry had died and his demons couldn't haunt him anymore.

Archie had continued to get up early for years and had eventually installed timers so the coffee was always brewed and the light was on when he came downstairs, just as it was when Henry was alive.

It was a pleasant view to the southeast from the window over the sink and Archie could watch the first suggestion of dawn or the first rays of sunlight as they came over the hill across the river in New Hampshire, an ideal way to start the day. No talking, no questions, nothing but quiet and a strong cup of coffee. When he let his mind go free, he sometimes heard his Uncle Henry rambling on about the nature of things, things most people care nothing about.

There had been another frost. Henry might launch into Ecclesiastes and quote the parts about a time to plant and a time to reap. Henry loved Ecclesiastes. Ecclesiastes may have been the one thing that gave Henry some sense of balance to the mysterious life in which he found himself.

Archie had accepted the Ecclesiastes philosophy as well and had never run out to cover garden plants with sheets when frost warnings were posted. It only worked occasionally anyway and it was a pain in the ass. It also looked as if the yard was full of ghosts when he looked out the window in the morning.

This frost was a hard one. He could see it in the driveway and on the garage roof. A frost like this would sweeten the Brussels sprouts. The kale and the chard would like it, too, but the summer vegetables were gone.

Archie had bought this house from his parents and married Ellen that same year. Their life together had been good, he thought, although the goodness of his life was not something Archie had ever examined too closely. Some things, he reasoned, were probably best left unexamined.

There was little passion in their marriage but neither was there anger or bitterness. All in all, he thought, the twenty-seven years with Ellen had been good ones. Their children, Mark and Janet, were grown, married, and moved away. Archie didn't know whether Ellen was happy or sad about that. Were they having lives that she wished she'd had? She'd never said and he'd never asked. Still, he wondered…

An addition to Archie's morning routine was Hank, a curious blend of hound, shepherd, collie, and lab. Herb Johnson's dog, Bonnie, had delivered yet another batch of pups seven years ago, eight of them, all from different fathers.

Archie had never been too tight with dogs but when he saw the puppies they were about six weeks old. A brownish short-hair with big paws and bushy eyebrows rushed over to greet him.

"There's something about this one, isn't there?" Archie said. "Works his eyebrows just like my Uncle Henry did."

"I remember Henry," Herb said. "Bit of an odd duck, but nice fella, I always thought. Lived with you, didn't he?"

"...until he died, yup. I was still in high school..." The puppy watched Archie as he spoke. "You don't suppose Henry's come back inside this dog, do you?"

"S'possible, I s'pose."

"Damned if he don't remind me of Henry."

"I know you don't connect all that much with dogs," Herb said, "but I'll tell you, Arch, you'll never be sorry you took this one."

And that was that. Henry sounded like a goofy name for a dog so Archie called him Hank instead. Now, seven years later, he couldn't imagine a day without him. Hank rode in the truck, he joined him in the diner or offices or stores in town, and everybody liked the quiet, friendly dog with the big eyebrows. Some kept a supply of little doggy snacks for him.

Every morning Hank ran out and went about his rounds, moving methodically from one bush or marking post to the next, always the same order. With everything inspected and marked, Hank would finally begin his search for the perfect place to take his dump.

This was Archie's puzzle. Why was finding the right spot so important? Hank always picked a place within sight of the kitchen window, as if he knew Archie would be watching, and then he'd turn his back and assume the position. What was that about?

This would be typical of the mysteries that Henry would often discover and then try to solve. If everything else about the morning outing was the same and predictable, why was it so important to Hank that he find a different right spot to move his bowels each morning? Was there a pattern? Would it be possible to predict the next one?

Earlier in the summer Archie bought some graph paper and created a scale drawing of his yard. Every day for three months he marked and dated each of Hank's contributions. In the end it revealed nothing, even when Archie connected the dots. It was one of those dog secrets. Archie and Hank were about as close as two creatures could be, but Archie had a feeling that even if Hank could talk he wouldn't tell, any more than his Uncle Henry would.

Only in retrospect did Archie realize he had spent the better part of the summer recording the location of fresh dog shit. It didn't help when Ellen found the map.

"This is the reason you get up so early?"

"No, it's just something I did for a while."

"Did you learn anything from it?"

"Can't say I did."

Thanks to his Uncle Henry, Archie had spent countless hours in his adult life trying to solve mysteries such as this, not because the solution would mean anything or even contribute to the betterment of mankind, but simply because it might be possible.

Hank bounded away from a great steaming pile on the lawn, fully refreshed. Only the worming pills could put more spring in his step. Archie wished his own bowels were as predictable and the results as rewarding. It had been a long time since he'd last felt a spring in his own step. Some mornings it was an effort to heave himself out of bed.

Archie rinsed his cup, refilled it, and went back to the window. Hank was out beyond the garden eating some of the long grass by the fence. Apparently this was one of the days when he wanted to throw up.

"Hmm," Archie said. "I wonder if there's a pattern to that…"

*

That same Thursday Luther Pike had begun to rake up leaves from the maples in front of the elementary school. Luther held several positions in town. He was janitor at the elementary school, sexton at the Congregational Church, and he was custodian at the town offices which included maintenance of the town common. After fifteen years in his role at three of the town's institutions his place in Grants Ferry was secure.

Luther was not a big man – about five foot six – but he was solid. Years of manual labor had kept him fit and given him a stamina few men could match. Luther didn't chat. If a question couldn't be answered with a yup or nope or maybe he'd simply go along, not always a wise choice, but in the moment Luther was unable to make that distinction. Confrontation reduced him to mumbles or grunts.

Luther was determined to finish with the leaves and be gone before Mary Louise Turner appeared. Luther hated Mary Louise Turner. Mary Louise

Turner was the new principal of the grade school, a driven woman who worked long hours, demanded extra effort and perfection from her staff, and refused to reduce her expectations. She'd found extra chores for Luther to do around the school that had never been part of his job before she came. She insisted, for instance, that he take the leaves away almost as soon as they fell. Luther had always raked them into big piles so the kids could jump in them during recess for a few days before he hauled them away. Now they had to be cleaned up nearly every day. Mary Louise Turner wanted to change everything.

She was from Massachusetts and she had letters after her name. That was all Luther knew about her and that was enough. She came to work early and she left late. He'd hoped to avoid her this morning but it was hopeless. Her lime green Volkswagen growled up the street, ground around the corner, and lurched into the school parking lot. Mary Louise Turner drove her car as hard as she drove her staff and she was a woman without mercy. Luther swiped at the leaves and tried to ignore her but there was no escape.

The Volkswagen creaked with relief as Mary Louise pulled herself out. Now aside from everything else, it has to be told that Mary Louise Turner had an ass that would fill a barn door. Luther often wondered, when he allowed himself to speculate about such things, just how she fit in the car at all. Once he'd actually stolen a glance at the front of her skirt to see if the steering wheel had worn a thin spot. She reached back inside to retrieve the several bags she always carried and her long skirt hiked up in the back to reveal the two stout tree trunks that were her legs, not something Luther expected or wanted to see. She unplugged herself from the Volkswagen, stood up, and set off toward Luther in a great swirl of skirts and handbags.

"Oh, Mr. Pike!"

Luther played deaf but it never worked because Mary Louise Turner was a driven woman and deafness was no excuse.

"Oh, Mr. Pike!" she called again.

That was another thing that pissed him off. Nobody called him Mr. Pike except Mary Louise Turner.

"Mr. Pike, I'm so glad I caught you," she puffed. "Isn't this just a glorious day? Thank you so much for cleaning up so well. We so appreciate all you do for us."

Christ, it's like listening to a saw mill.

"I wondered if you might stop by my office when you finish, Mr. Pike? I have a small list of things that need attention. Perhaps we could just run through the list before the classes start?"

Luther nodded dumbly. There was no way he could avoid it.

Inside.

Her office.

Alone.

The very idea soured his stomach.

"Thank you, Mr. Pike. I truly don't know what we'd do without you." Mary Louise Turner put her soft round hand on his arm.

Luther froze, overcome with a mixture of panic, fear, confusion, and an unexpected tingling in his loins. He was unable to breathe.

Mary Louise flashed a smile from those big round cheeks and steamed off across the yard to the schoolhouse. Luther let the dizziness pass, caught his breath, and was finally able to speak.

"God damn her," he said.

Luther attacked the leaves again, hurriedly gathered up the corners of the tarp, and dragged it to the bank behind the school. When he turned to empty the leaves he saw that in his haste he'd let go one side of the tarp and had left a trail of leaves clear across the playground.

*

The Congregational Church's most reliable fundraiser was the annual Harvest Festival and once again Archie Whitaker was chairman. The weeks prior had been filled with furious last minute preparations, meetings, and phone calls. Archie never physically did anything but he needed to manage people. Every year it grew more difficult and every year he swore it would be his last. Of course, no one else would step up and he'd figure if he didn't do it the whole festival would flop, the church would be in crisis, and it would be his fault.

His last few nights had been restless ones. He'd wake up and run lists, sometimes like a continuous loop. This year was it, though – time to hand it off to someone else, someone with more energy than Archie had anymore.

It was 9:15. He and Hank had settled into their booth at Dot's Diner, Archie on one side, Hank on the other. Dot plated up a doughnut and coffee for Archie and a doughnut on a plate for Hank and brought it all to the table.

"You know, one day Hank's gonna be sitting there at the table when the State Health Inspector shows up. He's not gonna like it."

"Yeah, well…"

"You got a call." She pulled a cordless phone from her apron pocket. "Alice Crowley."

"Hey, Alice."

"Archie," Alice said, "I'm over at Fanny's. I think she's baked her last bean."

"What?"

"Looks like she came down the stairs ass over bandbox," Alice said. "Made quite a mess of herself."

"Aw, Jesus…" What next? "You okay, Alice?"

"I'm okay but I've seen Fanny look a lot better."

"Well, have Dennis pick her up. Increase will want to know, too."

"All right. I'll take care of that. What're we gonna do about beans?"

"Jesus, Alice, I don't know." Archie took off his Red Sox cap and scratched his head. "I'll find somebody. Just make the calls, okay?"

Dot was still by the table.

"Fanny's dead," he said. "Alice found her."

"Oh, my God…"

"Yeah. One more thing…" Archie tossed down his coffee. It was damned inconsiderate of Fanny to just drop dead that way. Death had a way of distracting people from the business at hand, and the business at hand at the moment was the festival.

"If she was going to do a header down the stairs," he said to Hank as they left the diner, "why didn't she wait until next week, for Christ's sake?" One damned thing after another. This was his last year. No question. Half an hour of phone calls later Margaret Ingraham agreed to two batches and Monica Pierce said she'd do the third. They were young women, though, and Archie hoped they knew what they were doing. He usually started the young ones off with something simple like deviled eggs but just finding someone to say yes was reason enough to let them do it and they seemed eager and willing. He'd praise them up one side and down the other no matter what they produced so they'd be on board for next year even if they needed some subtle instruction in the art of bean baking from one of the masters.

*

Dennis Coombs had taken over the funeral parlor from his father, Otto. It was a small home with little opportunity to stage elaborate funerals but Dennis took pride in his work and his services were appreciated. Before he slid Fanny into the cooler, he made a quick assessment of the challenge he faced. The wizened ones are the hardest. He could always puff them up to make them look healthy and vibrant but how far do you go? Should he have her appear to be at peace or should he restore that pinched and bitter disapproving look she seemed to favor most of her life? And, of course, there was that depression where her head had apparently hit the newel post... Decisions, decisions...

*

Increase Houghton was in his office this Thursday morning, a comfortable space virtually unchanged over the forty odd years of his practice. His lone concession to the present day was the computer that sat on Irene Bills' desk in the outer office. Increase himself had never touched it and was confident he never would. Instead he left it to Irene, a round, red-headed dynamo who ran the computer and his office with an uncanny efficiency. Increase would freely admit that at least half of his reputation in Vermont law circles was due to the skill and dedication of Irene Bills. Irene knew as much or more about Increase's practice as he did, so when Irene had suggested it was time for a computer, rather than resist, which was his first impulse, Increase told her to research machines and software, get what training she needed to make the damn thing work right, and he agreed to pay for it. Thirty thousand dollars later, everything was bought and installed and Irene was fully trained. Increase was nearly sick at the cost of what he saw as nothing more than a fancy typewriter but true to his word and his faith and confidence in Irene Bills he simply signed the checks and never complained.

When Irene began to spit out lengthy briefs in minutes and created clean copies of edited documents even faster, kept the books, did the billing, and kept his schedule in fifteen minute increments, he considered the money more than well spent. He was especially satisfied after having spent countless hours and endless changes in details with Fanny Forbes and her will.

And Increase, via Irene Bills, had only recently discovered the research powers of the Internet.

Irene took the call from Alice Crowley.

"Increase!" In all the years she'd worked for Increase it had never occurred to Irene that she should get up and come to him. As intelligent and efficient and valuable as she was, she'd failed to take on the slightest suggestion of professional countenance. On the plus side, Irene could exhibit a formidable presence and a strong defense should someone unexpectedly slam into the office with an attitude. Not only was Irene an excellent secretary, she doubled as a bouncer. She was devoted to Increase and her job and Increase had no problem putting her rough edges aside.

"That was Alice Crowley," Irene said when Increase came to the door. "Fanny Forbes has finally checked out."

"Ah."

"Looks as if she took a header down the front stairs," Irene grinned.

"Oh, Lord…"

"Made quite a mess of her, apparently," Irene savored the details, immensely satisfied that Fanny had come to such an undignified end.

"All right, pull her file," Increase sighed, "and see if you can find a current number for Kenny Forbes. Last I knew he was someplace in New York City."

*

Kenneth Forbes and Simon Hirsh took their mornings slowly – coffee, the morning paper, and the last segments of the morning TV shows. In the antique business, at least the business they ran, nothing much happened before noon anyway. Staff opened the store at 10 and they'd go in around noon.

Theirs was a comfortable partnership. Simon was the curious one, the one who loved to learn the history of things, assess their value and cut the deals. Kenneth loved antiques because they endured but he never became attached. Everything in this business, even his personal possessions, was for sale. He had a discerning eye, an unwillingness to haggle, and over the past ten years he and Simon had gained an excellent reputation for honest, clean, and fair dealing.

In social settings, Simon would find the spotlight. Kenneth liked to seek out a corner where he could then enjoy a conversation with one or two other people. One on one, Kenneth was a solid and intimate friend. At a party, though, Simon quickly drew the attention

Kenneth had scrambled a couple eggs and waited for a frozen waffle to finish toasting. Simon had prepared a perfectly brewed cappuccino, the whipped milk on top in a perfect little swirl, dusted with just a hint of cinnamon, and had begun the precise spreading of mascarpone cheese on his gently toasted oat and honey bagel. Nothing could interrupt Simon during the spreading of his cream cheese until it was even. Kenneth usually stood and ate at the island. It was he who answered the phone.

"This is Kenneth."

Grants Ferry

Years ago he'd read someplace that "hello" had been made up especially for answering the telephone. Kenneth didn't know if that story was true but it was reason enough to stop using it altogether.

"This is Increase Houghton."

Kenneth felt his stomach turn. No call from Increase Houghton or anyone else in Vermont could be good news.

"Is this Kenneth Forbes, formerly of Grants Ferry, Vermont?"

"Yes. Yes it is," Kenneth said, determined to keep it pleasant. "'Formerly' being some time ago, I might add. How are you Increase?"

"Been better, but then the years have been adding up. I'm afraid this is not a social call, Kenny. Your Aunt Fanny is dead. They found her this morning."

"Oh, that's too bad…" Kenneth said. He covered the mouthpiece, threw his arms in the air, and screamed at the ceiling, "Yes! The bitch is dead!"

At this very moment Simon had sipped a bit of blistering hot coffee. In ten years he had never heard Kenneth raise his voice and the outburst so startled him that cappuccino splashed out of his delicate hand painted porcelain cup onto his priceless hand painted silk robe.

"Jesus Christ!" He jumped up. "Oh, shit, shit, shit…"

Kenneth grinned broadly enough to actually expose teeth, another rare event. He held up his finger for Simon to be quiet.

"I'm sorry, Increase," he said as he struggled to conceal his excitement. "I just spilled some coffee. What was that?"

"I was saying that Fanny had lived a full life."

"Yes, yes, she did. She had a full life. No question about that. Long and full."

"Indeed," Increase agreed. "Now, I've called so that we might discuss the final arrangements."

"I don't see how that could possibly concern me," Kenneth said. "We disowned each other years ago."

"Well, quite frankly, Kenny – "

"It's Kenneth."

"Kenneth. I'm sorry, Kenneth. The thing is, like it or not, Fanny has named you in her estate. I've been given authority over certain aspects of it but there are a number of requirements with a rather small window of opportunity that require your presence in – "

"Oh, no. No. Absolutely not." He hung up.

Simon was blotting his robe but he looked at Kenneth.

"What was that, some sort of obscene call?"

"In a manner of speaking, I suppose it was." The phone rang again. "All right, Increase, what is it?"

"Kenneth, please hear me out. I can't stress too strongly the importance of this information. I'm not permitted under the details of the will to tell you why. I can only do that with your presence in Grants Ferry, in person, and only following the funeral service." Kenneth took a deep breath and then exhaled.

"Anything else?"

"Fanny's directive was that the service and burial be held on the first Saturday following her death."

"Why, that's the day after tomorrow, for Christ's sake. Why don't you just fax the stuff to me? I'll sign it and FedEx it back overnight."

"Under the conditions, I'm afraid that's not possible, Kenny."

"Kenneth."

"Kenneth. I'm sorry, Kenneth. It's been some time. I've never known you as an adult. I still think of you as Kenny."

"I understand." Kenneth wanted to tell Increase he still thought of Increase as an old man, but he stopped himself. It wasn't Increase's fault he'd had a sour, mean-spirited bitch for a client.

"Thank you," Increase continued. "At any rate, the service is penciled in for 2 pm on Saturday with burial following. Once she's interred we take care of the reading. Fanny left specific instructions as to what was to follow her death and her will is very carefully worded. Much of what is contained therein was against my advice, but nonetheless. I can only say at this point that it will be in your best interest – and I can't stress this too strongly, Kenneth – as difficult and inconvenient as it might be, to do as she says one last time."

Kenneth considered this while Increase waited on the other end.

"Are you sure she's dead?" Kenneth asked.

"Quite sure. Dr. Morgan signed the certificate this morning. Dennis Coombs has her down at the funeral home and he'll be going to work on her this afternoon."

Kenneth was silent for what seemed to Increase like ten full minutes but Increase was a patient man. Finally, Kenneth spoke.

"Look, Increase. This couldn't happen at a worse time. Can't you just keep her in the cooler for a week or two?"

"I'm not able to do that, Kenneth. I'm sorry."

"What difference would that make to her?"

"None at all, but it could have a significant impact on you."

"Ah. Still in control, is she?" He watched Simon dab his robe with a wet towel for a few seconds. "How about they lay her out on a warm rock someplace? Reptiles sometimes respond to that. Then we can put her down later on when it's more convenient."

"You're talking about your aunt, Kenneth."

"That's right. Look, I know you're just doing your job. I'm not angry with you. Give me your number. I'll see what I can do."

Kenneth scribbled the number on a pad and hung up.

"Well, this kimono is completely fucked," Simon said. "You'll work what out?"

"I may have to go to Vermont this weekend."

"*Vermont*? You can't go to Vermont, you fool. The sale starts on Saturday!"

"I know. Maybe Roger can host it if we confirm all the arrangements – "

"Are you shitting me?" Simon all but shrieked. "Roger can't even put on white gloves and direct traffic. How the hell is he going to run an event where he might actually be responsible for something?" He stopped his rant to catch his breath. "Okay, who died?"

"My Aunt Fanny."

"Oh, stop it. Seriously. Who died?"

"My Aunt Fanny."

"Really?" Simon smiled. "What a delicious name. Was she a large woman?"

"Not particularly, at least not thirty years ago. She's the one I ended up with when my parents were killed. My Uncle Fred, her husband, died in the same car accident. She always acted as if I were somehow to blame. Christ, I was eleven years old. What did I have to do with anything?" He shook his head and took a deep breath before he continued. "I've waited over thirty years to hear the words 'she's dead' and even now it wouldn't surprise me if this were some kind of trick."

"Sounds like a real peach. So what's this shit about going to Vermont instead of hosting our biggest sale of the year?"

"Something to do with the funeral, the will, the estate – I don't know. I've been named executor, there are conditions, a small window of opportunity…"

"Well, as you might say if I brought you a similar story, it sounds like horseshit to me."

"Me, too. But I think I have to go."

"You get a call from some little hamlet in the hills and in ten minutes you're ready to run off to the woods and leave an event that pays most of our bills next year?"

"I've known Increase Houghton all my life and if Increase Houghton says this is important you can bet your ass it's important."

"Oh, well. Excuse me. If my ass is on the line…"

"As to the sale, I'll see if I can get Diane to come in to do the stage managing. That will leave Roger out front where he can schmooze and fawn all he wants. I know he's a fool but the heavy buyers seem to like him and Diane will make sure he does no real damage."

"Maybe I should stay," Simon said. "You go run around the woods with your hairy friends and I'll stay here and get the show kicked off. Then neither of us will have to worry."

"I'm not going back to that snake pit by myself."

"Okay, great," Simon said, although he didn't think it was great at all. "Pack the black powder and the plaid shirts and the snake bite kits and let's go to the woods."

"Look, if I spend the rest of the day making phone calls we can probably get everything in place."

"This is a big mistake," Simon said.

"Maybe it is. In any case, it's a long weekend and it's a beautiful time of the year in Vermont, probably the only thing about the place I really miss. We're due for some time away. Let's hand the event over to Roger and Diane, leave town, and forget about it. We'll drive up, find out what the bitch has done that can't wait, get it over with, and come home. If nothing else, we can get some decent apples and some maple syrup."

*

After a long call to Diane followed by several faxes with written assurances and guarantees it was done. The arrangement included written job descriptions, clear levels of authority and responsibility, and a written agreement which she insisted be read and signed by Roger who was appropriately insulted that Kenneth and Simon would even consider that such a thing was necessary. Roger wished he could run off to play in the woods but Simon waved a $100 bill at him and he signed the agreement without another word. Everything was in place by 2:30 on Friday afternoon and Kenneth called Increase to tell him he would be there for the funeral service. Increase confirmed the funeral was now set for 2 pm.

"Oh, by the way, Increase. Could you find a place for us to stay?"

Well, it was foliage season, of course, and Increase thought that under the circumstances Kenneth might stay at Fanny's house which was probably the only house in the state with spare bedrooms.

"You're kidding, right?"

"Not at all."

"You expect me to stay in that house while she drags chains around all night? Get serious, Increase."

"I really don't know – "

"Listen. *You* called *me* up and caused *me* to change *my* entire life around in twenty-four hours so *I* could drive clear the hell and gone up to Vermont on Columbus Day weekend. Find a place for me to stay."

"Very well," Increase said. "I'll do my best but Fanny's house may ultimately be your only option."

"Well it's a piss-poor one. We're not staying in some fleabag, either."

"Of course not."

"Good. See you tomorrow for the service. I can hardly wait."

His hand trembled as he put the phone back in its cradle.

Chapter Two

1960

Cheers, whistles, and applause rose up at the Community Theater on South Street in Springfield as the final curtain rang down on *You Can't Take It With You* after three curtain calls. Kenneth Forbes was there with his father and his Uncle Fred to see his mother, Amy, who had played Alice Sycamore, the granddaughter.

The cast had come out front to visit with the crowd a few minutes later and Kenneth worked his way to a place where he could see Amy. She was a pretty woman but this night, in this moment, in her makeup and costume, Kenneth thought she was the most beautiful thing he'd ever seen. She motioned for him to join her and held him close. He could feel her tremble with excitement.

"Did you like the show, Kenny?"

"I liked your part. You were beautiful."

"Thank you, sweetheart." She hugged him – a quick squeeze. "Did Tom and Fred like it?"

"I think so. They laughed a lot."

"I had such a good time. Oh." She stood on tiptoes. "Robert! Robert, come meet Kenny."

Robert Jordan Palmer excused himself from a small knot of people.

"Amy, Amy, my dear, my dear." Robert Jordan Palmer's voice was deep and resonant, the voice of God. "You were absolutely aglow tonight," he purred as he took her free hand. "No matter the scene, you were always bright, always convincing, always in character, always believable – pure music, a lovely melody. You simply threw open your arms and sang all night."

The compliments made Amy blush. "Thank you, Robert. Kenny, Robert is our director. Everything you saw tonight was because of Robert's wonderful vision and his ability to inspire us."

"Oh, my goodness," Robert said, as if it were actually possible to praise him too much. "If that gets around people will come to expect it and then where will I be?" Robert Jordan Palmer could easily listen to this sort of praise all night but he turned his attention to Kenneth. "Well, Kenny, did you enjoy the show?"

Kenneth shrunk from his huge voice. "Yes." Robert had to lean forward to hear him. "I especially liked Amy."

Kenneth's mother had always insisted that Kenneth use her given name instead of "Mommy". She was proud of Kenny and forever thankful for the joy he brought to her life, but she was also determined that she would never lose her own identity and become known only as Kenny's mom.

"Amy has a rare gift," Robert agreed as he straightened up again. He looked at Amy although he was speaking to Kenneth. "A gift which would make any son proud. It's given me a great deal of pleasure to discover it and bring it to our small community." He directed his attention to Kenneth again. "Now, may I ask, what is your given name?"

"Kenneth Scott Forbes."

"Ah. Kenneth Scott," he rumbled. "A fine name, a noble name. Might I offer a bit of advice, Kenneth Scott – and in the spirit of the evening we might even venture to offer it as direction – Kenny is a fine name for a *boy,* you understand, but one day – and I daresay that day will come soon – one day, you should become Kenneth. Kenneth Scott would be ideal but at the very least you should become Kenneth. Never underestimate the power and strength of your full given name." He stood up again and spoke to Amy. "A handsome young man, Amy. I see you're accomplished in this area as well."

"Thank you, Robert."

Robert took her hand by the fingertips and brought it to his lips while he gazed steadily into her eyes. "On the contrary, my dear. Thank you. Kenneth, I hope we see you again. Perhaps you'll audition one day." Kenneth shrank from the very idea. "Talent runs in families, you know, and we're always looking for new faces." He turned to Amy once more. "Thank you again, my dear." And with that he strode off to rejoin the small knot of people.

"Kenny, why don't you find Fred and Tom while I get changed? I'll meet you at the car, okay?"

"Can't I go with you?"

"I'll just be a minute. See if you can get them out to the car so we don't have to wait. I'll make cocoa when we get home."

Fred and Tom were with three other men at the back of the hall, all looking at a big woman on the far side of the room.

"Hard to believe every bit of that went in through her mouth," one of them said.

"You suppose you could even reach all the way around her?" one of them asked.

"Well, it depends whether it's firm fat or soft fat," Fred explained.

"What difference does that make?"

"Big difference. Soft fat sort of flops out over your arms."

"Oh, Christ, that's sick," the other man said.

This exchange was punctuated with the kind of laughter that always accompanies jokes made at someone else's expense. Kenneth squeezed into the circle and stood beside Tom.

"Hey, look who's here," Fred said, ending the conversation about the fat woman. "Wasn't your mom great tonight?"

"Yes, she was."

"Born to it, I say. A natural."

"Amy's getting her stuff," Kenneth said to his father. "She wants us to meet her at the car."

"Okay, pal," Fred said. "Let's go. Be good to get home. Been a long day. You ready, Tom?"

"Any time," Tom said.

Outside was cooler but humid.

"Christ, you'd think they'd get some air conditioning in that place, wouldn't you?" That was Fred Forbes again. "I mean, go to all the trouble to put together a show like that and then we have to sit in a goddamned steam bath."

"The theatre company just rents the space…"

"Well, the town or somebody ought to get its finger out of its ass and put in some AC. It would be a hell of an attraction on a night like this."

"You're right. It certainly would." Tom let his brother Fred be the know-it-all. He wasn't giving anything up with this strategy since he basically agreed with Fred ninety-nine percent of the time and the other one percent wasn't enough to argue about.

Kenneth shared Tom's reticence. He listened, though, seldom missed anything, and only chose to speak when it was "safe", whatever that meant.

Kenneth was ten years old, almost eleven, and had finished the school year at the top of his fifth grade class. His birthday came right on the cusp of the time when the authorities can make kids wait another year before they start school but after some consultation it was decided he would do well, even though he'd be younger than most of his classmates. To no one's surprise he had aced every subject in every grade. He was smaller than most of his male classmates and smarter than all of them, not an asset in a community heavily populated with big, slow kids.

He didn't enjoy school. The classroom with the desks in perfect rows, the endless list of rules, and the tediousness of the lessons which were always paced for the slower kids, left him bored and uninspired. He never mastered the throwing or catching of balls and struggled with most sports. He excelled at running, though, and had been the fastest runner in the school since the middle of second grade. School was a regulated, noisy, threatening place, especially when the school bullies decided it was time to prove themselves once again.

At home, on the other hand, he was free. Amy never talked down to him, never tried to hide things, never contradicted or corrected him in public, and generally respected him as an individual. They worked together on projects around the house. He often helped cook supper, she taught him to wash and iron his clothes and shine his shoes and they talked. Kenneth had missed her when she was gone to rehearse for the play. Tom Forbes, on the other hand, had always let Amy do whatever she wanted and her absence didn't seem to affect him one way or the other. He never would have said so but he found the silence rather peaceful.

Amy brought home tickets so that Kenneth and Tom could go to the show with Kenneth's Uncle Fred and Aunt Fanny. Kenneth liked Fred but didn't look forward to an evening with Fanny. Fanny fussed and complained all the time and she didn't like Amy which to Kenneth was beyond belief.

"Your mother always was the party girl," Fanny would sniff in a way that made it sound dirty. Fanny said it was a disgrace that Amy had taken up with "those people," meaning the actors who were "nothing but gypsies, after all."

Fanny developed a headache the night of the play. She'd have to stay home alone now, she fussed, and she didn't think it was right for Fred to go gallivanting off while she was nearly blind with the pain, etc., etc. Fred often said Fanny's headaches were one of her finer accomplishments and he was more than willing to let her enjoy them. Besides, he wasn't about to give up a Saturday night out with Tom and Amy and Kenny. During the show Fred laughed loud, he laughed often, and sometimes he slapped his knee. Tom enjoyed the show, too, but he only smiled and occasionally shifted in his chair, which for him was a display of extreme pleasure.

Fred bought cider and cookies during an intermission.

"So how do you like it so far?" Fred asked around a mouthful of brownie.

"It's good," Kenneth said. "Are there really people like that?"

"There may be," Fred said. "Known a few who've tried. Never seemed to make it last, though."

Later in the car Amy and Kenneth sat close in the back seat. She held his hand in both of hers.

"Did they really make fireworks in the cellar?" Kenneth asked.

"In the play, they did."

"Isn't that dangerous?"

"Probably, but a play is make-believe. In make-believe even danger can be fun. They lived their lives doing what they loved most and it was such a good story that the two men who wrote it won a Pulitzer Prize."

"What's that?"

"It's a special prize that's given to people who create wonderful things."

"But they all seem kind of wild and crazy."

"A little, I guess. But who would you rather spend an afternoon with, Tony's parents who want everything to be right and proper or the guys in the cellar who make fireworks?"

"I – I – "

Amy laughed and squeezed his hand. "You don't have to answer," she said, "but I think that's why this play won the Pulitzer Prize. Deep inside I think we all wish we could dance or play the xylophone or make fireworks in the cellar and whatever we want to do would be okay."

Kenneth hunched across the seat so he could lie down and put his head in Amy's lap. She stroked his hair and he thought about big families full of wild and crazy people and freedom and fireworks and dancing – and then he was asleep.

The fog which had begun to settle along the Black River grew even thicker when they reached Route 5 and the Connecticut Valley. Tom turned north and climbed the hill away from the river. Here the fog became intermittent, thick one moment and gone the next. The road was visible only for short distances and sometimes not at all. Tom nearly missed the turn to Grants Ferry. Fred had chattered steadily since they left Springfield but Tom had tuned him out, a skill he'd learned years ago.

A wooden guardrail suddenly loomed in front of them and the car broke through. Tom stood on the brakes, even pulled on the steering wheel to give him more pressure, but the bank was steep and the grass was wet and the Buick skidded sixty yards down the hill, gaining speed as it went, until it slid straight into a maple tree near the bottom.

*

State Trooper Harlan Otis had seen his share of accidents over the years and this one had fatal written all over it. He called in a report and hurried down the hill anyway, just in case. The carnage against the dashboard and through the windshield told the story.

Just like that, he thought.

Harlan Otis had been a State Trooper for almost fifteen of his forty-seven years but he'd never hardened to this part of his job. He closed his eyes for a moment, and without words – he wasn't a religious man and he could never think of words that would convey just what he was feeling – he imagined that this small gesture would somehow send these souls on their way, whatever that might mean. There was nothing left then except the grisly job of retrieval and cleanup.

A faint moan came from inside the wreckage. Kenneth's breathing was shallow and his pulse was weak but he was alive. Trooper Otis clawed his way back up to the road and radioed a second time, this time to advise dispatch that there was a survivor and to make sure they sent a paramedic team.

An ambulance screamed up the hill ten minutes later. The paramedics had unloaded their gear and were on their way down to the wreck when Sheriff's Deputy Burt Persons pulled up. Burt was thirty-five and relatively new to the Sheriff's Department. His entire deputy career until recently had been spent cruising around the county on the night shift.

"Hey, Harlan," he said as he climbed out of his cruiser. "What's up?" His new daytime uniform was pressed and spotless.

"Three fatals. One survivor, a kid."

"Know who it is?"

"No. I called in the plate number but I haven't heard back yet. Takes'em longer on Sunday, I guess."

Burt leaned over the edge of the road to get a look.

"Holy shit. I think that's Tom Forbes' car. Oh, Jesus H. Christ."

"Yeah. It's a bitch when you know them. That's why I transferred down from Orleans County. I knew too many people."

"Son of a *bitch*," Burt said.

"We ought to get down there," Harlan said. "The boy's still alive – or he was when I left him. They're going to need some help bringing him up the hill."

“Aw, Jesus, Harlan. I don’t want to do this. I mean, I went to school with Tom, you know?”

“I’ll tell you what,” Harlan said, “you got to let that go. Right now it’s all about the kid, you understand?”

“Yeah. Okay.” Burt took a breath. “Okay.” He stood at the edge and looked down. “God damn it.”

“Let’s go.”

Halfway down Burt fell and stained his new, pressed uniform on the wet grass. He jumped up and wiped at it frantically but the grass had done its work. The paramedics gently extricated Kenneth from the car. Burt stood out of the way but Harlan steadied the stretcher as they slid Kenneth on and strapped him down. When he was secured one of the paramedics looked up the hill and then back at the two officers.

“You guys give us a hand?”

“Sure thing,” Harlan said. “How’s he doing?”

“Pretty banged up. He’ll be in the hospital a while. Serious but not critical.”

“Well, I suppose we can be grateful for something.”

“Right. We’ll take him head first. Try to avoid bouncing him too much.”

“Burt. Give us a hand here.” Harlan said.

The four men pulled the stretcher along the wet grass as gently as they could. When one of them slipped the stretcher would jerk and bring a groan from Kenneth.

“Should’a thrown a line down,” the paramedic said. “We could’a pulled him up. Would’a been easier.”

They were all sweating and out of breath when they finally slid the stretcher gently into the ambulance and closed the doors.

“Thanks, guys.” This was Harlan Otis. Burt had gone behind his cruiser where he thought no one would know he was throwing up.

The ambulance tore off to the hospital in Springfield. Burt, unsteady and pale, came back to join Harlan. Both men leaned back against Harlan’s cruiser, their arms folded, and stared off away from the wreck as they waited for the wrecker to come and drag the car up to the road and for another ambulance crew to take the bodies away.

Harlan’s eyes were wet. He heaved himself off the cruiser and kicked a loose stone across the road. He had to take several deep breaths to keep from crying. He hated this part of his job.

*

The identities were confirmed when the bodies were removed from the demolished car.

"Who needs to be told?" Harlan asked Burt.

"I think all that's left now is Fred's wife, Fanny."

"Okay. I'll go by and tell her. Were these church people?"

"Yeah."

"Okay, you break the news to the minister. It's easier than telling relatives."

Harlan sat in front of Fanny's house for several minutes. He was always in a foul mood after he'd worked a fatal and he didn't want it to show. When he'd calmed himself he strode up onto the front porch and knocked. He stared vacantly at the porch floor, hands clasped behind his back. Fanny opened the door, dressed for church. She wore an apron and wiped her hands on a towel.

"Mrs. Forbes?"

"Yes."

"I'm Trooper Harlan Otis. There's been an accident, sometime during the night. Your husband, Fred Forbes – your husband was in the car and was killed."

"Really?" Fanny said, as if she'd just been told her order from Sears would be a day late. "I wondered why he didn't get home."

Well, that's cold, Harlan thought. "We think it was the fog last night. They went off the road on that bad turn by the Stewart Farm."

"Drinking, was he?"

"I – I don't think so. There didn't seem to be any indication of that."

"Thank you," Fanny said, and closed the door.

Harlan Otis had met some cool customers in the past fifteen years but never anyone quite as icy as Fanny. He wasn't finished, though, so he knocked again.

"Something else?"

"Yes. Ma'm. The other fatalities were Tom and Amy Forbes. There was a survivor, a boy. He's been taken to the hospital in Springfield."

Fanny let this information register. "Very well," she said. "Thank you again." She closed the door and threw the bolt.

Back in his cruiser Harlan Otis sat for several minutes. He couldn't remember a time when he'd been so pissed. He radioed in that he'd notified the widow, started the car, and drove away. It took all his willpower to stay within the 25 mph speed limit.

*

Burt Persons was no stranger to the church but he'd never had a reason to come inside wearing his uniform and his revolver.

"Oh, my word," the Rev. Gordon Nelson said when Burt broke the news. "Oh, my Lord in Heaven."

"Tom's boy, Kenny… Kenny's down to Springfield in the hospital."

Gordon Nelson sat bent over, elbows on his knees, hands clenched so tight the fingers had lost their color. "Oh, my word…" he said, shaking his head. He suddenly realized Burt had spoken again. "I'm sorry. You say the boy survived?"

"Yes, sir. He's been taken down to Springfield. A little broke up but the medics think he'll be all right."

"Thank the Lord." Gordon closed his eyes and took a moment to collect his thoughts. "You say the boy's in Springfield?"

"Yes, sir."

"Someone should be with him," Gordon said. "I wonder if I might impose on you, Burt, to drive Charlotte down to be with him."

"Sure thing."

"After church I'll go down myself. Does the boy know about his parents?"

"I don't think so. He was unconscious when we put him into the ambulance. They think he hit his head."

"All right. Thank you, Burt." Gordon's mind was racing now. "I should go see Fanny."

"Harlan Otis went to tell her."

"Of course, but this is a time – a terrible time, a time to offer solace. You understand."

"Yes, sir."

Gordon Nelson slumped back in his chair and let out a great sigh. Charlotte began to cry when he called and Gordon had to speak sharply so she would listen to his instructions. "Just go to be with the boy," Gordon said. "I'll be down later to tell him about Tom and Amy."

He had about 45 minutes before the service, very little time, but as a servant of the Lord Gordon Nelson should offer solace to Fanny, one of the Lord's children, a staunch and loyal member of the Grants Ferry congregation. He pulled on his jacket and ran to his car.

Gordon Nelson was a charitable man who sought the good in everyone but he knew Fanny Forbes could be a difficult woman. She motioned him in, gestured for him to sit down, and finished turning the doughnuts that were floating in the hot fat. Without speaking or asking, she took a fresh doughnut from the drying tray and served it up on a small plate.

Making a similar call on other parishioners, Gordon Nelson might offer a hug, a hug to comfort and console in a time of shock and grief. Fanny Forbes, however, had never been one to suggest appreciation of any physical contact so instead Gordon simply pulled out a chair and sat down at the table.

"Fanny, I – "

"Coffee?"

"Um – Yes, thank you." As a rule, Gordon avoided taking on fluids before the service, but this was not the time to be ungenerous. She dumped a spoonful of powdered coffee in a mug, poured hot water over it, stirred it a couple times, and brought it to the table. "Fanny, if there's anything we can do…"

There was no response. He started again. "Fred was a good man, Fanny, and – "

"What good is he now, Gordon? I ask you that. What good is he now?" She fussed with the doughnuts. When she turned to face him she saw that he hadn't touched the doughnut on his plate. "You want me to dust that with some powdered sugar?"

"No, thank you," Gordon said. He started again. "Fred's time with us – "

"Is over, that's all. It's done." For several moments the only sounds in the kitchen were the ticking clock over the sink and the doughnuts as they floated and hissed in the hot fat.

"I understand the boy's alive," Fanny said.

"Yes, thank the Lord."

"And what happens to him now?"

"The boy will be seen to," Gordon said.

"What does that mean?" she said without looking up.

"I'm not sure just yet. He's in the hospital in Springfield. I'll go down after church to tell him about his parents. Charlotte's on her way to stay with him."

Gordon waited then while Fanny removed the doughnuts from the fat to the drying tray and put some more in to cook.

"I expect they'll just send him off to some state home," she said, more to the floating doughnuts than to anyone else.

"He'll be in the hospital for a while," Gordon said. "We'll have plenty of time to make these decisions." He heard Fanny snort. "Again, Fanny, I'm terribly sorry about Fred. And Tom and Amy, a terrible blow… I'll do whatever I can..."

Fanny rolled her eyes. "Thank you, Gordon."

"And you know the church family is always – "

"Yes, yes, I know," she said, waving her hand while she poked at the doughnuts with a long-handled fork.

"Fanny, I thought I might offer up a prayer."

"Frankly, I don't feel much like praying just now."

Gordon had reached his limit in the solace department and moved on to business. "I'll be spending my time with Kenny this afternoon," he said, "if you'd like to come along…"

"I can't think of what use I might be sitting around a hospital room."

"I see. Of course. So it might be a good idea if we get together tomorrow to work out details for the services. Had you given any thought as to the day of the service?"

"Thursday."

She poked at the doughnuts.

Gordon waited but there didn't seem to be anything else.

"Very well," he said. "They've all been brought in to Otto Coombs, of course. It occurred to me that we might do all three at the same time since they were family – one service, and then the committals at the cemetery. Keep them together to the end, so to speak."

She didn't look up. "Whatever."

"Good. I'll have Margaret make the arrangements."

"Fine."

"And Fanny, if there's anything any of us can do…"

"Just send someone around for the doughnuts," she said. "I won't be going to church today."

The Rev. Gordon Nelson had been dismissed.

*

Church was an important part of Fanny's week even though she tended to disagree with the generally liberal tendencies of Gordon Nelson's sermons. Despite Gordon's rather weak spiritual leadership, Fanny viewed the church itself as a focal point of the community, a nucleus for the potential of Christian good. Participation in the church and its activities, along with an attempt to instill some moral values in the younger generations, was perhaps the only salvation for what was left of Grants Ferry. It was from that perspective that Fanny was a regular and active member. But today she would stay home. She wouldn't abide the sneaky glances or the stares, or the solicitous condolences. Instead she would organize a strategy for her looming widowhood.

She packed the doughnuts carefully into a towel-lined basket, folded the edges over them, and then laid another towel over the top. Her part was done. She reheated the water for tea.

From childhood Fanny's life had been filled with the church community and its activities. She was proud to be a Christian, even though she could never state just what that meant beyond not being a Jew or Muslim or even Catholic, since to Fanny, Catholics were not really Christians, either.

Her life had been one of duty, duty to family, duty to church, and when she married Fred, duty to Fred. Fanny and Fred had lived with her mother when they married – her father died when she was fifteen – and she inherited the house when her mother died. Fred, surprisingly, had put up with the two of them. It was a challenge few other men would have taken on but Fred tolerated Fanny and her mother with a remarkable good humor. The relationship was one of the town mysteries.

Still, Fanny felt little sadness that Fred was dead. Theirs had been an awkward marriage at best. She'd often wondered over their thirteen years together why he asked her to marry him in the first place. She hadn't invited it and wondered now what had led her to accept. It certainly wasn't love; Fanny had never been in love. As far as she could tell now she'd agreed because getting paired up and married is what people did and Fred had been the least objectionable from an assortment of losers. He was reasonably good looking, he had a playful nature, he was a hard worker, and fastidious with his hygiene.

Fred had been a steady and dependable earner and she had kept the house. As marriages go it was probably satisfactory. She had no strong feelings for Fred but neither did she dislike him. He appreciated the food she prepared, frequently went off to hunt or fish, and he worked around the house and yard on his days off. Of course, there was his ever-present need for sexual relief but as driven as he was in this department Fanny had nothing to suggest he'd ever taken this need to anyone else. If there had ever been a night in their marriage when he wasn't on her like a goat she might have wondered but in spite of Fred's determination, Fanny had never become pregnant. She had wondered about that from time to time but was quite content to remain childless.

The tea kettle whistled and she poured the water over the teabag.

Fred did drink, though, the one vice that got by her before she married him. Fanny had come from a long line of teetotalers and had been raised on horror stories about Demon Rum and all its cousins. Not until they were married did she discover that Fred Forbes not only consumed alcohol but consumed it regularly. Fanny refused to have it in the house. As a result, Fred usually swung by the Ferry Slip, the disgusting bar down at the old ferry landing, before he came home for supper. She suspected he had a stash of liquor hidden somewhere in the house or the barn but she was never able to find it.

Fred did not get drunk. He grew mellow, although no less horny. Fanny never knew whether he limited his consumption because of her or if a drink or two was really all he wanted. In her sentimental moments, which were few, she sometimes mused that it might be she who had kept him tolerable. In reality she admitted that she probably had little or no influence on Fred's behavior.

Fanny took the tea to the table. What would it be like, she wondered to herself, to actually go to bed secure in the knowledge that no one would climb all over her in the night? The mere thought opened her heart. The house had always been her domain and she didn't need Fred for that. On the other hand, he did bring home a steady paycheck and that would now stop.

There was no mortgage. Fanny had been careful and frugal with money all her life and had saved regularly. There would be some insurance and there were some things she could sell for cash. She had no cause for panic, but something would have to bring in money on a regular basis or she'd eventually be reduced to finding employment, a situation she found unacceptable. As occasionally frustrating as her marriage had been, Fred had provided a life free from financial stress.

How had she not seen this coming? Why he'd wanted to see some silly play was beyond her. Amy never should have taken up with those theater people. She'd run wild all her life and this play acting was just a chance to run off with the circus.

Amy had no sense of discipline or rules. What kind of mother teaches her son to cook and do his own laundry? And Amy seemed to draw men like moths to a flame. She'd flirt with all of them, married or not, openly and without shame. So of course they'd all be out with the child on a foggy night when everyone with any sense would be home in bed. Tom and Amy could do whatever they wanted, of course, but they'd taken Fred along as well. Oh, they'd invited Fanny, too – they always did – and then she'd come down with the migraine, nearly blind with the pain, and Fred had gone off and left her again.

Alice Crowley knocked on the back door and came in.

"Fanny, I just heard." The basket of doughnuts was by the door and there was no invitation to come further. "I'm so sorry, Fanny. What a shock. And Tom and Amy, too."

"Yes, well…"

"Thank God Kenny's all right…"

"That's what I'm told."

"I'll deliver the doughnuts. If you need anything…"

"No, I don't. I don't want people coming around, either. Tell them that."

"All right. Still, if you need anything…"

"I know, I know…" She waved her hand for Alice to go along.

Moments later Fanny's thoughts were again of Fred and Tom and even Amy. The brothers, Tom and Fred, were no more alike than anything. Fanny could remember maybe five times when she'd actually heard Tom speak. The man could sit for hours and never open his mouth. Fanny wondered if he might be deficient but Fred said he wasn't.

"He just doesn't have much to say and spends a lot of time not saying it," Fred explained.

They're gone now, Fanny thought. *Only the boy is left, heir to their property. Probably not a lot, by any means, but liquidated…* "Where will that money go now?" she asked the empty kitchen. *To the boy? To some foster home? An orphanage? And what about my support now they've taken Fred…?*

She drifted off in mid-sentence as the pieces fell into place. She took the empty cup to the sink. At the stove she poured the cooled but still liquid fat into a container for storage. She washed the pan, put it away, hung up the towel, and wiped down the area around the sink.

"The boy," she said as she hung her apron on the back side of the pantry door. "The boy is the key."

*

Chapter Three

Kenneth had no sense of time or where he was, his vision was fuzzy, he couldn't move, and Charlotte Nelson, the minister's soft, round wife was hovering over him. Even semiconscious the last thing he wanted was Charlotte Nelson but she was on him in an instant.

"Oh, look who's awake now. Should we try to go pee-pee, sweetheart?" Without waiting for an answer she pulled back the sheets, lifted his Johnny, grabbed his pecker, shoved it into the mouth of a urinal, and then held it as she waited for the trickling sound to begin. The minister's wife was actually holding his pecker. He managed to push out a couple spoonfuls and that seemed to satisfy her. She gave his pecker a little congratulatory squeeze and took the urinal away. In a flash she returned with a warm wet wash cloth and proceeded to spend several minutes to thoroughly "wash him up".

Any attempt to speak came out as a moan which only seemed to encourage her. He finally faked sleep again so she would leave him alone.

And he did sleep. When he woke again the Rev. Nelson, a tired, drawn man, was there beside his soft, round wife. Why were these people here?

"Where's Amy?" he said. His jaw hurt when he spoke.

Tears ran down Charlotte's round cheeks.

"Kenny," the Rev. Nelson began, "there was an accident…"

"We went to the play." He struggled to form the words. "People made fireworks in the cellar. And there was a Russian and a xylophone, and – "

"Yes, but after that, on your way home – "

"Where's Amy?" Kenneth interrupted again. "Where's Tom and Uncle Fred?" He tried to sit up but restraints held him down. In his confusion he began to cry and that hurt his ribs and stomach.

"There, there, sweetheart," Charlotte cooed between sobs. "There, there."

"Where's Amy?" he asked again.

"Kenny, you and your parents were in the accident," the Rev. Nelson said. "I'm afraid the others – the others, your parents and your Uncle Fred, were taken from us. You alone survived."

Kenneth didn't understand any of it. If Amy wasn't here whatever was going on couldn't be good. He couldn't move and this woman he didn't like was cooing over him and the Rev. Nelson was rambling something about the House of the Lord and being at peace and Kenneth fought the straps and the room got dark around the edges, something that happened those rare times when he was angry or confused. He could see straight ahead but the edges were dark and none of it made any sense. A woman dressed in white was there, a big woman with glasses and a white band around her head and it seemed as if she had simply appeared. He fought the restraints and he cried and it hurt again.

"I'm sorry," the Rev. Nelson said to the nurse. "I'm afraid I simply don't know any gentle way to tell a boy his parents are dead."

"Never mind," the nurse said. "We'll give him something so he can sleep." Kenneth felt the prick of the needle and in seconds he was sinking, sinking into darkness. He didn't want to sink into darkness, he wanted to see Amy. He didn't want to close his eyes, either, but as hard as he tried he couldn't keep them open. His one last thought before everything went away: at least he wouldn't have to listen to Charlotte Nelson.

*

Fanny dedicated the rest of the day to methodically purging the house of all things Fred. From the bathroom, from closets, from dresser drawers, she filled paper bags and cardboard boxes with clothes, toiletries, books, magazines, and anything else that was his alone. She carried it all to the barn where she tossed it into a heap on the far side of the sliding barn door. She couldn't find the key to Fred's gun cabinet or she would have emptied that and removed it as well. Fanny wasn't a big woman but she was wiry and driven by a fierce determination. By suppertime the worst of it was done.

After a light supper of Campbell's tomato soup and crackers, Fanny stripped the bed and pulled the mattress into the upstairs hall. Then she stripped the bed in the guest room, dragged that mattress into what was now her very own bedroom, and flopped it onto the box spring. She made the bed up again with a set of clean sheets and made up the guest room using the old mattress. Fred's mattress was good enough for guests, should she ever have any, but Fanny would never sleep on it again.

Satisfied, she went into the bathroom, plugged the drain in the tub and turned on the hot water. While the tub filled, she went downstairs to the kitchen, fixed herself a cup of tea, and brought it back to enjoy as she soaked and basked in a strange relief at the reality of Fred's death. While he was alive, the thought of life without him had never entered her mind. His death, in spite of some potential financial problems, had brought her a pleasant and unexpected peace.

Remaining traces of Fred continued to appear over the next few days, things she'd missed in her initial campaign. There were photos here and there and the chair he always sank into in the evening. She discovered his coffee mug in the pantry. His work coat and boots were in the shed. She'd walked past them time after time on her way to the barn and hadn't noticed them. And his tools in the cellar and the shelves of coffee cans full of nails, screws, and odd hardware. Fanny didn't know how to use most of the tools and couldn't identify some of the hardware but she'd keep the tools and supplies, even if Fred had touched each and every one of them. They were necessary to make repairs and she would learn. Everything else went to the barn.

The house was now hers. Fanny didn't hold much with ritual but as an acknowledgment of the change she lit up a balsam incense cone in each room. The pleasant scent of evergreen filled the house and served to rid the place of any lingering hint of Fred's scent. The purge was as good as complete.

The cleansing process had not been without interruption, however. Gordon Nelson had come by on Monday. She'd considered not answering the door but he kept knocking and calling to her. The only way to get rid of him, she realized, was to let him in, pour some coffee, and give him a doughnut.

Gordon sat at the kitchen table again as Fanny served things up. "I thought we might have a single service for the three of them," he suggested, apparently forgetting that he'd presented this same brilliant idea just over 24 hours ago.

"Might as well," Fanny said.

"My thinking…" Gordon's voice trailed off as he realized he wanted to reframe his suggestion. "To lose three well-loved people so suddenly and so violently, I believe, has left the entire town in a terrible state of shock and mourning. In times like this – "

"Do whatever you need to do, Gordon," Fanny interrupted. "Just keep it succinct. Just enough and no more."

A heavy blow. Gordon Nelson had already begun stories about all three of the deceased and had outlined a rather elaborate but touching service, a moving discourse about the mutual dependence we share as both family and community, a celebration of their lives in which he could present himself as a strong and inspirational leader in a time of crisis and mourning.

"But don't you agree that – "

"I want it short," Fanny said. "My personal preference would be for cremation and burial. I could dig a hole for the urn myself."

"Ah," Gordon Nelson was momentarily speechless and he stirred his coffee while he cleared his head. This nasty woman had stolen his moment. But confrontation was not in his nature and he sipped coffee as he struggled to find words of grace and forgiveness. "Very well, then," he said when his voice returned. "We've set the service for Thursday at two. Otto says they'll be ready for viewing after noon on Wednesday."

"Fine." Fanny had no intention of viewing anyone. She'd seen more than enough of all three of them while they were alive.

"If you need a ride down…"

"No, thank you."

"You might give Otto a call, then. Increase has been appointed by the court to see to Tom's and Amy's interests but I think you should connect with Otto as well. We all want to be on the same page…"

"Yes, I know." Fanny got up and held the back door open for him. "Thank you."

She would keep Fred's desk. It had belonged to his grandfather. Fanny was sure it was an antique and she'd always admired it. It was a large, dark, rolltop which occupied a convenient place in the side room off the dining room where Fred sat down to pay the bills each month. It was a repository for other important documents as well, such as insurance policies and savings account passbooks. At least, she noted as she went through them, they were all joint bank accounts and she was listed as beneficiary on the insurance policies (which pay double for accidental death, she was glad to confirm). There were no surprises but it gave her a sense of her assets. All told, she could count on about $50,000 in cash. She would sell Fred's car and his guns and fishing equipment and get some cash from those things as well. He'd owned little else save for that mess in the barn. There might be some widow's benefits and possibly something from his pension plan at the machine shop but it wouldn't be much.

While Fanny had never been included in the financial side of their marriage, she was pleased to discover that Fred, for all his annoying quirks, was meticulous in his record keeping. It would be a simple thing to keep his system running. As she slid the deep bottom drawer closed there seemed something odd about it. She pulled it all the way out. At the back was a compartment with a hinged lid. Inside she found two bottles of Wild Turkey and two small glasses. Both the bottles and the glasses were fit into felt lined cutouts that held them snugly so they didn't rattle. She'd finally found Fred's stash.

Fanny's mouth clamped shut. The muscles in her neck were so tense she could feel herself tremble. She slammed the compartment lid down and shoved the drawer closed. The bottom drawer on the other side had an identical setup. Unable in her fury to even touch the poison in the drawers, she closed the desk and went to the kitchen where she could attempt to collect her thoughts.

She was still raging several minutes later when the phone rang. It was Otto Coombs.

"What are the arrangements so far?" she asked.

"We're waiting to hear from you, Mrs. Forbes. Increase is acting on behalf of the others."

"I see."

"We have a few decisions to make about Fred. Would you care to come down so we could work out the details?"

"No, I wouldn't. I don't drive."

"Why don't I drop by, then? Would two-thirty be all right?"

"Any time."

*

For all her assertiveness, Fanny had never been involved in a large purchase like a car or a house and wasn't quite sure how to go about it. She did, however, anticipate an opportunity to negotiate and her fury over the discovery of the alcohol served to focus her during the final arrangements.

Fanny was still fuming when Otto Coombs arrived. A three-party funeral doesn't come along every day, she reasoned as soon as they sat down, and Otto Coombs should certainly be willing to relinquish a portion of this windfall in the form of a generous volume discount. Otto agreed that a triple service was rare but the best he could do was a piddling one per cent, as a gesture to a family that had suffered such a cruel blow.

"What do you mean, 'family'?" she snapped. "I'm it."

"Well, there's the boy..."

"Oh, poo," She said. "He's not paying the bill. He's not even an adult. This has nothing to do with him."

"Still, there isn't much room here, Fanny." Otto wasn't in the habit of negotiating for his services as if he were selling used cars. "It's not like we can stuff all three of them into one box," he said. "I have to arrange for two more hearses and staff from other homes. There are still three graves to dig, three body preps. Funerals, by their nature, simply don't allow room for volume discounts."

"Well, I think it's disgraceful," she said. The platform rocker made faint creaking sounds as she pushed it back and forth.

"I quite agree," Otto said, although he was referring to Fanny's incredible gall, not his discount policy. "I – uh – I wonder if I might take along one of Fred's suits."

"What for? The casket's going to be closed, isn't it?"

"If that's what you want. Certainly. But some folks like to come by the home for viewing, you know. It's sort of a last chance to say good bye."

Every bit of this circus was getting out of hand. Otto continued to add one expense after another, her source of support had been taken from her, she'd found Fred's liquor stash, and at the moment she couldn't even bring herself to speak.

Otto, for his part, employed a strategy he'd perfected some years ago. He simply sat and waited. It was best to let them see for themselves how inappropriate they are and silence was far more powerful than argument.

"I heard the three of them were all smashed up," Fanny said finally.

"Well, yes, that's true. We'll need to do some considerable reconstruction. Dennis, my boy, has been working with me the past few years. He's become quite accomplished. I think you'd be quite pleased."

Fanny considered this for a moment as she sipped her tea. Again there was a long silence, save for the creaking of the platform rocker, while Fanny reviewed her options. In the end she decided to simply get it over and done.

"His suits are out in the barn in the pile beyond the door," she said. "Help yourself."

"Thank you. A recent photo would help as well."

"Out in the barn with the suits."

After twenty years running the funeral home, Otto understood that grief often brings inappropriate behavior but this was a new one. Once again silence was his salvation. He waited as Fanny rocked and stared vacantly across the room. After a few minutes Otto stood to leave.

Fanny noticed the movement. "That's it, then?" she said.

"Yes. Thank you. The suit?" he said.

"Out in the barn. You'll find it."

"Thank you. I'll see to everything, Fanny."

"I'm warning you, Otto. You can have the whole town down to your place to gawk and cry over him as long as you want, but if you so much as crack that lid during the service at the church you won't get paid."

"Of course. Oh, I almost forgot. Increase Houghton called just as I was leaving to come over here. You'll want to come to an agreement about the service. I'll do whatever you two decide."

"Fine."

Fanny sat and rocked in silence until she heard Otto's car back out of the driveway. She considered her options again, running the list over and over. Tom and Amy probably had insurance and they had their house. There should be some value there, probably not as much as she and Fred had, but putting the two estates together might bring enough security that she could live in relative comfort. It was they, after all, who took away her sole source of support and she was certainly owed something for this loss, some sort of compensation. None of this had been her fault. Why should she suffer?

But the boy had survived. If she took the boy she might negotiate for Tom and Amy's estate... With Fred's cash management system and some careful planning she could probably make that last for years. The challenge, though, would be to persuade Increase Houghton to convince the court that this is how it should be.

*

By nine o'clock Saturday morning they'd stopped for breakfast outside Stamford, Connecticut. Only seven or eight words had passed between them since they'd got in the car.

Simon tasted his coffee and made a face. Kenneth took his black but he stirred it anyway. They both stared out the window.

"You fellas ready to order yet?" The waitress was a big woman with orange hair. The flesh on her upper arms made dimples of her elbows.

"I think I'll have the two egg omelet," Simon said.

"You want cheese?"

"On top or inside?"

"It starts out on top. They fold it over so it's on the inside and it leaks out onto the plate."

"Oh, yum. Give me the cheese, too."

She turned to Kenneth.

"How about you, sweetheart?"

"Two whole wheat pancakes, two slices of bacon, and scrambled eggs."

"You mean a number three?"

"Is that what it is? Yes, a number three."

"Warm those up for you?" meaning the coffee.

"Sure."

She topped off the cups and went back to the kitchen. They stirred and sipped in silence until the waitress returned with their orders.

"Okay, so what is it about this place that has you so up tight?" Simon said as he peeked inside his omelet.

"Long story."

"Let's have it. I'm tired of this silence."

Kenneth pushed his eggs around with bits of pancake. Finally he just shook his head. "You knew my parents were killed, right?"

"Right."

"But I never told you the story?"

"No."

Kenneth stirred his coffee again, ignoring the food. "So I was ten, almost eleven. My parents and my Uncle Fred – Fanny's husband – had taken me down to Springfield to see a play Amy was in, *You Can't Take It With You*, you know, the one with a houseful of crazy people. Amy had one of the lead roles. Fanny begged off with a headache or something. It was late – 10:30 or 11, which is late in Vermont – and it was foggy. My father drove off the road and straight down a steep hill into a maple tree."

"Jesus," Simon said.

"I was asleep across the back seat with my head in my mother's lap. Of course nobody wore seatbelts in those days and when the car hit the tree the others all went through the windshield. I was thrown into the back of the front seat, woke up in the hospital the next day."

"Jesus," Simon said again. "And you were what, ten?"

"I'd be eleven in another few weeks. Nobody had wills so everything was up in the air. Aunt Fanny played the stoic and wanted to 'do the right thing'. She said it was only right that she take me in. Family should take care of family, and all that. My parents' house was eventually sold and the money from that and whatever insurance they'd had was somehow doled out to her each month in return for her taking me in until I came of age."

"She got the money?"

"Well, I never saw any of it. I was only a kid and as the next living relative, if only by marriage, she became custodian. She never missed an opportunity to remind me that if my mother hadn't taken up with those theater people it never would have happened. She didn't like the way my father drove, and my mother so wild and undisciplined it was no wonder her house was such a mess, she couldn't imagine raising a boy in that environment. Now Fred was gone and she was left to fend for herself – that sort of thing."

"Damn. Was your mother wild and undisciplined?"

"She was fun, more like a big sister. But all I heard from Fanny after Amy died was how loose and careless she was."

"You take after your father, do you?"

Kenneth chuckled for the first time in two days.

"Yeah, I suppose I do. Amy was always planning things. I think my father just enjoyed the ride. They had a good time together." He looked out the window, lost in memories. "God, it's so long ago. When Amy laughed it was like music and my father – that's when he was happiest. I had a register in the floor of my bedroom to let the heat up in the wintertime and I could hear them talking and laughing long after I'd gone to bed. I don't think there was anyone who didn't like Amy, except maybe Fanny."

"You must have really missed her."

"Yeah, well… She really liked me, you know? And we played together. She was a big beautiful friend." Kenneth mused a moment and shook his head. "I don't think I've really played since."

He paid the check and five minutes later they were back on I-95 heading for New Haven and I-91 which would take them north to Vermont.

"When I was little," Kenneth continued, "before my parents were killed, I knew a wonderful freedom. My parents weren't highly educated, they may not have even been particularly smart, but I remember they enjoyed each other and they had a good life together. And they had fun with me, like it never occurred to them that I was only a little boy. Amy talked to me all the time… I don't know… Maybe it was never that way, but that's the memory I have of them, anyway."

"You were happy?"

"I never knew unhappiness before they died."

"And then there was Fanny."

"Yeah…"

"But that was thirty years ago…"

"Thirty-two."

"And now she's dead."

"Ah, but the rest of them are still there."

*

A small sign stood by the walk in front of the house.

Increase Houghton
Attorney at Law

While many professionals appreciate some considerable distance between their daily grind and their private time, Increase Houghton had found living above his office to be extremely convenient. Everything he needed for both his professional and private lives was contained in this building.

At noontime he simply climbed the back stairs to the kitchen where Judith had his lunch ready. It might be a sandwich, a salad, and iced tea in the summer or a hearty homemade soup and crackers in the winter. Leftovers often appeared in various disguises. He traveled when necessary but if he could manage it he would insist that people come to him.

His meeting room, originally the dining room, was lined with shelves full of case law and state statutes, each set with matching bindings and stored sequentially. These tomes held few secrets from Increase Houghton. The top shelf, however, was filled end to end with Readers Digest Condensed Books. He'd picked them up at yard sales and second hand bookstores, taken the paper jackets off, and put them on the shelf with their stripes and gold lettering in full view. He'd never read a single one, never intended to, and no one had ever noticed.

Increase had created a life in which he was surrounded by things that gave him pleasure, his wife Judith, his house, his community, and his 1955 Buick Roadmaster which he considered to be the last of the classics. His secretary, Irene Bills, who had just appeared in the meeting room doorway was also on that list. Irene seldom left her desk and the fact that she was up and in his office doorway was a sign she was ready to protect him from something.

Increase had hired Irene right out of high school. He'd asked for the fastest and most accurate typist in the class, sight unseen. She was a beefy, round-faced young woman with few social graces and a taste for clothes that were always too small. She could type like fury, though, and within a few weeks Increase discovered she possessed a natural intelligence and a talent for organization. He was never able to domesticate her but she quickly become a loyal and indispensable part of his practice. Much of his success in the years that followed was due to the support he got from Irene Bills and Increase, more than anyone, knew it.

"Fanny Forbes is here," she jerked a thumb over her shoulder, "and she's got a full head of steam."

A visit from Fanny had been expected eventually but Increase had certainly not invited one. "Give me a minute to finish up this one piece," he said, "and then send her in."

Having cooled her heels in the outer office for a full ten seconds, Fanny pushed into the room past Irene.

"What of the boy?" she demanded. "What of the boy?"

Irene had balled a fist, ready to reset Fanny's clock, but a look from Increase kept her in check.

"Morning, Fanny," Increase said, as much a signal to Irene as it was a greeting to Fanny. Irene just rolled her eyes and shook her head as she went back to her desk. Fanny stood across the table from Increase now, her face red. She gasped to catch her breath.

"What happens to the boy?" she demanded.

"The boy's interests will be seen to, Fanny."

"But surely he belongs with family." Her panting made it difficult for her to speak. "He has family, after all. I know he's technically an orphan, but he still has family. I should take the boy in. It's only right that he be with family."

"We all want what's best for him, Fanny."

"I know what the state will do, Increase. They'll have a committee review the situation and they'll meet forty times and finally decide to send him off to some heartless foster home where people will mistreat him and feed him porridge."

"Fanny, I – "

"That's not right, Increase. It's not right."

"There's been some mention of Kurn Hattin…"

"Oh, nonsense. Nothing against The Kurn Hattin Home, but the boy should be with family. I can take him in."

"Malcolm and I and the court will come to a satisfactory arrangement, I'm sure."

"Malcolm? What's Malcolm MacArthur got to do with this?"

"Tom and Amy had no wills. Their assets, or, more correctly the proceeds from the liquidation of their assets, will be put in trust for Kenny."

"A trust?"

"That's correct. Kenny as next of kin is the legal heir but of course as a minor he can't yet take possession. The trust will protect these funds until he comes of age. The trust would also be available to see that his needs are met."

"I see," she said. "So the money would be locked up for ten years?"

"To be precise," Increase explained, "the trust assures that the money is protected from misuse."

"But the boy," Fanny said, not wanting to appear to dwell on the money. "Surely he should be with family. I'm more than willing to take him in. It would be a hardship, of course, since I've been left with so little, but as family…"

"These arrangements take time," Increase said. "I'll do what I can to expedite things."

"He can't just be shoved around like furniture, Increase. Let the boy come home with me. He should be with family."

"The boy's still in the hospital. He may be there for a couple of weeks."

"Oh." She absorbed this information and reconsidered her time frame. "Well," she started again, "I know the Nelsons have taken over but between you and me I've never really trusted clergy," she snorted. "They're little more than transients. They come and they go. I know they're supposed to be good Christians, but – "

"Have you been to see the boy, Fanny?"

"What?"

"Have you been down to Springfield to see the boy?"

"Why, no," she said. "I've been busy here with the funeral, making arrangements and all."

Increase took a moment to adjust some papers on his desk.

"The 'good Christians' have been down there with him every day, Fanny. You might want to think about that."

"Wuh," she huffed. "You know I don't drive. How would I get there?"

"Perhaps the good Christians could find room in their car."

Fanny set her mouth, stood up, and left the room without a word. Five seconds later the photo of Increase's parents rattled on the conference room wall when Fanny slammed the front door.

Increase chuckled quietly to himself and caught a glimpse of Fanny as she steamed back up the street toward her house. He sat down, took off his glasses, rubbed his eyes, and pondered the fate of young Kenneth Forbes.

Irene Bills was in the doorway again.

"You're not going to let that sour bitch take that nice boy, are you?"

"These things are never simple, Irene. The courts like to keep the child with family if possible. We could argue that Fanny is not technically family but she's as close as he's got and that's going to carry some weight. She's also announced a willingness. Let me see what I can come up with."

Increase concluded the best he could do was to oversee the liquidation of Tom and Amy's assets and create a trust that would dole out a maintenance allowance to Fanny or anyone else as long as Kenny remained in their care. He drafted a proposal of the plan and had Irene Bills type it up so he could send it to the court as a starting point for the discussion and eventual ruling.

"So she gets the boy?" Irene said when she'd finished.

"Along with a modest stipend. You and I both know it's the money she's after. This way she has to earn it."

"And the boy serves a ten year sentence while she dips into his inheritance? Good work, Increase." Irene threw the papers on the table and went back to her desk.

It was now five minutes to noon. Increase came out of his office.

"I'm going up for lunch. Can I bring you anything?

"After the past hour I'm not hungry."

"It's not over 'til it's over, Irene."

"Tell that to Kenny. I'm sure he'll feel a lot better." She slammed a drawer shut.

Increase had a gift for arguing law but he'd never won an argument with Irene Bills. As he reached the back stairs he heard the front door slam.

Twice in the same day, he thought, and continued up the stairs.

"What was all the banging around?" Judith asked as he sat down at the table.

"One was a client, one was the help." He took a bite of his BLT, chewed it thoroughly, swallowed, and wiped mayonnaise from the corner of his mouth with a clean, crisp cloth napkin. "Some days," he said, "I just piss people off."

*

Most of the mourners were contemporaries of the deceased, middle-aged, married, with families of their own, and had known them since grade school. The rest, from an older generation, were people who always went to the funerals, no matter whose it was. Funerals were entertainment. The attraction this time, of course, was the thrill of a triple header, three corpses in concert so to speak. After days of anticipation, there was considerable disappointment among the hard-core mourners when they realized the caskets would remain closed.

"Well, Christ," Wendell Billings muttered. "S'hardly worth the trip."

Still, it was a fine opportunity for theater in a town with nothing in the way of formal theater. Kenneth was still in the hospital so it fell on Fanny Forbes alone to represent the survivors of this enormous tragedy. She sat, a forlorn and singular figure draped in black, separated from the rest of the crowd by two empty pews. Head bowed, alone in her grief, she milked it for all it was worth.

The Rev. Gordon Nelson held a pose of silent reflection at the front. The draft of his five page eulogy for the deceased lay abandoned on his desk, a piece, he thought, that was, with the help of God, his best work but the moment had been snatched away. As a humble servant of the Lord, however, he would respect the wishes of his parishioners, no matter how narrow and selfish they might be, and the service, as Fanny had directed, would be brief.

At the stroke of two Ruth Bennett, the organist, improvised a conclusion to *In the Garden* and Gordon Nelson approached the pulpit. He was about to begin when Ruth's foot slipped and the organ honked a deep low G.

"Sorry, Gordon."

Gordon Nelson let the snickering in the sanctuary subside and then spoke about each of the deceased, assured everyone that all three would "want us to continue on" even though they were "no longer with us". He offered a prayer, invited the congregation to join in singing *Abide With Me*, and closed with a short benediction. Split three ways, taking out the time for the hymn, it came to about three minutes each. He concluded with a reminder that the social committee would host a memorial reception in the community room downstairs following the committal and burial.

The old hymn tunes again flowed from the organ and the mourners shuffled out. A few came by to offer condolences to the small shrouded figure in the front row.

"Thank you," Fanny said. "Thank you so much, but my concern now is for the boy. Thank you." People who had never seen Fanny so contrite were nevertheless generous enough under the circumstances to attribute it to shock and loss.

"Oh, I'll get by," she said, "but I just weep for that poor boy. I'll be fine, of course. I'll make do. I only hope the court doesn't dump him in some cold, heartless foster home. It would just be a shame to take him away from family…"

"Of course," they'd say, "of course," and head for the door for some fresh air. Fanny, who had never looked up through her veil as people came by, continued for several seconds after the last of them had left.

"Fanny." It was Otto Coombs.

"What?"

"Everybody's gone," he said. "We're ready to load'em up."

"Fine." She stood and tossed back her veil. As she surveyed the empty sanctuary Gordon Nelson came back down the aisle. "Who set up that reception?" she hissed.

"The social committee always hosts a little do after a funeral."

"Don't they even ask? I'm not going to any reception. Is there any way to stop it?"

"I shouldn't think so." He looked to Otto who shrugged his shoulders.

"There are people in this world," Otto said, "who are driven to make coffee and serve cookies in times of crisis. There's nothing we can do about that."

"Just get me out of here. Are there people out front?"

"A dozen or so, waiting for the caskets to come out the front door. That seems to fascinate some people. Why don't we let the boys get to work?"

"Can I go out the back?"

"Of course. Just let me bring the car around." Otto bustled up the aisle and out the front door. Normally he moved slowly and deliberately in an effort to present an air of solemn dignity. But, as with any theater – and a funeral was certainly an opportunity for high theater – it was entirely appropriate and often necessary to hustle behind the scenes to push things along.

Gordon Nelson hovered nearby. "I'm, ah… I'm going to head on out to the cemetery, Fanny. Was the service concise enough?"

"I could have done without all eight verses to the hymn."

"Yes, well… I should have shortened it. I'm sorry about that."

"Never mind, Gordon. Just get out to the cemetery and get'm buried."

Otto took Fanny out the back door, put her in the rear seat of the flower car where she could hide behind the smoked glass windows, and brought the car around front again.

When the caskets were loaded the hearses and limousines whispered off to the cemetery, trailed by a small assortment of private cars and pickup trucks with their headlights on.

A smattering of mourners gathered as the caskets were removed from the hearses and Gordon led the procession into the cemetery where he stood at the head of each grave as the caskets were placed on the riggings that would eventually lower them into the ground. Fanny sat at the side of each grave through the three brief committal services. Gordon Nelson again reminded the mourners about the reception at the church. Fanny gestured to Otto.

"Take me home," she said.

Otto had by this time taken more than his fill and readily agreed. Neither of them spoke on the drive back into town.

"Don't bother to pull into the driveway," Fanny said as they turned down her street.

"Should I come to a complete stop or just slow down so you can jump out?"

"Don't get smart," she said.

Inside, even though the day was quite warm, Fanny built a small fire in the kitchen stove. When she was satisfied it was burning vigorously enough she took off her black mourning costume, and threw it into the fire, shoes and all.

"And that," she said, "is that."

*

Chapter Four

Blessed with both youth and resiliency, Kenneth healed quickly and his release from the hospital was scheduled for the Monday following the funeral. He still needed care, however, and this would come in the soft round form of Charlotte Nelson. She'd been with him tirelessly every day, after all, and knew the routine.

"Can't I go back home?"

"Oh, don't be silly, sweetheart. We have a room all ready for you at the parsonage."

"But I want to go home."

"I know you do, honey," she stroked his forehead and patted a few stray hairs into place, "but there's no one there, no one to care for you, and you can't stay alone."

"But I don't want to go to the parsonage. I want my own room."

"I know, dear, but for a few days you'll come live with us."

Kenneth was ready to argue the point but a nurse came in with a wheelchair.

"All ready to go?"

"All dressed and ready," Charlotte chirped. "Aren't we Kenny?"

Charlotte had measured him up and bought him a complete set of new clothes, including underwear and socks. This morning she'd arrived early, gave him a thorough washing, rubbed him dry, carefully helped him dress, and combed his hair. The shirt barely fit over the cast on his arm. The leg splint was wrapped around the outside of the new chinos. She'd bought new white sneakers, too, and a belt with a cowboy buckle and a metal tip. She chattered non-stop as she pulled and tucked and lifted and adjusted and tied to prepare Kenneth for his "big day".

Charlotte Nelson was not to be stopped. To the contrary, she seemed to take a particular pleasure in his helplessness. No one, not even his mother, for instance, had ever been so obsessed with his bowels. The day he finally managed a dump in the bedpan appeared to be one of the great moments in Charlotte Nelson's life. Kenneth was both amazed and amused that a bowel movement could make anyone so happy. She lifted him off the pan and took several moments to inspect and praise his turds – even gave him a little congratulatory peck on the cheek. Then she rang for the nurse so they could all celebrate the product of his efforts. The nurse, while satisfied, simply took the bedpan and emptied it while Charlotte drew a basin of warm, soapy water to clean Kenneth up once again, paying particular attention, as always, to his genitals. Her constant attention annoyed and confused him but with one arm in a cast and his leg in a splint, he couldn't get away.

And he was about to live in this woman's house.

"Well, Kenny, ready to go home?" The doctor had come in.

"I can't go home. I have to go to the parsonage."

"Ah, a literalist."

"My parents are dead. I can't go home," Kenneth said again.

"Yes, that's true – it certainly is – but you'll need someone to help you for a few weeks. We didn't think you'd have much fun in a nursing home with a lot of really old people. At the Nelsons' you'll be back in Grants Ferry where your friends can visit."

"How soon can I walk?"

"That depends. Don't try to walk around without the splint until I tell you, though. You don't need the splint when you're in bed, and you can bend your knee as long as it doesn't hurt. But don't get out of bed without the splint. Okay?"

"Okay."

"If you had both arms available we'd have you on crutches and you'd be up and running but as it is… Well, you'll be coming in again the first of next week and we'll see how you're doing. One step at a time."

Kenneth was transferred to the wheelchair and then rolled out to the car where the nurse positioned him to rest his splinted leg on the seat. He was glad to be in the back and out of Charlotte's reach. She chattered constantly as she drove and Kenneth just let it flow over him like an annoying buzz he couldn't shut off.

They passed the broken guard rail and the temporary barriers and he sat up to get a better look.

"Is that where they died?"

"Yes, dear, I'm afraid it is. I didn't want you to see it but this is the best way home."

"Can we stop?"

"Oh, I don't think that's a good idea, sweetheart."

"I want to see. Go back, please."

At the next driveway, Charlotte turned the car around and went back but now they were on the wrong side of the road.

"I want to see over the edge."

"Really, dear, I don't – "

"I want to see where they died!" he yelled. Charlotte quickly put the car in gear.

"All right, honey," she said, "just let me turn the car around again." Charlotte stopped the car near the temporary barriers.

"I need to get out."

"Oh, sweetheart, this is not – "

But Kenneth had opened the door and hunched across the seat. Before Charlotte could get out and around the car he had both feet on the ground and by holding onto the car door he worked his way to the barriers where he could look over the edge and down the hill. He was very still. Marks went from the road, down the hill, and straight to the maple tree where a great section of bark had been torn off. He knew he had been there, with them, in the car when they died but as hard as he tried he couldn't remember any of it. He wanted to feel something of that moment but there was nothing.

"Did it hurt?"

"I don't think so, dear." Charlotte put her arm around his shoulders to comfort him but he shrugged her off. "It all happened very quickly. It was terrible. They didn't expect to find any survivors. You were very lucky."

"I should have died, too," he said.

"Oh, that's not true, Kenny. You have your whole life ahead of you."

"Oh, right," he said. "And Amy's dead. What kind of life is that?" He hobbled back to the car and slid in across the seat. For the rest of the drive Charlotte had the good sense to keep her mouth shut.

The Nelsons had rented a wheelchair but Kenneth wanted to walk into the house. Supported between them he was able to slowly climb the front steps to the porch and then to the room they'd prepared for him on the first floor. The Nelsons had obviously gone to some trouble and he thanked them.

"Can I get you anything, sweetheart?"

"I'm really tired," he said. "I think I'd like to lie down."

"Of course, dear." The Nelsons helped him onto the bed. "When you need anything, just ring the bell." She jangled a small bell on the nearby table.

"Okay. Thank you."

Alone at last, Kenneth stared at the ceiling. There were small cracks in the plaster but if he let his eyes relax everything went out of focus and it became a big, white, blank screen. Images of the skid marks and the damaged tree came and went and Kenneth tried to imagine what it must have been like in those last seconds as the car fell down the hillside in the dark and the fog. Did Amy and Tom and Fred know they were going to die? Had Amy, in those last moments, tried to protect him, knowing full well that she couldn't protect herself? The scene ran over and over and over but it never changed.

And then he cried.

*

Curtains softened the light from the one small window and shelves of books lined the walls. He tried to sit up but the cast on his arm threw him off balance and he fell back again.

"Well, my sakes, look who's awake," Charlotte Nelson was there, watching. "And guess who has company," she chirped. She put another pillow behind him, patted his hair and straightened his shirt. When she finally moved out of the way to open the curtains Kenneth saw Ellen LeClaire standing in the doorway.

"Hi," Ellen said. Her eyes were big and her voice was small.

"Now why don't you two just have a nice little visit? I'll get some milk and cookies," Charlotte said. "Visits are so much nicer with a little treat, don't you think?" Without waiting for an answer, she pushed past Ellen and went to fetch the snack.

"Hi," Kenneth smiled. Ellen was the first good thing that had happened in the past week. They'd been playmates since before first grade. Both were small for their age, among the youngest in their class, and were exceptional students. Neither was popular among the others so they had found each other. Ellen lived only four houses away from Kenneth and they easily walked back and forth.

Ellen was not just a small child, she was also skinny, with arms and legs that looked as if they might snap if you hugged her too hard.

"How are you feeling?" she asked.

"Sore."

Ellen put a paper bag on the bed.

"I brought you some books. I don't know, you might not like them, but I thought you'd like something to read."

"Thanks," Kenneth said. He looked through the titles with his good hand. There were three Nancy Drews, a Hardy Boys, and a couple others he didn't know. At home he had some Zane Gray westerns. He could easily read some of those again, but these would do for now.

"These are some I had," Ellen said. "I'll go to the library if you want something else."

"These are good." Kenneth wasn't sure he could read a book with just one hand but maybe Charlotte Nelson would leave him alone if he was reading something. "There's nothing to do here except listen to Mrs. Nelson so these will be good."

"These are kind of girl books but I can get – "

"Here we are." Charlotte Nelson carried a tray with glasses of milk and two small plates with store bought ginger snaps. "Isn't this fun?" She put Kenneth's snack on the table by the bed where he could reach them easily. Ellen's were put on a table across the room. "There you are, darlin'," she said. "Now you two just sit and have a nice little visit." She fluffed Kenneth's pillow again, smoothed the bedspread, and bustled out.

Ellen picked up her milk and cookies and brought them to the table near the bed. She slid all the cookies onto one plate, put the full plate on top of the empty one, and brought a chair close. Neither of them cared about the snacks. Ellen's hands were clasped so tightly in her lap the blood couldn't reach the ends of her fingers. Kenneth saw that violet hue in her eyes that appeared when Ellen struggled with her emotions.

"I – I'm really sorry about your mom and dad," she said. "I cried."

No one had actually said this to him. They'd said lots of other things but not this. It wasn't until he heard the words that he realized they'd been missing. His throat constricted and it was difficult to breathe. Kenneth was afraid he might cry again but he didn't want to cry in front of Ellen. He took a deep breath and stopped it.

"…and I wanted to do something for you," Ellen said, "but I…" She looked down at her hands again. "So I brought some books… I didn't know…"

"Thanks."

Ellen was quiet again, this time for what seemed like several minutes. When she spoke again her voice was small.

"Was it awful?"

"I don't remember."

"I've been crying all the time," Ellen said.

"Me, too. Sometimes."

"I try to imagine what it must have been like and I – "

"Me, too. I can't."

There didn't seem to be anything more to say about that so they just sat with each other.

"Where will you live?" Ellen asked finally.

"I don't know. They won't let me go home."

"What about your Aunt Fanny? She's family, isn't she?"

"Well, yeah, by marriage. Does that count?"

"I don't know. I think so."

"I don't want to live with her. Jesus. Don't I have any say?

"Kid's don't have much say in anything."

"Amy let me choose," Kenneth said.

"Amy was special. You know that."

"Well, you always said that."

"Fanny's creepy."

"Well, yeah."

"It would be a longer walk to see you then."

"Yeah." Kenneth tried to imagine a life with his Aunt Fanny but it was too awful. He changed the subject. "Can you come again?"

"I can come every day."

"Good. Come every day and stay for as long as you can. Mrs. Nelson is driving me crazy."

"Okay." This is what she wanted to hear. "We can talk and we can play games – whatever you want."

"Okay. Good," Kenneth said. Ellen smiled and wiped her eyes. There had been tears, but she was smiling. He lifted himself up and motioned for her to come close. "I have to get out of here," he whispered. "I hate that woman."

"Mrs. Nelson?" Ellen whispered back.

"Yeah. She won't leave me alone."

"What do you mean?"

"She's always touching me. I hate it."

Ellen looked back at the doorway. "What do you want me to do?"

"When I can walk, maybe next week, we'll go for walks."

"Walks?"

"We'll say we're building my strength. I'll talk to the doctor about it so Mrs. Nelson won't give us any trouble. As long as I'm careful – "

Charlotte appeared in the doorway.

"What are you two whispering about?" She leaned between Ellen and Kenneth to gather up the dishes. "We don't whisper in this house, dear."

Kenneth sank back against the pillows. "Sorry."

"Me, too," Ellen said.

"Now," she addressed Kenneth, "what was that all about, sweetheart?"

"Well," Ellen said, completely sincere, "I asked Kenny about – about the night of the accident, and – "

Charlotte knew she wasn't getting the truth. "I think that might be enough for today, dear. Why don't you run along now? You can come again for a little while tomorrow."

Kenneth, with the slightest movement of his eyes, one that Charlotte Nelson couldn't see, told her to agree.

From the earliest days of their friendship, Ellen and Kenneth had created this secret language. They could communicate with each other through very slight facial expressions, mostly with their eyes and eyebrows and the bond between them became even stronger.

"Okay. I'll come by tomorrow," Ellen said.

"Not too early, dear. We want to be sure he gets plenty of rest, don't we?" Ellen left and Charlotte Nelson looked at the uneaten snacks. "I guess you two weren't very hungry. Should I leave these for later?"

"Yes. Thank you." Kenneth had to take a whiz but he knew if he said anything Charlotte Nelson would grab his pecker again. He decided it was time to do it on his own.

"Where's the bathroom?" he asked.

"What, dear?"

"The bathroom. I'd like to go to the bathroom."

"I'll get the urinal, sweetheart, you just relax. I'll be back in a jiff."

"I'm going to use the bathroom."

"But your leg – "

"The doctor said I can walk on it as long as I wear the brace. I'll be careful."

"Well, I don't – "

"Help me out of bed, please." She made no move to help him so Kenneth rolled around, pushed himself up with his good arm, and swung his legs off the bed."

"Kenny, now you stop that."

"I'm not using that urinal any more." He could stand by himself as long as he held onto something but he wasn't sure he could keep his balance if he tried to walk. "Help me, please." He took a shaky step and began to go down like a tree but she caught him.

"Now, Kenny, I don't think – "

Determined, he took another step and she helped him shuffle to the bathroom.

"Do you want me to – "

"No."

He closed the door, leaned against it, and took several deep breaths. The short walk had exhausted him but he hadn't let Charlotte Nelson see. He positioned himself at the toilet and struggled one-handed with the zipper, fought with the fly in his underpants, and finally brought the little fella forth to enjoy his first private whiz in over a week.

Finished and satisfied, he took two full minutes to get everything closed again. The zipper would only move if he pushed his good leg against the toilet to hold his pant leg down. It took several tries but he got it zipped. Charlotte Nelson was waiting outside, of course, listening the whole time.

"Well, dear. Aren't we making progress, though?"

Kenneth didn't answer. All he wanted now was to get back to the bed where he could rest, be alone, and read Ellen's books whether he liked them or not. He'd have her go to the library and get some Zane Gray books eventually, but right now it was enough to just hold something that was hers.

*

Kenneth was up, dressed, and sitting in a chair with his leg up on a stool when Ellen came.

"You're up?"

"Yeah, and I'm staying up," Kenneth said. Since he'd managed by himself in the bathroom the previous afternoon he'd had enough of bed, enough of Charlotte Nelson fawning and pawing him and washing him, and he was determined to do things for himself and get out of this house.

"Is it okay… for you to be up?"

"It feels okay. Nothing hurts. The doctor said as long as nothing hurts." He was clearly feeling better. "You can move that little table over and we can play a game or something, except she won't let me play cards."

"Why not?"

"Who knows? Something to do with gambling."

"We're not going to gamble."

"Doesn't matter."

"Does she have games here?"

"She brought a stack of them in the other day. I don't know what they are." Ellen found them on the floor behind the door, games like Chutes and Ladders and Candyland, games that would be an interesting exercise for kindergarteners but nothing that would challenge a couple of fifth graders with ninth grade reading levels.

"Doesn't she have any word games?"

"I don't think so."

"I can bring Monopoly tomorrow."

"Good. Thanks."

"I've got Checkers and Scrabble, too."

"Good."

"I've got some jigsaw puzzles. Would she let us set that up?"

"I don't know," he said. "It won't hurt to try."

"Won't hurt to try what, dear?" Charlotte Nelson was in the doorway. For a big woman, Kenneth thought, she could certainly move quietly.

"Ellen said she could bring a jigsaw puzzle. I thought we could set up a card table or something."

"We'll see, dear. Right now you have company. Look who's here. Surprise!" As she stepped aside Kenneth's Aunt Fanny appeared in the doorway.

"Well," Fanny said, looking at everything in the room but Kenneth. "Here you are." She attempted a smile but it looked a bit freakish. Kenneth shot a glance at Ellen. "I saw that," Fanny said, looking at him for the first time. "Who's your friend?" as if Ellen wasn't there.

"Ellen LeClaire."

"LeClaire?" Fanny's eyes were as cold as two pieces of slate. "Your father's the Frenchman that works down at the sawmill?"

"Yes, he's the head sawyer," Ellen said.

"He's the one who keeps that pack of hounds?"

"We have three hunting dogs."

"Come down across the border, did you?"

"What border is that?" Ellen said.

"Canada, of course."

"Oh." Ellen knew where this was going. "My grandparents came from Nova Scotia to Maine and then to New Hampshire. It was all a long time ago. I was born in Grants Ferry."

Ellen remained polite and answered everything but confrontation heightened her clarity and her answers became quick and precise.

"My mother's an Allen," Ellen said.

Fanny grunted her disapproval. *Of course*, her manner said. *No wonder she settled for a Frenchman.* This reaction was not lost on Ellen.

"And your father? When did he come?"

"I think you should ask him," Ellen said.

Fanny turned to Charlotte. "Does she come here often?"

"Yesterday and today." Charlotte deferred to Fanny's rudeness, even in her own house. Kenneth and Ellen were suddenly invisible.

"I'm not so sure that's a good idea," Fanny said.

"Why, I – "

"At the very least we should work out a schedule."

"Well, I – "

"The burden has fallen on me now. I'm the only family he has left, after all."

"He's been no trouble…"

"That's beside the point," Fanny said, all business. "The wheels are in motion. I'll come for him when it's settled." And with that she turned and left the room.

"Well," Charlotte Nelson said, suddenly at a loss for words. "Well," she stammered again. She patted her hair and pulled nervously at her clothes. She looked around the room as if that would inspire her to say something, anything at all. Nothing helped. Ellen was the next to speak.

"Mrs. Nelson, I've only been here a few minutes. Is it all right if I stay?"

"Of course, dear. Now let me see if I can find the card table. You two just visit." Charlotte tugged at her clothes again and left the room.

"See what I mean?" Kenneth said.

"What?"

"She's come to get me. Help me to the bathroom before Mrs. Nelson gets back."

*

Chapter Five

Kenneth gained strength and stability as he learned to shift his weight and keep his balance. The doctor confirmed his progress on the following Monday and he was encouraged to walk, outside if he liked, but to take it slow and not get tired. He could even try without the brace as long as someone brought it along should he need it. He couldn't use crutches with his arm in a sling so the people at the hospital gave him a cane and taught him to use it properly, how to negotiate steps, one leg at a time. By the end of the week he and Ellen were out for two hours or more. He took frequent rests in the folding lawn chair that Ellen brought along.

These were good times and Kenneth made them last. One day Ellen brought a deck of cards and her father's copy of *According to Hoyle* and they walked clear to Audrey's Diner on Main Street where they ordered milkshakes and spent several hours learning the rules to new card games.

Audrey didn't like kids to hang out at the diner but like so many others in town she'd easily made an exception for Kenneth and Ellen. Adults always treated him well. They noticed his progress, told him how they'd loved and missed his parents, and complimented Ellen for being such a help. They all seemed to know him, know the story, and this is what they did when they didn't know what else to do.

Some of the boys, on the other hand, were merciless. They liked to come up behind Kenneth and Ellen at full speed on their bikes and then scream as they tore past to see if they could startle Kenneth enough to lose his balance.

The worst of them was Archie Whitaker, a born bully with a solid reputation. From the day Kenneth began kindergarten, Archie had pushed him around, knocked over blocks that Kenneth was trying to make into a house, or spilled his milk at lunchtime. Archie would do these things in a way that made Kenneth look clumsy and leave Archie blameless. Archie

Whitaker was the main reason Kenneth hated school. He could have dealt with the regimentation and the boredom but Archie and the ever present threat of his bullying was something else again.

He and Amy had long talks about this and her advice had been to let it go. Nothing, she said, is gained by fighting. She liked to quote a rule she had read years before in the Pogo comic strip. "He who strikes the first blow loses the argument." So Kenneth had remained noncombative and continued to suffer the indignities of Archie's pranks.

Archie's rules of confrontation were similar, the primary rule being that the other person had to make the first contact. Contact in this case could be a bump or a nudge or a shove so Kenneth's nonresponse only intensified Archie's efforts. The verbal abuse or the pranks were only teasing, Archie reasoned, not actual fighting. Even the slightest contact, however, would free Archie to pound him senseless.

School vacations meant Kenneth could stay out of Archie's path for ten whole weeks and this had promised to be another such summer but during his recovery walks he and Ellen were exposed nearly every day.

For Archie, this opportunity was too good to pass up. He liked to hide behind a bush out of view from the parsonage and jump out when they came by.

"Hey, I see the cripple's got a girlfriend," he'd say.

They'd ignore him.

"This your girlfriend? I guess cripples have to settle for the boney ones."

No response.

"Hey, Crip. Got a girl holding you up?"

This or a variation of it happened several times over two weeks. Archie was verbally abusive but never physical. Kenneth refused to respond, no matter what Archie said. Finally, in his frustration one day, Archie snatched Kenneth's cane. Technically, this still fell within Archie's rules of no first contact, although, one could make a strong argument that he had finally crossed a line he himself had drawn. For Ellen, the argument was strong enough.

"Give that back," Ellen said.

"Whoa. Cripple's got a girl speaking for him now?"

"I said give it back," Ellen said again, this time a little louder.

"I'm not talking to you, toothpick."

Ellen reached for the cane but Archie held it over his head.

"Give it," she said through her teeth, but Archie swept her away with his other hand. She landed in the Randalls' front yard. Archie laughed in

Kenneth's face and held the cane just out of reach, knowing full well Kenneth couldn't take a step without it.

"Come on, crip, here's your cane. Come get it. Come on, crip."

Ellen flew up off the lawn and landed on Archie with a ferocity seldom seen in human beings. The cane fell to the ground. Archie tried to shake her off but Ellen was wiry and fast and furious. She clawed at his face and pulled his hair and pounded his ear. Archie could have been standing over a nest of yellow jackets for all the defense he had against Ellen LeClaire.

Ellen bit hard into the side of Archie's neck and he howled with pain. She scratched at his face, barely missing his eyes. She pounded his ear again and he lost his balance and fell over. He tried to roll away but Ellen was on him again and she punched and kicked and pulled his hair. Archie flailed his arms in a feeble defense but Ellen was so quick he was only able to deflect a few of the blows that rained down on him

"You give up?" she said?

Not likely.

"Crazy bitch," he said.

Ellen punched him in the mouth. His lip split and blood sprayed over both of them.

"Give up?" she said again.

Archie shook his head.

Ellen drove her knee into his ribs and his breath was punched out in an ugly grunt.

"Say 'Uncle'," she said. Archie shook his head. Ellen hit him again. "Say 'Uncle'. I'm warning you." Archie was unable to speak. He was on his back and Ellen had straddled him, holding him down. He shook his head again. Ellen delivered a blow to his jaw that snapped his head to one side. There was his left ear.

Ellen bit it. Hard.

"Ow! Jesus!"

Ellen sat back on her heels, her small chest heaving. The top of Archie's ear hung from a small cartilage hinge. Blood was everywhere.

"What are you doing?" Archie cried, his defenses completely gone.

"I'm getting you to say 'Uncle'."

"I'm not – "

Ellen grabbed the little finger on his left hand and bent it backwards.

"Ow! Ow! Jesus! Uncle, for Christ's sake! Uncle!"

Ellen let go his finger and stood up. Archie felt his ear.

"Jesus, you bit off my ear."

"Did not."

"Yes, you did. You bit it off."

"Did not. It's still hitched." She spat blood onto the grass.

Archie moaned and sobbed and rolled back and forth. He held his ear and blood ran out between his fingers.

"Oh my God, Oh my God...."

"You notice anything else?" Ellen said.

"What?"

"You notice anything else?"

"Notice what?" he said.

"You seem to have wet your pants." She wiped her hands on the grass and the legs of her shorts, picked up Kenneth's cane, and gave Archie a smart rap on his leg. "Get up and get out of here."

Archie moaned. She prodded him with the tip of the cane and rapped him again.

"Now," she said, "Move it."

Archie got up, still holding his ear. His wet pants clung to his legs and he was sobbing.

"Get out of here," Ellen said again.

Without looking back, Archie shuffled off toward home.

It was over in far less time than it takes to tell about it, a display of savagery that left Kenneth slightly nauseous, although with a surprising wave of satisfaction at the result. The efficiency and clarity with which Ellen had expressed herself couldn't be denied. A new and hidden Ellen LeClaire had surfaced, an Ellen LeClaire who would only be pushed so far.

"Kenny."

Kenneth jumped when he heard his name. Ellen was holding his cane and spattered with blood.

"Let's get back to the parsonage," she said.

"He's bleeding."

"Good. Let's get out of here." She turned Kenneth around but he looked back. Archie, in his wet pants and a hand over his torn and bleeding ear, was running for home.

"He'll tell, you know."

"No, he won't."

"Yes he will. That's what he does. You're in big trouble."

"No, I'm not."

"You can't bite somebody's ear off and not be in trouble."

"I didn't bite his ear off."

"Well, excuse me. Hanging by a thread."

"Doesn't matter. It's not off."

"It's almost off and it's bleeding. They're going to come and get you."

"Wanna bet? Three people know about this. I'm not saying anything, you're not going to say anything, and Archie certainly isn't about to tell anybody a girl beat him up."

"So how are we going to explain all the blood to Mrs. Nelson?"

"She's not going to see it. I'm going to get you back to the parsonage and go home. You can tell her I wasn't feeling well."

"What about your mom?"

"I'll think of something. I'll get cleaned up and come back after lunch."

Ellen watched until she was sure Kenneth was up the steps and able to get into the house, then she ran home the back way through the woods. Ellen's mother was in her garden where she enjoyed the precision and tedium of weeding carrots or thinning beets or tying up tomato plants. Ellen ran inside and upstairs to the bathroom, peeled off her clothes, got a wash cloth from the cupboard, and stood at the sink where she soaped and rinsed and soaped and rinsed until she was sure she was free of anything connected to Archie Whitaker. She brushed her teeth for several minutes but she could still taste Archie's ear and the salty stickiness of his blood. She'd spit repeatedly on the way home but it hadn't helped. She hated the taste but she rinsed and gargled twice with her father's Listerine. Then she held a mouthful for a full minute. That seemed to do it.

She pulled on clean clothes, carefully wiped up the few blood stains on the bathroom floor, got three days' worth of newspapers, wrapped up the bloody clothes, and took the bundle out to the garbage pail in the garage. Satisfied that she'd covered her tracks, she went out to the garden to see her mother who was now weeding the green beans.

"Hi, Mom."

"Oh. You're home?"

"Yeah, Kenny wasn't feeling well. He wanted to rest. I'm going back after lunch."

"Oh."

"So I guess I'll have lunch here today."

"All right. Let me finish this row and I'll make some tuna sandwiches."

*

Charlotte heard Kenneth hobbling up the steps and was in the hall when he came in the front door.

"What happened to your little friend, dear?" Charlotte seemed unable to call Ellen by name.

"She didn't feel good."

"Oh, my. That's a shame."

"She went home to lie down. She might come again this afternoon."

"Oh, that'll be nice. Would you like some lunch, sweetheart? Why don't you get comfortable here in the parlor and I'll bring a tray with a nice tuna sandwich."

*

Archie, covered with blood and smelling of urine, sobbed all the way home. Now he knew how their cat felt after it had been clipped by a car and it hid under the bed for three days. That's all he wanted to do – just go someplace and hide until he was better. Of course, the cat had eventually died under the bed and he had to pull it out with a rake and bury it in the back yard, but that wasn't the point. The cat had gone where it could suffer in peace. On the other hand, Archie was so frightened of his ear being torn that he just kept running until he was home.

"My word," his mother said. "What on earth happened?"

"Big kids," he sobbed. He'd decided on the way home, when he wasn't thinking about hiding, that he had been set upon by a gang of big kids. "There were three or four of them, Ma. They were on me for no reason."

"Land sakes. Why would anyone do this? Oh, my word."

"I don't know, Ma." Blood had run down his arm and off his elbow.

"What's happened to your ear? Oh, my word. Oh, my word."

"They bit it, Ma. One of them bit my ear. It won't stop bleeding. I can feel a piece just hanging there."

"You sit," she said and she grabbed the dish towel and told him to hold it against his ear to catch the blood. Then she wrapped up some ice cubes in another towel. "Here. Put this on it. I'm calling the doctor."

"I wet my pants, Ma. I couldn't help it."

"There, there. We'll get dry pants. Just let me call the doctor." Mrs. Whitaker made the call and then brought Archie some dry clothes. He wouldn't take his hand away from his ear, though, and she had to change his pants for him. Archie hadn't had someone change his pants for almost ten years and even though it was his mother the very thought of it made him furious.

"This is not right" she said. "I – I think I should call the police."

"I don't want to do that, Ma."

"People can't go around biting people's ears, Archie. This won't do. It won't do at all."

"I don't want a lot of fuss, Ma." Archie's self confidence was coming back. Mrs. Whitaker washed the dried blood off his arm and got him a clean shirt. "If we make a big deal out of it," he said, "they'll just come back again. It's better to let it go."

"Well, your father will settle this," she said finally, which is how Mrs. Whitaker put an end to any disagreement. Archie stopped arguing because he knew it was now pointless.

The ice numbed the pain but Archie continued to whimper all the way to the doctor's office. He was taken straight into the exam room, followed by Mrs. Whitaker.

"Ah, yes," Doc Wilson said when he'd uncovered the ear. "We'll just have to put that fella back on again, won't we?" Archie's sobs soon turned into screams while his mother held his head still so Doc Wilson could clean the ear with antiseptic and sew it back together.

"Quite an art to get ear pieces lined up," Doc Wilson explained over the screams. "I had a couple of these in Korea. Shrapnel leaves an awful mess, you know. You just have to do what you can with what you've got." Archie struggled and squirmed with each stitch.

"Would have been a lot easier if we could just use a stapler," Doc Wilson went on. It took six stitches. "Well, there," he said when he'd finished. "Either that will take or it'll dry up and fall off. Now, I'm going to put a couple pads on there to catch the bleeding and then we'll hold'em in place with a bandage around your head. Once the bleeding stops, probably by tomorrow morning, you can take the bandages off and give it some air."

With the ear patched, Doc Wilson took a look at the bite on Archie's neck, clearly a human tooth pattern.

"Human bites are much worse than animal bites you know." Doc Wilson liked to drop this kind of news on people as if he were advising you on the best time of year to separate your peonies.

Archie didn't like the sound of that. "They are?"

"Oh, much worse," Doc Wilson said. "A lot of animal diseases won't transfer to humans. Human diseases and bacteria and so forth have a straight shot. Much more dangerous," he said. "Besides, you don't know where their mouths have been, do you?" He chuckled at his own wit. "I think we'll give you a little tetanus shot, too, just to be on the safe side…"

Archie started wailing again. He squirmed and tried to get off the table but his mother was a big framed woman and strong and she held him fast until the shot was delivered. Archie continued to whimper while Doc Wilson wrote out two prescriptions, one for a mild painkiller, and the other for a salve.

"Once the bandage comes off," he said, "you can put some of this salve on there. It will help it heal so the scar's not so noticeable. Come back next week and we'll see how it's doing.

*

When Archie's father came home that evening Mrs. Whitaker started right in.

"Hugh, Archie was set upon by some boys, some hoodlums."

"So?" Hugh Whitaker had done his time as a kid in Grants Ferry. He'd had to work it out for himself and had no sympathy.

"One of them nearly bit his ear off."

"Really?" For some reason, Hugh Whitaker found this amusing. "All of it?"

"No, just the top."

"Oh, well…."

"Doctor Wilson's sewn it back on, but – "

"Good for him."

"Hugh, I can't have this. There was blood all over. He had to get a tetanus shot because it was a human bite."

Hugh Whitaker chuckled.

"I said we should call the police" she went on, "but Archie said no, and I said we'd settle it when you came home. Don't you think we should call the police?"

"No, I don't. For once in his life, the kid's right. Leave the police out of it," Hugh Whitaker said. He knew Archie's reputation as a bully and had always assumed that one day someone would take him down a peg or two. Mrs. Whitaker couldn't believe what she was hearing.

"What?"

"Little bastard probably had it coming."

"Why, I – "

"Archie's right. Let it go."

He left her standing in the kitchen with her mouth open, took the afternoon paper into the living room, poured himself a slug of Jack Daniels, sat in his chair, lit his pipe, put his feet up, and let the entire episode slide out of his mind.

*

Archie's had his mother tell his friends he was sick all the next week, which, he reasoned, was not exactly a lie. Still, he could only be sick for so long and when he did go out again he would need to explain the ear. Maybe, he thought, he could say a dog bit it. That would sound good. A big dog. A big, mean dog.

He crafted his story. It would be the Reeds, wild rustic members of his mother's family from over in Proctorsville. They were an unruly bunch, exactly the kind of people to keep a mean dog. This would be a perfect story. The same guys who'd have little use for someone who'd been beaten up by a girl would be extremely impressed that he'd survived an attack by a Doberman. Yeah, it would be a Doberman. With his story secure and the bandage off and the stitches out, Archie again ventured out among his pals.

"Jesus, what happened to your ear?" Eddie Harris asked. Eddie was quick to notice things like torn and stitched up ears.

"Dog," Archie said.

"Dog, my ass," Eddie Harris said back.

"No, really. My mother's people from over in Proctorsville came by for a visit. Remember the Reeds?"

"The ones that jack deer and sell the meat to restaurants in Boston?"

"Yeah, wild crazy people. They showed up about a week ago along with my cousin Mike and his Doberman."

"They've got a Doberman?"

"Yeah, big and black with a little brown around his face and patches here and there. Mike's dog. Bluto, he called him."

"Bluto?"

"Yeah. They keep him on a chain and he's always trying to get loose. Mike thinks it's funny that people are afraid of him. I wanted to show him I wasn't scared so I went over to the dog with my hand out and just like that, he went for me – yanked the chain right out of Mike's hand."

"You were attacked?"

"By a Doberman?"

"Yeah."

"Man, those things are mean."

"Unpredictable, too."

"Oh, wow. What was it like?"

He had'em now.

"Well, you know," Archie said easily, having rehearsed his story several times, "they jump on you and try to bite you. And there's a lot of snarling."

"And he jumped on you?"

"Yeah. Knocked me down on my back. They try to go for your throat, you know." This, in the parlance of twelve-year-olds, is known as a basic truth.

"Oh, yeah. They know to do that. It's instinct." Another basic truth.

The others chimed in.

"They're born killers, you know."

"Great pets, though."

"Yeah, but who'd want one?"

"I would."

"You shit, too."

"No, no. Really, I would."

Archie could see their attention wandering and he wanted to finish the story. "So he was trying to get my throat," he said again. "He lunged at me and I must have turned my head or something because he only got my ear. Then my Uncle Jim pulled him off."

"They always foam," Benny Munson said, another basic truth. "Was he foaming?"

"I don't know," Archie said, as he realized he should have included foam in his story. "I didn't see. People were all around me and there was a lot of noise. My cousin Mike was laughing and the women were screaming. I heard the dog snarling and barking. I remember it was wet," he said. "Maybe that was the foam."

"Yeah, maybe,"

"Then I saw my father with his .45."

"His Colt .45?"

"Yeah, you've seen it. He'd brought it out of the house and handed it to my Uncle Jim. The dog was yelping and snarling still – still wanting to get me, but Uncle Jim kept ahold of his collar and dragged him out behind the barn and shot him."

"Jesus, he shot the dog?"

"Yeah, two shots. It wasn't even loud. It was kind of a pop, pop. I thought there would be more noise."

"You sure it was a .45?"

"Yeah. It's my father's," Archie said. "Of course it was a .45. I know what a .45 looks like."

"Damn."

"And I thought my cousin Mike might be upset but all he said was, 'Well, there. I guess that sumbitch won't bite anybody else.' He was still laughing, though, even when Uncle Jim got a shovel out of the barn, gave it to Mike, and told him to bury the dog."

"He had to bury his own dog?"

"Yeah. Out behind our barn."

"Wow."

"Jesus."

"Attacked by a Doberman."

"Yeah. And my ear was torn half off. It was pretty gross, just hanging there. Doc Wilson sewed it back on."

"It still looks gross to me."

"Yeah, but at least it's back on."

"Yeah. Hey." Eddie Harris remembered something which was not an easy task after this story. "Your mother said you were sick all last week."

"Yeah, well, my folks didn't want the story getting around about the dog, you know?"

"Why not?"

"Well, having to kill it and everything. Some people don't like to hear that. Some people can cause trouble. I told you guys because I can trust you but you gotta keep it to yourselves."

"Oh, sure. No problem," they all lied, as Archie knew they would.

"What about other people? You can't hide that ear."

"It's all just a story, understand? It'll be best if we just don't talk about it again. I don't even think I should show you guys the grave," he said, knowing full well they'd all sneak out behind his barn and find the hole he had dug and filled.

And with that, the gang moved on.

"Hey, Archie," Eddie Harris said. "I saw Kenny and Ellen out for their walk again. Let's go scare the shit out of them."

"Nah, I'm tired of that," Archie said.

"Tired of it?"

"Yeah, I don't want to do that anymore."

"You get attacked by a Doberman and you don't want to do that anymore?"

"Nah." He turned and left before he had to explain further. This behavior stirred a twinge of suspicion among his friends, but Archie had historically set the lead in their activities and if Archie had lost interest in tormenting a cripple so had the others. With that pleasure gone they once again resorted to hanging out on the common, talking about cars, movies, Randolph Scott, trucks, guns, heavy equipment, and the intelligence of various dog breeds, all of which generally reinforced an endless list of basic truths according to the accumulated wisdom of twelve-year-old boys.

*

Kenneth's arm healed and the cast came off the week before school opened. Most of the strength in his leg had returned and the limp was nearly gone. Charlotte Nelson still fixed his meals and saw to his laundry but her offers to help with other things were put off as firmly as Kenneth could manage. Even so, Charlotte could usually find an excuse to straighten a collar or pick off a piece of lint and finish up with a couple pats or a light brushing away. There wasn't a day that went by that Charlotte didn't touch him at least once. It was annoying but just as Kenneth began to feel a sense of normalcy again Fanny arrived unannounced.

"It's settled," she said. "I'm named as your guardian. Gather up your things."

Kenneth and Ellen saw this as the worst possible option even though they had nothing to replace it. Kenneth's only possessions at the parsonage were things that Mrs. Nelson had bought for him over the summer. He'd never gone back to his own house for his stuff. Fanny stood silent, her black purse hanging from her folded arms. Mrs. Nelson went about gathering his clothes and packed them into two battered suitcases. Tears ran down her round cheeks and she took a hanky from the sash on her skirt and wiped her eyes as she worked. She couldn't bring herself to look at Fanny and she made a long job of it, delaying the inevitable as long as she could.

"The suitcases will make it easier," she said when she'd closed them and snapped the latches. "You can bring them back after you're settled in."

When Kenneth stood up Charlotte Nelson swept him into her arms and buried his head between her big soft breasts. She was sobbing. As much as he disliked her he felt badly that she was crying over him.

"Oh, for pity sakes," Fanny said. "I haven't got all morning." She picked up one of the suitcases and left the room. Kenneth and Charlotte stood stunned. It had happened so fast. Five seconds later Fanny was back. "Get the other bag and move along," she said. Kenneth picked up the bag with his good arm and followed her out of the parsonage and up the street to her house.

It never occurred to Fanny that she might arrange a ride and she strode off with determination, a woman on a mission. When she reached her front door, she was disgusted to discover Kenneth just coming into sight. Kenneth was angry, scared, and exhausted but he kept his mouth shut. Fanny waited by the door while he came up the front walk, climbed the steps using his good leg one step at a time, and finally took the last step into the house.

"Upstairs," she said.

Kenneth followed her up the stairs, down the hall, and into a small room toward the back of the house. A single bed was against the wall, a dresser stood just inside the door, and there was a nightstand with a lamp and a wind up alarm clock. A worn and faded rug was on the floor.

"Your room," she said as she put the bag down. "Lunch is at noon. Supper's at six." She walked out, closed the door, and her footsteps faded down the hallway.

Kenneth had never felt so alone in his life. He thought for a moment he was going to cry but he refused to give Fanny the satisfaction even if she couldn't see him. Instead he sat on the bed. It was hard and a little lumpy, not as good as his bed or even the one at the parsonage. The walk had left him shaky and tired and his mind swirled with unknowns. He couldn't hold onto one thought before another pushed it aside and took its place. Trying to imagine what he had ahead of him wouldn't get him anywhere, though, because it was sure to be worse than it had ever been before the accident.

His Zane Gray books had taught him to survey the lay of the land. He put his few things in the dresser drawers. The closet was small but he didn't have anything to put in it anyway, at least until he had a chance to go home and get stuff. He heard pans and dishes being moved around downstairs and saw the register in the floor, just like he'd had at home. It was closed but if he opened it he'd be able to see through the grillwork and hear anything going on in the kitchen. He might even be able to hear things in other parts of the house as well. He wouldn't open it now, though, because Fanny might hear it and the noise could tip his hand. There was no rush.

It had been a long time since the room had seen paint or fresh wallpaper. It smelled unused. A small door, an access door, was set in the back wall. He tried to work the latch but it was stuck shut. He'd deal with that later as well. From the window he could see the driveway, the big sliding door on the barn, the side yard, and bushes beyond that marked the boundary of Fanny's yard and the neighbors.

The barn, he knew, was an amazing place. Uncle Fred had let him go in there sometimes just to poke around. Fred had collected things for years. Anything he came across that might have some value came home.

Fanny used to grumble about the barn full of junk but Fred knew it wasn't junk and Kenneth agreed with Fred. To Kenneth, it was like one of the archeological digs in far away places he'd read about. Everything in the barn, Kenneth knew, had a story. Someone had owned it, used it, and maybe even cherished it. He'd often thought it would be a wonderful adventure to trace each piece back through its life and the people who had touched it. There would be stories for several books.

Kenneth's Uncle Fred and Fanny and his parents had all come through the Great Depression when people kept everything because they knew times when there might not be any more. You used things up, you wore them out (after patching them several times), and you saved what was left, just in case. Fred had gathered books, tools, furniture, and stuff Kenneth couldn't begin to identify. Now he was living here he'd get a chance to examine Fred's stash more thoroughly.

He went back to the bed, took up one of the library books Ellen had brought and began to read. He really wanted some of his comics or a couple of his western novels but this would have to do.

The door opened and woke him up.

"We'll have no lie-a-beds in this house," Fanny said. "Your lunch is ready. Now." And off she went.

Lunch was Campbell's tomato soup, a tuna sandwich, and a glass of milk. Kenneth tasted the soup while Fanny was still wiping the surface around the sink.

"I see you need to be taught some manners," Fanny said. "The proper thing is to wait until everyone's seated before you begin to eat."

Kenneth put the spoon down.

"We're going to have an understanding right now," Fanny said, which was as good a way as any to spoil his lunch. She picked up her own spoon. Kenneth supposed this was the signal to begin. "I took you in because you're family and it's a family's responsibility to look after one's own," she said. "I certainly didn't expect to be burdened with a child at this point in my life, especially a sickly child. Still, as family, it's an obligation." They ate in silence, the only sound being the spoons against the sides of the bowls. "I just want you to understand the situation."

Kenneth continued to eat, concentrating on the food. The soup seemed watery. The sandwich was thin, too. Fanny's reputation as a good cook was facing a serious challenge with this meal.

"Did you hear me?" Kenneth looked up and nodded. "Then say so. The correct response is 'Yes, ma'am,' or 'Yes, Aunt Fanny'."

"Yes, ma'am." He would not use her name.

"You're going to earn your keep," she went on. "I'll make a list of chores. Some will be every day, some will be from time to time, but I expect them to be done well and done promptly, is that clear?"

"Yes, ma'am."

"I'll make allowances until you get your strength back but there is no free lunch in this house."

"Yes, ma'am."

"And stop clanking your spoon against the bowl all the time. Save some of your milk to go with a ginger snap." A single ginger snap? This didn't seem like much of a lunch but if he was going to live here he'd have to make it work. He wanted his own stuff, though.

"Can I go to my house and get my things?"

Fanny rolled her eyes. "I'll get Luther Pike to come around with his truck."

"Why don't we just go over in Uncle Fred's car?"

"Because I don't drive, that's why." An adult who didn't drive was unbelievable. Who would not want to drive? Kenneth supposed all adults could drive a car.

"You don't drive?"

"No, I don't. And besides, I sold it."

"You sold Uncle Fred's car? The Hudson Hornet?"

"Yes, I did, and good riddance."

"That was a great car."

"It was as big as a bus."

"But... But it was a Hudson Hornet. It was so cool. How will you get around without a car?"

"Shank's Mare, I expect."

"What's Shank's Mare?"

"I'll walk. Or I'll find a ride. Now that's enough. The car's gone. Finish your lunch. I've got a list of chores for you this afternoon."

*

Chapter Six

Archie was at the common by 7:30 to make sure everything was ready. Cold at first, it quickly became one of those perfect Vermont October days that are featured year after year in the pages of *Vermont Life* – cool, crisp, and dry, with a slight breeze. Brilliant red and orange and gold in the maples around the common cast a warm glow over the festivities.

Ellen had sold her pottery at the festival for several years and each year Archie helped erect her canopy and assembled the shelves. Ellen then carefully unwrapped each piece and set it out for display, a job that never took less than an hour. When she'd finally set up the table for her calculator and credit card machine, Archie returned with coffee.

The morning chill was gone by ten and the first of the foliage tour buses rumbled into town by eleven. By noontime the common was full, the food tent was busy, and the Morris Dancers had performed with their sticks and hankies and bells. Archie found time around 1:30 to grab a hamburger and a cup of coffee for himself and a couple hot dogs and a bowl of water for Hank. He dropped onto an empty bench where he could look out over the crowd. It felt good to sit for a few minutes. He'd only stopped for a quick whiz around eleven and hadn't put anything in his stomach except for the coffee he'd had with Ellen. The Festival was rolling, goods and money were changing hands, and he could finally relax enough to take a break.

Between bites of his hamburger he held a hot dog for Hank. Hank had never snatched and gulped his food. He'd wait until it was offered and then only take a small, gentle bite which he then chewed and savored, yet another characteristic of Archie's Uncle Henry. They ate at the same pace and finished together. Archie tossed the wrappers and the empty hot dog buns into a trash barrel and each, the man and the dog, released a long and satisfying belch. Archie sipped his coffee. Hank slopped up some water, shook his head, and climbed up on the bench to lie down.

The product of Archie's labors was a happy crowd, satisfied vendors, and a festive atmosphere. The pressure was gone. It was happening.

A hearse crept up the street and stopped in front of the church.

"What the hell?"

Archie was off the bench and through the crowd like a snow plow. Hank trailed along in his wake. A flower car pulled up behind the hearse. Dennis Coombs, in his official black, emerged from the hearse. Increase Houghton was there, too. The Rev. Peter Rodman opened one of the double doors.

"Oh, God, here he comes," Dennis muttered. Dennis Coombs hated confrontation. Confrontation by its nature led to raised voices and raised voices destroyed the dignity and calm of his services.

Increase cleared his throat.

"Hi, fellas," Archie said cheerfully.

"Archie…" Increase said.

"Somebody got a party going here that I didn't hear about?"

"I, uh – I wouldn't call it a party," the Rev. Rodman stammered. "It – it's Fanny. We'll be doing her service at two o'clock,"

"Not today you won't." Archie turned to Dennis and pointed at the hearse. "Get this god damn thing out of here."

The Rev. Rodman was not unfamiliar with profanity. He'd occasionally succumbed himself in moments of extreme stress. He was more offended that someone would attempt to interfere with the decorum and respect he thought proper for a funeral service.

"Look, Peter," Archie said. He turned to the Rev. Rodman and leaned in. "We can't be wheeling a wizened up old corpse into the parlor while they're fixing the bean supper in the kitchen."

"But – "

"'But' my ass!" Archie roared. Dennis flinched. He knew this would happen. Archie always raised his voice, whether he needed to or not. "What's the rush?" Archie turned on Dennis. "Put her back in the cooler and bring her out on Monday or Tuesday after all these people are gone," he said. "They're out there looking for ways to spend money. The last thing we need today is a funeral."

"I can't – " Dennis stammered, "I – I don't – "

Increase cleared his throat again. "Archie, the service will happen today…" Archie turned to argue "…and it will happen at two o'clock."

"Who says so?"

"I say so."

"Since when do you schedule the funerals, Increase?"

"Actually, this is Fanny's schedule, not mine."

"Christ," Archie said through his teeth with as much venom as he could generate without first taking a breath. "First she dies before she bakes the beans and then she wants her funeral in the middle of the festival?"

"I doubt she planned it that way, but she insisted that her service would be at 2 pm on the Saturday following her death and I can tell you it's very important to the town of Grants Ferry, the church, and everyone involved that her wishes be carried out to the letter." He checked his watch. "Dennis now has about fifteen minutes to get her inside."

Archie was getting nowhere with Increase.

"What's this all about, Dennis?"

Dennis threw up his hands. "I just wheel'em in and wheel'em out. I don't know anything," he said as he watched Hank lift his leg against the rear wheel of the hearse. Dennis didn't care for dogs and this was one of many reasons.

"Son of a *bitch*." Archie knew full well the futility of arguing with a lawyer, especially when a clock was running. The others would buckle in a second but Increase was like a rock. "All right," he said. "Get her inside and get that hearse out of sight. And make sure everybody parks out back and comes in the back door."

The Rev. Peter Rodman quickly opened the other door.

Dennis signaled to the flower car and his two part-time associates, Luther Pike and Delmar Hawkins, got out and removed the polished wooden casket from the rear of the hearse. This struck Archie as rather extravagant for a skinflint like Fanny. He supposed she'd have insisted on a cardboard box.

"Come on, you guys, step it up."

The walk sloped gently up to the first of three granite steps. The top step was deeper, about three feet, and then a final step up through the double doors. At the front end of the casket, Luther picked up the pace. At the rear, Delmar, who didn't care whether he pleased people or not, struggled to keep up.

"Come on, a little hustle there," Archie snarled.

Luther took a big step up into the church which yanked the casket along after him. Delmar wasn't expecting this and tripped on the second granite step. His end of the casket went down with a great hollow thump. Delmar, a large man not given to quick response times, followed it down and landed on top. Dennis heard the sound of breaking wood.

"Well, shit," Delmar said.

The activity on the aft end of the coffin shook the fore end out of Luther's grip and it, too, fell on the oak threshold with another hollow thump. This thump, though, was amplified in the empty vestibule and sent back out through the front doors of the church five-fold, a magnificent sound. People in distant lands who communicate with drums would envy the power and range of this hollow wooden thump and it was this amplified thump that finally drew the attention of the crowd on the common.

Hank got in the spirit of things now and began to bark encouragement. His voice, unused for months at a time, grew louder and more powerful with each delivery and once begun it was all but impossible to shut off.

"Oh, Christ, Hank. Knock it off," Archie said, but Hank only became more intent. "Get her inside," Archie yelled, "and fast." The four of them grabbed the coffin, heaved it inside onto the vestibule floor, and the Rev. Rodman slammed the two front doors. Hank continued to bark on the steps but the door snapped open again, a flannel covered arm reached out, grabbed his collar, yanked him inside, and slammed the door shut again. Hank was delighted with the acoustics of the front vestibule and the sanctuary and began to explore their possibilities while the casket was moved into place.

"Hank, will you knock it off, for Christ's sake?"

Increase Houghton had wisely remained apart from the activity around the coffin. With the others inside, he climbed to the top step just to the right of the door. He barely turned to face the common when the door flew open again, Luther and Delmar rushed out of the church, jumped into the hearse and the flower car, started them with a roar, and then laid a pair of smoking patches down the street to the church driveway where they careened in and quickly disappeared. No amount of pottery, hand crafts, stained glass, leather vests, or knit goods could compare with this entertainment but it ended as quickly as it had begun and the fair goers soon returned to the task of pawing through hand crafts and running up their credit cards.

The front door opened again. This time the Rev. Rodman stepped out, followed by a few notes from an old hymn.

"Everything is prepared, Increase. Dennis says the casket is cracked but it's on the side that won't show."

"Fine."

"Dennis did a fine job on her. You'd hardly know it was Fanny."

Increase considered this.

"But it is, isn't it?"

"Oh, yes, yes. Just younger looking. You know – fleshed out."

"I'm sure she's a sight to behold."

"The fall shook her down to one end of the casket but Dennis got her back in place."

"Glad to hear it." Increase checked his watch. 1:58. Kenneth was nowhere in sight. He kneaded the muscles on his neck. One of his primary irritants was people who seemed to have no integrity around punctuality.

"Peter, go tell Evelyn to keep playing. I don't want you to start the service until Kenny's inside and seated."

"Right." The Rev. Rodman went back inside and closed the door.

Increase checked his watch. 1:59. Damn. He reset the watch for 1:55 just as Archie and Hank came outside again. The hymn was *Abide With Me* and the soft music had calmed Hank who was finally silent again.

The steeple clock struck two.

"Two o'clock," Archie said. "We gonna get this show on the road or what?"

"Clock must be fast," Increase said. "I've got 1:55."

"Clock's not fast. Your watch is wrong. The clock just struck. Let's get it over with."

Increase held up his watch for Archie to see.

"The stem's out, Increase. The watch is stopped."

Increase Houghton was not often caught in some slight easing of details to make things come out right. He cleared his throat.

"I'll tell you this once, Archie," he said, "and if it ever goes any further than these steps I'll deny under oath that I ever said it, understand?"

"Go ahead."

"One of the conditions, in addition to Fanny's funeral being today at this hour, but certainly no less important, is that Kenny Forbes be present at the service."

"Kenny? Christ, he's been gone for thirty years."

"Thirty-two, in fact, but he's assured me he'll be here. For the record, Archie, now and forever, Kenneth will arrive at 1:55. Is that clear?"

Dennis Coombs slid out and shut the door quietly.

"Everything is ready, Increase, just as you instructed." Dennis seemed always to speak "in private".

"Thank you. I'll let Peter know when to start."

Dennis had heard the clock strike but deferred to Increase. He'd done his part. He backed away three steps and stood with his hands clasped in front of him. Patience, service, discretion. After all, Increase was the one to okay the final disposition of the account…

They waited.

Hank hoped there would be more entertainment.

The door opened once more, this time releasing a bit of *The Old Rugged Cross*. Luther and Delmar lumbered out and closed the door.

"We're all set up."

"I know. Thank you."

"People are still comin' in."

"Fine."

Luther and Delmar nodded and then backed slowly to the side of the door. Now there were six men on the church steps, standing and waiting. Delmar cleared a gob of phlegm from his throat and spit it into the bush beside the steps. Dennis glared at him.

Luther looked at Hank who sat beside Archie and studied Luther. Luther liked dogs but he'd never understood this one.

Delmar didn't care anything about dogs. He wanted a cigarette but Dennis wouldn't stand for it. That was the worst part of this job, aside from the waiting around. Dennis had this thing about smoke. He didn't like the smell, he said. There was no hint of this aggravation in Delmar's normal gloomy expression, though. In this job he was a professional. He could hover in the background for hours, if necessary.

So they stood – waiting – the undertaker and his crew, the pastor, the lawyer, and certainly not the least among them, First Selectman of Grants Ferry and Chairman of the Congregational Church Annual Harvest Festival, Archie Whitaker. Under different circumstances, there might have been some discussion of the approaching deer season or the merits of horse manure on asparagus or rhubarb, but today they were all of the same mind and nothing they might say about this situation would change things (or as Archie and Increase knew, would start the clock again) so they stood – mute. They watched. And they waited.

Delmar thought about beer. Well, a cigarette, a beer, and maybe a good piece of cheese. Good strong cheddar, dry and crumbly, and a bag of those thick crinkly potato chips, the ones with big hunks of salt on them. On second thought, maybe two beers…

Luther decided Hank was either stupid or rude – maybe both.

So they stood, silently, and listened as the sad, faint strains of the pipe organ leaked through the front doors as Evelyn Goss ground through her repertoire.

*

Kenneth steered the pearl white Beemer Z4 off the Interstate and backtracked a short way down Route 5 before he turned onto Ferry Road where they wound their way along the brook that ran between the hills to Grants Ferry and the Connecticut River. A particularly dangerous stretch had rock ledge on one side and the brook on the other. Repeated pleas to the legislature over the years to widen and straighten the road had gone unheeded. The shoulders were broken down, the pavement dried and cracked, and save for a thin coat of paving laid on by the state every three years or so and the annual painting of the lines to help drivers navigate the road at night, the road had been as good as ignored by highway crews for years.

Hills on either side kept this narrow valley cool and sheltered in the summer. The brook was an excellent trout stream but these same hills prevented the sun from warming the pavement in winter. During a cold snap in January or February the road could be covered in ice for weeks. It was once estimated that state highway crews dump more salt and sand per mile on this short stretch than any other road in the state, including the Proctorsville Gulf. Long, dangerous spells occur each winter when the ice only melts enough to let the sand sink beneath the surface before the road freezes over again to a glaze of ice.

On this day, though, the road was dry, the air was warm, with no hint of the dangers that lurk there in wintertime. The trees were bigger now and Kenneth could see stumps where there had been an attempt to open the road to sunlight in the winter but it was little changed from when he left. The fog lines on the edge of the pavement were new – they weren't doing that 30 years ago – but it was the same winding road.

When the terrain opened up again there was a smattering of houses. A few were newer style ranch houses but as they got closer to town they became the familiar story and a half homes with small sheds attached. Most had a garage. All had clotheslines with laundry drying in the October sunshine.

Kenneth made the last turn to cross the iron bridge where the village proper began. He groaned and braked the car.

"Oh, God…"

"What's the matter?"

"I'd forgotten about the Harvest Festival. It's always this weekend. The place will be mobbed." His breathing became quick and shallow. "I've got to pull over."

"You all right?"

"I think so." He got out of the car. "Jesus." He took a deep breath. "Ah, shit." He walked around to the shoulder. Simon got out, too, and both of them went to the front of the car where they could look down the street into town

"I thought you said nothing happens here," Simon said.

"Well, this does."

"We're going straight to the funeral, though. This won't matter, will it?"

"The funeral is at the church and the church is right in the middle of that."

"Oh."

Kenneth checked his watch.

"And we're late, too. Increase will hate that. He was always a bug on punctuality." Kenneth began the square breathing technique his therapist taught him. In on a count of four, hold for a count of four, out on a count of four, hold for a count of four. Sometimes, if he had the time, Kenneth could build it to a seven or even an eight count. The controlled breathing slowed him down.

"Take as much time as you need," Simon said. "If they give us any shit, let me deal with them. You think they're ready to go up against a total queen?"

"Look, don't go all freaky on me. I've got enough to deal with here."

"Let's have a plan, then."

"Okay. Give me a plan."

"We make an entrance. We drive up and we expect them to be waiting for us. Stand up straight, look'em in the eye."

"Listen, they don't know – "

"I'm talking celebrity. You've been away, you're back. You expect to be welcomed and you behave that way."

"Okay…"

"And we're dressed for the part."

Kenneth finally smiled. "Well, you're right about that. You can bet your ass no one else is going to this funeral in white." Calm had returned. All it took was a plan. He slid in behind the wheel. "Let's do it."

And so, nine minutes from the time Increase pulled out the stem on his watch, officially on the stroke of 1:55, the pearl white Z4 turned in from Main Street, worked its way through the crowd that had spilled out onto Laurel Street, and pulled up in front of the church. Increase pushed in the watch stem and the entire delegation came down the church steps to greet them.

Kenneth and Simon were stunning in the October sunshine – white open neck shirts, white cardigans, white ducks, white and brown saddle shoes – a total throwback preppy image, a fun way to go to the country.

Kenneth, now in character, was the first to speak.

"Sorry we're a bit late," he said. "I hope we didn't miss anything."

"Not at all," Increase said. "As a matter of fact, you're right on time. Welcome home."

"I may be back, Increase, but I'm not home," Kenneth said. "My partner, Simon Hirsh. Simon, this is Increase Houghton, my Aunt Fanny's attorney."

"Simon. A pleasure."

"I'm sure it is," Simon said with a bit of tease in his voice. He looked back at the festival activities. "Fanny must have been a pistol for you to throw a bash like this."

"That's our annual Harvest Festival" Archie explained. "Fanny got added on at the last minute."

"Wonderful. I'm Simon, by the way." Simon held out his hand and with just enough hesitation, Archie took it. Simon could sense his discomfort and held the handshake while he sized Archie completely up and down. Archie blushed and tried to pull his hand away but Simon held it firmly with both hands.

"Archie Whitaker," Archie stammered.

"Archie. What a great name – so – so butch," Simon said. Kenneth gave him the elbow and slick as anything Simon looked back at the common again, still holding Archie's hand. "So Fanny was added onto your party? I think surprises are often the most fun, don't you, Archie?" Simon had dropped Archie's hand but moved close and linked their arms.

Archie looked to Increase who ignored him and changed the subject.

"You remember everyone, I suppose?" Increase asked Kenneth.

"I think so. How could I forget Archie, the school bully?"

"A bully?" Simon gasped in horror. He held Archie's arm even tighter. "Oh, my gracious!"

"Ah, Christ, Kenny. That was a long time ago…"

"Yes, but the memories linger," Kenneth said. "Did you even know what a faggot was in those days?" For the first time in years Archie began to rub his damaged ear. Kenneth moved on. "Dennis, of course," Kenneth continued. "Long time, Dennis."

"Hi, Kenny."

Kenneth stopped at the minister, an unfamiliar face.

"Peter Rodman," Peter introduced himself.

"Peter," Kenneth said. "Whatever became of Gordon Nelson and that soft round wife of his?"

"I understand he left the ministry and they went into foster care. He died about five years ago, someplace in Ohio. One or the other of them had family there…"

"I had an incredible weekend in Wapakoneta back in the late 70s," Simon said.

"Wapa-what?" Archie said.

"Wapakoneta. If you think Ohio is all corn fields and Spartan white churches you ought to spend a weekend in Wapakoneta."

"I'll remember that."

"It will change your life," Simon said.

Dennis stepped in. "Of course you remember Luther and Delmar," he said, gesturing to the two behind him.

"I do," Kenneth said. "Good to see you, Luther. Long time. Delmar." He walked past Dennis to shake their hands. This gesture alone, he knew, elevated the workers and demoted the principals, an equalizing strategy Kenneth liked to employ at any opportunity. "My partner, Simon," he said. Both Luther and Delmar dutifully took Simon's small white hand in their big rough paws but were clearly unsettled. This pretty little guy talked awfully fast and they were both confused about two guys dressed in white for a funeral.

Increase cleared his throat. "It's not my intent to rush you Kenny, but everything is ready inside."

"Oh, good," Kenneth said jovially. "All laid out, is she?"

Dennis winced.

"Sorry, Dennis," Kenneth continued. "She must be a picture of loveliness, all cold and still that way."

Dennis didn't care for that, either.

"Sorry again," Kenneth said, laughing. "I seem to be overcome with mortuary humor." He turned to look out over the common, the familiar trees, the white clapboard buildings, the bandstand, the civil war statue, the old hotel on the corner. The sky was cloudless and a particular clear, pure, Vermont-in-October shade of blue. Kenneth felt thc crisp, clean air, so different from the air in the city. "I should apologize for the trouble I gave you on the phone, Increase. This is an absolutely gorgeous day."

"No trouble at all."

"All right," Kenneth said. "Let's do it." He and Simon went up to the top step where Kenneth turned to look out over the common one more time. His anxiety was gone. He was back. Delmar and Luther were peering into the Beemer.

"What are they doing?"

"They'll put the car out back," Dennis said.

"Of course. Have Luther move it for me, would you?" He handed the keys to Dennis who in turn gave them to Luther. Kenneth turned to Simon. "Shall we view the remains?"

The Rev. Rodman held the door and the funeral party followed Kenneth inside. Archie and Hank went back to the fair.

Light streamed in through the south windows. Evelyn Goss plowed through another old chestnut.

"What *is* that hokey music?" Simon asked.

"One of the old time hymns. *Sweeter as the Years Go By*. Fanny loved the old ones."

"It really swings, doesn't it?"

Kenneth observed that the the sanctuary had been freshened with a coat of paint at some point but it was the same room Fanny had dragged him to every Sunday, a space used by generations past.

One of the pipes vibrated and buzzed when Evelyn played a low note. *They haven't fixed that in thirty years*, Kenneth, thought, nor had Evelyn Goss improved her skills at the keyboard. It amazed him that something could remain virtually unchanged for an entire generation. For a moment it was as if he'd never left but the feeling passed as quickly as it came.

Individually, he knew, these were fine, rather simple people who lived uncomplicated lives. As a community, however, they represented narrow, small town minds locked against change and a suspicion of anything from more than forty miles away.

Dennis took his arm and guided him down the aisle to the second row, an empty pew customarily reserved for the family of the deceased. Kenneth hated to sit in front but was determined he would not make a scene.

The next row back was empty but the fourth row was filled with women on both sides from one side of the church to the other. They were middle aged to well-seasoned and appeared somewhat disheveled, certainly not in funeral attire. Kenneth let Simon into the pew and turned to Dennis.

"What's the deal with the women?" he whispered.

"The kitchen crew," Dennis whispered back. "They're all working the supper downstairs. Fanny baked beans for the suppers, you know…"

"Of course. Fanny's Famous Beans."

"She died before she made them this year but they thought they should come anyway."

There were faces he didn't recognize but he gave them all a pleasant smile. A few smiled in return. Two of them glared. A last woman came in the side door wearing yellow rubber gloves. She stood at the end of a full pew until the others hunched together to make room for her. Once settled she proceeded to remove the rubber gloves with great elastic sucking sounds. Oblivious to the congregation, she turned them right side out again and blew into each to make the fingers spring back out in ten little pops.

There were maybe fifty people in all– mostly really old folks – scattered through the rest of the pews. They were Kenneth's parents' generation or older and he could no longer remember their names, but there they were – retired, old, and saving their energy for each other's funerals.

Dennis eased him into the pew. Simon had been too busy rubbernecking at the inside of the church to pay attention to anything but Kenneth had heard the whispers and felt fifty sets of eyes staring at the back of his head.

Dennis slid quietly back up the aisle and the Rev. Peter Rodman took his place in the dark, high-backed chair just to the right of the pulpit. The pulpit itself was a high, narrow, elegant affair rising from the raised platform. Of all the details in this church the pulpit had always been a point of fascination to Kenneth. While the rest of the house was rather austere, the pulpit had been carefully crafted from fine grain walnut and was always oiled and rubbed every week so that its moldings and details caught the light from any direction. It was a truly magical sight during the candlelight service on Christmas Eve.

Behind the pulpit was the choir loft, sheltered by a short modesty rail – high enough that no one could peek up skirts but low enough that the choir couldn't get away with any monkey business during the sermon. The old Congregationalists trusted no one.

Beyond the choir rose the pipe organ where Evelyn Goss followed the action and took her signals through her rear-view mirror.

"She's not very good, is she?"

"Never was. She seems to have reached a plateau and stayed there. When she makes a mistake she'll go back and play it again. You never know how far back she'll go, either. Sometimes it's an entire line, sometimes it's only a bar or two. I remember she once played the same line four times before she was satisfied and moved on."

"Why don't they get somebody else?"

"They tried a couple times while I was still here but she claimed God had called her to play the organ and put up such a fuss the music committee finally gave up. It was easier to put up with her playing than to cross God and push her off that organ bench."

"Amazing."

"Sometimes you could hear her curse."

Evelyn began to bounce her way through *I Love to Tell the Story* and Mildred Noyse appeared through the side door.

"Oh my God, Mildred Noyse is going to sing."

"Who?"

"Mildred Noyse. Up in the choir loft."

Simon had begun to think this was some sort of surprise party, a funky theme weekend Kenneth had set up as a treat. He nudged Kenneth.

"We could probably get $400 thou for that pulpit."

"Forget it."

"And those chairs – Thurston Gardner would pay a small fortune for those. He loves that dark overdone Elizabethan majestic stuff for his place out in the Hamptons."

"Behave, will you?"

"What's the matter? Have they been blessed or something?"

"It wouldn't surprise me."

Evelyn picked up the tempo.

"Oh, wow. Don't you just want to get up and dance?"

"Stop it."

Kenneth had avoided the open casket from the time he'd entered the church, but there she was, less than eight feet away, white, grim, and not looking well at all. Kenneth thought he could see traces of a mustache. He'd heard hair continued to grow after one died. He didn't remember Fanny with a mustache but in retrospect he thought she might look good with one.

Evelyn finished the hymn and the Rev. Rodman got his signal from Increase. Slowly and deliberately he walked to a space on the platform behind the coffin.

"We gather here this glorious October afternoon" he droned, "to honor and celebrate the life of Fanny Forbes, a life-long member of this church and this fine community. We remember her for her careful and precise manner in any of her many pursuits, her baking (especially the hundreds of pounds of beans she baked for us over the years), her devotion to this Christian family, her love of her beloved birthplace, Grants Ferry, and its place in our history…"

As far as Kenneth was concerned, it was all horseshit. Fanny was a bastard. Bastard was the only word he had to describe her. Fanny's bastardness transcended gender. Any image Kenneth could pull up around the word "bastard" had Fanny's face on it. Paint her any color you want and you still end up with a bastard.

*

Mildred Noyse's signature song was *Jesus Calls Us* and Fanny had specified it for her service. Mildred could swoop from one note to another like a tin slide whistle. Mildred's other skill was the ability to sing while Evelyn Goss accompanied. If the organ stopped because Evelyn got her fingers stuck in the keys, Mildred would simply plow ahead, sliding from note to note, and leave Evelyn to catch up. Sometimes they ended together, sometimes they didn't. One never gave the other an inch.

"Is she for real?" Simon whispered.

"You bet your ass," Kenneth whispered back.

"Amazing."

"Isn't it?"

There were some readings of scriptures, a closing prayer, and the service ended with Evelyn worrying *Sweet Hour of Prayer*, Fanny's favorite. Kenneth remembered it, too, especially the last verse. It was one of the few verses of a hymn he remembered.

"... 'til Mount Pisgah's lofty height
I view my home and take my flight;
This robe of flesh I'll drop and rise
To seize the everlasting prize;
And shout while passing through the air,
Farewell, farewell, Sweet Hour of Prayer."

Kenneth found the image absolutely bizarre but when Fanny sang it on the occasional Sunday morning she envisioned the Rapture, her reward for all the hardship and suffering she endured in this life. Fanny never considered that her general nastiness might somehow make her ineligible for this voyage. Nastiness in the name of the Lord assured her final reward.

The music stopped and Kenneth started to get up but felt a hand on his shoulder. Dennis had come down the aisle again.

"Let the others leave first. It'll just take a minute."

Kenneth settled back into the pew and Evelyn took up at the beginning of her repertoire to provide some cover and mood music as people shuffled out. Some people came by the casket for a last look. Most, however, headed for the door. Those who lingered found themselves in line for the bathrooms.

When the house was finally empty and the music stopped once and for all, Dennis, Delmar, and Luther set about preparing the casket for the trip to the cemetery.

"Just a minute," Kenneth said. He went to the casket for a closer look. "Looks like hell, doesn't she?"

"I did what I could, Kenny. She'd grown rather gaunt the last few years and then I had to cover up the bruises from the fall. I don't know if they told you but the whole side of her head was pushed in. They think she hit the post at the foot of the stairs."

"Ah, the details make the story, don't they?" Kenneth smiled. "Don't worry. You did fine." He took a small mirror from his pocket.

"What are you doing?" Simon said.

"Just being sure," Kenneth said. "I saw this trick in that movie *Charade* when all those guys showed up at the funeral and had different ways to check to see if that guy was really dead." He held the mirror under Fanny's nose.

"That's the sickest thing I've ever seen," Simon said, backing away.

"You never saw her alive."

"I'm not watching this." Simon wandered up into the choir loft, where he could check out the organ, the chairs, the pulpit, and the stained glass windows. Dennis, Luther, and Delmar kept a discreet distance.

Kenneth was determined to hold the mirror in place for at least three minutes. He knew she couldn't hold her breath that long. He counted off the seconds and time began to shift and change. He was young again and holding the mirror became a stealthy and daring thing. He waited for the tell-tale fog that would prove this is only another of her tricks, another way to bend his mind, another way to control him. He's counting, counting and he's watching for the mirror to steam, waiting , waiting, for any – and suddenly there's a shriek and Fanny's hand snatches his wrist and he yanks it away and jumps back and he's eleven years old and screaming and screaming –

But the corpse hadn't moved.

"You okay, Kenny?"

"I – I – "

"Just take your time. Catch your breath. There's no hurry here."

Simon ran down from the choir loft.

"What happened?"

"A flashback or something. I'm okay. Go ahead, Dennis. Close it up," Kenneth said.

"All right. We'll meet you outside."

"Not a chance," Kenneth said, his voice stronger. "I want to watch. Close it up."

Dennis produced a small crank and inserted the end into a device in the corner of the casket by Fanny's head. When he turned the crank, Fanny settled slowly into the casket.

"So that's how you do it."

Dennis smiled. "It's a lot easier than when we used to have to lift'em up and slide blocks under them, especially if we got a 300-pounder.

"Very clever." Kenneth watched them close the casket. "Is there any chance you can glue it shut and screw it down? I want to be sure it stays closed."

"Not really. There's a latch…"

"Can she work it from the inside?"

"No, I don't think so…"

"I'm surprised she went for this wooden casket," Kenneth said. "I'd have thought she'd buy the cheapest thing you had."

"Well, that's what she wanted but she insisted on that adjustable platform and it doesn't come in the cheaper models."

"She always fussed about open casket services," Kenneth said. "Funny she wanted it open for her own."

"I just do what they pay me for," Dennis said. "I don't try to analyze them."

"I suppose she just wanted to be sure I got one last look…"

"It was all arranged a couple years ago. Not pre-paid, you understand, but arranged. Increase will settle up."

None the worse for the short drag race it had endured earlier, the hearse now waited in front of the church. Kenneth's Beemer was right behind it, followed by the flower car. Dennis leaned toward Kenneth.

"She was a mean-spirited bargainer, though."

"You come out okay?"

"I'm okay," Dennis smiled, "but this is not the gig that will let me retire."

The casket was loaded and the big rear door was closed.

"Okay, Dennis, take her home."

*

A short drive out Laurel Street and then up Linden Street led to the top of the hill where folks were laid to rest with a nice view of the Connecticut River Valley. A perfect site for a few luxury homes had instead become the ultimate subdivision. Headstones revealed the evolution of the tombstone industry. First there was slate, available locally and easily carved when still soft from the quarry. Marble came later, still easily carved, but brought over from Rutland. And finally granite, polished stones from Barre that would retain their sheen long after the inscriptions on the slate and marble stones had been eaten away by acid rain.

The procession stopped a short distance from the open grave. Off in a far corner, Elmer Fisk sat on his backhoe, waiting to finish the job he'd started this morning. Luther and Delmar carried the casket to the grave. A brief service, a few words of completion, some scripture, and the coffin was lowered into the void. A brief benediction was delivered, and the few people who had accompanied Fanny on her final trip wandered back to their cars.

Kenneth remained.

"We'll take care of the rest, Kenny," Dennis said. "You can go along."

"I'm not leaving until the hole's filled."

"Well, we have to pick up our things, and then Elmer – "

"Do what ever you have to do. I'm not about to miss this part."

Dennis's men quickly gathered up their trappings which exposed the open grave, the pile of dirt, and the lid to the concrete vault. Whatever had been subtle about the event was now gone.

"Well, I don't need to stay for this," Increase said. "Stop by the office when you're done."

"Fine. See you later."

Dennis signaled to Elmer and the tractor sputtered to life.

The burial had been strangely more moving to Simon than the service at the church. This, after all, was truly the end of the road. He'd managed to avoid funerals all his life. There were occasional memorial services but he'd never actually gone to the cemetery. He only knew this scene from the movies where there's usually a single mysterious individual standing far off, perhaps in a mist, away from the proceedings. He'd looked around during the committal but the mystery figure hadn't appeared.

Now, though, as he saw the raw soil, the size of the hole, and the concrete container at the bottom, he wondered for the first time at the inefficiency of this custom.

He nudged Kenneth. "Do people get cremated here?"

"I expect it can be arranged but Fanny will burn soon enough."

Elmer used the backhoe and a chain to lift the cover to the vault. Once it was in the air he jumped down and opened a can of black, gooey sealant that he troweled around the edge.

"Gotta keep'er dry," he grinned. A gob of the sealant dripped onto Elmer's hand. "Oh, fuck me," he said. He wiped his hand in the grass, and then took out his handkerchief to clean as much as he could off his hand. A brown stain remained. "That shit's gonna be on there for a week," he said.

When he finished he got back on the tractor and eased the lid down onto the vault. He unhooked the chain and then turned the tractor around to push the stony soil back into the grave. Stones bounced on the concrete vault lid, an odd hollow sound. Once the vault was covered, the only sound was from dirt falling on dirt. Elmer got off the tractor between loads and jumped into the hole with a shovel to push the dirt into the corners and tamp it down with his feet.

When the grave was filled, Elmer raked it smooth so he could replace the sod. Kenneth was finally satisfied.

"Think that will keep her down, Elmer?" he asked.

"Never had one come back up," Elmer said.

"That's good enough for me." He gave Elmer a $50 bill. "Keep an eye on her, just in case."

"You betcha," Elmer said.

Kenneth jammed his hands in his pockets as he and Simon walked back to the Beemer arm in arm.

"You okay?"

"Yeah." He stopped. "No. No, I'm not done yet." He led Simon across the cemetery to the graves that held Tom and Amy Forbes.

"Oh, wow," Simon said.

"Yeah. Long time ago. Sometimes I have to look at those old photos to remember what they looked like." The cemetery was still, save for Elmer cleaning up. "They were nice people, Simon."

"Yeah. You want some time alone?"

"No. No, it's all right. I used to come out here a lot but then it was less and less. I never thought to come by to say good-bye the night I left town. I've always regretted that." They stood for several minutes. Elmer started his tractor again and waved as he drove away. "They were both young, you know," Kenneth said, "younger than we are."

"Yeah…"

"I mean we all expect our parents to die before we do, but we don't ever think about a life without them, do we? We expect them to be around to see what they've produced once we've grown up, you know?" He wiped his eyes. "I would have had a great time with them. Especially Amy."

Simon was weeping. He held Kenneth tight. "I'm so sorry," he said.

"Yeah. It's a bitch," Kenneth said, and he closed his eyes. They held each other for a few minutes. Then Kenneth sighed and pulled himself together. "Let's go see Increase."

They were back in the car before Kenneth spoke again.

"You know, I've dreamed of this day for years. I thought the world would look different without her." He shook his head. "Maybe I was just expecting too much."

*

Chapter Seven

Fanny finally hired Luther Pike to bring things from Kenneth's parents' house.

"But I'm not having any of your clutter downstairs," she said. "Whatever you bring has to be in your room or out in the barn."

Luther had been out of school for a few years and earned his living doing odd jobs and hauling. Luther's father had done hauling, too, but Luther had added grounds-keeping and wood-cutting jobs to his services. He wasn't a tall man but he was compact with large shoulders and thick arms and to Kenneth he seemed incredibly strong.

On the first trip they gathered all the things from Kenneth's room, his clothes, his books, his radio and lamp and chair and bed. The second trip was things from his parents' room, some pictures of them together, a couple of his father's hats and ties, some of Amy's scarves and jewelry. He wanted her sewing machine, her iron, her step stool, even some of the bowls and utensils from the kitchen, not because he had plans for them but she had touched them and used them and some small part of her remained. He couldn't bear the thought of his parents' things being handled and mistreated by strangers.

"Mr. Pike?"

"Christ," Luther snorted. "Call me Luther."

"What will happen to the rest of this stuff?" he asked.

"Sold, I expect. Auction, prob'ly."

"Oh."

Taken away, just like that.

"But what if I still want it?"

"I don't know. I was told three loads."

"I know, but…" Kenneth felt sick. Everything was being taken away. "Where could I find out?"

"We'll go see Increase," Luther said.

*

Irene Bills typed so fast on her electric typewriter it sounded more like a buzz than individual letters hitting paper.

"Hi, Luther. Kenny, how're you doing?" Her voice was sharp, almost cutting.

"Fine, thanks."

Luther felt clumsy and out of place in offices and it didn't help that Irene obviously had her eye on him.

"Increase in?"

"INCREASE!" Irene yelled. Kenneth flinched and took a step behind Luther. Irene could shatter glass with that voice and it was always a shock to the uninitiated. "Luther Pike and Kenny are here."

Increase appeared in the doorway. "Luther. Kenny. Come in, come in. Sit down. What can I do for you?" Increase's voice was soft, a gentleman's voice.

"Kenny's askin' about his folks' stuff," Luther said.

"Ah, yes." Increase said. He noted that Kenneth had come with Luther and not Fanny. "Well, Kenny," he explained, "the usual process in these circumstances is to liquidate the estate, sell the house and contents for the cash value."

"Isn't it mine?" Kenneth said.

"In a way, yes, it is. But, you see, your parents died without wills and when that happens the courts have to decide how the estate will be settled. Money from the sale will be put in a special fund to take care of your needs at least until you finish school. As Fanny has been named as your guardian she'll be given a monthly stipend toward your care."

Kenneth didn't like the sound of this at all.

"She gets money from my parents' house?" He could feel his stomach churning.

"No. Well, not all at once. The judge and I worked out the terms. The stipend continues only as long as you're in her care."

"But she gets the money?"

"Actually, you get the money, but through your Aunt Fanny. It seemed the fairest way all around, Kenny. Your Aunt Fanny lost her husband in that accident, too. This way the survivors of this tragedy are able to support each other."

"And everything gets sold?"

"Most everything, yes."

"But it should be mine," Kenneth said.

"I agree. But even if we kept the house and everything in it, Kenny, you'd be unable to maintain it and keep it in good order."

Kenneth saw where this was going. He would end up with nothing and Fanny would get it all. His eyes were wet. Everything was being taken away.

Luther saw the problem. "Give us a minute, Increase?"

"Surely." He went to the outer office and closed the door.

"What am I going to do, Luther?"

"Lemme think," Luther said. He stared out the window for a solid two minutes. "So," he said, "it looks like they have to sell the house, right?"

"Right."

"Suppose you get to keep anything that's inside."

That would do it. Kenneth could keep or sell whatever he wanted. It would be his choice.

"Okay," he said. "But where would I put it?"

"Let's see." Luther opened the door and Increase joined them again.

"So what have you come up with?"

"Kenny says he'll let go of the house if he can keep everything that's inside," Luther said.

"That so, young man?"

"Yes, sir."

"Fanny's been after me to clean all Fred's stuff out of her barn," Luther said. "With that gone, there'll be plenty of room for Kenny's things."

"I see. Well, the main value is in the real estate, after all. I'll run it past the judge. If he agrees, I'll drop the news on Fanny." He turned to Kenneth. "You do understand, I hope, that I've tried to do my best for everyone here."

"Yes, sir. Thank you."

"It's really little enough. You fellas run along. I'll take care of it."

Luther stood up. "Thanks, Increase."

"Not at all. You've done the right thing, Luther. And Kenny, if there's anything I can do for you, come by anytime."

"Thank you."

Kenneth was a bit light-headed as he walked out to Luther's truck. For the first time since Tom and Amy died two adults had actually listened to him. The ride back to Fanny's house was the most fun he'd had in months.

*

Committees at the church began to meet again in the fall. Fanny wasn't comfortable leaving Kenneth alone on the occasional evening but her committee work won out. Fanny would never miss a committee meeting. There was no telling what the others would do if she were absent.

With Fanny gone for a couple hours Kenneth took this time to explore the house. The first thing he did was pry open that small door in his room. It led to a dark attic space over the shed between the house and the barn. There was just a bit of light coming through cracks in the door at the other end. When he opened that door he was on the second floor of the barn. There was a stairway to the first floor, he knew, and a back door in the barn. From there he could run unseen down to the brook. He wasn't planning to run away but having the option to escape gave him a huge sense of relief. Any of the Zane Grey cowboys would have loved this setup.

He went back to his room. The little door creaked when he closed it. He'd need to find some oil to make it quiet. He spent the rest of the evening in his room with a book.

Whenever Fanny went to her meetings he'd explore another part of the house. In the cellar were Fred's workbench and his tools along with solvents, glues, powders, and oils that he used to fix things. A door in the back wall led to the root cellar which seemed to be under the shed. An oil fired furnace stood in the center near the chimney and one wall had shelves full of canning and preserves.

One room at a time, he familiarized himself with the entire house. The last room was the parlor, a mysterious room hidden behind two large doors that disappeared into the wall on either side. He tried to slide them open but they were locked and the shades were drawn when he peeked in the windows from the front porch. The parlor would have to wait.

It took three evenings of searching before he found a key to the parlor doors hanging from a nail in the closet under the front stairs. The next time Fanny left he got the key, unlocked the doors, and slid one open just enough to look inside. The rest of the house was furnished with solid, functional furniture but the parlor was the formal sitting room. Chairs in here were elegant and plush and the lamps had ornate glass shades with shining, dangling crystals hanging around the bottom. It was a room to receive and entertain guests in style. Who would come to visit Fanny, he wondered. Maybe the minister. It's part of the minister's job to visit people. Would Fanny bring the minister in here?

It was a wonderful, magical room. Footsteps on the front porch. Fanny was back. He squeezed through the opening and carefully slid the doors shut.

He hardly dared breathe. A few moments later he heard the front door close and when he peeked out the window Fanny was on her way back to the church. Too close. Just before he slipped out of the room again he saw the organ. He'd heard about Fanny's organ but had never seen it. He sometimes wondered if it existed at all but here it was. The details of its tall, dark cabinet were barely discernible in the dim light but he could make out the two keyboards and a long row of stops. The plaque in the front identified it as an Estey Organ from Brattleboro, Vermont. He wanted to try it out but he'd already had one close call and wasn't going to risk another. The organ would have to wait. He slipped out of the room, locked the doors, and put the key back under the stairs.

*

"Come in, come in." Increase greeted them in the front hall.

"We were a bit rushed before, Increase. My partner, Simon Hirsh. Simon, Increase Houghton."

"Simon. How do you do?"

"I'm well, thank you." Simon was tired of the gloom and in the mood to play. "I must say, this is an absolutely charming little town, Increase. And the name – Grant's Fairy? I love it."

"Grants Ferry." Increase pronounced it correctly. "It was one of the earliest ferry crossings from New Hampshire to what was then commonly known as the New Hampshire Grants."

"Ah, right."

"That's why 'Grants' has no apostrophe. It's often assumed the town was named for someone named Grant."

"Right. I haven't heard Increase as a name before. Is it old?"

"Not especially. I've only used it a little over 73 years." He led them into the conference room. "Kenny, I should advise you that the few portions of the will that I've been instructed to read to you concern matters of – ah – considerable delicacy. If this might cause any discomfort…"

"Simon can hear anything I can hear."

"Very well," Increase said. "As you know, Kenny – "

"It's Kenneth."

"Yes. Kenneth. I'm sorry. Sit down. Please." He cleared his throat. "As you know, Kenneth – oh, I've got some cider, about a week old now."

"Coming along, is it?"

"Quite nicely, yes. Can I offer you a glass?"

“I’d like that. Let’s introduce Simon to cider.”

Increase left the room and came back shortly with a tray and three tall glasses of a cloudy brown liquid. Kenneth smelled it, much the way he would sample wine.

“You’re right. It’s coming along.”

Simon held his glass up to the light. “Am I supposed to drink this?”

“Of course. Unpasteurized cider, a seasonal delicacy.” He took several swallows.

“I see.” Simon took a sip and made a face but gamely took another drink.

Increase opened a thick file.

“Now, as you probably know, Kenneth, your Aunt Fanny died without issue…” Simon snorted into his hand and Kenneth rolled his eyes. “…and this had been of some concern to her in recent years, especially as she considered the disposition of her estate. Fanny was nothing if not a careful and canny woman. At the time of her death, a rough accounting shows her net worth in the neighborhood of $1,500,000.

“One million, five hundred thousand dollars?”

“More or less. It may well be as much as $2,000,000. Now as you haven’t been to Grants Ferry in some time…”

“Wait a minute.” Kenneth held up his hands. “That nasty old woman was worth two mil?”

“More or less.”

“More or less…”

“At any rate,” Increase continued, “one of Fanny’s primary annoyances, if we assume for a moment that any one of her annoyances would stand apart from the others, was that Grants Ferry’s young people often leave town when they graduate from high school, if in fact they graduate at all. You may recall it was her strong belief that anyone who was fortunate enough to be born here should remain and contribute to the future prosperity and fortunes of the community.”

“I certainly heard that often enough.”

“She also clung to a rather strict and unyielding attitude toward what she saw as a moral decline of our society.”

“I assume,” Kenneth said, “that this preamble has something to do with the will.”

“That’s correct. I – um…. I must say I advised her against some of the language but she was adamant. I think, however, you’ll find it legally complete and binding.”

“Fine,” Kenneth said. “Let’s just get on with it.”

"I'll skip over the preliminary paragraphs. Also the paragraphs regarding some rather minor bequeaths to local institutions such as the library, and the church, and the historical society."

"The historical society?"

"Fanny created it a few years ago to display many of the artifacts she'd collected." Increase flipped through the will to the part he was to read.

"I'll give you a copy of the entire document when we're finished but Fanny insisted that I read this section." He paused and cleared his throat again. Reading now: "The balance of my estate, after the aforementioned items have been distributed, shall go to my nephew Kenneth Forbes, including properties in Grants Ferry as follows:

"1. My residence and family home at 14 Sycamore Street known as the Deacon Hitchcock House.

"2. The property known as the Wheeler House."

Increase interrupted himself. "Each of these properties has the address listed, but in the interest of time…"

"That's fine."

"3. The Allen Place."

"4. The William Frye House.

"5. The Enoch Potter Homestead.

"6. The Greene Family Home.

"7. The Judge Holmes Estate.

"8. The Ellis Rogers farm consisting of some 650 acres, more or less, along River Road and bordering the Connecticut River, possession to be taken when Ellis Rogers retires from farming.

"9. The Grants Ferry Hotel, known locally as The Intercourse House (and its outbuildings) on the corner of Elm and Main Streets – "

"The Intercourse House?" Simon covered his face in mock horror. "Here in little old Grants Ferry? Oh, my goodness, Kenneth. You never told me." He clapped his hands together. "The Intercourse House. Oh, this is just too precious. I love it."

"It's just a hotel," Kenneth said. "That was a nickname."

"But The Intercourse House? Oh, gracious me!" Simon fanned his face and pulled at his collar. Increase cleared his throat.

"A fine old word, intercourse," Increase said. "…fallen into some disuse of late…"

"Kenneth, you actually own something called The Intercourse House?" Simon swooned. "Oh, my God, I don't think I can stand another minute of this."

"It's just a hotel."

"Oh, tell me, tell me."

Increase cleared his throat. "If we could continue?"

"Sorry, Increase. Go ahead."

"By all means," Simon said. "I was just swept up. Sorry."

Reading again: "The above, along with all remaining assets after the previously mentioned have been disbursed and all outstanding debts have been paid, shall pass to my nephew, Kenneth Forbes, under the following conditions."

"Here it comes," Kenneth said. Increase cleared his throat again.

"1. That he (Kenneth Forbes) give up his disgraceful and degenerate life in Sodom and return to wholesome surroundings where he can reestablish his roots, relinquish his past life of degradation and shame, and live as the good and decent human being he was born to be."

"There's the Fanny I knew," Kenneth said.

"You were degenerate?" Simon said. "Should I get tested?"

"Quiet."

"2. That he continue, by accepting the terms which follow, to live in Grants Ferry and use his considerable intelligence to support the strength and growth of this community."

"Of course…." Kenneth said.

"3. That his residence from this point forward and as long as his physical health shall allow, shall be at one of the above named properties."

Increase looked up for a comment but Kenneth waved him on.

"4. That Kenneth Forbes will undertake the renovation and restoration of the Grants Ferry Hotel, shall acquire all necessary licenses and permits, and be prepared to serve meals and take guests within one calendar year from the signing of the attached agreement of acceptance."

"She wants me to restore the Intercourse House?"

"It was Fanny's belief that the restored hotel would inspire an elegance that has been missing from Grants Ferry for some years now. The hotel, along with the other properties she acquired over the years, represent the finest examples of Grants Ferry architecture in its heyday. She saved them from destruction. Now she wants them restored."

"And if I don't agree?"

"The alternative, of course, is contained in paragraph five."

"Of course."

"5. That should he refuse or fail in any of these conditions, all the above named assets, including the real estate, shall no longer be entrusted to him but shall be passed instead to the ministry of the Rev. Jerry Falwell and the *Old Time Gospel Hour*."

"Jesus H. Christ."

"Whoa," Simon said. "Slick move."

"I knew there was some reason the world didn't look different with her buried."

"6." Increase continued, "That Kenneth Forbes, should he choose to accept these conditions, if not removed from a life of sodomy and personal degradation, will have the opportunity to redeem himself in the bosom of the community into which he was born and assure his eventual and eternal residence in the House of the Lord."

There was an awkward silence when Increase stopped reading.

"Is that it?"

"Essentially, yes. There are some minor details and the formal agreement about the restoration of the Intercourse House. I'll leave them for you to read at your leisure."

"It just sounds so dirty when you say it out loud, don't you think?"

Increase shuffled some of the papers.

"So let me get this straight," Kenneth said, "if Fanny wouldn't mind me using that word. For me to inherit two million dollars…"

"…more or less…

"…more or less, I'm required to spend the rest of my life in Grants Fucking Ferry?"

"Grants Ferry must be your primary residence, yes."

"And I've got to restore and reopen the Intercourse House within a year?

"That's correct."

"And I can't sell off the properties – even the Intercourse House?"

"You want to sell the Intercourse House?" Simon said. "You'd actually sell something called the Intercourse House?" Kenneth ignored him.

"No, you can't," Increase said. "But you might mortgage them once the conditions are met and they are yours. All but the Judge Holmes Estate and the Intercourse House are free and clear."

"And if I don't agree to all the conditions everything goes to that bigoted bastard Jerry Falwell?"

"That's correct. It was originally Jim Bakker, but then he went to prison…"

"Of course. It's nice to see she had *some* standards. How did she happen to know about my life in Sodom, by the way?"

"Yes, well. When Fanny first came to work on her will a few years ago she asked me to find you and see what you'd been up to all these years. Irene made a couple phone calls, we paid a rather stiff fee, and were given a full accounting of your previous ten years. I still have the report if you'd care to see it."

"I don't think so. I was there, remember?"

"Well, it's in the file if you change your mind."

"So when do I have to let you know my decision?"

"I'm afraid there's a very small window. Within seven days of your being notified of the conditions of the will, roughly this time next Saturday."

"Well, Jesus."

"Fanny was insistent."

"How like her. And what will you need as proof that I've become a resident of Grants Ferry?"

"Oh, the usual," Increase said. "Change of address forms, registering to vote, registering your car in Vermont…"

"Christ, I can't get all that done in a week."

"I'll grant you that," Increase said. "Accept the terms by next Saturday and I'll consider it as good as done as long as you proceed with some diligence to make it fact."

"Once I'm here, do I ever get to leave again?"

"Of course. It must be clear, however, that this remains your primary residence. I must say, Kenneth, if you choose to accept this inheritance and succeed in meeting her conditions you will be the owner of some of the finest real estate in Grants Ferry."

"The Intercourse House? Are you kidding?"

"It was quite the place in its day. Could be again."

"Yeah. No doubt. Is there any place in town where we can all get a drink?"

"I expect the Ferry Slip is open but it's a pretty rough place. Fanny was trying to get it put on the National Register of Historic Sites."

"The National Register? That dive?"

"Yes, given its history and the role it played in the early years of Grants Ferry. The paperwork is down at the Historical Society in the Judge Holmes house."

"I own the Historical Society, too?"

"Only the building where it resides as a registered non-profit – rent free, I might add."

"Of course."

Increase handed Kenneth a copy of the entire will.

"Somehow I don't think Simon and I would fit in at the Ferry Slip."

"Nor I," Increase said. "Come on back." He took them through what had once been the kitchen, past the back stairway, and on to the shed that connected the house to the barn. It was a large, low room filled with comfortable chairs including a leather recliner, wide pumpkin pine paneling, lamps that provided a soft and mellow glow, a TV, full bookshelves, and as they saw when Increase opened a dark, carved cabinet, a well stocked bar.

"Judith calls this my lair," Increase chuckled. "Cider's all right for an afternoon," he said as he opened a bottle of Irish whiskey and poured generous servings for each of them. "Bút at the end of the day…" He handed out the drinks. "To Fanny. Long may she rest." Increase took a swig of his whiskey, savored the flavors a moment, and let it slide down.

"Frankly," Kenneth said, "I don't much care if she rests at all as long as she stays buried."

"Touché," Increase said.

"I love this room, Increase," Simon said. "It just shouts 'butch' doesn't it?"

"I find it a nice place to relax, if that's what you mean."

"I couldn't help but notice your whip," Simon said. "Do you play with that much?"

"It was my grandfather's. He dealt with animals – livestock. My father got the whip when Gramp died and then he left it to me. I tried to make it work once when I was about fifteen but it came around and caught me in the back of my leg. Hurt like a son of a bitch. I have it up there now to remind me that many things have the potential to work against me, suddenly and unexpectedly."

"But what if you've been naughty?" Simon asked.

"I beg your pardon?"

"Well, a whip is just such a delicious punishment – with some leather restraints, maybe a hood…"

"Simon, knock it off," Kenneth said.

"Well, he has a whip. Don't you just wonder what he keeps in these cupboards?"

"Will you stop, for Christ's sake?"

"I'm just trying to be one of the boys." He made a face and walked to the other side of the room to study an old yellowing map of Grants Ferry.

"You seem to have done well over the years, Increase," Kenneth said.

"For the most part," he said. "I've managed to pick my battles carefully. And when I couldn't pick'em I made damned sure I was well paid."

"Any regrets?"

Increase studied Kenneth for a moment. To a Vermonter a question like that borders on prying.

"Professionally, none that matter. Personally, Judith and I never had children. We will die without issue, to use an expression of the trade, and I've always felt I missed something incredibly valuable. It must be a great gift to have a hand in guiding a young soul into adulthood. I think I would have enjoyed that."

"Fanny didn't enjoy it much."

"Ah, well. To Fanny's struggles."

"Yeah. Long may they wave," Kenneth said.

"The end of an era," Increase retrieved the whiskey bottle and refreshed their drinks. He refreshed Simon's as well.

"Thank you," Simon said. "I'm sorry, Increase. I get carried away."

"There's nothing to be sorry for, young man. We come from different times and different places – different worlds, really. It's understandable that we might not always speak the same language."

"Hey, Kenneth," Simon said. "Maybe the old guy's okay."

Increase smiled.

"Don't be too hasty with your judgment, Simon. I'm afraid, Kenneth, I couldn't find a room for you tonight. The only option seems to be Fanny's house."

"Ahhhh, Jesus."

"I sent Margaret Collins over to clean and change the linens and freshen things up. It was rather a mess after Fanny took her fall but Margaret's very thorough. Luther Pike took the cats and said they can stay at his place unless you want them back."

"She had cats?"

"Two big ones. Doted on'em apparently. I don't expect Margaret's left any trace of them."

"Good."

"I also told Margaret to stock the cupboards and the refrigerator." He looked at Simon. "Including fresh fruit."

"Okay, that's it," Simon laughed. "Open the cupboards."

Kenneth waved him off and turned to Increase.

"You're serious, right? I'm going to have to spend the night in that house?"

"I'm afraid so. It's really quite comfortable."

"Did you grow up in that house?"

"No, I didn't."

"Then don't talk to me about comfort." Kenneth rubbed his forehead. "You wouldn't happen to know an exorcist who wants the challenge of his life, would you?"

“Take this along,” Increase said, offering the rest of the whiskey. “I’m sure you won’t find anything like it in Fanny’s house. Go ahead, take it. I don’t know about you but I’ve had a bitch of a day. Make good use of it. It’s not on the bill.”

“Thanks,” Kenneth said. “Come on, Simon. We’re off to the Addams Family mansion.”

“But Increase hasn’t shown us his closets.”

“Some other time,” Increase said. “Incidentally, I bought a couple extra tickets to the bean supper down at the church. Judith and I are going for the 7 o’clock sitting. You’re welcome to join us.”

“A bean supper?” Simon said.

“It’s a church supper,” Increase explained. “Not fancy, but a wholesome and plentiful meal. Virtually all you can eat.”

“Christ, I don’t know…” Kenneth said.

“Oh, let’s do it,” Simon said. “It’ll be a hoot.”

“It sure will.”

“Why don’t you fellas go on over to Fanny’s and get settled. Judith and I will be by the back door to the church about ten to seven.”

Kenneth and Simon agreed. Increase tossed down the last of his drink, showed them out the side door, and went upstairs.

*

The Deacon Hitchcock house was one of the first to be built on Sycamore Street. It sat solidly behind a broad, deep lawn. Massive maples stood on either side of the front walk and a wide, sweeping driveway led beyond the house to the barn. The roof over the porch that stretched from corner to corner across the front of the house was supported by large turned posts. A bit of fancywork and moldings added an air of elegant detail.

In the twilight Kenneth could just make out the two porch rockers to the left of the door. On the other side a glider hung by chains from the ceiling. In the gloom the house was like a live, waiting thing and the old memories rose up as Kenneth turned into the driveway.

“I hate this place,” he said.

Inside, there was only a faint glow from the three 15 watt bulbs in the kitchen ceiling light. Except for an updated electric stove and refrig-erator, the kitchen was unchanged from thirty years before, a room without cupboards or counters. The stove, the refrigerator, and the iron sink with a built in drain board all stood apart and alone, a Hoosier was against another wall. A large work table and two chairs sat in the center of the room. A cord hung from the light fixture on the ceiling and the end of the cord had an outlet to power appliances on the table. To one side was a generous pantry. Another door led to what would have been the creamery in years past when the family had owned a couple of milk cows. Now a huge chest freezer sat against one wall and a path led between shelves and boxes to a connecting shed and then to the barn.

Kenneth went from room to room switching on the lights as he went. No bulb in any lamp was larger than 15 watts and they did nothing to lift the pall that hung over the place.

"So when does the organ music start?" Simon asked.

"Any minute now, after werewolves in the cellar wake up. We're lucky the moon isn't full. We'd need a armful of sharp sticks to drive through their hearts."

"Isn't that for vampires?"

"Right. Silver bullets kill werewolves. Where's the Lone Ranger when you need him?"

"Distracted. I always thought he and Tonto had something going."

"Can't you leave any legend alone?"

"Well, they spent a lot of time alone… And the Lone Ranger liked to dress up sometimes…"

The small room off the dining room still had Fred's roll-top desk with banker's lamp on top. An envelope stuck up from between the slats. It was addressed to Kenneth in Fanny's careful script.

"Did she know you were coming?"

"Of course she knew. She'd set it all up. Even buried she's able to pull people's strings."

He took out the single sheet of paper and turned on the banker's light. It was dated, he noticed, just over a week previously. Aside from an occasional shaky spot, it was a young woman's handwriting, very graceful, with occasional flourishes. Kenneth read aloud.

Kenneth –

I've felt rather poorly these last few weeks and may well be reaching the end of my life. Agreements are in place with Increase Houghton and Dennis Coombs for my final disposal.

By the time you read this, you will have been offered an opportunity to own some of the choicest pieces of real estate in Grants Ferry. I've worked my last years to acquire them in the hope Grants Ferry might regain its former grandeur but I seem to have run out of time.

There was a time when Grants Ferry was grand, before the flood, before the elms died, before the decline. You turned your back on Grants Ferry years ago. You can now choose to complete the work I've begun or run away again.

I've set the stage; the choice is yours.

Fanny

"Just in case Increase didn't make it clear, I guess," Kenneth said.

He handed the note to Simon.

"What are you going to do?"

"I don't want to think about it."

They wandered into the living room. Little had changed since the day Kenneth left. Antimacassars were still on the sturdy stuffed chairs and the windows were dressed with the sheer curtains from 40 years ago. Twice a year Kenneth had watched Fanny wash them, bleach them, starch them, and then dry them on a curtain stretcher before they were put back up. It was a process that could spread out over weeks, depending on the weather.

The furniture, the shelves, the lamps, were all well cared for, and clearly dated. Most were oak or walnut with an occasional small piece of mahogany. A single small gate-leg table had been handcrafted from birds-eye maple, the only blond piece.

The house held the smell of old things and the furniture cream that Fanny used to buy from the Boy Scouts every spring whether she needed more or not. Kenneth hated the sweet creamy smell. He could also detect a faint essence of cat.

Kenneth slid open the double doors to the parlor for the first time in almost forty years. The dim light from the six 15 watt bulbs working together in the ceiling fixture made the parlor the brightest room in the house.

"Wow," Simon said from the doorway. "What a wonderful room."

"Yeah, pretty much the way it was when I left."

"We could get a fortune for this stuff in the city."

"I know."

"And you knew this was here all the time?"

"Well, sure, but I'd put it all out of my mind…"

"But look at it. You sure she wasn't gay?"

"No question at all, believe me. We need to buy some light bulbs."

Upstairs the small room that had been Kenneth's appeared to be unchanged as well. His clothes were still in the drawers and his high school yearbook photo sat in a frame on the dresser. It was as if Fanny had never opened the door after he'd gone.

"Whoa," Simon said as he picked up Kenneth's high school photo. "Is this you?"

"Yeah. Looks a bit unfinished, doesn't he?"

"God, you look so straight."

"Actually, at that point I didn't know."

"Did anyone ever share that bed with you?"

"No."

"Want to share it now?"

"No."

"Which one will we share?"

"I don't know but it won't be this one and it certainly won't be Fanny's."

"I could show you a great time on this braided rug."

"Not tonight you won't."

"Well, shoot. You're no fun."

Simon spotted a black and white framed photo on the wall.

"That's Amy," Kenneth said.

"She's lovely."

"She was beautiful. I got a camera for my birthday. We'd gone on a picnic and I shot two rolls of film, mostly of Amy. I could never really capture who she was, though. That was the best."

"We ought to have it out where people can see it."

"Yeah, maybe."

Kenneth turned on the lights in the bathroom and Fanny's bedroom and opened the windows. Then he went back downstairs and opened the windows in the living room and the kitchen and got a jar of spice from the pantry.

"What's that?" Simon asked.

"Sage. Fanny used to put it in the sausage she made. We'll let the place air out and when we come back from supper we'll close the windows again, light a dish full of sage, and smudge the place. I know she's still hovering around in here. If we can chase her away I'll get some sleep tonight. What time is it?"

"About 5:30."

"Good. Let's see if the local store has some light bulbs."

"And wine?"
"Sure, why not?"

*

Kenneth bought every 60 and 75 watt bulb in the store. At the counter, Paul – not someone Kenneth knew – added up the charges.

"What're you doin' there, lightin' up a football field?"

"Haunted house," Kenneth said. "Lights keep vampires away."

Simon had found two bottles of New York State wine.

"What do you think? A red and a white. Is that a challenge?" He turned to Paul. "Or maybe you could make a recommendation."

"Not much of a wine person, myself," he said, "but the wife and I like to try'em all. That red's pretty rugged but I find the white a little too tart. There's a few folks in town that like it, though."

"Well that's good enough for me," Simon said.

"We also got a couple cartons back there." He pronounced it "caht'ns". "Come with a little tap on'em. Quite handy."

"Next time. These will do for now."

Back in the car Kenneth couldn't leave it alone.

"You actually bought wines because they were described as 'rugged' and 'tart'?"

"Well, with all the hair sticking out of that guy's nose I wasn't about to ask him about the bouquet."

*

Chapter Eight

Wood smoke in the air brought it all back. Cold nights, wood fires, and church suppers were all timeless and familiar to Kenneth. They found Increase in the crowd behind the church.

"Kenneth, you remember Judith?"

"Yes, I certainly do. It's been a long time, Mrs. Houghton." Judith Houghton was Mrs. Houghton and it never occurred to anyone to suggest otherwise.

"Indeed it has," she said. She held out a tiny hand. Judith Houghton was a small woman, about four and a half feet tall, one of those people who is small proportionately as opposed to being dwarfed. Standing by herself with no reference, one would be unable to determine her size. What Mrs. Houghton lacked in size, however, she more than made up in manner and style. She was trained as a teacher and although she hadn't been at the front of a class in years, she still maintained a teacher's precision in her speech and her movements. Her silver hair was stylishly short with a soft wave that gently framed her face. Her rimless glasses gave the impression her eyes were twinkling. "How are you, Kenneth?"

"I'm well, thank you. This is my partner, Simon Hirsh."

They exchanged greetings. Judith Houghton took Simon's arm and turned him toward the church, taking them apart from the others.

"I think, Mr. Hirsh," she said, "that we should leave these old-timers to reminisce."

"I agree."

"Now, tell me," she put her other hand on Simon's arm, "how do you know Kenneth?"

It had been some time since Simon had run into anyone so smooth and direct without being rude.

"Well," Simon said, "Kenneth and I own and run a rather upscale antique gallery in New York – quite successfully, I might add."

An excellent answer to some other question.

"Good for you," she said, patting his arm.

"In addition," Simon continued with the second half of his answer, "for the past ten years or so, Kenneth and I have known each other in the Biblical sense as well."

"And what is that like?"

"Well," Simon said. "Like anyone, you find someone you want to spend your life with, you play and laugh and work together, you have a nice home, and a safe place to spend the night."

"And do you have all this, Mr. Hirsh?"

"Yes, we do. And I think our lives would be complete if we only had a neighbor such as yourself."

"You are quite the rascal, Mr. Hirsh," Judith Houghton chuckled. "Now if I might be a bit bold, I'll ask for the pleasure of your company during dinner this evening."

"This evening, Mrs. Houghton," Simon said as he looked back at Kenneth and Increase, "I can't think of anything I'd enjoy more."

The 6 o'clock crowd trickled out of the church, well-fed, happy, and chatty, trailing smells of warm rolls, baked beans, and strong coffee. Serving crews inside scrambled to clear, tidy, and set up for the final sitting. Crumbs were whisked off the tables, clean dishes and silver were brought from the kitchen still warm from the sinks where women had washed and dried them as fast as they came in from the tables, places were set, salt and peppers were lined up, and in less than ten minutes the room was ready again. Only then were the doors thrown open.

Mrs. Houghton led them to the far end of the room where she claimed the end of one of the long tables. Kenneth remembered it all, the pine paneling on the walls, the cheesy fluorescent lights on the tile ceiling, even the shuffleboard lines painted on the concrete floor. It hadn't changed in thirty-two years.

Archie Whitaker came up the far side of the table, followed by an attractive woman Kenneth couldn't place.

"Kenny," Archie bellowed, "you remember Ellen…"

"Of course," he said. Had she noticed he hadn't recognized her? "How could anyone forget Ellen?"

"Hello, Kenny," she said. Ellen might be the only person in the world who could call him Kenny and it would still sound good to him. She'd been really thin when they were in high school when the "look" in the 60s still favored the rounder figures and round faces. The years had not been kind to many of the other women Kenneth had seen in town but Ellen possessed a classic elegance that would serve her well into her nineties.

Christ, he thought. *She's stayed here all these years.*

Archie took up what seemed to be a continuing discussion about town affairs with Increase, Simon and Mrs. Houghton chattered away at the end of the table like a couple of teenagers, and Ellen busied herself with minor adjustments to her plate and napkin and cutlery. When she discovered Kenneth watching her heart gave a little flutter.

Kenny Forbes was back and he looked good, too. The years had rounded him out a bit, put a dash of gray in his hair, and once again she was reminded how much she had missed him, how furious she had been that he hadn't told her he was leaving or even said good-bye. She'd been beside herself for months.

Kenneth hadn't actually run out on her. They'd had no agreement. They were never boyfriend/girlfriend. In fact they'd never been on an actual date. They'd been good friends, though, close friends, and they could talk for hours on end but nothing had ever suggested that Kenny would simply disappear.

In the fourth grade they'd been Mary and Joseph in the Christmas Pageant and Kenny had been naturally and genuinely protective in his role as Joseph. From that moment on Ellen had loved Kenny Forbes. And while certain romantic notions came with this love, it was as much around the comfort she felt in his company as anything. Time would pass without notice. And yet it wasn't a physical relationship. Once they were walking along the river and she took his hand in hers. She immediately sensed his discomfort and as soon as she could find a way to make it appear to be about something else she'd let go and hadn't tried again. And then there was the night after graduation while they sat on the common and she'd kissed him goodnight after he'd walked her home. But that was the limit of their physical intimacy.

Ellen had supposed once school was over they would become closer, perhaps even marry, but then he was gone – just disappeared during the night. And now, after how many years and how many tears later, here he was, with those same sensitive, intelligent, penetrating eyes, eyes that still took her breath away

Kenneth looked from Ellen to Archie and back, meaning "married?"

He was using their secret communication again. She looked down at the table and blinked slowly before she looked back up.

Kenneth pursed his eyebrows slightly and his eyes opened a bit wider: "Why?"

Ellen gave him another small blink with an equally small shrug which answered everything and said nothing. Then Ellen glanced from Kenneth to Simon and back, meaning "him?" Kenneth shrugged an acknowledgment of his own, watching Ellen carefully to catch her reaction. To his relief there didn't seem to be any.

Kenneth refused to accept that a just and loving God would allow a genetic throwback like Archie Whitaker to take the lovely and delicate Ellen LeClaire into his bed. It confirmed once again that life in Grants Ferry was bizarre, even bordering on insane, and was all the more reason to have left and a damned good reason to stay away.

"How are you, Kenny?" Ellen asked as casual as if instead of thirty-two years he'd only been gone for the summer and just got back. Kenneth began to answer but the room had filled up and the serving dishes arrived. The din rose to a level that made conversation impossible unless you were directly beside someone and could lean in. Kenneth didn't want to yell so he pointed to his ear and shrugged, meaning "later".

Simon was fully into the spirit of things, trying it all, gesturing, laughing, and having a great time with Mrs. Houghton. Increase and Archie, from what Kenneth could hear, were deep in the finer points of zoning law and land use but with the buzz in the room Kenneth couldn't follow it and didn't care anyway. Ellen quietly ate her meal and studied Kenneth. That wonderful sensitive boy she knew in high school had become an incredibly attractive man. It was an effort to keep from staring.

After the meal, Ellen worked her way through the crowd until she was next to Kenneth. She took his hand and to her surprise, he took hers in both of his and pulled her next to him as they left the church. She was equally surprised to discover that this contact left her as light-headed as if she were sixteen again.

"So how long are you staying?" She tried to keep calm in her voice as he let go her hand and pulled her in close.

"Just the weekend," Kenneth said. "I didn't want to come at all but Increase insisted so Simon and I took the whole three days."

"So it's you and Simon, then?"

"A little over ten years now."

"That's not why you disappeared is it?"

"No, it's not."

That's as far as she would pursue it, at least for now.

"Will we have some time before you leave?" she asked.

"I'll make time. We'll probably spend most of tomorrow looking over Fanny's holdings," he said, "you know, the real estate. Increase mentioned the Historical Society and Simon's all excited about that..." She watched him, trying to make up all the lost years. "Apparently she got Ellis Rogers' farm, too," he went on. "And of course Simon wants to cruise the craft booths at the fair. We'll probably head back to the city Monday afternoon."

"I have a booth at the fair," Ellen said, "so I'll be busy all day tomorrow, but maybe Monday?"

"You have a booth at the fair?" Simon said. "What do you do?"

"Oh, Simon." Kenneth said. He'd not seen Simon join them. He pulled Ellen in closer. "This is Ellen. Ellen was the best friend I ever had in Grants Ferry before I left."

Oh, really? Ellen thought. *And you left without saying good-bye, you bastard?* Instead she said, "Oh, I create pottery things – whimsical stuff – nothing much. I took a couple classes in Springfield about fifteen years ago and started playing with clay. Archie bought me a wheel and a kiln. After that I just experimented and developed a style of my own."

"We're doing the fair tomorrow," Simon said. "I'd love to see it. We'll be sure to look you up."

"Oh, good. So, Kenny – our time – Monday morning, then?"

"Monday morning?" Simon said. "Why don't you come for breakfast? There's enough food in Fanny's house to run a Navy boot camp for the entire winter. Let me fix breakfast. About 9?"

Ellen would have preferred to have Kenny alone for a couple hours but she was curious about Simon. She looked to Kenneth who just shrugged and nodded. Simon seemed pleasant enough in a funny, elfin way. Mrs. Houghton had certainly been taken with him, a good omen indeed. And Kenneth was holding her close.

"Breakfast would be nice," she said.

"Wonderful." Simon said. "I can't wait to dive into Fanny's pantry." Ellen giggled and that was all he needed. "I want to fondle her utensils, dip into her goodies, rummage through her drawers, sample her preserves..."

Ellen burst into that big, wonderful, deep-throated laugh that Kenneth loved. She was still chuckling when Archie joined them.

"Now tell me," he said, "was that a meal or what?"

"Hasn't changed in forty years, has it?" Kenneth said.

"Nope, you find a winning formula, you stick with it. Remember Coke – how they tried to change it? Big mistake. Cost'em big time. You stick with what works. You ready, Hon?"

Hon? Kenneth thought. *Ellen lets this clown call her "Hon"?*

"Just a sec," she said and turned to Simon. "So Monday at 9, then?" Simon, she'd decided, was both the social secretary and the host.

"9 a.m."

"What's Monday at 9?" Archie asked.

"Kenny and Simon invited me to breakfast."

"That so?"

Simon batted his eyes.

"What can I say, Archie? We simply have too much food. And these two apparently need to catch up."

"Oh." Archie wondered what he'd missed while he was inside but he wasn't about to exhibit anything resembling suspicion. "Oh, good. Well, long day tomorrow." They said their good nights. Ellen and Archie walked to Archie's pickup truck and Ellen, they noticed, had to open her own door and push a dog out of the way before she climbed in.

"So," Simon said. "You and Ellen, huh?"

"Coulda been."

*

Archie yanked his truck out into the street so hard that Ellen was thrown against the door and Hank, who was sitting between them, threw out a front foot that landed on the inside of Ellen's thigh with the claws out.

"Ow! What are you doing?" Ellen said.

"Driving home. What's it look like?"

"Well, don't jerk the truck around like that. My stock's in the back and I don't want it broken."

Archie didn't answer but he slowed the truck.

"What's going on?" Ellen said.

"I don't know. Something's happening."

"Happening? What's happening?"

"Just a string of things. Fanny died – I suppose she couldn't help that, Kenny shows up out of the blue, Increase is being very cagey…"

Archie thrived on inside information and manipulation. As first selectman he considered it part of his job to keep a finger on everything. He was a politician, after all, a label he would deny, and no piece of information was trivial. It was all a puzzle to be solved, not unlike Hank and the dog shit map. Once he had all the pieces together he could then guide things in the right direction, whatever he decided that was.

Ellen, on the other hand, was still aglow with the memory of Kenneth's touch.

"Wasn't it nice to see Kenny again?"

"I don't know yet."

"What do you mean you don't know yet?"

"Because his showing up here today means something," Archie said. "We couldn't even start Fanny's funeral until Kenny got here."

"Fanny's funeral was today?"

"Jesus, didn't you see that circus in front of the church this afternoon?"

"I guess I missed it."

"Well, you were the only one. What a friggin' side show. You wait. Fanny's got something going, God damn her."

"Fanny's dead. What could she have going?"

"She may be dead but she's not gone. I bet it has something to do with all her properties."

"Her properties?"

"Yeah. I tried to buy them for years, especially the Intercourse House, and she wouldn't sell'em. Said she was afraid I'd tear them down."

"Well, wouldn't you?"

"Probably." A couple beats. "Eventually."

"Well, there you are."

"God damn it," Archie said. They rode in silence for about half a mile. "I really wanted to get my hands on the Intercourse House."

"Whatever for?"

"To get rid of eyesores like the Intercourse House and bring in some new business, something useful and classy, right in the center of town where it counts."

"Are you back on that Rite-Aid thing?"

"What's the matter with Rite-Aid?"

"As a convenience, nothing; as the future of Grants Ferry, everything."

"Look, they build new stores in depressed towns. They're big, they're bright, they're clean, they're new. They'd come here, too. Trouble is they only want the corner where the Intercourse House sits. It would be a great thing."

"No, it wouldn't. It would be a disgrace."

"Disgrace? How can something new and fresh in this town be a disgrace? Look around. The place is worn out."

"Every dollar we'd spend there except for taxes and what little they pay the help would leave town. Secondly, it doesn't belong here. It would be awful, as bad as that Post Office you built, a cement block shoe box with brick on one end. It's ugly. It's embarrassing."

Archie looked past Hank to see that Ellen was glaring at him.

"You're not helping, Ellen."

"I'm not going to help you tear down the Intercourse House, if that's what you mean."

Archie tried another angle.

"You're going for breakfast Monday. See if you can find out what those guys are up to."

"I'm not going to spy for you, either."

"Jesus, did I say 'spy'? Just see if you can find out what's going on," Archie said.

"The only reason I'm going to breakfast is to hear what Kenny's been doing since he left."

"We know what he's been doing. Christ, just look at that little faggot he's brought back with him."

"That's enough."

"Jesus, Ellen – "

"I said that's enough."

Archie pounded the steering wheel. A cold shudder ran around his shoulders and down his back. Ellen was pissed and Archie didn't know anyone colder than Ellen when she was pissed. He absently rubbed his left ear, the second time today.

Hank tried to lick Archie's face but it didn't help. Conversation had stopped. They drove the rest of the way home in a cold and brittle silence.

*

Increase and Judith whispered home in his Buick. They were well away from the church when Increase broke the silence.

"Well, my dear, what do you think?"

"Simon's a delightful little man," she said.

"And…?"

"They'll stay."

"He said that?"

"It never came up."

Judith had perhaps the most powerful instincts for reading people that Increase had ever known. She could glean information from a conversation that had never even been hinted to Increase.

"Well," Increase said finally. "A good day's work."

He backed the Buick into the barn, turned off the engine, and went around to open the door for Judith. When she got out, he gave her a peck on the cheek and stroked her face with his thumb, a gesture of endearment he'd made often since before they were married. The single bulb overhead cast harsh shadows over everything but Increase had never seen Judith in a light in which she wasn't absolutely stunning. Her twinkling glasses looked like tiny jewels.

"Thank you, my dear."

Increase slid the heavy door shut and followed her inside.

"A good day's work," he said again.

*

Back at the house Kenneth immediately set about changing light bulbs. The rooms grew steadily brighter until the house glowed in the night as if it had come to from a long, drugged sleep.

"Hey, Simon."

"What?"

"Come outside for a minute."

"What's going on?"

"Just come out front."

Out in the street they turned back to look at the house.

"What'dya think?"

"About what?"

"The house – the lights."

"It's a house with all the lights on," Simon said.

"Years ago – I was in junior high, maybe – one of the old timers here, Clayton Roberts, told me that he always liked to see a house with the windows lit up. It was a little wasteful, he said, and it cost a little more, but he just thought it looked pretty."

"Who was Clayton Roberts, a poet?"

"Not that I know of. He raised chickens – thousands of them. He had a place out on the Willowbrook Road."

"He raised chickens and he liked the lights on?"

"That's what he said."

"Fascinating. I'll be in the kitchen." Kenneth followed a couple minutes later.

"I can work with this for a while," Simon told him, "but we're going to need to make some serious upgrades."

Kenneth took a tumbler out of the cupboard.

"What are you talking about?"

"Well, the spices are old and flat. I'll need some bread flour and yeast and a couple vanilla beans. There's no Tamari or soy sauce or fish sauce or rice wine vinegar or sea salt or Tabasco…"

"Fanny wouldn't even know about Tamari."

"Look what they got us for coffee." Simon held up a small jar of powdered IGA brand instant. Kenneth found some ice cubes and put half a dozen in the tumbler. "And there's tea, of course, and bouillon cubes. And three boxes of these Royal Lunch crackers. What are those?"

"Crackers and milk on Sunday night."

"Crackers and milk?"

"Big dinner at noon on Sunday. At suppertime it was either popcorn or crackers and milk." Kenneth poured a generous dose of whiskey over the ice. "You want some of this?"

"No, thanks."

"Well, here's to it."

"Look," Simon said. "Aluminum pans. They'll have to go. And that electric stove – I mean, it works but it's a total piece of shit. And the only coffee maker is this thing with the glass knob on top that lets you watch the coffee perk. And the lights in here… I've started a list."

"We're only here for the weekend," Kenneth said.

"We'll be back."

"What makes you so sure?"

"Are you going to let Jerry Falwell have $1.5 million?"

"Oh, well, there's got to be some way around that."

"It didn't sound like it to me."

Kenneth sipped his whiskey and watched Simon and his lists. "There's something else. What is it?"

"Something else?"

"Well, it's not just Jerry Falwell. What's going on?"

"Ellen."

"Ellen?"

"Yes, the lovely Ellen, who was feeling you up behind the church."

"Oh, for Christ's sake."

"Tell me about Ellen."

Kenneth waved him off. "Ellen was thirty-two years ago."

"The Ellen I saw was twenty minutes ago."

"Listen. We were always really good friends but it was more like buddies or favorite cousins or something. If there had been one single reason to stay here thirty-two years ago, Ellen would have been it, but with all the rest, I couldn't do it."

"But now you're back."

"Right. And she's married to Archie and coming to breakfast Monday morning. You don't need to spend a lot of time on this." Kenneth put down the glass and rubbed his eyes and his forehead. "Christ, I'm tired. I think we can use the bedroom across from the bathroom. It was always a guest room and I never slept in it so it's as close to neutral territory as I can get in this house. I'm going to crash."

"Okay. I'll be up in a few minutes."

"Oh, the smudge." Kenneth took the sage, a saucer, and matches. "Can't be too careful," he said.

"Yeah. Good luck."

"Leave a couple lights on when you come up."

"You got it, Clayton."

Kenneth put the saucer with the sage on a small table in the center of Fanny's room and closed the window. He pinched the powder into a cone and used three matches to get it lit all around base. When he was convinced it would keep burning he blew out the flames and the room filled with a heavy, pungent smoke.

Kenneth's head throbbed, his shoulders ached, and he was exhausted. He looked for some aspirin. He found a few prescription bottles but no pain killers. Of course, there wouldn't be. Fanny would rather push through pain and emerge triumphant on the other side than take anything that would afford her some relief or make her life easier. Perhaps there was virtue in that somewhere but Kenneth had never learned to appreciate it.

He crawled into bed exhausted and restless. Part of the restlessness came from seeing Ellen. She had actually married that goon, Archie Whitaker, of all people. Kenneth couldn't get his mind around that one. He finished the whiskey and then sucked on one of the ice cubes.

She looks really good, though, he thought. She hadn't taken on that resigned, worn out look so many rural women have. Images floated in and out, scenes from years ago and from the last few hours, intermixed and without a pattern, clear but fleeting. Ellen was in all of them, the younger Ellen and the older Ellen and each brought another question. Did she have kids? Sired by that bastard? He'd never thought to ask. Could Ellen LeClaire be a grandmother now? Granny Ellen in a rocking chair knitting socks? There was no story, just random thoughts, images…

When Simon came upstairs five minutes later, the lights were still on but Kenneth was asleep.

*

Kenneth found Simon at the stove the next morning. He was wearing one of Fanny's faded aprons while he whipped up a country breakfast. Sausage – great hamburger-like patties – were already browned and warm on a back burner. As Kenneth came into the kitchen Simon poured six perfectly round four inch pancakes onto a sizzling hot iron griddle.

"Coffee?"

"Is it that instant stuff?"

"No, I found some store-brand ground something-or-other on a back shelf in the pantry," Simon said. "I managed to take the edge off with a pinch of salt and a shake of cinnamon. It settles out after a minute or two."

Kenneth tested it.

"Better than I expected."

"In the meantime, we've got this wild and woolly local sausage, and blueberry pancakes coming up. I found Fanny's personal cookbook in the pantry. Handwritten recipes."

"If the house were on fire, Fanny would brave the flames to rescue her recipes. She might then go back for her Bible but I would have been toast."

"She must have known what she was doing."

"Fanny could cook when she put her mind to it. It wasn't gourmet but it was always good."

"You want eggs?"

"Just pancakes and sausage, I think."

"Brown eggs. Are they okay?"

"Of course. Probably came from Rhode Island Reds."

"Oh." The answer wasn't as interesting as he'd hoped. "We've got orange juice."

"Okay."

"Apple butter, jam, maple syrup…"

"Syrup."

Simon flipped the pancakes and pushed the sausage around in the pan. "Man, she's got a ton of stuff in the freezer – meat, frozen pies, bags of fruit…"

"Been down cellar yet?"

"Yeah. Stuff in glass jars. Looks like pickles and string beans and tomatoes, mostly."

"Well, that's life in the country."

Simon served up the pancakes with a couple sausage patties on each plate. He poured more pancakes onto the griddle, and brought both plates to the table.

"What's that creepy, dank room behind that big wooden door, a dungeon?"

"A root cellar. Things like potatoes, carrots, beets, and turnips will keep through the winter in there."

"Or wine…"

"Or wine." Kenneth poured syrup on his pancakes. "I see she had some of the good stuff."

"Good stuff?"

"The syrup. Fancy grade is very light and delicate and it usually comes from an early sap run. Did you realize it takes as much as 40 gallons of sap to produce a single gallon of syrup?"

No, he didn't. Nor did he care. Besides, his mind was on the house.

"Well, the place is a little frumpy," Simon said. He got up to flip the pancakes. "But it's big, it's solid, and it could be quite the place. It's like stepping back into the 40s without having to create it."

"I haven't decided anything yet," he said

"Fanny's got you by the short hairs and you can't get out of it. You really have to admire how she's set you up. I mean, think of it."

"I have."

"Well you can fight it, or you can make it work," Simon said.

"What about the store?"

"We could sell it."

"Sell it?"

"Sure. Roger and some of his queer friends think they know it all. Sell'em the inventory and let them take over the lease."

"Are you serious?"

"Why not?" Simon said. He sat at the table again. "Look, we've just been going through the motions the last couple years anyway. I think it's time for something new."

Kenneth finished his pancakes and coffee. "Okay, but does the something new have to be here?"

"Look out the front window," Simon said as he stood up again. "Jerry Falwell's out on the front porch and he's about to ring your chimes."

Simon cleared the table, rinsed the dishes and left them in the sink, wiped his hands on the towel, and returned to his "to do" list where he added "dishwasher".

*

Stacks of old newspapers and magazines lined the walls in the shed on the way to the barn. There were also bins where Fanny, the good citizen, carefully separated her trash. A corner at the far end held a collection of old brooms and mops.

"What's the deal with the mops?" Simon said.

"Oh, you keep those in case you ever need a handle for something."

"What would you use them for other than a handle for a mop?"

"I don't know, but we always kept them, just in case. If you went around to all the houses in Grants Ferry right now you could probably fill a good-sized dump truck with wooden mop handles."

"Fascinating."

"Yeah, well stick around."

In the barn Kenneth went straight to the far side of the door, removed the wooden block that served as a lock, heaved the heavy door open, and day-light poured into the barn.

"Oh, wow," Simon said.

"Well, I'll be damned," Kenneth said. "There it is."

"Was that hers?"

"Sure was – a 1960 Plymouth Valiant. Kitchen Blue. I remember when she bought that car. Made it last, didn't she?"

"Does it run?"

"Let's see."

The keys were in the ignition. Kenneth got in, turned the key, and it started immediately. The car had vinyl seats and rubber floor mats.

"This looks like it came from a government motor pool," Simon said.

"I heard the dealer had to order it special, the cheapest version she could get. The only extra was the automatic transmission."

"It's in great shape."

"She probably never drove it in the winter. Salt would have eaten it up by now. She didn't even know how to drive when she bought it. I don't think Fanny ever had a happy relationship with the car, though. She didn't drive it so much as she aimed it. Everybody gave her plenty of room when they saw her coming."

"We ought to take it out for a spin."

"Why not? The whole weekend has been a total time warp so far. A ride in a 1960 Valiant will be just one more thing." Kenneth turned off the engine. "Let's see what else she has in here."

The barn, they discovered, was no longer empty as it had been when Kenneth left town. Behind the car, carefully stored in stalls on either side of the center area, were wardrobes, dressers and mirrors, chairs and tables, and bed frames with carved headboards and tall posts, all draped with big sheets of dust covered plastic. An envelope taped to one of the dressers in front said, "Front Door – Hotel".

"What do you suppose that means?" Simon asked. Kenneth took the envelope.

"You remember her note and the part about coming back to complete the work she'd begun?"

"Yes…"

"Well, this is it. I'll be a son of a bitch if she hasn't set me up."

"A barn full of furniture?"

Kenneth dangled a key.

"Looks like you're going to get to see the Intercourse House."

"Great."

"First, though, I want to see if my stuff is still here." They went upstairs and it was just as he'd left it, except for thirty years of dust on the plastic sheeting. All the things from his parents' house plus the few of his Uncle Fred's things that he'd kept when he and Luther cleaned out the barn. "I'll be damned," he said. "She couldn't wait to get rid of Fred's stuff when he died, and yet she left all of this."

"You think it was deliberate?"

"I don't know. Maybe she thought I'd be back when I came to my senses and then just forgot about it. I doubt she ever came up here."

"Damn."

"Well I can look this stuff over later," Kenneth said. "Right now you're going to get to see the Intercourse House."

Kenneth eased the little powder blue car out of the barn. Out on the street the tiny engine whirred like a lawnmower.

"Is this fun or what?" Simon asked.

"Not yet, but the day's young."

Another couple minutes.

"Kenneth…"

"What?"

"Do I smell urine?"

"Christ, I hope not."

*

Chapter Nine

Kenneth and Luther emptied the barn of Fred's things over several weekends. Kenneth had a great time. He got to ride in Luther's truck and look through Fred's entire collection, piece by piece. He was also out of Fanny's sight.

Fanny told Luther to take it to the dump, get rid of it all, and Luther agreed to do it for $10 a load. Instead, they hauled load after load to Herm Fairbrother's Salvage Yard and Second Hand Emporium up in Windsor. Herm had an eye for value in most anything so to be presented with Fred's inventory was a bonanza. Herm paid cash, too.

Kenneth kept some old phonograph records and Fred's record player, a ukulele, and a few odd pieces of china and tools he thought were interesting. These things he put upstairs where he would eventually store the things from his parents' house. When they finally delivered the last load Herm Fairbrother gave them a hand-written list of everything he'd bought along with the price that he'd pay. The total: $2,625.

"You fellas okay with cash?"

"Cash is always good," Luther said. "Split it in two. Kenny gets half."

Kenneth rode back home with $1,312.50 in his pocket, more money than he'd ever seen in his life. Luther didn't need to warn him to keep it hidden from Fanny. He put the money in a tobacco tin with a snap lid that he'd found in Fred's stuff and hid it in the space over the shed behind his room. The next Saturday they swept the barn clean and brought the rest from Tom and Amy's house. It required several trips and they worked hard but Luther made Kenneth laugh and the time went quickly.

They arrived with the last load of Tom and Amy's things, pushed open the barn door, and found the Plymouth Valiant sitting inside, ready to go.

"Well, ain't that precious," Luther said.

Kenneth was nearly speechless. "But – but she doesn't even drive," he said.

"I'll have to learn, then, won't I?" Fanny was in the doorway to the shed. "I told them to leave room for you to get by," she said. "Make sure you don't scratch it." The door banged as she went back inside.

They carried the last of Kenneth's things upstairs and then covered everything with a big sheet of polyethylene.

"Keep the dust off," Luther said. "Mice'll get into the couch and stuffed chairs, though. I'll find somebody to buy'em." Kenneth got another $100 for a few pieces of furniture he'd discovered he didn't care that much about anyway – even Tom and Amy's mattress and box spring. He kept the bed frame, though. Once he had a choice, the need to keep it all was gone. Besides, $100 seemed like a great deal of money for a few pieces of second hand furniture which wouldn't store well.

*

At supper Kenneth was full of questions.

"Is it new?"

"Yes."

"How'd it get here?"

"Had it delivered."

"How much did it cost?"

"Never you mind."

"How big is the engine?"

"No idea."

"Did you ride in it?"

"One like it."

"Why'd you get blue?"

"The other colors were awful."

"Are you going to learn to drive it?"

"Of course."

Kenneth laughed.

"What's funny about that?" Fanny said.

"Nothing," Kenneth said. "Who will teach you?"

"Finish your supper," she said. "Gracious, you've chattered half the evening away."

Through the summer Fanny had managed a weekly ride for supplies into Springfield or Windsor with other people who were going. The little grocery in Grants Ferry was all right for occasional things, but Clarence Bemis charged far too much for just about everything. She liked the local beef and chicken and eggs and was willing to pay a bit more for them, but felt he overcharged for everything else.

Fanny hated to be dependent on the whims and schedules of others, though, and resented the two dollars she offered to pay for part of the trip. They were going anyway, she reasoned, and her being in the car didn't add to the cost. There were two incidents that forced her decision to buy her own car and both were because of Myrtle Powers. They'd been to the grocery store and then Myrtle wanted to run a few more errands as long as she was in town. Fanny spent a furious hour in the car while Myrtle shopped. Two weeks later Myrtle had promised they would go to Springfield but didn't tell Fanny she'd changed her mind until Fanny showed up on her doorstep with a shopping list.

If she couldn't depend on people to keep their word, Fanny raged as she walked back home, there was no reason to depend on them at all. As much as she'd resisted the idea, she would need her own car. It would be small, though, American made, simple, and as cheap as she could buy it.

She would also need someone to help negotiate with the car dealer and it must be someone trustworthy. There were several men in town who could help in the purchase of a car but none with whom she would spend half a day alone. It should be someone of substance, someone with integrity, someone who would bring a degree of authority to the negotiations. The only person who came to mind was Malcolm MacArthur. He was stodgy, fussy, and fastidious, he sang in the church choir each Sunday, and had been the church treasurer for almost as long as she could remember. He was an odd, awkward man, but his reputation in the community was solid.

*

Malcolm was still in high school when he began at the bank as a part-time teller. His father, August MacArthur was the president and general manager. Malcolm quickly moved to full time after high school and then became a personal banker, as they like to call themselves, with a desk, a phone, and the authority to make small loans. He soon reached the level of vice president. With this title on his resume he could have easily found a lucrative job in some big city bank. The money was tempting but his future had been set years before. When he reached a level of proficiency that convinced the senior MacArthur that Malcolm could take over it was arranged for the directors to formalize this appointment when the time came.

That following spring Malcolm's father was struck down with a massive heart attack while shoveling six inches of wet, heavy snow from his driveway and at the tender age of forty-one Malcolm found himself in charge.

His future was secure. The workings of the bank, the tallying of numbers at the end of the day, the secure sound of the vault door closing each night – these were things of which Malcolm never tired. There was security in the sameness and the routine. He served the bank and in turn the bank provided for him as it had provided for his father and his father's family before him. Malcolm's function was one of oversight and development, the creation of long-term vision. He was determined, nevertheless, to remain humble.

Malcolm had nothing against marriage, he'd just never felt a need for it. Besides, Malcolm found touch uncomfortable. Hands, especially other people's hands, were just mobile germ factories. Malcolm washed his hands often. His first official order as president of the bank, was to have a washroom built next to his office. He stocked it immediately with germ-fighting soap, Lysol spray, and several cases of paper towels.

Malcolm's social life was his participation at the church. He was a deacon, he sat on the board of trustees, he volunteered for numerous ad hoc committees throughout the year, and he brought a strong and vibrant baritone to the bass section of the choir every Sunday morning. He was elected each year to the office of Church Treasurer and kept a complete and thorough set of books.

Malcolm, and by extension, the bank, held mortgages on nearly every property in Grants Ferry. He was gracious when people suffered unexpected tragedies or financial difficulties and let them make it up when they could. Sometimes it took years and he often waived the accrued penalties and fines that even to his banker's heart were too much like kicking a man when he's down. These people were his neighbors, after all, and helping them in times of crisis was the Christian thing to do.

Malcolm's personal needs were few. He grew orchids in the greenhouse just off his kitchen, and he enjoyed good food and good wine. He was not a greedy man and he didn't make demands of others.

A broad, solid man, he wore vested suits, his shoes were always shined, and his rimless glasses sparkled and projected an air of confidence and security. His light brown hair was thick, wavy, and cut short. His full mustache, with some oddly reddish highlights, completely obscured his upper lip but was always impeccably trimmed. There was occasional speculation about

Malcolm's bachelor status but no one was ever heard to utter a word against Malcolm MacArthur's character.

Malcolm didn't like surprises or challenges that had no precedent. Sudden exposure to the unfamiliar brought immediate lower intestinal gastric distress. No matter where he was or who he was with, Malcolm would suddenly cut a penetrating, noxious, eye watering fart, caustic enough to make strong men weep and raise blisters in lead paint.

Malcolm appeared to be oblivious to the pain and discomfort he caused in others. It was advisable, therefore, to avoid putting Malcolm MacArthur in a stressful situation unless one appreciated the considerable entertainment value of his condition.

Fanny and Malcolm had never mixed socially. Malcolm knew the story of the accident, of course, and found it admirable that Fanny would take on the raising of a child not her own.

From this perspective of relative isolation and chronic bachelorhood Malcolm was both surprised and flattered one Sunday morning when Fanny asked if he would drive her down to Springfield and help negotiate the purchase of a car and then teach her to drive it.

"Of course, I'll pay you," Fanny said.

"No, no. That won't be necessary."

"I'll not take charity, Malcolm MacArthur."

"Of course not."

"I need someone to assist me in the purchase and then show me how to make it behave. This has value. I'll pay you." She didn't want to pay for any of it but she wasn't going to be beholden to this man.

"I didn't mean to imply…"

"What do you consider to be a reasonable fee?"

"I have no idea, Mrs. Forbes. I don't want your money. I – "

"All right, then," Fanny said, "we'll barter."

"Barter?" This was not a banking term and Malcolm detected a faint rumbling in his bowels.

"You help me negotiate the purchase of a car and teach me to drive and when I get my driver's license you come to dinner at my house each Friday until you decide we're even."

Malcolm's bowels relaxed and the deal was done. He enjoyed a good meal, enough that he'd occasionally drive as much as two hours to find a restaurant that could leave him sated and impressed with both the food and service, not to mention a hefty charge on his credit card. These dinner excursions might also include a night at a nearby motel which allowed him to also enjoy a bottle of wine with dinner and not have to face a long drive home.

A capable and occasionally creative cook himself, Malcolm seldom spent a lot of time in the kitchen. Instead he spent tireless hours with his orchids. Food preparation was a chore. Orchids were a gift from heaven. Fanny's offer, with her solid reputation as a good cook, was too good to pass up.

The salesman at the car dealership made several phone calls and found a model that met government motor pool specifications with no frills at all, except for an automatic transmission which was standard so anyone could drive one. They were cold, spiritless cars and that suited Fanny. She wasn't buying a car to make a personal statement, she said, unaware, of course, that this was exactly what she'd done. Who else, given a choice, would want a car designed for a government motor pool?

Fanny was a determined learner, attentive and alert. She knew the driver's handbook, inside and out. She appeared to absorb and understand Malcolm's instructions as well but much of what she'd heard couldn't find its way to her hands and feet once she got behind the wheel. To Fanny, the Valiant was a wild thing to be subdued and controlled. The notion that with a little practice the car would effortlessly do her bidding and give her a freedom she had never known was unavailable to her. The Valiant could turn on her at any moment and she was determined to be ready for it.

It was not an easy time for Malcolm, either. Once, when he spoke sharply to her because she had wandered across the center line into the path of a log truck, she was ready to kill him. She swerved to avoid the log truck but then slammed on the brakes, stopped in the traffic lane, and refused to drive another inch. Inside the car was very still but the excitement of facing down a load of logs had brought Malcolm a state of considerable anxiety. The results were immediate.

"Pee yoo," Fanny said. "Land sakes. You need to go home and wash up?"

Malcolm's face flamed red. He opened his door and got out. After a few minutes, Fanny slid across the seat to the passenger side.

"All right, the car's aired out. Take us home. I've had enough," she said.

Malcolm drove the car back to Fanny's house and as soon as the car stopped she got out, slammed the door, went into the house, slammed that door, and threw the lock.

Malcolm arrived the next week at the usual time and they began the lesson as if the previous week had never happened. Fanny easily passed the written test and the vision test but she would only agree to a driving test on days when the streets were clean and dry. Most of the winter passed before she was willing to risk it. Even then it took three attempts and three different testers. The first two refused to test her again. She finally got her license, though, and the following Friday she invited Malcolm for his first dinner.

*

Kenneth knew something was up when the good dishes were brought out, the silver had been polished, a pie was baked, and the smell of herbs and roasting chicken spread through the house. Dinner with Malcolm would be dinner with Malcolm, however, and at six o'clock Fanny put out a plate of hot dogs and baked beans for Kenneth in the kitchen.

"Hot dogs and beans? I smell chicken."

"Don't you sass me, young man. Finish that up and go to your room."

"It's only 6 o'clock," Kenneth said.

"Six o'clock is suppertime. You know that."

"But I never go to bed this early."

"You hush. I have to fix dinner for Malcolm MacArthur to pay for my driving lessons."

"You have to cook him dinner?"

"He wouldn't take money so I bartered. I should have known better. The man's a bottomless pit. I'll be in the poorhouse by the end of the year."

"From one dinner?"

"Not just one dinner; one dinner a week until we're even, probably for the rest of my life unless I find a way to kill him first."

"How come I can't stay up?" Kenneth asked.

"Because I don't want to upset him," she said. "When this man gets upset he loses control."

Kenneth had a vision of this man throwing a plate of food across the room. "Wow. He gets mad?"

"No, no, no. Good Lord, what are you thinking? He cuts wicked smelly farts." Kenneth giggled. He'd never heard a woman say a word like fart and was surprised Fanny could even think it. "T'ain't funny, McGee," Fanny said.

"Why would I upset him?"

"I have no idea, but I'm not taking chances. We'd never get the smell out of the curtains. Now finish up and go upstairs. I don't want to hear any more out of you. Go on. Shoo."

Malcolm's dinner included roast chicken, gravy, string beans, summer squash, and mashed potatoes, finished off with blackberry pie and vanilla ice cream, not to mention candles on the table. It wasn't gourmet by any means but Fanny, whatever else anyone might say about her, could lay out a wholesome, well-prepared meal when she put her mind to it. Malcolm, who would seldom fuss like this at home, savored every mouthful, helped himself to seconds without them being offered, and exhibited complete enjoyment and satisfaction. Fanny watched carefully. As far as she could tell, the display was genuine. Malcolm MacArthur, like any man, certainly had his faults but apparently deception and guile were not among them, at least when it came to food.

Kenneth listened carefully at the register in the floor to see if he could tell what was happening. All he could hear after they sat down at the table was eating sounds. There was no conversation at all, just things like, "Gravy?" "Yes. Thank you." "Delicious, Fanny, absolutely delicious." Kenneth soon lost interest and went back to his book.

When Malcolm had cleaned his plate for yet a third time, and polished off two pieces of blackberry pie, Fanny stood to clear the table.

"Go and open the parlor," she said. "I'll bring coffee."

The meal was clearly over. Not that Malcolm was complaining, but he could have easily gone around again if there had been anything left. He lifted himself from the table.

"A delightful meal, Fanny," he said. "You deserve every bit of your reputation as a fine cook."

"Oh, go on with you. Open the parlor. I'll be right in."

Malcolm slid the heavy doors into the walls on either side. When Fanny brought the coffee tray into the parlor she found Malcolm sitting at the organ, running his round pink fingers over the oiled woodwork.

"This is an Estey Organ," he said. There was surprise and amazement in his voice, perhaps even a hint of reverence.

"Yes, it is. My grandfather bought it for my mother years ago."

"It's beautiful. I didn't know they made these tall ones."

"It's the Renaissance Model," she said

"Do you play?"

"Lord, no. I never had the patience for it. My mother played, though. She was very skilled."

Malcolm's fingers were itching to get at the keyboard.

"Do you mind?" he asked.

"Go ahead," Fanny said. *Just keep him happy*, she thought, and bent over the low table to pour the coffee.

Malcolm adjusted the bench slightly, worked the pedals, and began to play an old hymn from memory. Not only, it seemed, did Malcolm possess a fine baritone that rumbled out of that big trunk of his, but he was also quite accomplished at a keyboard. Fanny brought an old hymnal from the bookcase and Malcolm spent the next hour and a half playing and singing their favorite hymns. Fanny rocked gently in her mother's rocker, closed her eyes, and sipped her coffee. Her mother was the last person to bring such lovely music out of that old organ and that had been years ago. Remembering this, Fanny actually enjoyed herself, a sensation so unfamiliar it left her a bit lightheaded.

They must be in the parlor, Kenneth thought when the music started. Music was an alien sound in this house. Fanny didn't own a radio or TV and as far as he knew she didn't have a record player, either. Uncle Fred had owned a lot of that stuff but it had all been swept out of the house and into the barn with every other trace of him after he'd died. What Fanny didn't know, however, was that Kenneth had kept Fred's records and the phonograph and a big old radio and had them stored with all his own things in the barn.

He crept quietly out of his room and sat at the top of the stairs. The old hymns flowed out of the parlor and throughout the house. He wanted to sneak downstairs and get a better look at the instrument that produced these sounds but he knew better. Once Kenneth had been sent to bed Fanny didn't want to see him again until morning and Kenneth wasn't about to seek an exception to this rule tonight. Besides, there was always the chance he could upset Malcolm MacArthur.

The next day, though, at breakfast, he had to ask.

"You have an organ?" He didn't want to give her any hint that he'd found a way through the sliding doors.

"Yes, I do."

"In the parlor?"

"That's right."

"Were you playing last night?"

"That was Malcolm."

"He's pretty good, isn't he?"

"He'll do."

"I didn't know we had an organ."

"'*We*' don't have an organ. *I* have an organ and you're not to touch it, you understand? You stay out of that parlor."

"But I – "

"That organ was my mother's, bless her soul, and that room is off limits to you." Fanny's voice was rising. "You stay out of that room, you hear?"

"Yes, m'am."

But he resolved that one day when she was safely gone he'd find a way to inspect the organ. There were lots of things he could do that Fanny wouldn't know about. The parlor was a special case, though. He'd have to be really careful with this one.

Each Friday he'd be given a quick and early supper and sent upstairs. Malcolm MacArthur would arrive sometime later, the candles would be lit, the lights would be turned down, and Malcolm would methodically Hoover up several helpings of everything. There was always dessert, of course, a treat that was seldom offered to Kenneth, after which Fanny and Malcolm would slide open the parlor doors and the music would flow for another two hours or so. Malcolm was tireless at the keyboard.

By the fourth dinner, Kenneth was confident he had at least two hours when Fanny would be so engrossed that he might escape unnoticed, so when the hymns started he opened the small door to the space over the shed, went through the barn and out the back door. It was a short walk to Ellen's house.

"What are you doing here?" Ellen asked the first time he showed up.

"Fanny and Malcolm MacArthur are in the parlor making music."

"What?"

"I'm not kidding. Malcolm taught her to drive and now she cooks dinner for him on Friday nights."

"So you get a real meal once in a while?"

"No way. I get hot dogs and mashed potatoes or soup in the kitchen. He gets roast chicken and gravy on the good china in the dining room." He could see the fire come up in Ellen's eyes. "It doesn't matter," he said. "Hot dogs or stew or hash is fine. It's no big deal. I don't go hungry. Anyway, turns out Malcolm can play so they started with hymns and now they're working their way through some old song books or something. It's awful stuff but they're always at it for a couple hours. I can sneak out through the barn and get back before she ever knows."

It wasn't as good or as frequent as the time they had when he was staying at the Nelson's but it was a lot better than nothing.

*

After three months of Friday dinners, Malcolm acknowledged that he had been more than well paid but suggested they might continue with the dinners and the music on the condition that he supply the ingredients. This took a considerable financial strain off Fanny and as she rather enjoyed cooking for someone who appreciated it as well as the music afterward, she agreed. Malcolm then took Thursday afternoons to drive to a small grocery in Keene, New Hampshire, where he could select prime cuts of meat, often raised locally and cut to order, the freshest produce, and whatever fresh fruit Fanny might make into a dessert. He'd turn up at Fanny's house later that day, bags bulging with his purchases, already salivating at the thought of the meal he would enjoy the following night. Given a choice, Malcolm would have also brought a bottle or two of wine as well, but he knew what Fanny thought of alcohol. It was a small enough price to pay for an excellent home-cooked meal.

Fanny felt as if she were cooking for a party of eight, but she cooked it all anyway. Malcolm would eat his fill every Friday and there were leftovers to feed Kenneth and herself through much of the week.

The dinners became slower and more relaxed. Fanny still found Malcolm to be a rather stuffy man, but over a series of good meals he gradually softened. Their conversation grew freer.

"Do you remember how this town used to be grand, Malcolm?"

"I do."

"And look at it now. What's happened to it?"

"Well, there was the bridge…"

"Oh, for pity sake. Bother the bridge. That's just been an excuse to give up."

"I think folks are doing the best they can, Fanny."

"And the best they can do is let the place fall down around them? What do you see when you look around this town?"

"Well, I – "

"What happened to the prosperous downtown and the lovely old residential streets, the things that made Grants Ferry grand. What do you see when you look at that?"

"Sometimes," Malcolm said, "it reminds me of photos of old movie stars long past their prime. I see a – a suggestion of their former elegance and style, but now… Now it's as if the structure is still there but I see tiredness. Sometimes I see hopelessness as well."

"I see it, too," Fanny said, "and it makes me sick. I've so wanted it to be the way it was, back to the way I remember it, but – but I haven't the means."

"The means?"

"Money," she said, as if any fool, especially a banker, should be familiar with the euphemism. "But," she went on. "I'm not even sure if I had the means I'd know what to do." She felt vulnerable after sharing her dream. The months of dinners and music, however, let her believe Malcolm MacArthur could be trusted, trusted with something as dear to her as her dream of a grand and proud Grants Ferry. She took a breath and went on. "I've dreamed of creating something," she said, "a legacy that Kenneth can continue when I'm gone. I don't have a clear vision of it but it would preserve some of the best examples of Grants Ferry when it was grand."

"Preserve them? Properties?"

"Yes. Acquire them and preserve them, to prevent them from being destroyed at the very least."

"I see."

"It would be wonderful to be able to restore the hotel, for instance – there were such happy times there – but I don't know. It's only a dream, a dream I've had for years. I see the result, Malcolm; I can't see the means." She drifted away for a moment, staring at the dining room window as if her dream was complete and sitting on the other side. "This town used to be grand," she said again, "a thriving and happy community…" Her voice drifted off. Suddenly she stood and began to clear the table. "Oh, land sakes," she said. "Dreaming never got anything done. Go on into the parlor. I'll bring the coffee."

*

Malcolm gradually grew accustomed to Fanny's lament about the decline of the town. He sympathized but his realist banker instincts doubted it would ever happen. Still, he was interested in maintaining the relationship with this woman who took him into her home each week for a fine home cooked meal, something he'd missed since his mother died.

Gossip around town had it that Fanny Forbes and Malcolm MacArthur were a bit of an item. A couple of the more vicious gossip-mongers even sat across the street for several Fridays to see if the light ever went on in Fanny's bedroom before Malcolm left for home. Much to their disappointment, it never did.

Romantic notions were the farthest things from Fanny's mind and if Malcolm had ever considered an increased level of intimacy he wouldn't have known where to begin. In the many months he'd come to dinner, Malcolm had never so much as unbuttoned his vest, even in summer. On warm nights he'd ask if he might remove his jacket, but that was as familiar as he was likely to get. His shirtsleeves always remained buttoned. In situations where protocol was established, like the bank or at the church, Malcolm knew his role and managed it comfortably. Matters of a personal and unpredictable nature, matters that required some of the softer social graces, were unfamiliar to Malcolm and could cause immediate anxiety and the resulting flatulence that, even sneaky and silent, could never be hidden or ignored. Both Malcolm and Fanny, therefore, were careful not to move into an area where Malcolm might feel uncomfortable or stressed.

One night Malcolm was at the Estey, working his way through a soulful rendition of *When You and I Were Young, Maggie*. Fanny began to sing along and absent-mindedly rested her hands on Malcolm's shoulders while she leaned in to read the words to the fourth verse. Malcolm immediately stumbled over notes and in less than five measures he released a noiseless but nevertheless eye-watering fart. The music stopped and the room fell silent. Fanny dropped her hands and left for the kitchen. When she didn't return after several minutes, Malcolm put on his coat and went home. He showed up with the groceries the next Thursday, though, on schedule. Under the circumstances, that seemed best. Let the air clear, so to speak, and start again.

Malcolm had been dining at Fanny's house for six months before he asked if he might use the bathroom, a request far too personal for mixed company. In fact, he wouldn't mention it in unmixed company if he could help it. He didn't like to think of himself as ever using the toilet and to mention it in front of a lady was absolutely beyond his limits. This particular Friday, however, he'd had a long afternoon board meeting where he had absentmindedly sipped his way through three cups of coffee without a thought to the consequences. It was over four hours since the last cup of coffee and he'd now finished a full meal. He stopped playing.

"Fanny, I'm sorry. The – um – the bathroom?"

"Upstairs. To the right."

Totally embarrassed, his face flaming red, Malcolm eased himself off the bench and moaned through his teeth with each gingerly step up the long flight of stairs. So great was the pressure that he nearly lost all control as he fumbled to make the lock on the bathroom door work. He finally gave up in desperation and stood with his back to the door, aiming sideways into the toilet in case Fanny should burst into the room. He'd worried for nothing. The last thing on Fanny's mind was Malcolm's pecker. Still, he was careful to not let his eyes wander. It was not his nature to snoop into a lady's personal belongings.

It was an unsettling episode, using Fanny's toilet, but thankfully it hadn't been so uncomfortable as to generate one of his blistering farts. From that day forward, though, he became very careful about his fluid intake at the Friday board meetings.

*

Chapter Ten

Fanny often settled into bed with one of her favorite books, *Fifty Years in Grants Ferry, a Pictorial History, 1885 – 1935* by Leonard P. Hopkins.

Leonard Hopkins had been a photographer with a small portrait studio just off Main Street when Fanny was a girl. He hired out for weddings, individual portraits, and large family photos. He also contributed occasional streetscapes to *The Grants Ferry Herald.* It had never been a lucrative profession but Leonard Hopkins had few interests aside from his photography. His shelves had held thousands of prints and negatives, an extensive photographic record of activities in Grants Ferry over decades. He'd also acquired collections from earlier photographers' estates from which he sometimes made prints. It was from this combined collection that he published his book in 1937, a limited printing of virtually no interest to anyone outside Grants Ferry. Leonard sold what he could and sent copies off to libraries around the state, as well as the Library of Congress and each of the New England states' libraries. The rest were stored in his studio. Leonard framed the thank-you letter from the Library of Congress.

Many photos in Leonard Hopkins' book were of local businesses but it was the earlier photos that interested Fanny, photos which featured architectural details and the scale of buildings, the grace and elegance of the streetscapes with the towering, over-arching elms that lined the residential streets, the well-maintained fences, the spacious front lawns, or the variety of trees around the common. Even in the sepia tones of the early photos the people possessed a style and manner long lost, pride of community, a comfortable life celebrated in an elegant and dignified environment.

But the town slid into decline and few people had money to keep places up. On the other hand, they had no money to tear them down, either, a hidden blessing. Nearly thirty-five years after Leonard published his book, many of the buildings remained. The elms had succumbed to Dutch Elm Disease but the essence of rebirth survived. All Fanny needed, she knew, was the means to bring it back. She could inspire others (which she considered hopeless) or she could take it on herself.

If she couldn't physically bring the town back to its former luster she could at least collect the information and historical materials to document what it had once been. Her search sometimes took her away for hours at a time and this suited Kenneth just fine. Food was always available, even if it was only a peanut butter and jelly sandwich or a can of soup. He was content with anything that filled him up. There were always leftovers after Malcolm's Friday night feed. There might even be cake or pie.

Life with Fanny was a constant balancing act. There was never a suggestion of friendship or hint of family intimacy and little conversation. Fanny let Kenneth know where she was going and always inquired about his going out. Fanny was not above courtesy, after all, as long as she ultimately got her way.

She would go to Windsor, she told Kenneth, to do research at *The Vermont Journal*, a weekly newspaper in Windsor. The *Journal* had bought up *The Grants Ferry Herald* years ago only to shut it down six months later. All the old copies of the *Herald* were still preserved and on file in Windsor and that's where she'd be most of the day. Kenneth was to do his chores and stay out of trouble.

As soon as she drove away Kenneth called Ellen.

"She's going to be gone all day," he said. "Come on over."

"Where's she gone?"

"Windsor."

"What for?"

"Something about old newspapers. Who cares?"

"Did she say when she'd be back?"

"She said she'd be gone most of the day."

"Why don't you come over here?"

"I want to show you something. Come on over. Then we'll go back to your house."

"Okay. I have to help Mom for a while, then I'll come."

It was almost noon when Ellen arrived. Kenneth made sandwiches, poured milk, and they ate at the kitchen table.

"So what is it you're going to show me?"

"Surprise," Kenneth said.

"Right. Is it going to be something creepy, like down cellar where it's full of spiders?"

"No. Better than that."

Kenneth washed the dishes, wiped them, and put them away. In Fanny's house he lived without leaving a trace.

"Okay," he said when he'd hung up the towels. "Come in here and I'll show you." He got the key to the parlor doors from under the front stairs. "This is great. Wait 'til you see this." He unlocked the parlor doors and slid them wide open. Even with the curtains drawn, the day outside was so bright that the parlor was softly lit."

"Oh, wow," Ellen said. "I've never seen this room."

"She keeps it locked. It took me weeks to find the key."

"Have you been in here before?"

"Once. I found out how to get in here a couple months after I came here but she doesn't know." He pulled her into the room and turned her to face the organ. "Look at that."

"Oh, wow," Ellen said again.

"Yeah, it's an Estey. They made them down in Brattleboro."

"This is Fanny's?"

"Yeah. Her grandfather bought it for her mother. Malcolm plays it every Friday after they've had dinner. I asked if I could see it and she told me I was to stay out of here."

"Don't you think we should get out, then?"

"Why? She's gone. She'll never know. Besides, I want to see how this thing works." He slid onto the bench and gently pumped the pedals. He touched a key and the organ sounded a reedy A. "This is great," he said. He tried several combinations until he found a chord. He pulled out one of the stops and another voice was added. He pulled another stop and a third voice joined the others.

"Kenny, we ought to get out of here."

"Wait. I want to try this." He pulled out all the stops and all the voices sounded at once like a huge choir. "Wow," he said. "It would be great to learn to play something like this, wouldn't it? Come on. Sit here on the bench and try it out."

"Kenny, I – "

"Come on. Just for a minute. You have to see what this feels like. It's really great."

He showed her which keys to press and they each played the same chord but at different octaves and Kenneth worked the pedals and increased the volume. They were so intent trying the different stops and key combinations that they never knew Fanny was there until they looked up and saw her standing in the doorway, white with rage.

Ellen was off the far side of the bench in a flash but Fanny tore into the room, grabbed Kenneth by the collar, and pulled him off the bench. It happened so quickly he couldn't get his footing. He fell and Fanny came down on top of him. Ellen bounced around the room like a rabbit and the instant she found an opening she streaked into the hall, out the front door, and home.

"You'd better run, you little tart," Fanny shrieked after her. "And don't you ever come in my house again. *Ever!*"

Kenneth fought to escape but Fanny gripped his shirt with all the ferocity of a bulldog and just as determined. She yanked him to his feet and dragged him out through the kitchen to the shed where she took one of Fred's old belts off a hook. In no time she'd doubled the belt back on itself and then, with a fury Kenneth had never seen, she brought the belt down across the backs of his legs. The pain was so intense he could only gasp.

He'd been afraid when Fanny appeared in the parlor doorway but now he was terrified. No one had ever hit him, much less whipped him with a leather strap. Amy and Tom didn't believe in spanking and with Amy's counseling and instruction he'd always managed to avoid fights at school. The first blow from the strap landed with a sharp crack as the two pieces of leather slapped against each other and the sound and the pain were one. Pain seared along the backs of his legs and sent them into spasm. He'd lost the ability to make them move.

Fanny let fly the strap again. This blow came before he'd caught his breath from the first and fell across his lower back. His body contorted involuntarily. He still made no sound save for a sharp intake of breath. The third blow struck his legs again. His vision was cloudy. He couldn't breathe. The fourth blow landed on his calves. The fifth struck his hip. By this time his fear had swelled into rage and hatred. He refused to cry. He held his breath on purpose. He wouldn't give her the satisfaction. The sixth and last blow struck him across the buttocks and he nearly screamed from the shock and pain but kept silent except for his gasping to disguise his sobs.

Fanny finally let go of his shirt and leaned back against the door frame, exhausted and breathing heavily. Kenneth trembled on the shed floor.

"I told you time and again you were to stay out of that room," she said, gasping for breath, "and this is the thanks I get for taking you into my home. I leave the house and you sneak around like a thief. I should put you out, send you off to some state home. You don't deserve any better. See how far you'd get sneaking around there."

Kenneth lay still, breathing deeply so he wouldn't cry. He couldn't speak, even if he wanted to, and besides, he was afraid anything he said would invite another lashing.

"You get on up to your room," Fanny said when she'd got some of her breath back. "And don't come down again until I call."

Kenneth struggled to his feet. His legs were shaky and he held onto things to steady himself. "Move along," Fanny said. She tried to sound threatening but her energy was spent. Kenneth couldn't hurry in any case but he kept moving. He expected another bite from the belt but it didn't come.

There was no call for supper that night but it didn't matter. He had no appetite anyway. Any movement during the night was painful enough to wake him. The next morning Fanny called him to breakfast and busied herself at the sink while Kenneth ate his cereal and toast. He finished his juice and went to the door.

"You won't send me away," he said.

"Think so, do you?" Fanny didn't look up from the sink.

"Yes."

"And why's that?"

"Because if I don't live here the money stops." He backed through the doorway so he could escape if he needed to. "And don't ever touch me again," he said.

Fanny was now furious. "Don't tell me what to do in my house, you little brat."

"If I go, the money stops," Kenneth said. "If you ever touch me again I'll tell Increase Houghton." Kenneth was poised and ready to hit her if she came for him again but she turned back to the sink without another word.

He was right and she knew it. She could lose the stipend and without the stipend she could lose everything else. She'd have to work out a plan. In the meantime, she'd call the Whitaker boys and arrange to have a new lock put on the parlor doors.

One of the Whitaker men came by that afternoon, a repulsive man who continually snuffed and wiped his nose on a disgusting gray handkerchief. He had the lock changed in less than an hour. He gave her the new keys which she washed at the kitchen sink as soon as he'd left.

She wore the new keys on a ribbon around her neck.

*

Kenneth sneaked out the back and ran over to Ellen's house the next Friday evening as soon as Malcolm began playing the organ.

"Hi," she said. There were tears in her eyes. "What happened? What'd she do?"

"She dragged me out to the shed and whipped me with a belt."

"Oh, God… That's awful. I thought you said she was going to be gone all day."

"That's what she said. She may have set me up."

"What do you mean?"

"She never tells me when she's coming home. I should have known better."

"And she whipped you?"

"Yeah. Big leather belt, probably one of Uncle Fred's. I thought she'd got rid of all his stuff. It's probably the belt she uses to hold the pail when she goes berrying."

Ellen's mother brought in a bowl of popcorn and two bottles of cold 7-Up. Kenneth never got 7-Up at Fanny's house.

"How you doing, Kenny?"

"I'm okay."

"Good. It's nice to see you again. You come over anytime."

"Thank you." She went back to the kitchen and the kids began on the popcorn.

"She's really strong, you know."

"Fanny?"

"Yeah. I couldn't get away. Even when we stood up, she kept me off balance and wouldn't let go of my shirt. Then she had the belt. After she hit me the first time I couldn't move at all."

There were tears in Ellen's eyes again.

"I shouldn't have come over. It's my fault."

"No, it's not," Kenneth said. "I talked you into it and I'm the one who got the whipping."

"But if I hadn't come – "

"It would have been something else. Don't worry. It won't happen again."

"Why not?"

"Because I told her I knew the money would stop if I didn't live there and if she ever touched me again I'd tell Increase."

"What'd she say when you told her that?"

"Nothing. But she won't touch me again."

*

It was the domestic equivalent of a cold war. Kenneth gave every appearance of compliance and cooperation. He completed the chores she laid out and he did them well and on time. Fanny continued to cook and do his laundry and see to his basic needs, all done with a minimum of conversation. Each watched for subtle ways to gain some advantage over the other without the appearance of having done anything.

Fanny believed labor in the name of God might bring salvation to his sneaky little rebellious soul and volunteered Kenneth's services at the church at every opportunity. This work was on top of the usual household chores, like adding ten years to an already unreasonable sentence, but Kenneth never let his irritation show. He never complained or argued because he knew that a constant display of happiness and contentment drove her crazy.

Working along side adults helped Kenneth develop a level of maturity far beyond that of his peers. Other boys his age would rather be hunting or fishing or knocking each other around in a ball game. He did chores and volunteer work. Archie liked to call him the "Ladies Aid".

The church women loved this courteous young man who cheerfully set about whatever had to be done. Fanny had also unwittingly given Kenneth back to Charlotte Nelson as well if only for a few hours now and then.

"Such a fine young man," Charlotte would say. "Your dear mother would have been so proud," and she'd smother him in a big, pillowy hug. Charlotte had grown even rounder since he'd lived at the parsonage and it was like being pushed into two big warm gelatin pillows. From a distance, though, Kenneth noticed that Charlotte's breasts moved when she walked and he was surprised that this interested him.

He hadn't seen a woman's breast since Amy died. Amy hadn't romped around the house naked but neither had she hidden herself. If he'd happened to walk in when she had no top on she'd just say, "Hi" and finish dressing. It was a normal and natural thing. Amy's breasts had been smallish, though, and didn't move very much. Charlotte's were like big flesh colored water balloons and for a teenage boy who only knew breast shapes constricted behind heavy, harness-like bras, to see Charlotte's flesh roll around under a thin knit top was a fascinating thing. Her breasts hadn't moved like that when he'd been at the parsonage. Was it the extra weight? Something to do with her age? Or was it that she had begun to wear scoop neck tops that often revealed a generous dose of cleavage. Or perhaps in the parlance of some of the novels he'd read, this was "an ample bosom". Ample seemed like a good description.

Time ground on, seasons had passed with a grueling predictability, the same events replayed again and again. Kenneth and Ellen were both sophomores now and their friendship was a welcome constant, a refuge, and, as always, they could speak frankly about anything.

"Jesus," Kenneth said, "have you noticed Charlotte Nelson's boobs?"

"What about them?"

"They're big and they move around when she walks, like – like water balloons rolling around on a shelf."

"Well, what do you expect? They're just blobs of fat tissue. You expect a blob of warm fat is going to sit still?"

He hadn't thought of them as blobs of warm fat. It struck him as quite a discovery.

"I guess not," he said. "I just thought it was interesting, that's all. I hadn't noticed it before."

"You've never seen boobs?"

"Not big ones that moved."

"You've seen boobs, then?"

"Well, yeah. Amy's sometimes, but that was a long time ago. They didn't move like that, either."

"Of course not. Most women make some attempt to control them. I don't know what's got into Charlotte Nelson lately but people don't dress that way unless they want people to notice. Keep that in mind."

Ellen's curiosity was piqued. Had something finally awakened in Kenneth that drew his attention to female body parts? If other boys were any measure it was certainly late in coming with Kenneth. Ellen had sometimes felt their friendship had the makings of a romantic one but she'd never picked up the slightest interest in that department from Kenneth. Now he was talking about Charlotte Nelson's breasts.

"Do your boobs move?"

"None of your business," Ellen said.

This was a conversation in which Kenneth could easily find himself over his head. He let it go.

*

The top of Archie's deformed ear listed at an odd angle and the scar had turned purple. Folks in Grants Ferry were used to it but the summer before he started high school in Springfield, a day trip to a reconstruction specialist in Hanover straightened it out and reduced the size of the scar. It wasn't perfect but he began to wear his hair longer to cover it. He'd rather be teased about long hair than a misshapen ear.

Archie had grown to appreciate Ellen as well. She wasn't much to look at, even now – he'd begun to have an interest in that direction – and she generally avoided him, but when he thought about it, she was quite something in that cool, distant way of hers. She'd clearly beat the shit out of him but by keeping it to herself she'd both preserved his reputation and guaranteed he wouldn't bother either her or Kenneth again. He admired that.

Kenneth and Ellen were easy prey for the gang mentality that ruled some of the remaining bullies but Archie found he could direct their interests away from Kenneth and Ellen without having appeared to be defending them, a skill that would serve him well in the years ahead as a community leader.

*

Kenneth and Ellen had a solid friendship in which gender seemed to not play a part, something few people in Grants Ferry were able to understand.

Boy+girl+together = Item.

But what they had wasn't as simple as that. Theirs was pure friendship which had grown and become more secure each year. Given the slightest opportunity, they'd avoid their classmates and find a quiet place where they could read or talk. They sometimes went to the town library for a couple hours to do their homework and see whether Harriet Gould Brown, the librarian, had any new books for them.

The Grants Ferry Library had a pitifully small inventory of its own books, a situation that was unlikely to improve given the focus of the town budget on things like road repairs and plowing snow. But Harriet Gould Brown was not simply a custodian of books. Her mission was to get books into the hands of people who would read them and take nourishment from the knowledge they held. A closed book was a book unused, mute and waiting. It distressed her that so many young minds were directed toward other things, minds wasted when they could so easily absorb the incredible and vast knowledge contained in books.

Her salvation had been the Vermont State Library system which could bring nearly any book she might request. Harriet fashioned her weekly request to the state library according to the interests of her patrons. Kenneth and Ellen, at least, were curious about the world outside and seemed willing to grow beyond the dreary life waiting for them in Grants Ferry. With enough enticement they would both escape to a world where they could grow and explore and contribute. It would be criminal for Kenneth and Ellen to remain where there was so little potential. Harriet Gould Brown had hoped all her professional life to find and serve individuals like Kenneth Forbes and Ellen LeClaire and she felt her life finally had purpose after all.

Ellen was fascinated by the way things worked and she marveled over details and schematics, power generation, engine functions, heat transfer, or plumbing. She asked for books that explained about locks and clocks and radios and electric motors. Without hesitation she'd opened and repaired her mother's sewing machine. She then took up sewing and Kenneth was amazed at the way she could design her own clothes and sew them together so quickly. The cloth and the curves all made sense to her while it made none to Kenneth. Once at a church supper he found her discussing the merits of diesel engines versus gasoline engines with a couple of local loggers.

Kenneth, on the other hand, was drawn to stories of people and places other than Grants Ferry. He loved novels set in cities, the bigger and more complicated the better, convoluted stories that involved interesting personalities. He found the whole idea of ethnic neighborhoods and different languages and strange smells and quaint customs exciting. He was curious about the steamy underside of big cities, dark alleys, places that were open all night, music, lights, smoke, and people who wouldn't care who he was or why he was there. Books became his companions on those nights when he couldn't otherwise escape Fanny's scrutiny. He sometimes read late into the night.

Ellen's vision of her life was in Grants Ferry. Stability, familiarity, and consistency were a comfort to her. She had a clear concept of the rest of the world but was more than content to let it be. She would bring what she needed from outside. Catalogs, mail order, and access to anything was available if she did a little research. She briefly considered training as a nurse when her mother became ill and Ellen had realized some satisfaction in caring for her. But her mother recovered and Ellen's thoughts of nursing school disappeared. She was content to watch the rest of the world from afar. Ellen read magazines, saw an occasional movie, watched a little TV and that was enough. Nothing she saw suggested she should leave Grants Ferry for something better.

Catalogs told her all she needed to know about current styles. She and her mother made a trip to one of the big malls in Massachusetts a couple times a year but she was never comfortable there. Too many people, too much traffic which moved too fast, and the constant noise was distracting.

For groceries they drove to either Springfield or Windsor or occasionally down to Keene, New Hampshire. These trips were more than enough adventure for Ellen LeClaire.

Except for his friendship with Ellen, Kenneth couldn't see anything positive about the town at all. He liked the springtime when everything was green again and the last hurrah in the fall when the colors came in October, but other than that it was tired buildings, tired people, evidence of making do, and an endless series of church suppers, the annual harvest festival, school, and chores. There was nothing that he could see in the years ahead that looked or felt the least bit positive or different.

On the rare occasion when Fanny chose to talk with Kenneth about anything other than his chores and scheduling, she would reminisce about the way the town used to be, a time of pride and energy, a place that provided comfort and a sense of place, not just shelter at the end of the day. Fanny's vision of the past glory of Grants Ferry was one of community, of celebration, a time of general prosperity. Everyone agreed it must have been wonderful but the hopelessness of the task overwhelmed them and Fanny's dream would fade once again. It was just too big. "Nice idea and everything, but these days, with the way things are…" And this included Kenneth. He was still in high school, after all. Except for Whitaker's lumber mill and dry kiln, there was no industry. Virtually everyone, save the people who scratched out a living in a few local shops, worked at the mill handling logs and lumber or somewhere else that involved at least a half-hour commute each way. It was common for both adults in a family to work which often required two vehicles as work schedules never coincided. Parents with young children also had the expense of child care if grandparents weren't available.

Luther Pike, however, like his father before him, had cultivated a string of local people who would hire him for hauling rubbish to the dump, occasional yard work, and general cleanup jobs. He was steady, he was honest, and he sometimes hired Kenneth to help him out. Luther taught Kenneth how to lift heavy things, to use the weight of the item to advantage, to feel the motion of the person on the other end of something heavy so he could work with them and not against them. Kenneth wasn't as strong as Luther – he didn't know anyone who was – but Luther never asked him to take on more than he could handle.

Ellis Rogers hired Luther to paint his barn and Luther asked Kenneth to help him out. It was soon apparent that Luther had no facility with liquids and brushes. At the end of the first day he had as much paint on himself as the barn and was too pissed to even speak on the way home. Kenneth had only a few spots on his hands and that pissed Luther off even more. He left the entire job for Kenneth to finish. He drove him to the job in the morning, brought him lunch around noontime, saw that he had whatever he needed, and took him home at the end of the day, usually stopping to buy him a cold soda from the machine in front of the gas station.

"How'd it go?"

"Good."

"Mmm." Belch. "Good."

The entire barn was going to be red but Kenneth suggested to Ellis Rogers that it might look nice if they trimmed it with white and painted the doors and window sash a really dark green. Ellis liked it so much when it was done he gave Kenneth a $200 tip and said he thought he might have him paint the house next year. On the way home Kenneth handed the $200 to Luther.

"What's that?"

"Ellis gave it to me. He liked the way the barn came out."

"That's yours, then."

The work with Luther was sporadic, and sometimes groaningly tedious, but Kenneth was always well paid and while he was working with Luther Fanny didn't seem to be interested in what he was up to. He and Ellen found snatches of time to go for walks, or to the library, or grab some TV on the Fridays when Fanny and Malcolm were having their music fest. It was uncomplicated and predictable. Fanny never let up with her complaints and criticism. Kenneth never talked back.

During his senior year in high school Kenneth began to wake in the night and wonder at his future. Whatever he thought of school, it brought a routine to his life that would no longer exist when he graduated. He supposed he'd be expected to find work in Springfield and join the commute back and forth each day. He'd hate that, though, and it wouldn't be like working with Luther. Kenneth faced a life of tedium. It was all tones of gray, not a single bright spot, and it left him sleepless and exhausted.

"What's going on?" Ellen said. Kenneth had been uncharacteristically quiet. They were walking home from a spring cleanup day at the church.

"We're about done with school."

"I know."

"And then what?"

"What does it matter?" she said. "You hate school. It's almost over."

"Right."

"I should think you'd be happy."

"That's what I always thought but at least while we were in school I knew what was coming next. It's like everything was planned around that schedule and all I had to do was show up."

"Yeah," Ellen said. "But now you've got choices."

"I wonder," he said.

The uneasiness increased steadily, right through his final exams. There was a general euphoria among his classmates who seemed to relish the new freedom. Some of the kids from Springfield, he knew, were going off to the University of Vermont, some to technical schools, a few to the military. He'd never asked Fanny about money for college and really didn't expect it in any case. Even if college had been in his future, he didn't want to make that choice right now. He needed a year or so to sort it out, to decide what he wanted to do with his life. He wanted to know, to have a goal and focus on reaching it, or he wanted it totally open and wild and unpredictable and free. He certainly didn't want to become another of the tired, worn down people of Grants Ferry.

On graduation night Fanny had another of her "headaches" so Kenneth rode down to Springfield with Ellen and her family. It was a clear, warm night and the ceremony was held outside on the baseball field.

On the positive side Kenneth took comfort that he might never see most of his classmates again. On the negative side was the fear that he would, and often. He fumbled with his program, rolling it first one way and then the other, as the proceedings continued to plod through each item.

A man with white hair got up to speak, a serious sort, no doubt one of Springfield's prominent citizens.

"Welcome graduates," he said, "and congratulations." He acknowledged this milestone, congratulated them again on having reached it, and couldn't stress too strongly its importance in the rest of their lives.

"Tonight," he said, "you leave the protective halls of Springfield High. Before you now are the challenges, the opportunities, and the events that will form your life. Go on to school if you can," he said, "make a contribution to the rest of the world if you're able, prosper and multiply wherever you are, but never forget the place that gave you the gift of life in the first place. Always remember," he preached, "your obligation to the community that has supported you from the cradle to this moment. In return for this support, as true Vermonters, we all have an obligation to help our birth communities to prosper and grow, to see that they become better places when we leave this earth than they were when we arrived. There is no greater gift, or ultimately one more appreciated, than the support and energy you give to your own community. Join the service organizations, participate in your churches, volunteer for worthy causes, run for local elections. Service comes in many forms and all communities, large or small, depend on people who take on the tasks that need to be done.

"If your plans include more schooling, good for you. A community needs many skills. Bring your knowledge home and put it to work. If, on the other hand, your plans are to stay and join the local work force, then you must work hard, work honestly, and give some of your money or your time to your community.

"Life's greatest opportunities await you – right in your home town. Seek them out, support them, and both you and your community will be the better for it.

"Go now, with your school's blessing. Your communities await and the future is yours.

"Thank you, and Godspeed."

Most of the applause came from the families, not the graduates. The school officials went through the dispensing of the diplomas, the class president, John Harrison, stood in front of the class and coordinated the switching of the tassel from one side of the mortar board to the other, a great cheer went up, the band struck up *Pomp and Circumstance* again, and the class marched out.

It was over.

*

The LeClaires let Kenneth and Ellen out at the common so they could go to the hotel where they took a small table by the front window and ordered ice cream. A car went by, horn blaring and kids yelling out the window. No doubt they'd got hold of some beer and were off to the river where they could party and be as loud as they wanted. After the ice cream Kenneth and Ellen went out to sit on the bench by the cannon. Content and happy, Ellen hunched over, slid her arm through his, and took his hand in both of hers. Kenneth was mildly surprised. In all their years of friendship he'd considered them buddies, not girlfriend/boyfriend. It felt good, though, and he liked it, but it was an unfamiliar level of intimacy.

Kenneth expected her to start talking about something – the future – anything, but she seemed content to simply sit close and be still and that was fine. He wasn't in a mood to talk. He'd not really listened to the speech at graduation but now it was running through his mind, over and over: duty, obligation, good citizen, work, volunteer, give back to the community, be a good citizen, make a contribution…

He looked down Main Street. The tired buildings only confirmed the struggle Grants Ferry faced every day. If there was potential here, Kenneth couldn't see it.

Ellen put her head on his shoulder. He could smell her shampoo and he liked the way her hair felt on his neck.

The church clock struck eleven, late by Grants Ferry standards. They got up then and he walked her home. At her door she pulled him to her, took his face in both hands, and kissed him.

"Good night." She was inside before he could respond.

He and Ellen had never had that kind of contact or relationship. He didn't object to the kiss, but neither had he expected it. As he walked home, he wondered if it had meant anything or if it were simply affection, or maybe just a celebration of graduation.

Fanny's light was out when he got home. Upstairs in his room, half undressed, he stopped and sat on the bed. *Commitment, obligation, work, community, service, duty, volunteer, prosperity, work, volunteer, obligation...* He couldn't shut it off. Careful to avoid noise he retrieved the metal box with his money from the space over the shed. Besides what he got from selling Fred's stuff and the things from his parent's house years ago he'd earned more helping Luther Pike. He had just over $3,700 now, most of it, unfortunately, in small bills. Still, it would be a start. He retrieved a suitcase from the barn, one of Fred's that he'd liked, packed a week's worth of underwear, socks, a couple shirts, a pair of cords, and a second pair of shoes.

He'd need food. He didn't want to use the front stairs because he might wake Fanny so he went out through the shed and the barn and then back into the kitchen where he made up an entire loaf of bread into peanut butter sandwiches and stacked them carefully back inside the bread wrapper. Back upstairs he packed these into his bag as well. The bulkiness of the money bothered him so he broke it down into small amounts, wrapped some around his ankles and pulled his socks up around it. He put some in his wallet, more in his front pockets, and finally, he wrapped some inside his socks in the suitcase. If he lost any part of it, he'd still have some to fall back on. At some point he'd find a bank and put it in traveler's checks.

It was just after one a.m. He packed an unframed photo of his parents and a small one of Amy by herself, grabbed his father's hat and a jacket, and went out through the shed to the back door of the barn. The moon was bright and he didn't need the flashlight so he put it in his pocket. He went up to the street, past the common, and began the long walk to Route 5 and Springfield and whatever he might find beyond.

*

Chapter Eleven

Kenneth stopped the Valiant in front of the hotel. Across the street a sheriff's deputy, an older guy with his pants worn high, said something to his partner and gestured toward the Valiant. The partner, a young blond man, crossed the street. His uniform was new and crisp. Kenneth cranked down his window.

"I'm sorry, sir, but you're not allowed to park here today."

"I just inherited this fine vehicle," Kenneth said as he patted the door below the window. "I thought I'd show it off a bit."

"Yes, sir," the deputy said, "but I need you to park someplace else."

"I just want to go into the hotel for a few minutes. We shouldn't be long."

"Yes, sir," the deputy said again. "I need you to park behind the church or behind the Grange or there's space behind the hotel."

"No problem. Thanks." They drove around the corner and behind the hotel. "Official sort, isn't he?" Kenneth said.

"I think he's cute. I always had a thing for boys in uniforms."

"Yeah, well, leave'em alone. You don't know where they've been."

"…with the stripes and the creases…"

"Yeah, yeah…"

"…and the belts and the sticks and the guns and handcuffs…"

"I know. Shame we didn't bring all that stuff with us."

"Well I really didn't have time to pack properly. What'd you expect?" Simon saw Ellen pulling boxes out of a pickup truck. "Let's go see Ellen," he said.

"She's busy setting up her stall. We'll see it later."

"I want a preview. Besides, we can't talk when there's a crowd around. Come on."

Ellen was surprised to see them. "What are you two doing out so early?"

"Kenneth's going to show me the Intercourse House. Won't that be a kick?"

"Might be," Ellen said. "I haven't been inside in years – maybe three times since our high school graduation dinner. Twenty-one Grants Ferry kids that year. Remember, Kenny?"

"Yes, I do, and the dinner was definitely the last time I was in there."

"We had ice cream after graduation. Have you forgotten that?"

"That's right. The ice cream. Well, it was some time ago."

"Yes, it was."

Simon had gone inside the booth to inspect her pottery, an earthy style of vases, mugs, planters, and sculptures. Most were heads with hair, ears, and expressive features. Every one was different. The men usually had some facial hair, the women were usually wide-eyed and innocent. Some had similarities, clearly features that made them members of a family, but each piece was unique.

"These are great, Ellen."

"Thank you, Simon."

"Really clever," Kenneth agreed. "I always thought you had an artistic streak."

"I beg your pardon?" Simon said. "An artistic '*streak*'?"

"You know: talent."

"Yes. Talent," Simon glared at him. "Don't call it a streak. Jesus, you know better than that."

"Yes, I do. I'm sorry, Ellen."

"Thank you." She took another box into the booth.

"Where do you sell your work?" Simon asked.

"Oh, I set up here at the fair every year and there are a few gift shops up and down the river that take things on consignment."

"What do you think, Kenneth? Isn't this the sort of thing the Schmidts would like?"

"It's hard to tell with those two. Maybe…"

"Let me take a few pieces back to New York," Simon said. "I think you could really sell down there. Even wholesale you'll do better than this. These prices are way low, you know."

"Really?"

"It's a common mistake craft people make," Simon took her arm to get her full attention. "It's not your time you're selling, it's your creative inspiration, your muse. We'll take some samples to show Ben Schmidt. He's got a great shop, lots of foot traffic. People with money are always in there looking for something new and a little funky. I bet he'll take all you can make."

"Well...."

"We'll talk tomorrow. At breakfast. Come hungry, okay?"

"Okay."

"We'll be back later. Can you believe he never told me about this place?"

"Yes, I can," Ellen said.

"Was he always this secretive?"

"No, not always, but I've had a chance to rethink that over the past thirty years or so."

Kenneth could see where this was going.

"Well, see you later, then," he mumbled.

"We'll talk tomorrow," she said. "You will be there, won't you?"

"Of course."

"Simon, will you see to it?"

"Oh, count on it. I wouldn't let this go by for anything. Oh, did you know about Fanny's organ?"

"Jesus, knock it off," Kenneth said.

"I remember her organ, yes," Ellen said. "I even saw it once."

"Really? Very few people ever saw Fanny's organ, you know. It was a very private thing. Do you know that Kenneth once touched it?"

"Oh, Christ..."

"Yes, I do. I touched it, too. Fanny was furious."

"That's what I hear. Apparently, Fanny only liked to have her organ touched by a pink round man who came to dinner on Fridays." Ellen laughed and Simon plowed on. "Do you suppose that's what made her so mean?"

"I think it started long before the pink round man." Still laughing she reached into the truck for another box.

"We'll come back after the hotel tour," Simon said.

"Okay. I'm here until four."

"Why'd you have to bring that up?" Kenneth snarled as they walked away.

"Bring what up?"

"The organ."

"I thought it was fun. Besides, I wanted to hear Ellen laugh. I have a feeling Ellen doesn't laugh enough." They stopped at the street while a fire truck was moved into place toward the rear of the hotel. "Is something on fire?"

"They stand by in case there's an emergency. They're also after donations for the fire department."

"Donations?"

"It's a volunteer fire department. They're always looking for money."

"Oh." Simon considered this for a moment. "So," he said, "do you?"

"Do I what?"

"Think Ellen laughs enough?"

"There was a time," Kenneth said, "when Ellen's laugh was the most beautiful thing I'd ever heard."

"…and…"

"I'd say she may not have much to laugh about."

"Right. How about we change that?"

"We can try."

"Good. You got the key?"

*

With facades on two streets, the hotel loomed over the downtown, a huge, weathered hulk. Above the two story porch the mansard roof rose up, sloping in gently, its surface interrupted by tall windowed dormers spaced precisely over the second floor windows all the way around.

The entrance was at the corner where countless feet had trod the granite steps. The lettering on the old sign by the door was faded but still legible.

The Grants Ferry

An Hotel and Tavern

Host to Vibrant

Social and Commercial

Intercourse

"As you might surmise," Kenneth said, "this is where the common name came from."

"That's so great. It's also authentic. That's the key, isn't it?" Simon said. "Authenticity. We could have that replicated and printed on stationery and napkins and brochures and the website." He grabbed the key, unlocked the door, and disappeared inside.

The front doors opened to a foyer with built-in coat racks, a bench, and a tall mirror. The floor was marble, worn and uneven from years of traffic. The woodwork was walnut or stained to look like walnut and beyond was the lobby with a manager's desk, a stairway that led to the upper floors, and French doors to the left and right. A cheap light fixture with a square glass shade clung to the center of the embossed metal ceiling. Peeling paint hung down in palm sized sheets. Years of accumulated dust covered everything. Even in the dim light that filtered in through the dirty windows it was clear the hotel had once dripped with mid-19th-century elegance and had fortunately escaped the art deco phase much of the rest of the country had suffered.

The long, large dining room looked out over the street and back down the east side of the building. Traces of its former life were evident but it was now a dusty, gray, empty space. Simon pulled a torn and decaying curtain aside and saw a neglected and overgrown garden with a rotting, eight-sided gazebo slumped in a far corner, a mere suggestion of a more prosperous time.

The romantic in Simon swept away the dust and torn curtains and imagined fresh linens, and soft lights, the woodwork cleaned and rubbed with lemon oil, and visualized a grand salon with elegant appointments, a bustling kitchen run by a clever chef, and platters of well-prepared meals being delivered to discerning diners as they listened to gentle melodies being played on the baby grand piano in the front corner or maybe some strings…

"What about the other side?" he asked.

"The tavern," Kenneth said. "Both were served by the same kitchen."

Wood panels on the tavern ceiling softened the sound and gave a feeling of privacy, even with all the hard surfaces. What light came in through the windows facing the common seemed to be sucked into the wood before it had a chance to illuminate the room. A magnificent mahogany or cherry bar, at least 30 feet long took up much of the inside wall. Behind the bar were racks and shelves and mirrors.

Simon pushed open a door that led to a smaller, private room in the rear.

"Any stories about this room?"

"Probably, but I can't recall any."

"In New York this place would be a gold mine."

"Well, we're not in New York, are we?"

"No," Simon said. "What's upstairs?"

"Rooms."

Simon was out the door and up the stairs.

The second floor had sixteen guest rooms. Eight had access to shared baths. The others shared two toilet rooms at the back of the building. The only light in the hall came from windows at either end.

"We'd have a little trouble getting stars in the triple A guide with this setup, wouldn't we?" Simon said. "Nobody I know is going to stay where they need to share a bathroom down the hall with a dozen strangers. Maybe in Ecuador or Bolivia but not in this country. We'll need a lot of plumbing – and new wiring, and sprinklers."

"Listen to me," Kenneth said.

"What's above this?" Simon interrupted.

"The ballroom."

"The ballroom? Are you kidding? A *ball*room?" Simon shot up the last flight of stairs.

The third floor was indeed a huge open room. The stairs came up on one side, a small bandstand was in the corner, and the rest of the space was open, thanks to an ingenious roof system as carefully engineered as any bridge. Since the walls sloped inward, the actual span of the roof framing was smaller than the footprint of the building, a rather clever solution. Remnants of heavy damask curtains hung in several of the tall dormer windows.

When Kenneth finally came up the stairs Simon was waiting.

"Would the gentleman care to join me in the grand march?"

"No."

"Perhaps allow me a minuet, a waltz, or even a reel?"

"No."

"One of the peasant dances, then? A polka? A schottische?

"No."

Simon smiled and shook his head. "One of these days," he said as he passed Kenneth to go back downstairs. "One of these days," he said again, as he reached back and ran an index finger down Kenneth's nose. "One of these days…" and he left Kenneth at the top of the stairs.

A few minutes later Kenneth found Simon sitting in a dusty old chair at a small table in the tavern. He was looking out the window.

"What are you doing?" Kenneth said from the doorway.

"I'm taking my ease at the Intercourse House, a fine old inn on the green of a grand old New England town. Look at this place. It's wonderful."

"Listen, I – "

"I should have brought the camera," Simon said. "I'm going over to Paul's and get some of those throwaways. I've got to get pictures of this." He jumped up ran out.

Kenneth sat at the table. Everything was filtered through a nagging fear that he was caught up in something he couldn't control. This whole weekend, and maybe even the rest of his life, was like some sort of runaway train. It was that same feeling he'd had before he'd left town all those years ago.

For most of the thirty-two years he'd been away, he'd managed to avoid this trapped feeling. There had been difficult situations, a couple had even been rather dangerous, but he'd always had choices. As an adult in New York, in both his social and professional life, he'd gained considerable skill in protecting himself from both the expected and the unexpected. Back in Grants Ferry again he was a child, and Fanny, god damn her, was coming for him again.

Simon burst into the tavern.

"He had ten and I bought them all." He ripped open the package to one of the cameras. "You coming?"

"No."

Kenneth watched Simon through the dirty windows as he ran across the street to snap pictures of the outside from several different angles. The camera flashed uselessly in the daylight. Ellen had customers already.

Simon came back inside and snapped away in the foyer and then the lobby. Kenneth could hear the click and the ratchet to set the next frame each time.

"Two dead soldiers," Simon said. He tossed the spent cameras into the bag, tore open another box, and put yet another in his pocket. "Now for a little human interest…"

"Oh, no. Forget it."

"Sit. Look like you're having a good time."

"Yeah, right."

Simon found an old dirty glass behind the bar and handed it to Kenneth. "Look as if you're enjoying a nice relaxing drink at the end of the day." Kenneth rolled his eyes. "Just look out the window and take in the small town charm. Be three thousand miles away at the Guinness factory if you have to. No, no. Don't look at me. Just settle back and enjoy." He took a couple quick snaps. "Perfect." He ran off to the dining room. A couple minutes later Kenneth heard him dashing around in the kitchen. There was a loud ringing sound, like a gong.

"Ah, fuck," Simon moaned. Another crash, this time it was longer, a series of metal things tumbling to the floor.

Kenneth jumped up and ran to the kitchen. As he pushed open the swinging door the camera flashed in his face.

"Gotcha!" Simon said and ran out through the dining room, through the lobby, and on into the tavern where he grabbed another camera before he ran up the stairs two steps at a time. Kenneth went outside and sat on the front steps. Simon came out about ten minutes later.

"I'm telling you, Kenneth. This could be a gold mine."

"Yeah, well…"

"We'll talk, right?"

"No doubt."

"Let me get the cameras. Then we can lock up and do the fair."

*

Fire Department personnel were in the street with buckets, looking for donations. Kenneth spotted Luther Pike.

"Luther, how you doin'? Didn't get a chance to chat much yesterday."

"Dennis don't like us chattin' while we're workin'."

"Quite a day, all considered. Oh, Luther, this is Simon."

"Hi, there," Luther said.

"Luther used to hire me from time to time, gave me a chance to earn some money. How you been, Luther?"

"About the same," Luther said. "I keep busy."

"Good. Good for you."

"Ayuh. Pays the bills." He held out the bucket. "I know you're just back for a visit but you feel like helping us out, Kenny?"

Kenneth took five twenties out of his wallet and tossed them in the bucket.

"What's the project this year?"

"New truck. That one's over thirty years old." He looked into the bucket. "Jesus Christ, you sure you want to do that?"

"I'm sure," Kenneth said. "By the way, you suppose you might drop by the house tomorrow before we head back?"

"Sometime after lunch?"

"That would be good. I'll give you a call tomorrow and we'll set a time."

He and Simon crossed the street.

"A hundred dollars?" Simon said. "I thought you didn't like these people."

"I don't much. But I like Luther."

"What makes him different?"

"Luther's a good man. Aside from Increase, he may be the most valuable connection we have here."

"And Ellen?"

"We'll see."

*

Simon was a thorough shopper. He explored everything, tried things on, talked with the vendors about their techniques, their suppliers, and where they sold their things. He seldom left without having purchased something. Kenneth could never think of anything to say to these people and avoided eye contact. Simon wandered into the stalls to inspect the goods and chat while Kenneth waited outside.

Simon bought a hand-knit angora slouch hat and a matching scarf and wore them immediately. Accessory bonding, he called it. Two minutes later he'd darted into another stall to study the hand work on some embroidered kitchen towels and aprons.

"Kenny. How you doin'?" Archie and Hank had come up on his blind side.

"I'm fine," Kenneth said.

"Good crowd today," Archie said, assuming Kenneth cared. "Still early, though." Hank sniffed Kenneth's shoes. "Sundays are always a little chancy with church and everything but if the weather holds I think we'll do okay."

Kenneth looked up through the trees. The sky was perfectly clear with no indication this would change any time soon.

"Looks like you got a day for it," he said.

"Well, you never know…"

Hank, having collected the available information from Kenneth's shoes, sat down beside Archie where he could give Kenneth a thorough inspection.

"Interesting dog," Kenneth said.

"I know. He reminds me of my Uncle Henry – damnedest thing. You remember Henry?"

"Vaguely. Kinda kept to himself. Worked at the lumber yard, right?"

"Ayuh, ayuh. The yard and home. That was about it. Ayuh. Lived with us, you know."

"I guess I did know that."

"Damned if this dog don't remind me of him for some reason."

"Interesting," Kenneth said, although it wasn't.

Hank yawned and studied Kenneth. Kenneth, in return, studied Hank and understood the bond. Archie would be naturally drawn to an animal that suggested intelligence and absolute devotion with no capacity to ever argue or contradict him.

"Yeah, damnedest thing," Archie said again. "You fellas must have got up early. Saw you while Ellen was settin' up."

"Thought we'd take a look at the Intercourse House."

"Kind of a mess, ain't it?"

"Certainly is."

"'Course it's been empty for years now. I tried to buy it, you know, but Fanny beat me to it."

"Really? What were you going to do with it?"

"Tell the truth, Kenny, I always thought that big old empty hotel was one of the things holding this town back, you know? Big ugly thing, right here on the Common… I ask you now, is that a shining symbol of depression and failure, or what?"

"It's seen better days," Kenneth said.

"Sure as hell has."

"Fanny might call it a sad reminder of our past glory."

"Yeah, that sounds like somethin' she'd say." Archie scanned the crowd to make sure things were moving smoothly. "Goddamned eyesore, is what it is," he said. "I think if we were to take it down and replace it with something new, something classy, I think that would spur a lot of new activity in Grants Ferry, don't you?"

"It might," Kenneth said. "What'd you have in mind?"

"I think one of those new, classy Rite-Aids would be just the ticket." Kenneth was speechless. He didn't think even Archie could be that stupid. "I've seen some of the new ones," Archie went on, warming to his vision of prosperity, "you know, big and clean and bright colors – big lit-up sign, pharmacy in the back, film processing… I think that would brighten up the whole town, encourage people, you know? Maybe they'd try to keep up."

"You're kidding, right?"

"No, no. Look, if the Intercourse House is yours now, or gonna be yours, maybe we could talk, you know, about making some changes here, something to bring some life into town."

Simon had bought and donned an apron with big embroidered sunflowers. He carried an armful of matching towels.

"Hi, Archie. Kenneth, I know the apron clashes with the scarf, but what do you think?"

"Very nice."

"Oh, what a quaint dog. Don't you just love all these wonderful ruffles, Archie? I mean, after all, most of the aprons today look like they should be worn by some brute on a construction crew. Who wants to eat a meal that's had a lumberjack dripping sweat and shaking sawdust into it for half an hour?"

"I – I don't know," Archie said.

"Would you, doggie?" Simon said to Hank. "No, no, no, no. We don't want sticky, salty, crunchy things in our soufflés, do we?" Hank just stared back. "Do we, Archie?"

"No. No, I – I shouldn't think so," Archie said.

"Absolutely not. Gets caught in our teeth. Makes us spit." Simon said. "Come along, Kenneth. We need some of Ellen's mugs to go with the towels." He took Kenneth's arm and they walked away, leaving Archie and Hank to stare after them.

"So," Simon said when they were out of earshot. "What did Mr. Red-Knuckles want?"

"He wants the Intercourse House."

"Really? What would he ever do with it?"

"He wants to tear it down so Rite-Aid can build a new store there."

"Are you shitting me? A Rite-Aid?"

"That's what he said."

"What's the matter with him, anyway?"

"Same thing that's always been the matter with him. He's a fool."

"Would you sell it to him?"

"As I understand the will, I don't think I can. And even if I could, I wouldn't."

"Well, I'm glad to hear that. Let's find Ellen and get some mugs."

On the way they passed a booth with canvas tote bags and Simon bought the biggest one they had to carry his purchases.

*

The single bagful was Simon's limit and he'd stuck to it: four coffee mugs, a creamer, and a sugar bowl from Ellen, a pair of leather gloves, a sheepskin vest and cap, a pair of heavy wool socks, and some wooly boots for wearing around the house when the floors are cold, plus the apron, the towels, the scarf, and the hat.

"All very practical," he said.

They bought some coffee at the food tent and Kenneth took Simon to the corner of the Common. The bench was still there, about fifteen feet away from the cannon which pointed down the street toward the river.

"Ellen and I sat on this bench the night we graduated from high school."

"Really?"

"Yeah. Strange night. We'd always been friends, you know, but that night it seemed like she was moving on to something else."

"Sex?"

"No… No, I don't think so. I think it was more about the natural progression of things: high school, graduation, engagement, marriage, family. We'd never discussed any of those things and it felt like I was suddenly being cornered, having choices made for me. It was almost claustrophobic."

"What'd you do?"

"Nothing. She was sitting very close, she'd put her arm through mine, and even put her head on my shoulder. Eventually I walked her home. Then she kissed me good night. That had never happened before, either."

"Upgrading?"

"I think so. About two o'clock the next morning, I packed a bag, took my savings, and left town."

"You didn't tell her?"

"No."

"Well, Jesus. I'm surprised she speaks to you at all."

"Yeah."

"Did you tell anybody?"

"No, I just left. All I could see that night was the hopelessness of this place and I knew I couldn't become trapped here. I was scared shitless but I knew I had to leave."

"Wow. Just disappeared."

"Yup."

Simon considered that as he looked at the hotel and on down the street.

"Man, they sure let this place go, didn't they?"

"Sure did."

"Why?"

"A combination of stubbornness and apathy, I think."

"Well, that doesn't make any sense at all," Simon said.

"Nobody ever said it made sense. See that cannon?"

"Yes."

"Well, there's a reason it points toward New Hampshire. You have no idea how these people can hold grudges. Read the plaque on that rock."

Simon sipped his coffee while he read.

This fine cannon played a major role
in the noble defense of
Grants Ferry and lands which now
comprise the great State of Vermont
from a misguided few who launched
a pitiful, futile, and unauthorized
attempt to claim these lands
for the State of New Hampshire
on or about midnight, 18 August, 1789

"Okay, what's that all about?" he said when he sat down again.

"Vermont was an independent republic for about ten years. The story goes that a few guys from New Hampshire launched a raid one night to take it back for New Hampshire, tried to sneak across on the ferry. Word had got out, though and people on this side were waiting for them. The invaders apparently bailed over the side and swam back to New Hampshire and the ferry continued to this side with muskets and a New Hampshire flag on the deck. No one in town would admit to anything but there were rumors and all the stories in all the variations always included a cannon, a cannon that had mysteriously disappeared along with the defenders.

"A hundred years later, about 1888, long after the principals were dead someone found this cannon, taken apart and hidden in a shed. The legend was reborn, the cannon was restored, set up here with a big ceremony, and that plaque was unveiled. New Hampshire was insulted and insisted the cannon be removed. Grants Ferry refused.

"But that doesn't explain the sorry state the town's in now."

"No, it doesn't. These things take time. By this time a covered bridge had replaced the ferry and Grants Ferry was still one of the popular river crossings. The Intercourse House was a comfortable and charming place to meet and cut deals or to stay on a trip from Boston to the interior. Then in the early 1900s electric companies began building dams across the Connecticut River to generate power and this leads us to another quirk of history which involves the boundary between New Hampshire and Vermont. Normally, a boundary is the center of the stream, not one bank or the other. In this case the boundary is on the Vermont shore, a situation set up when the king established the colony of New York."

"Oh."

"Now, all these years later, Vermont claimed the center of the river as the boundary so they could collect taxes from the electric companies. The dispute went to the Supreme Court and in 1932 the court recognized the original boundary set by the British Crown and also affirmed a decision by George Washington who recognized the boundary when Vermont gained Statehood in 1791.

"As owner of the river, though, New Hampshire would be almost entirely responsible for the building and maintenance of bridges, in retrospect, a much better deal for Vermont."

"Okay. So what's the cannon got to do with any of this?"

"Well, 1938 was the year of the hurricane and the great floods. Trees were blown down, roads disappeared, the Connecticut River rose up, and the bridge from Grants Ferry to New Hampshire was swept away."

"Uh-oh."

"Yeah. New Hampshire refused to rebuild the bridge and overnight, a town that had always been on the way to somewhere was now at the end of the road. There were a few good years during the Second World War when there was a call for lumber, and there was lots of work at the machine shops in Springfield as they supplied the war and the early space program but after that it slipped downhill. Then the machine shops in Springfield – Precision Valley, they used to call it – began to close in the 60s and skilled machinists couldn't find work. The town was already in decline while I was in high school. It's only gotten worse."

*

Back in the Valiant, they went to see Fanny's other properties. All showed clear signs of age, but the essence of the structures remained. It was easy to imagine them in their prime. Large, well groomed yards, barns or carriage sheds, deep wraparound porches, and just enough gingerbread to make a statement.

"Fanny certainly had an eye," Simon said as he snapped away with the cameras.

"Yeah. She didn't love much but she loved her vision of how this town used to be, at least as it was represented in the old photos. 'It used to be grand,' she'd say. Malcolm MacArthur must have heard that line a thousand times. I could hear it from my room over the kitchen."

"You had the dining room bugged?"

"No, no. The register in the floor to let the heat up in the winter. I could lie on the floor with my head on the register and hear just about anything.

We had a setup like that in my parents' house, too. I used to listen when they thought I was asleep."

"Why, you sneaky little bastard."

"Not with my parents. Some nights all they did was play cards at the kitchen table. It was comforting to hear them and know they were there. When I moved in with Fanny I realized I'd need all the information I could get if I was going to survive. She never spoke to me much so I learned a lot by listening to her conversations with other people. She and Malcolm MacArthur talked a lot about the old days."

*

Simon packed a picnic to take with them for the drive out to view the acreage by the river. A short walk took them to a hill where they could look out over the valley. The river, New Hampshire on the far side, and a harvested cornfield were all in front of them. They spread a blanket, opened the bottle of New York red wine Simon had bought the night before, and unwrapped the sandwiches.

"Well, Paul was right about the wine," Simon said. "It's rugged."

"Probably the best compliment it's ever had," Kenneth said.

Simon chattered about the Intercourse House, the houses, the fair, the people, the town… Like his vision of the hotel, he could see grace and elegance behind the peeling paint. There was potential here, he thought, even profits if it were managed well. Kenneth had fallen asleep. Simon poured himself another glass of rugged red, sipped at it for a while, and then lay down himself.

When they woke later Simon picked up where he'd left off.

"The point is, it's been handed to us. All we've got to do is arrange to have it done. We can liquidate everything in the city, and borrow the rest."

"And then?"

"We'll either have the potential for more than we ever had in New York or we'll have nothing."

"You're really serious."

"Damn right."

Ellis Rogers appeared in his pickup as they were putting the picnic stuff back in the car.

"Afternoon, fellas. Heard you were in town, Kenny."

"Ellis," Kenneth said. "Good to see you again. This is Simon. Simon, Ellis Rogers."

"Wonderful piece of land, Mr. Rogers."

"Ayuh, it is that."

"Fanny bought this from you?" Kenneth asked.

"Ayuh. 'Bout six, seven years ago now. Fanny and Malcolm. Quite the pair, they were."

"You still farm it, though."

"That's right. They bought the farm, I kept the business."

"You're still farming?"

"Ayuh. Still at it. Twenty good milkers and I lose money every year."

"You lose money?" Simon asked.

"Just don't know when to quit, I guess. That's a Vermont farmer's idea of success, you know; work longer and harder, lose money, and stay on the farm."

"Why do you do it?" Simon asked.

"I'm 84. What else am I going to do?"

"You ever think of taking it easy?"

"Oh, I've got a couple young fellas who help out and I get a few minutes after supper to read the paper. Besides, there's the cows. They're both dependents and employees, don'tcha know?"

"So you sold to Fanny and Malcolm?" Kenneth asked again.

"Well, Malcolm knew I was about at the end of my rope. The cash bailed me out and they get the place when I'm gone. 'Course, I'd had that little stroke earlier that year – left me a little gimpy. I suppose they thought they wouldn't have to wait long. But they're both gone now and I'm still here." He chuckled at the thought.

"Funny how these things work out."

"Don't seem fair," he agreed.

"Well," Kenneth said, "it seems Fanny left everything to me. Lots of strings, of course, but I'll honor any arrangement you made with Fanny and Malcolm."

"I sure appreciate that, I truly do. Quite a relief, frankly. Good to see you again. Barn still looks good. Colors come out nice this year, didn't they?" Ellis shuffled back to his truck, turned it around, and drove off.

"You do realize," Simon said, "that to honor Fanny's agreement we have to move here."

"I know that," Kenneth growled. He leaned back against the Valiant and took in the view. "Ellis sold all this, a big piece of his life, so he could continue to work sixteen-hour days. I mean, imagine that." The sun was lower now and it bought out a deep orange in the leaves. It was the Vermont he remembered and he was suddenly aware how much he'd missed it. He pushed himself up off the hood of the car.

"God damn it," he said.

*

Back at the house, Simon put his purchases on the kitchen table. "Feels more like home already," he said.

Kenneth poured himself a generous portion of Increase's Irish whiskey and took it into the parlor where he sat very still and tried to imagine this place as home.

*

Chapter Twelve

The aroma of fresh coffee mingled with the cinnamon and yeast in fresh-baked rolls. Ellen hung back by the door.

"Come in, come in. Sit," Simon said.

"I – I haven't been in this house since – "

" – the day we were playing the organ?" Kenneth finished.

"Yes. I don't think I've ever been so frightened, before or since."

"That was the day Fanny took the leather strap to me," Kenneth explained to Simon. "Right out there in the shed."

"Oooo. Fanny was into leather? Do you suppose her equipment is still here?"

Ellen giggled. "Did you ever tell anyone about that?"

"Just you and Simon," Kenneth said, "and I only told him a couple days ago."

"Somebody should have been told," Ellen said. "It could have been your ticket out of here."

"Maybe…"

"You two sit." Simon said. "I'll serve this up in a minute."

Ellen took in the spread on the table. "Does he always cook like this?"

"When he knows someone's coming."

"I found Fanny's personal cookbook," Simon said. "These are her cinnamon buns. The rest is from supplies someone bought for us." He dished sausage and scrambled eggs onto each plate. He put a platter stacked with warm cinnamon buns in the middle of the table, took a last look to be sure everything was ready, and sat down.

"Well, Ellen, if His Rudeness here isn't going to mention it, welcome to our home."

"Your home?"

"We're trying it on," Simon said. "And I must say you're looking absolutely lovely."

Ellen blushed and glanced at Kenneth "I haven't heard that in a long time. Thank you."

"Don't wait for him to compliment you," Simon said. "It's not his nature."

"I know, but he was always a really nice boy."

"I've seen the high school photo. We might have been rivals."

"You think so?"

"No question. Of course I would have been about five or six years old. I wouldn't have had a chance unless he liked'em really young."

Kenneth let him talk. The chatter helped avoid the conversation he knew was coming.

"I'm surprised he didn't stick around," Simon said.

"Me, too," Ellen said. "Why was that, Kenny?"

"Well, I – "

"You ran away in the middle of the night, you bastard. You never hinted you were going to leave, never said good-bye, or invited me to come with you."

Kenneth stared at his plate.

"I loved you, Kenny. I've always loved you. We were so close I even expected we might marry and have a family and spend the rest of our lives together."

"Ellen, I – "

"Do you have any idea how many nights I cried myself to sleep?"

"I had a few, myself."

"Why? Did someone run out on you?"

"No. I was alone and afraid."

"You didn't have to be alone."

"I know. But you were always going to stay here."

"So?"

"I couldn't stay here. I was afraid I'd become one of these sad, tired people. Tom and Amy's house had been sold and the new family was trashing the place. I wanted something I'd never find in Grants Ferry."

"What about us? I loved you."

"Would you have left your family?"

"I – I don't know."

"You had family. You'd never looked beyond Grants Ferry. My family had been dead for seven years."

"But you could have become part of my family. We could have talked about it. That night after graduation, when we were sitting on the common, did you know then? When I kissed you good night, did you know then and not say anything?"

"No. It was later. I couldn't get to sleep. All the talk about obligation and duty to community from the graduation ceremony kept running through my head. There was no future that night, only more of the past."

"And now?"

"Now? You mean Grants Ferry? I've been here two days and the place is even worse than I remember it. The same people are here and a different generation is running things but nothing much has changed, has it? And Fanny's set me up, God damn her."

"Set you up?"

"Yeah. Turns out she was worth 1.5 to 2 mil, mostly in real estate, including the Intercourse House."

"Really? I had no idea. I knew she'd bought some properties over the years but I never thought anything about their value. So how are you set up?"

"It's all mine if I meet certain conditions. I have to move back and live here, for instance."

"That's it?"

"No, of course not."

Ellen smiled and looked at Simon who had split open his cinnamon roll and spread a perfect layer of butter.

"Don't you just love to watch him squirm," she asked.

"They're some of my happiest moments," Simon smiled.

"Okay, what else?" Ellen laughed.

"I've got a year to renovate, restore, and reopen the Intercourse House."

"A year? Can it be done?"

"No idea."

"Would it even support itself if it was open again?"

"Maybe the dining room and tavern, but even then… Financial success wasn't mentioned, only that it be restored and reopened."

"Anything else?"

"Of course. If I refuse or fail it all goes to Jerry Falwell and the *Old Time Gospel Hour*."

Ellen suddenly took a fit of giggles. When she saw Kenneth wasn't the least bit amused it tickled her even more.

"Clever bitch, wasn't she?" Simon said.

"Fanny knew about you and Simon?"

"Apparently Fanny had Increase do some investigating," Kenneth said. "She may not have known about Simon but she learned enough."

"So what will you do?"

"I've got until next Friday to let Increase know."

"We're gonna do it," Simon said.

"Really?"

"Don't count on it," Kenneth said.

"Oh, don't pay attention to Mr. Libra here."

"It would be nice to have you home again," Ellen said.

"Aren't you pissed off?"

"I was furious and hurt for a long time. But I've missed you – all these years. I've never had a better friend. Even the other night at the bean supper, the first time I'd seen you in over thirty years, it was as if we could pick up in mid-sentence where we left off." Ellen's mention of the bean supper brought up another point.

"And you married Archie Whitaker? I mean, Jesus."

"Well, did you ever give me any clue you were coming back? I always thought we were pretty close but you couldn't even tell me you were going to disappear. Why was that?"

"That night. I knew the kiss suggested we might move to a different level."

"You read that right."

"And – and – I'd always loved you, too, Ellen. You were the only real friend I had. I loved you then and always have. But I wasn't *in* love with you."

"Really?"

"Come to think of it, I don't think I've ever been *in* love with anybody."

"Hel-LO?" Simon jumped in. "Never been *in* love?"

"I don't think so, no."

"What was the last ten years, then?"

"Well, you can love someone and have a great relationship with them and not be *in* love. I think it's simpler, cleaner somehow."

"What the hell does that mean?"

"Yeah," Ellen said. "What *does* that mean? I'd like to hear this one."

"Look. When people are *in* love they tend to make a lot of irrational choices," Kenneth said. "I think simply loving someone for who they are makes it much easier for a relationship to work. You don't go in with a list of rules or conditions. You simply love them without being *in* love."

"That," said Simon, "is horseshit."

"Not to him," Ellen said. "He was always able to do that. It keeps him attached but removed somehow."

"You're right," Simon said. "It explains him completely."

"If anything can," she agreed. She turned to Kenneth again. "But why didn't you tell me you were going to leave?"

"Because," Kenneth said, "you were the one person who could talk me out of it."

"And if I had?"

"If I'd stayed something in me would have died."

Ellen understood but she didn't want to argue anymore. Simon took the plates to the sink.

"We could have had beautiful children, Kenny," she said.

"Oh, Christ, Ellen…"

"I used to dream about the children we'd have. We'd have fun the way you and Amy had fun together. We would have been good parents, Kenny."

"Yeah, well… And you and Archie?"

"Two, grown and gone now. I even have three grandchildren."

"They didn't settle here, then?"

"No. I made sure of it."

"Why's that?"

"I expected to be here forever but I wanted a bigger world view for my kids."

Simon topped off the coffee cups.

"So, you and Archie. How'd that happen?"

"Oh, I don't know… You were out of the picture, I wanted children, and he'd been after me for several years…"

"But Archie Whitaker? I mean, Jesus."

"I know…."

"You bit off his ear, for Christ's sake."

"Is that what happened to that big brute's ear?" Simon jumped in.

"Archie pushed me too far one day when we were kids and I beat him up."

"Came totally unhinged," Kenneth said. "I've never seen anything like it."

"Years later he told me he always respected us for never telling anyone," Ellen said. "He even asked me out a couple of times while we were still in high school."

"You never told me that," Kenneth said.

"It was too laughable to even mention. Anyway, when you didn't come back he started sniffing around again. He was always polite, never threw his weight around, and he treated me well. Eventually, I came to like him a bit."

"Enough to marry him…"

"Well, eventually. Given my other choices in town, Archie was the best of the lot. I came with a list."

"A list?"

"I bargained for security. The house, for instance, is entirely in my name. I've had my own car – whatever I've wanted – a new one ever three years, he's put money into my bank account every month and doesn't question how I spend it. And I insisted that when we had children, they would eventually go to college, long enough to pursue PhDs if they wanted to, and he would see to it."

"And he agreed?"

"Didn't even negotiate. He's never resisted any of it. He's treated me quite well, considering."

"Considering what?"

"Well, it's not been a passionate marriage, but neither has it been terribly unpleasant. I've managed the house and raised the kids and he's been free to do his work and his politics. He's been gentle with me, he's always considerate, and I'm as financially secure as anyone in town. I'd have been happier with you but I could have done a lot worse. He's a bit clumsy but he does the best he can, I guess." She finished her coffee.

"Well," Simon said. "Let me show you around." Kenneth stayed to clean up while Simon led Ellen through the house and talked about changes he'd like to make, thoughts about decorating. Kenneth heard the word plumbing several times, and colors and a word or two about lighting. He began to scrape the baked sugar off the cinnamon roll pan and saw they were outside. Their breath was visible as they laughed together.

Inside again, Ellen hugged herself against the chill.

"Sounds like you're coming back," she said.

"If you listen to him, it does," Kenneth said.

"Ellen says there's a bunch of hotel stuff at the Historical Society," Simon said.

"A couple of the upstairs rooms are full of boxes and odd lamps and linens," she said, "some pieces of furniture…lots of papers. I've got a key. We could go over right now."

"We were going to head back, avoid the traffic…"

"Stay another night and drive back in the morning," Ellen suggested.

"Good idea," Simon said. And to Kenneth: "I like her."

Kenneth hated it when people managed his time and his choices. On the other hand, as an antique dealer he was curious and Ellen's suggestion was workable. Coming from someone other than Ellen, even Simon, he'd have put his foot down, if only on principle.

*

"So Fanny collected all these things?" Simon asked. They were in the front room at the Historical Society.

"Most of it," Ellen said. "She'd always had an interest, of course, but when Malcolm died it became an obsession. One thing just led to another."

Sepia toned photos gave a general sense of Grants Ferry in its heyday. Residential streets were lined with towering elms. Except for an occasional horse and carriage, or an occasional automobile, the streets were empty. Only a few photos included people.

Some were clearly portraits of the homes themselves, a photographic record, accompanied by a page or two of typed background data – the date the home was built, the original owners, the various owners since, and any stories associated either with the people or the house.

"And this was Fanny's dream?" Simon asked.

"She wanted to preserve the memory of the Grants Ferry that's been lost," Ellen said. "If it couldn't be brought back she felt it should at least be remembered. Some of these buildings are now gone, for instance, a couple terrible fires, maybe fifteen or twenty years ago. Remember the Millers?" she asked Kenneth. "Their little girl died when their house burned. And then the Pierce Homestead – you remember that big old house on the Main Street end of Cherry Street. Archie bought it, tore it down, and built that awful concrete block shoebox to rent to the Postal Service. I was disgusted. Fanny was appalled. I think Archie and the Post Office were what really inspired her – the realization that these once grand buildings could disappear so quickly. The fires were accidents but the Pierce Homestead was deliberate and that bordered on criminal."

"So she and Malcolm McArthur…"

"Yeah. Archie was convinced Malcolm was bending some rules inside the bank to finance their operation. He wanted to buy the hotel so he could sell it to Rite-Aid but word got back to Fanny somehow… Anyway, Fanny and Malcolm bought it out from under him. He hadn't even seen that coming."

"And they had no plans for it?"

"Only to keep it from being torn down. From what I've heard, the previous owners had no plans for the hotel either, but they didn't want it replaced with a drug store."

"So," Kenneth said. "In spite of Fanny you volunteered here."

"Yeah, I liked the idea and wanted to help, but only when Fanny wasn't around. The hotel things are upstairs."

She took them to a large room that looked out to the street over the porch roof. Some boxes held old linens, some had remnants of drapery material. There were other boxes with odd pieces of glassware, china, and silverware, albums, and loose photos. One album was a collection of yellowing newspaper clippings with stories of visits by various dignitaries over the years.

"Wow," Simon said. "Where'd she get it all?"

"She'd never tell anyone. Apparently there were a lot of people in town who'd had some connection to the hotel when it was running and one source led to another. When the hotel closed for good there was an auction of the furnishings and dishes and things, broken up into small lots – samplers, really – so people could have souvenirs – sets of dishes and linens, things like that. Fanny had bought some things at the auction and later she just began to track things down and buy them back."

"That explains all the furniture in the barn, then," Kenneth said.

"Furniture from the hotel?"

"I think so."

Simon took a thick yellowing roll of papers out of a box in the corner and carefully opened the roll on the floor. The front page was a rendering of the main entrance corner of the hotel with elevations of both street sides drawn in great detail. The date in the bottom corner was 1868.

"Holy shit," Simon said. "Are these genuine?"

"I don't know," Ellen said.

"They look like the construction drawings," Simon said as he flipped through the sheets, "maybe even the originals, right down to the interior details. If these are real, half the work is done. An architect can take a look at these and know exactly how the place was put together. Look. Even the woodwork details for the ceiling in the Tavern are here."

"You'll do it, then?" Ellen asked.

"I don't know," Kenneth said. "We could spend huge amounts of money and lose it all. Can we take this to make copies?"

"Of course."

Back in the car Kenneth pointed the Valiant out of town along the River Road and then turned on the road to Springfield.

"Where're we going?"

"One more place I want to see." A few minutes later Kenneth pulled off the road and parked.

"This is where they died, isn't it?" Simon said.

"Yeah. Come take a look."

They crossed the road and looked down the slope in silence.

"The tree's gone now," Kenneth said finally, "but it was right down there. It began to fail that summer and a couple years later it, too, was dead."

"Jesus," Simon said.

"It was a maple, a big one. Somebody got a lot of good firewood." Ellen hugged him and he put his arm around her. It was comforting and welcome, a kind of closeness he'd not felt in a long time.

"You remember anything about that night?" Simon asked.

"Well, we'd been to see the play down in Springfield and Amy – I'd never seen her so happy. And on the way home I was trying to understand the guys in the cellar with the fireworks and the guy who played the xylophone and the wrestler and the girl who made candy. Amy said people in the Sycamore house were happy because they were free – pursuing dreams, really." He stopped. It was coming back now, almost as if he was in the car again, "And I remember… I remember she asked me whether I'd rather be with Tony's parents, full of rules and propriety, or the guys who were making fireworks down in the cellar."

"What'd you say?"

"I couldn't answer. The guys in the cellar were way too unpredictable, too wild. On the other hand, I knew, even then, that they – the whole Sycamore family – were alive, totally into inventing and solving problems and new ideas. They didn't just live, they played. And Amy, by being in the show, was playing and it was wonderful. My life had been like that before I started school. Remember that book called *Flow* by Mihali Whatshisname?"

"No," Ellen said. "I don't know that one."

"It was all about getting so caught up in something that time almost ceases to exist. It can happen to artists or it can happen to skiers, downhill racers, where time actually slows down for them so they can make all the sudden changes to stay on course. When I was little I remember freedom like that, like the guys in the cellar. Kids, small kids, really don't have a sense of time. When they play, they're in flow, one of the reasons it's so hard to get them to come for a meal. They've been so busy they don't realize time has passed."

"That's happened to me a few times with the pottery," Ellen said.

"That's what Mihali Whatshisname called Flow. Before I started school I could do that. I don't think I've ever been as free or happy since."

"Well, now's your chance," Simon said. "You've got 1.5 million dollars and a whole town to play with. I say let's play."

"You're serious, aren't you?"

"It's been handed to you. Fanny wanted the town fixed up – let's fix it up. We'll restore the Intercourse House and then go to work on the others."

Kenneth felt the way he had in the car that night with Amy. The idea was just too big, too unpredictable. This was not play. This was big and expensive and risky.

"Maybe we'll even make some fireworks," Simon continued.

"Grants Ferry could use some fireworks," Ellen said.

"This doesn't feel good at all," Kenneth said. "It's too big. I like to know where I'm going."

"None of us knows where we're going," Simon said. "The best we can do is try to influence the outcome. Christ, you're the one who taught me that."

"But in Grants Ferry? I mean, Jesus. If we go down in Grants Ferry…"

"It's where she's brought us and I say we go for it."

Ellen held her breath.

"Well…" Kenneth mumbled, "I've got to talk some more with Increase."

"Is that a yes?" Ellen asked.

"It's as close as we're gonna get this afternoon," Simon said. "This morning he had his bags packed. Now he's willing to talk. Get behind the wheel, big fella, and take us back to town."

*

"Oh, I almost forgot," Ellen said. "I brought some pieces you can take to New York. It's basically a full place setting and a few planters and pots."

"Great," Simon said. "People down there will love'em. I'll negotiate a good price but you'll get to okay it before you start taking orders."

"Well, okay," she said, unsure just how this would play out, whether she could keep them supplied and happy. "I just – "

"They're gonna love it," Simon said again. "You'll see."

*

Benny Munson ran the family garage and filling station. Years ago it had been a gleaming Tydol station but under Benny's care since his father died it had become a greasy, cluttered eyesore on the main street. Most of the women in town refused to go there for gas. Benny was as dirty as the garage and he kept a strange dog that had somehow lost all its hair and only came out of the garage long enough to inspect and whiz on customers' wheels.

"I see Kenny's back," Benny said when he'd set the nozzle in the filler pipe in Archie's truck. He wiped his hands on a filthy rag as he came back to the window so they could visit while the pump ran.

"Came back to bury Fanny," Archie said.

"Waited a long time for that day, din't he? Saw him drivin' around in her Valiant."

"That so?"

One of the reasons Benny had not gone over to self-pumping like so many places was that it gave him an excuse to visit with people who came to buy gas.

"Ellen was with him," Benny went on.

"She was?"

"Yep. Front seat. Between Kenny and another guy."

"That would be Simon. Came up with Kenny. Ellen was with them?"

"Yup. Took him no time at all, did it? You think Fanny left him everything? I always supposed she hated him."

"Somethin's goin' on," Archie grumbled. "Fanny never gave anything away. There's a hook there somewhere."

"Didn't Kenny and Ellen used to have somethin' goin'?" Benny said, not one to miss an opportunity to stir up old stories.

"Oh, Christ, that was years ago," Archie said.

"She looked pretty comf'table to me," Benny offered.

Archie gave that some thought. He'd expected Ellen and Kenny would be catching up. That's what the breakfast was all about. But now Kenny had that little faggot in tow. If Kenny was queer there couldn't be any threat where Ellen was concerned but it certainly didn't look good. That was the unsettling part. In all the years they'd been married he'd never known Ellen to step out of line but now she was riding around in Fanny's car in full daylight and it would be all over town in no time. As handy as Benny was as an information source, his gossip was spread equally to all customers.

"Yeah, well, they were friends years ago," Archie said, not wanting to show concern. "She had breakfast with them this morning. They prob'ly just wanted to drive around so Kenny could see what the place is like now."

"Musta seen most of the town already, then. They headed out toward the highway," Benny said.

"Oh, yeah?"

"Yep. You suppose there's somethin' goin' on?" Benny grinned.

"Oh, somethin's goin' on, all right, but not what you think."

*

"Okay, explain the rules for this thing again," Kenneth said. They were settled around one end of Increase's conference table.

"I'll give you a written list of the conditions that must be satisfied," Increase began, "but basically you must accept the challenge by this coming Saturday afternoon."

"Okay."

"Grants Ferry must, with due diligence, become your primary residence."

"Okay."

"During the course of the challenge you will have the right of occupancy to Fanny's house, rent free. If you meet all the conditions of the challenge within the specified time, all her accumulated real estate, bank accounts, and other investments, become yours."

"Other investments?"

"A few mutual fund stocks."

"Are we allowed to work on Fanny's house – fix the place up?" Simon asked.

"You're free to treat the place as your own. If you fail to meet all her conditions, however, you stand to lose the cost of any improvements."

Simon looked at Kenneth who simply shrugged.

"Fanny set a deadline of midnight of the day one year from the time you sign the agreement. The hotel must be renovated, brought up to current codes, restored as closely as possible to the original, with allowances for modern requirements, of course, acquire necessary permits to allow the operation of the dining room, and a certificate of occupancy to receive overnight guests on the second floor."

"And the tavern?" Kenneth asked.

"Interestingly, there's no mention of alcohol," Increase said. "I doubt she forgot it, but she may have simply recognized that without an alcohol license it would be unlikely to attract enough patrons to survive."

"And the ballroom?"

"There's no mention of the ballroom."

"Do you think it's possible to do all that in a year?"

"I truly don't know. There's nothing that prevents me or anyone else from helping you, however. I'm more than willing to take care of any legal work or dealing with local, state, or federal requirements, approvals, or permits. The state may present one of your biggest hurdles but I still have some influence in Montpelier."

"And when does the clock start running?"

"The latest you can sign the agreement will be this coming Saturday afternoon. The clock starts then."

"You understand we've got a life to wrap up in the city."

"Of course."

"Can we have Luther keep an eye on things?"

"Or course. I can pay him if you like. Technically, the properties are still in the estate. He can be paid from that."

"Okay. Good. Whatever he charges, increase it by half."

"Very well."

"And don't let him argue about it, either," he said. "By the way, I'm not sure it matters, but how did Fanny end up with all this property?"

"Ah, yes. Well, when you left town Fanny's stipend from the trust stopped. She was quite alarmed at this loss of income so she and Malcolm hatched up this plan to acquire some of the finer examples of Grants Ferry architecture with a goal of preserving and one day restoring them."

"What's that got to do with the stipend?"

"It was a rather clever scheme. She wanted the money from the trust as well as the equity in her own house to provide her share of the partnership with Malcolm. Since it was my duty as trustee to not only protect the trust but to see to its husbandry I wouldn't give it to her. Instead, I became a silent partner in that I let them use it as collateral as long as the investment was secure and that its value would continue unharmed. Malcolm, of course, was able to make some very attractive financial arrangements through the bank. Between them they would quietly buy these houses and then rent them out, sometimes back to the previous owners. They kept the buildings in reasonable repair over the years but never had any extra money for the restoration Fanny dreamed about. In return for managing the properties, Fanny was paid for her services which more than made up for the loss of the monthly stipend."

"So they both owned them?"

"As joint tenants in common. Malcolm had no heirs and when he died, Fanny owned the lot, free and clear, including Malcolm's house. I suggested she might want to make arrangements for the properties following her own death and I insisted that since her fortunes were made possible in part by your trust fund, you should have claim to the properties in any case."

"With conditions," Kenneth said

"With conditions," Increase agreed. "In actual fact, they're in a trust and the management of the trust is left to you. Basically, you get to treat them as your own. I suggest you form a corporation at some point through which any of your business enterprises would be run, separate from the trust. The trust then stays intact but your corporation would have full access. I can work it up if you'd like."

"Okay," Kenneth said. "I'll let you know."

*

"So you got Fanny's house, then," Luther said.

"Not yet," Kenneth said. "Come on inside."

"Piece of work, she was."

"Hi, Luther." This was Simon.

"How you doin'?"

Luther was normally hesitant around new people but if this little guy was a friend of Kenny's he was all right in Luther's book.

"So how've you been, anyway?" Kenneth said.

"'Bout the same. Thirty years older, that's all."

"...looking good..."

"Yeah, well... Don't believe everything you see. Takes more effort to get up every morning"

"You married then? What've you been up to?"

"Yup. Married. 'Bout twenty-two, twenty-three years now. I lose track."

"Anybody I know?"

"Remember the Cramers, out on the Clay Pit Road?"

"Cramer? Worked on the highway crew?"

"That's him. Red Cramer. Mean son of a bitch. Wife shot him."

Simon dropped a pan in the sink. "She shot him?"

"Twelve times."

"Jesus," Kenneth said.

"Just wanted to be sure."

"Well, yeah."

"We all thought she'd get the chair but they decided she was crazy instead and sent her up to Waterbury."

"She shot him twelve times?" Simon said.

"Yup. Used Red's own double-barreled 12-gauge and double-ought buck," Luther smiled again. "Had to reload five times, you know. Made quite a mess of him."

"Jesus," Simon said. "And they said she was crazy?"

"She wan't too bright but she sure was pissed." Luther said. "Told'em she'd just had enough. The kids were put out to foster homes. No surprise to find out they'd all been abused for years."

Kenneth had always suspected some of those outer fringe people had gone feral.

"My folks took Yvonne in," Luther went on. "She was the youngest. Red had totally fucked her over."

"Bastard."

"Yeah. My folks and me, it took some time but we got her settled down, turned around. Time she was eighteen, she'd turned out kind'a pretty, I thought. Then my mother died and Yvonne had no place to go so we got married. Seemed like the thing to do."

"Good for you." This was Kenneth.

"She don't like crowds much but I get her to the grocery store once a week – late Thursdays when hardly anybody's there. She's a good woman. Tends the house, the garden, the animals… Don't talk much. Makes good company."

"By not talking?" Simon said.

"Well, after all those years we've pretty much said it, don'tcha think?"

"I never thought of it that way."

"If she likes somebody, she'll talk their ears off. Don't know where that comes from. Some sort of instinct, I guess."

"Any kids?" Kenneth asked.

"Nope. After those years with Red Yvonne don't like to be touched."

"Oh, too bad," Simon said.

"Yeah, well… She's good company, though," Luther said again, totally content with his situation. "Not many folks married twenty-two years can say that, can they?"

"Probably not."

"No complaints."

"Well, that's good," Kenneth said. Simon was still curious.

"So in – what – twenty-three years – you've never had sex?"

"Well, Yvonne don't like to be touched…"

"And that's worked?" Kenneth asked.

"So far."

Simon just shook his head.

"Well, listen," Kenneth moved on. "Everything's up in the air around Fanny's estate. I asked Increase to have you look after things."

"No problem. I used to help Fanny out now and again."

"Do whatever you need to do. Give your time to Increase every week and he'll see that you're paid, okay?"

"Sure. Oh, what should I do with Fanny's cats?"

"Well, I don't want them back here."

"You don't want a cat?" Simon said.

"Not those two. If we ever have a cat we're going to start fresh. Can you deal with them, Luther?"

"They're pretty wild but Yvonne's good with animals."

"As long as I never have to see them."

Luther got into his truck. "We had some good times, didn't we, Kenny?"

"Sure did."

"Good to have you back." He backed out of the yard, and drove away.

"That was interesting," Simon said.

"Luther was like an older brother after my parents died. He's a good, honest man, salt of the earth. Giving him some responsibility and paying him for it is the sort of thanks he can accept," Kenneth explained. "If I offered him cash without expecting something in return he'd be insulted. Hiring him is the only honorable thing."

"So we've got a hired hand?"

"Not yet, but he'd be a good one."

"Does he come with a double-barreled double whatever it was?"

"Possibly."

"Would he show it to us?"

"I don't think that's something Luther flashes around."

*

"Well, that must have been some breakfast," Archie said when Ellen came home.

"It was nice to see Kenny again," Ellen said. "We had a lot to talk about."

"I'll bet."

"Simon made cinnamon buns. It's been years since I've had fresh cinnamon buns."

"So what's going on, then?"

"Going on?"

"They gonna be selling Fanny's properties or what? Any suggestion he might sell the Intercourse House?"

"I really don't know."

"Christ," Archie said, his voice getting louder, "you were over there for at least five hours. Didn't he tell you anything?"

"I didn't go to spy for you and don't raise your voice."

"Well, you didn't spend five hours eating breakfast. Benny said you all drove out of town in Fanny's Valiant."

"Isn't it nice you have Benny keeping an eye on things for you," Ellen said. "Kenny wanted to show Simon where his parents died, that's all. And before that, I took them down to the historical society. Oh, and I took some of my pieces over to them. They think they know someone in New York who could sell them in his store. It could be a chance to make some real money instead of working craft fairs."

"I thought that was just a hobby."

"Well, it has been. But now the kids are grown and gone I was thinking I might expand it – build a small business."

"Right," he snorted, "with all you know about business."

As soon the words were out in the open and on their way across the kitchen Archie knew he'd made a big mistake. He saw it in her eyes before they even landed. Ellen didn't speak, nor did she need to, but Archie knew he was toast before she turned and left the room.

There was a strange tingling in his left ear.

*

"You know," Simon said as they cleaned up from supper, "I think we need to stay here this week."

"I never thought I'd hear myself saying this," Kenneth said, "but I was thinking the same thing. There's no way we can make a decision from New York."

"Where do we start?"

"We need to find an architectural firm that specializes in historic restoration with connections to contractors who are organized enough to work fast and still do good work. If Increase has the Internet, perhaps he'll let us work out of his office."

"You've actually been thinking about this."

"We've just got to find the right people and be willing to pay for it."

"And the store?"

"Unload it," Kenneth said. "The condo, too."

"Whoa. The condo, too? Where'd that come from?"

"Well, we could lease it out, but we'll probably need the cash."

"Jesus. Three days ago you didn't even want to drive up here."

"Yeah, well, things began to fall into place when we were out where my parents died and I got to thinking again about those people in the play, that crazy kind of freedom they had. I want to feel that way again. It's been a long, long time."

"And…?"

"Jerry Falwell, of course. I'm damned if I want to give it all to that bastard."

"If we lose, he gets it anyway."

"Right but if we don't try, he gets it by default," Kenneth said. "You and I both know that as soon as Increase dropped that bomb we were hooked."

"It crossed my mind. How many people do you suppose know about that twist?"

"Would it matter?

"I don't know."

"Irene would know…"

"Irene?"

"Irene Bills, his secretary, but she's no gossip. She's devoted to Increase."

"What about Ellen?"

"We'll see."

*

Irene had just turned on her computer.

"Why little Kenny Forbes," she bellowed. "Look at you, all grown up."

"Hi, Irene." The voice didn't scare him the way it had when he was a boy but to Simon it was like shattering glass.

"I'll be damned," Irene said. She came out from behind her desk and gave Kenneth a big, beefy hug that pinned his arms to his sides.

"This is Simon, my partner," he said when she finally let him go.

"Gladda meetcha," she said. She shook his hand with a grip that was surprisingly gentle after the way she'd grabbed Kenneth.

"Likewise," Simon said.

"Increase said you was coming back. God, what's it been, thirty-two years?"

"That's right."

"Can I get you fellas some coffee? Increase should be down any minute."

"Actually, we just had breakfast."

Irene glanced at the wall clock.

"Little late, innit?"

"We got into some bad habits in the city. Stay up later at night and get up later in the morning." In Irene's world this bordered on sloth. "Increase still pretty busy?"

"Not like it used to be. We're down to four days a week now and he's taking a lot of pro bono work. Sometimes I think it's just to give me something to do." She looked toward the door where Increase would appear, put her hand up to hide her mouth if Increase should come in, and whispered, "He ought to retire and take it easy."

As if on cue, Increase came into the room.

"Hi, fellas. Thought you were heading back to the city."

"Well, we'd planned to go back," Kenneth said, "but there's too much to do before we decide. We wondered if we might work out of your office this week."

"Certainly," Increase said. "Certainly. Set up in the conference room. Irene, see that these fellas have anything they need. We don't have anything pressing this week so just consider you're working for them. You mind?"

"'Course not." She went into the conference room and began to pick up books and papers.

"She's priceless," Increase told them. "Don't know what I'd do without her."

"Hey, Increase," Irene yelled from the conference room, "you want me to file this stuff or just pile it someplace?"

Increase left them to see what she was talking about.

"Pile it someplace?" Simon said.

"Just leave it all over there by the window," he told her from the doorway. "I'll get back to it later." He gestured toward the conference room. "All yours."

"Thanks," Kenneth said. "And you must be hooked up to the Internet."

"Yes, we are. Don't have the faintest idea how to use it myself but Irene's a wizard. She'll be invaluable. Don't hesitate to use her. She loves a challenge."

"Okay," Irene was back, rubbing her hands together. "What do you fellas need?"

*

Chapter Thirteen

Irene found several New England architectural firms that specialized in historic restoration. Seven, from their websites, seemed to her the most promising and she printed out informational pages and contact details. Settled around the speaker phone, Kenneth and Simon explained the project to each firm, always finding enthusiastic interest until they mentioned the one year deadline. By noon the list had been exhausted with the same response from every call: impossible.

"What the hell's the matter with these people?" Simon said

"No luck, huh?" Irene was in the doorway.

"Not yet," Simon said. "But these can't be the only choices."

"Oh, there was others," Irene said, "but they just didn't feel right."

"They didn't feel right?"

"Nope. Anyway, I got to thinking and what I was thinking was I'd been looking in the wrong place, big names, with big projects in cities and stuff, right?"

"Right…"

"So I was thinking maybe we should look for someone with a good solid reputation but who's just starting out, someone who's maybe just as hungry and desperate as you are."

"You think we're desperate?"

"You kidding? I can almost smell it."

Simon squirmed in his chair.

"And did you find someone?" Kenneth asked.

"Well, there's no guarantees, of course, but I'd put my money on Clancy Matthews."

"Who's Clancy Matthews?"

"You want us to call a guy named Clancy?" Simon said.

"I printed out some pages from the website," Irene said. Each page included detailed photos of exquisite old New England heritage sites, both public buildings and great sprawling mansions that overlooked the sea, a mountain lodge built by one of yesterday's millionaires which had now been restored and converted to a luxury executive retreat, and another that had been restored and converted to an inn, all excerpted from a trade magazine, *Architectural Restoration*. The commentary gave credit to Bingham Haskell & Foster, one of the first firms Kenneth and Simon had called, but it was clear from the article that Clancy Matthews had been the driving force on the featured projects. Matthews, the article said, "*has a particular gift for meeting current codes and safety requirements without compromising the integrity, elegance, and grace of the original structures*."

"Clancy looks pretty good, doesn't he?" Simon said.

"Yeah." Kenneth looked through the pages again. "You say he's just starting out?"

"Yeah, about six months ago, not long after the article was published, apparently. Worked for Bingham Haskell & Foster before that, the first outfit you called."

Kenneth studied the photos in the magazine story. "So this Clancy Matthews no longer works for Bingham Haskell and what's-his-face?"

"There's all sorts of reasons for leaving a job. You gonna dial or you want me to do it?" Irene said.

"What the hell?" Simon said. "Go ahead."

The phone rang twice and a woman's voice said, "Clancy Matthews."

"Could we speak with Clancy Matthews, please?"

"This is Clancy."

"I'm sorry," Kenneth said, thrown off for a second, "I didn't realize – "

"No problem. I get that all the time."

"There was nothing on your website to suggest – "

"I know. You'd be surprised what a difference that makes in the length of time people stay on the site."

Irene grinned and gave him a thumbs up from the doorway.

"Well, I – I'm sorry. I'm Kenneth Forbes."

"What can I do for you, Kenneth?"

Kenneth explained the situation.

Quiet from Clancy's end. They waited.

Then: "You're kidding, right?"

"I wish I were."

"And you think this can be done?"

"I have no idea. Several firms including Bingham Haskell & Foster have assured me in no uncertain terms that it can't."

"No surprise there."

"I never got a chance to tell them that we have what we think are a complete set of the original construction drawings."

"Really. Are you sure?"

"Well, I'm not an architect but the date on the drawings seems right and there don't appear to be any significant changes to the structure – a few interior modifications, maybe, but not much. It seems to have avoided that awful modernization phase in the early 1900s. It'll need to be brought up to current codes, of course, along with some plumbing and heating, and a new kitchen. The rest, we think, is cosmetic."

There was silence for a full minute on Clancy's end of the line.

"And you say there's a clock running?" she asked finally.

"That's right. I have to complete it within a year of this coming Saturday afternoon or lose it all."

"There must be something else," Clancy said.

"Well, yes, there is. If I walk away now or if I try and fail, the entire estate goes to Jerry Falwell and *The Old Time Gospel Hour*."

"Are you making this up?"

"Not at all."

"Jesus Christ," Clancy said. It was silent again while she thought it through. "How'd you get into this mess, anyway?"

"Long story."

"I'll bet. And you're able to finance this work?"

"We think so. Of course, it depends how much we'll need."

"Good point." Another silence. Then: "Okay, give me an address I can put into MapQuest."

Simon clamped his hands over his mouth to keep from yelling. Irene pumped her fist back and forth.

"Of course," Kenneth said, very calmly. He gave her the street address.

"So how far away are you?" Clancy asked.

"About two hours from Boston, maybe two and a half."

"Okay," Clancy said. "Okay." Another short pause. "I can be there between nine and ten tomorrow morning. Will that work?"

"Perfect," Kenneth said. "We'll have the coffee on. Thank you, Clancy."

"Don't thank me yet, Kenneth. I may decide you guys are out of your minds."

The cheer that rose up in the conference room brought Increase out of his office.

"Good news, then?"

*

Archie hunkered over the newspaper, his coffee cooling on the table. Hank munched his pieces of doughnut. All in all, the Harvest Festival appeared to have been success, even with spectacle of Fanny's funeral on Saturday. The church had replenished its coffers for another year and the town had settled back into its daily routine.

Every year Archie vowed he'd never do it again and every year he sat here when it was over thinking of changes he'd make for the next one. Of course, there had been some strange stuff this year. Kenny Forbes turned up after thirty years and Increase wouldn't start Fanny's service until Kenny got here. Something was going on. People don't just show up for funerals after thirty years, although, he realized, in Fanny's case confirmation she was really dead might be reason enough.

Increase's role was clear. He was often called upon to take care of estates and last details, but Kenny was a wild card.

If anybody had access to Kenny Forbes and what he was up to it would be Ellen. They were all snuggly after the supper on Saturday and then she was over there with them for five or six hours on Monday but she'd been no help at all.

"Breakfast, my ass," he grumbled to no one in particular. He'd always supposed that Kenny's running off thirty years ago would have pretty much soured that friendship but they seemed to have picked up where they left off. And Kenny brought that little queer with him. Maybe Kenny was queer himself. Archie wasn't sure just where that detail might fit.

And Ellen. He'd never seen her ice up the way she had after he made that crack about her business venture. He rubbed his left ear. It tingled sometimes lately.

He put the *Rutland Herald* aside, picked up the *Keene Sentinel*, and scanned the headlines. Sometimes he'd read a paragraph or two to get a few basic details of a story and then move on to something else. He always read captions under the photos, skimmed their bleeding heart editorial, and checked out the whining letters to the editor.

It was habit as much as anything. None of it ever stayed with him. He was ready to check the obituaries, his favorite section, when a movement outside caught his attention. It was only a passing car but there was something about it, the unusual motion he noticed, not the fact of the car itself. A silvery gray Volvo station wagon crept up the street, driven by a woman with big red hair. Archie knew all the cars in Grants Ferry and this wasn't one of them. No one here had big red hair, either. Massachusetts plates, he noticed.

The Volvo turned by the hotel and went out of sight only to reappear a few minutes later after driving around the common. It then crawled back past the diner where Archie got a better look at the Maureen O'Hara red hair.

"Now who the hell comes gawkin' around Grants Ferry in the middle of the week?" he wondered. Hank followed Archie's gaze out the window.

"Freshen that up, Archie?" Dot said, meaning his coffee.

He always said "'bout half" and she always topped it up.

"'Bout half," he said, and she topped it up. "You ever see that car before, Dot?"

Dot leaned over the table to get a look just as the Volvo went out of sight. She'd steadied herself with a hand on Archie's shoulder.

"Nope," she said, "but then cars all look pretty much alike to me."

"That one's from Massachusetts."

"Somebody leftover from the weekend?"

"We don't have leftovers. They come, they shop, and they go. That's the point."

"Well, beats me," Dot said. She went back to the kitchen.

It was things like this, Archie groused, that upset the natural order in town: strange cars, Kenny turns up, and Ellen wants to start a business.

He rubbed his left ear again, realized it, and put his hand on the table.

"What do you suppose is goin' on?" he asked Hank.

Hank looked back at him with those Uncle Henry eyebrows. Even if he knew he wouldn't tell.

*

H.R. Wright & Co. had been one of those old fashioned hardware stores that carried anything you might need to make repairs around the homestead from shovels to harness hardware. They sharpened knives and saws, made keys, tuned up lawn mowers, and could find a bolt or screw that would put anything back together again. The big chain stores, the home centers, even though they were some distance from Grants Ferry, had eventually brought H.R. Wright down. Everyone thought it was a shame, even as they drove to Springfield to the home center for any of the big ticket, high profit items like electric tools that might have prolonged the life of H.R. Wright.

Ellen had always admired the ironwork across the front. It was all façade, of course, but it gave the appearance of columns and lintels entwined with vines. H.R. Wright had painted it all a solid dark green but Ellen visualized it stripped clean and painted again. Ivory for the columns, maybe with some marbling, and greens for the vines. She thought the blossoms might be morning glories and the flowers against the other colors would make a nice contrast and a bright and pleasant entrance to the shop.

Two big windows flanked the door. She could create a generous retail space in the front and still have a large work area in the back, sealed off to keep the dust away from the merchandise. There was plenty of room there for her wheels and kilns, not to mention the loading dock with a big overhead door which would be handy for shipping. There was an apartment upstairs, too, where she could put her office. All in all, with some investment in both time and money, it would be perfect.

The silvery gray Volvo drove by. Not a local car, Ellen noticed. The Massachusetts plates confirmed it. And it was Wednesday, a strange day for people from out of town to be here. No one in Grants Ferry had red hair like that, either.

The car turned down Sycamore Street and was gone from Ellen's mind almost as quickly. The Realtor's sign had a Springfield number. She would call from home.

*

Kenneth was at the kitchen door as Clancy got out of her car and stretched.

"Come in, come in. We've just made a pot of coffee and Simon's baked up some goodies. Give you a chance to unwind before we get to work."

Sweet rolls, a bowl of fruit, and juices were on the table, and a pot of water bubbled on the stove in case Clancy preferred tea. Kenneth made the introductions.

"Whoa," Clancy said when she saw the food. "That looks great. First, though, a bathroom."

"Oh. Right." Kenneth apologized. "It's upstairs." He led her through the house to the stairs.

"Nice decor," Clancy said. "Do it yourself?"

"My aunt's place, basically unchanged since I escaped over thirty years ago. Upstairs on the right."

A few minutes later they were all back in the kitchen. Simon poured coffee, plates were filled, butter was spread, fruit was dished, and cream was dolloped.

"I assume there's a story here," Clancy said.

"I lived here with my Aunt Fanny after my parents were killed.

"Oh, I'm sorry."

"Yeah. Thanks. I survived the same crash. I was almost eleven. Fanny was not a nice woman."

"I see."

"Her funeral was Saturday. Turns out while I was gone she'd managed to amass a sizable real estate portfolio – several big old houses like this one, the hotel, and a big farm that overlooks the river. It could all be worth as much as $2 million."

"She did well."

"It can all be mine if – "

"– you restore the hotel."

"Within a year."

"And, of course, there's Jerry Falwell."

"Of course."

"I drove around a bit when I got into town. There's nothing here, is there? I mean, even if the hotel were restored, what's the point?"

Kenneth gave a truncated history of Grants Ferry and what seemed to inspire Fanny to preserve what she could and keep the memory of the golden days alive.

"She wanted Grants Ferry to be proud again, the way it used to be, even though most of the good times were before she was born. I think she believed she was born too late."

"I've run into people like that," Clancy said. "They forget that many of the comforts and support systems we have today didn't even exist. The hotel, for instance, will only be grand if it meets today's hygienic and safety standards."

"I always thought it was a dump," Kenneth said, "but my time with antiques the last few years has given me a different perspective."

"So who would support this place when it's done?"

"I don't know. With some promotion the restaurant and the tavern could probably generate enough to cover basic operating costs. Hiring out the rooms would be a bonus, I think. Ultimately, and we haven't really thought it through yet, I think the hotel could be the first step toward a general renaissance in town. Her other houses could be great B&Bs. No doubt you noticed there are empty store fronts and spaces for new shops. It will take some time but there are possibilities. And then we've got the farm, 650 acres out along the river, which we get when the guy decides to stop farming or dies. River frontage – golf course, country club, marina, small conference center… But I agree, there's got to be more than the hotel to bring people here."

"And what do you need by Friday afternoon?"

"Someone who will agree to manage the restoration and tell me how much money I need."

"Fair enough." She tested the coffee. "How'd you happen to call me?"

"Increase Houghton's secretary found you on the Internet. You used to work for Bingham Haskell & Foster?"

"I did."

"It looks as if you did some good work for them."

"I did great work for them, always under budget and on time."

"What happened?"

"Oddly, it was that article in *Architectural Restoration* that did it. Bingham Haskell & Foster doesn't like individuals to get credit. That dislike is exponential if the individual is also a woman."

"Oh."

"When they discovered that John Flaherty who wrote the piece is a friend of mine they thought I'd put him up to it."

"Did you?"

"No. I knew he was going to do the article and so did Bingham Haskell & Foster but I didn't know it was going to be such a personal showpiece. Anyway, I got called into Bingham's office and each of them took a turn to tell me what a naughty girl I'd been."

"Because you did a good job?"

"No, because I got recognition. I never got thanked for doing a good job. So I apologized, assured them it would never happen again, emailed my resignation to all three of them with a cc to everyone else in the firm, picked up my laptop, and left. Over the next couple weeks I set up Clancy Matthews. That was just about six months ago."

"How'd it work out?"

"Harder than I thought, quite frankly – scary, to be honest – but those three misogynistic bastards will never scold me again."

*

Kenneth rolled out the plans on the dining room table.

"Here it is: The Grants Ferry Hotel, known locally as the Intercourse House."

"The Intercourse House?"

"Fine old word, intercourse," Kenneth deadpanned. "…fallen into some disuse of late…"

Clancy giggled.

"They actually called it that?"

"Most of the natives."

"Was it, like, a whorehouse or something?"

"No, at least I don't think so. The original owners were talking about social and commercial intercourse, a perfectly noble and honorable pursuit." He opened the plans to the page with the sign detail. "The nickname came about almost the instant they unveiled the sign."

Clancy flipped through the plans and scanned each page. "Well, these certainly seem complete. If they're genuine and there aren't a lot of undocumented changes it will make life a lot simpler. Can we get inside?"

"Thought you'd never ask," Kenneth said. "There's more, though. Come out to the barn."

He slid open the heavy barn door.

"Wow," Clancy said. "What is that?"

"1960 Plymouth Valiant. It's not the car I wanted to show you, though. Check out this furniture. I haven't been through it but I suspect most of it originally came from the hotel or is very similar in style to what used to be there. Most of it was auctioned off when the hotel closed. Fanny seems to have tracked it down and bought a lot of it back."

Clancy lifted the plastic sheet to get a better look. The piece in front was a solid oak dresser with a marble top, still in excellent condition. "You know, this is almost too handy. I can't decide whether it's a gift or a trap."

"No shit," Kenneth said.

*

"There's that car again," Archie said to Hank as they drove past the hotel. "Let's go in and see what's goin' on." He parked behind the Volvo and voices inside led him to the tavern.

"Kenny," Archie said. "I thought you'd gone back home." He was talking to Kenneth but looking at the woman with the red hair.

"Not yet. This is Clancy Matthews."

"Howja do?"

"Grants Ferry's first selectman, Archie Whitaker," Kenneth continued.

"What a gorgeous dog," Clancy said. She reached down to scratch behind Hank's ears. Clancy loved dogs.

"Name's Hank," Archie told her.

"Hi, Hank. How you doing, fella?" Hank squirmed happily.

"Didn't get enough of a look around the other day, then?" Archie said.

"Not quite."

"Hi, Archie." Simon said. "Our friend leans a bit more toward your gender preference, doesn't she?"

"Why, I – " Archie stammered.

"She's come to help," Simon went on. "We were just *way, WAY* over our heads, weren't we, Kenneth?"

"Way over," Kenneth agreed. "Clancy's an architect."

"That so?" Archie supposed that would explain the Volvo. He'd not met many architects but they all drove Volvos. "You thinkin' about hirin' an architect?" he said.

"Well, we just have to if we're going to bring The Intercourse House back to her former glory," Simon purred as he slipped his arm around Archie's.

"You – you thinkin' about bringin' it back? I mean, it's a wreck. Look at it. Should have come down long ago to make room for something new, don'tcha know. I got people interested," Archie tried to separate himself but Simon held on. "Now Fanny's gone maybe we could talk."

"About selling the hotel?"

"Well, yeah. You know. Out with the old, in with the new. Long overdue."

"I agree it's overdue," Kenneth said, "but the hotel's not for sale."

"Well, now," Archie smiled and chuckled as he oozed into his horse-trader-deal-making mode, a skill he'd honed to an enviable success rate over the years, "you and me, Kenny, we're both old enough now to know everything's for sale. All we have to do is agree on the price."

"Not this time," Kenneth said. "It's not mine to sell."

"It's not? Whose is it, then?"

"Still Fanny's, I think. She's locked it up in a trust."

"A trust?"

"That's right."

"Wasn't that clever of her?" Simon said. He was still holding Archie's arm. Now he gave it a little squeeze.

"Sure was."

"She wants me to restore it and reopen it by next year."

"Reopen it?"

"That's the deal. Then I get to keep it."

Archie's head began to buzz. He'd always assumed if he waited Fanny out he'd be able to move on the Rite Aid deal. Now there was this trust, however that worked, and now these two (or maybe three) were talking about restoring the damned thing.

"You've got a year? And what if you don't get it finished?"

"I lose."

Well, that sounded better. It would be a pleasure to watch Kenneth go down in flames – serve him right, showing up out of the blue the way he had. Archie might even find a way to influence that outcome.

"And then what? Will it be for sale then? Auction or something?"

"Afraid not. If I lose, the hotel, all Fanny's houses, the Ellis Rogers farm, all of it, goes to Jerry Falwell and *The Old Time Gospel Hour*."

"Falwell?" Archie sputtered. "The TV preacher? But – but what would he do with it?"

"No idea" Kenneth said. "I only know what I need to do. Clancy will tell us whether we should even bother."

"Well, shit," Archie said.

"You see? Fanny's set us all up," Kenneth said.

"I mean, who's gonna come to stay in Grants Ferry?" Archie sputtered.

"On the other hand," Simon said, "The tavern will be open again, a nice place to meet friends for drinks, and we'll have that lovely dining room and interesting meals."

"Well, yeah, but – "

"I know it's a little out of the way and it probably can't compare with those famous church suppers with the vats of baked beans and tubs of yellow squash but it will be lovely," Simon went on. "Now, Archie, this chat has been very nice but we've got a lot to do." He held Archie's arm and led him to the door. "So if you and the doggie just run along and interview someone else, we'll get back to work."

"Bye, Hank." Clancy gave him a last tussle.

Hank reluctantly pulled away and followed Archie.

"Has he always been like that?" Clancy asked when they were gone.

"Pretty much," Kenneth said. "When we were kids he was a bully. Now he's first selectman, sort of an adult version of the same thing."

"Wonderful dog," Clancy said. "I've never seen one quite like him."

"You'll probably never see another," Kenneth said. "Archie thinks it might actually be his Uncle Henry."

Simon took Archie all the way to the sidewalk. "Sorry we're so rushed, Archie. We'll just have to find another time when we can sit and talk, won't we? Bye, now." He went back inside, closed the door and rejoined the others, "Well, that was refreshing, wasn't it?"

"Will he be trouble?" Clancy asked.

"He'll probably try but he's no match for Increase Houghton."

"What happened to his ear?"

"Juvenile justice."

*

Clancy pulled two large flashlights from her bag and the three of them inspected the building from the depths and far corners of the cellar to the ballroom on the third floor. There were very few changes from the original plans. Sprinkler systems, the electrical upgrades, the telephone lines, the Internet and TV connections and anything else that guests might expect in a nice inn would have to be designed and installed but most of the rooms simply needed a good scrub, some paint, wallpaper, and soft furnishings. The hotel kitchen would be completely stripped and rebuilt.

"Well, it must have been quite the place in its day," Clancy said.

"I can picture it already," Simon jumped in. He'd kept quiet through most of the tour but now it seemed like a good time sell the vision. "Even when we walked through the other day, I could see it, all clean and gleaming and smelling of lemon oil. Flowers on the tables, piano in the corner of the dining room. And The Tavern with draft beer and artisan ales, glittering glassware, and a big mirror behind the bar… It could be a gem."

"Yes," Clancy agreed, "it could be. And if it were someplace else it would probably thrive but here it is in a little town that maybe fifty people in the entire world have heard of." She started the car. "Back to the house?"

"Want to see the other properties?"

Clancy checked her watch. "Are they part of this project?"

"If we finish the hotel on time they will be," Kenneth said.

"How many are there?"

"Half a dozen. Most are here in town but the farm overlooking the river is about ten minutes away."

"Well, as long as I'm here…"

Kenneth directed her past the other properties, telling some of the stories, some of the history of each place. Finally he had her drive out to the Ellis Rogers farm and the field where he and Simon had taken their picnic and looked down over the Connecticut River into New Hampshire. The hills on the other side of the river were still bright reds, yellows, and oranges, glowing in the afternoon sun.

"The whole farm is something like 650 acres," Kenneth said, "and it's almost all rolling hillside. The only level part is that big area down by the river."

"Beautiful spot," Clancy said. "Any idea what she had in mind for it?"

"I suspect she wanted to protect it from industrial development or a mobile home park. I don't know. It won't remain a farm once Ellis is gone, at least not a dairy farm. Simon and I see possibilities for a golf course, a club house, maybe some sort of marina and restaurant down by the river. There's woodland as well. It could be developed for hiking or cross country skiing – all pie in the sky, big investment, long term. Ultimately, I think, most of the land should remain undeveloped and preserved."

"Not to mention the historic district," Simon said.

"Historic district?" Anything with historic significance got Clancy's attention.

"Oh, yeah," Kenneth said. "The old ferry landing, just upstream a bit, was one of the first river crossings from New Hampshire to the New Hampshire Grants. Fanny applied to have that whole area listed. There's not much there now except a broken down pier, a boat ramp, and the Ferry Slip, of course."

"There's still a ferry?"

"No, The Ferry Slip's a bar. Rough place. Been there since the days of the ferry, though. The tavern in the hotel will be a nice, civilized alternative. There's also an application to put the hotel and the other buildings in the center of town in another historic district."

"Quite the challenge," Clancy said.

They drove Clancy down to the old ferry landing, showed her what remained of the bridge abutments, and took some more time to drive around the rest of the central part of the town. Kenneth related the story of the early days of the settlement, the years of the Vermont Republic, the legend of the aborted raid, the cannon on the common and the loss of the bridge, and the amazing ability of New Englanders to hold grudges. If nothing else it might help Clancy understand why Fanny would go to such trouble. It was late afternoon when they got back to the house.

*

"Can I make some coffee," Simon said as they pulled into the drive, "or even supper?"

"Oh, I don't think so, Simon," Clancy said, "that's very sweet, but – "

"I'm sure I can find something. Fanny was all stocked up for winter. The freezer's full of stuff."

"Well…" Clancy knew if she gave in around supper it would be a long, late trip home. She wanted to get on the road.

"For that matter you could camp here tonight and head out first thing in the morning, couldn't she, Kenneth?"

"Sure."

"I didn't come prepared for overnight," Clancy said, trying one more excuse.

"Well, we've got the room and the food and the hot water. I thought we should at least make the offer," Simon said.

"Well, okay," Clancy agreed. "Frankly, I'm whipped. It'll be a much easier trip in the morning."

"Okay," Simon continued when they were inside. "I'll see what Fanny's put aside for us. In the meantime, we have a single bottle of New York State white wine – a Reisling, I think – or we have Irish whiskey courtesy of Increase Houghton, Fanny's lawyer."

Clancy and Kenneth chose whiskey; Simon decided to try the wine. He put the drinks together while Kenneth took Clancy to the parlor.

"Wow," Clancy said. "You could put a velvet rope across the doorway to this room and charge admission."

"I know." I think it's probably pretty much as it was when Fanny's mother put it together eighty or ninety years ago. This was her mother's Estey organ, built down in Brattleboro."

"Fabulous," Clancy said. "Do you play?"

"No. Simon does, though. That trunk is full of old sheet music."

"You mind? Can I just…"

"Go ahead."

She adjusted the bench, pumped the bellows and experimented with some of the stops as she played different chords. When she was satisfied, she began to play Yum Yum's song from *The Mikado*. Simon arrived with the drinks.

"Nice," Simon said, meaning the music. He dropped into one of the bigger chairs, leaned back and closed his eyes. "Wonderful," he said. "The wine's not bad, either." They listened to Clancy play for a few minutes. "I found what looks like chicken pieces in the freezer. They're sitting in a bowl of hot water. I'll throw something together."

Clancy finished the piece, slid off the bench, took her shoes off, and folded her legs up in the chair. She suddenly looked smaller, younger.

"So tell me," she said. "You guys a couple or what?"

"Sometimes it's 'or what'," Simon said before Kenneth could answer. "Partners, certainly, but, yes, we're also a couple."

She turned to Kenneth. "So what made you leave in the first place and what's changed that makes you think you want to come back?"

"By the time I finished high school the prosperity that had created the hotel and the big old houses was long gone and the people seemed just as tired and run down as the buildings. I didn't want to become one of them."

"Probably not very attractive to a gay man, either."

"Well, I didn't know about that yet. I just knew I'd die if I stayed here."

"And now?"

"Well, Fanny's still pulling my strings but as an adult I have a choice."

"Even with Falwell?"

"Well, there's that, of course. I could just walk away and let him have it, but it was the damnedest thing. Going to the church, the cemetery where my parents are buried, the place where they were killed, and then seeing Ellen again…"

"Ellen?"

"Yeah. Ellen was my best friend while I was growing up. Now she's married to Archie, of all people. When we saw each other again it was like I'd only been gone on vacation. But here I am thirty-two years later and I'm thinking why not?"

"That's it?"

"You ever see the play, *You Can't Take It with You*?"

"I vaguely remember the movie with Jimmy Stewart, something about a crazy family and fireworks."

"But that's the point. They weren't crazy, they were free. The people in the Sycamore house did what made them happy. Their lives were play. I used to play before I started school, before I learned our lives are full of rules. Maybe this is a way for me to play again."

"You realize, of course, it's going to be expensive."

"All the more fun," Simon said, his eyes still closed.

"And we'd have to depend on contractors and suppliers. There are no guarantees."

"I understand."

"On the other hand," she mused, "it might actually work." She sipped her whiskey. "Iffy, though…"

"True enough." Simon agreed, "but Jerry Falwell and his Soldiers of the Cross are banging on the gates."

"The trump card."

Simon got up to fix supper. "Fanny knew when to play them."

"Need help with anything?" Clancy asked.

"No, I got it."

Simon left.

"Okay," Kenneth said, "tell me about you."

"Well," Clancy said. "Where to begin? My full name is Sarah Clancy Matthews. I grew up in several coastal towns north of Boston. My father was a building contractor, mostly new homes. The Massachuetts coast is littered with historic buildings and I lived among some of the grandest designs of colonial New England. That's what got me interested in architecture. And then, in the 50s and 60s there was that pattern of deliberate and systematic destruction of some of these magnificent old buildings that led me to specialize in historic preservation. When I discovered my father had been a moving force behind one of these tragedies in the late fifties it put a strain on our relationship that existed until he died. It was a marvelous old building, a library, an outstanding piece of architecture," she said. "I still have photos. The town had built a new library and my own father had demolished this wonderful piece of history to build an incredibly ugly retail space that became a WT Grant store. I decided to do what I could to make up for that sort of commercial madness."

"You think the hotel's worth it?"

"Of course it's worth it. It's always worth saving our heritage. Making it economically viable, now there's the challenge."

Kenneth agreed. He poured a bit more Irish whisky. Clancy went back to the organ and played a selection of Stephan Foster tunes.

"Stephen Foster was a melodist," she said. "He had a great gift for the tunes but needed someone else to write the arrangements."

*

It had been an unsettling afternoon and Archie needed time to think. Dot closed after the lunch rush so Archie had nursed three beers and munched his way through a couple bowls of bar nuts down at the Ferry Slip before he came home. The house was dark except for a light in the cellar so he assumed Ellen was down there with her pottery. She'd been cold and silent the last couple days and he wasn't about to get in her way. He found some leftover macaroni and cheese in the refrigerator. He dug out a portion, stuck it in the microwave, grabbed another beer, and went off the living room where he dropped in front of the TV. When Ellen came upstairs an hour and a half later, Archie was asleep. A documentary about the migration of snow geese was on the TV. His macaroni and cheese was still in the microwave.

Ellen got into bed, grabbed a notebook, and wrote down some thoughts about her new shop. The whole idea of a studio and a shop and classrooms away from the house, a place to go to work each day, refreshed and energized her. She seldom dwelled on the past, but she now regretted she'd not done this years ago. *Never mind*, she thought. *Focus on now. The past is gone.* She hid the notebook under the mattress, turned out the light and was asleep in minutes.

*

"What do we do if she doesn't come on board?" Simon asked as they got into bed.

"I think we tell Increase we're going to do it anyway. If nothing else it keeps Jerry Falwell out of town for another year."

"We could just walk away, save ourselves the trouble, and let it happen."

"Like hell we will."

*

"All right, I'm almost in," Clancy announced the next morning.

"Just like that?" Simon said.

"Not quite, but I think it's possible," she said. "I worked it out while I was playing the organ last night. It's a mental trick I use sometimes. I do something that takes all my conscious attention and my subconscious works through problems for me. Melodies like Stephen Foster's tunes seem to invite order and possibilities. Mozart will, too. It began to take shape last night but I can see it all this morning. I'll have to load it into my project management software to be sure. Nothing in that building is very complicated; we don't have to invent anything. It's coordinating and scheduling around what we've been given."

"That's it?"

"Well, I'll have to design the bathrooms on the second floor, and I'll need to get some help with a heating and hot water system, the kitchen, and the sprinkler systems, but I know good people and I can get them started. I'll also need some money up front to get things moving."

"How much are we talking about?" Kenneth said.

"At least $100,000 to start, I should think, for retainers to get these people on board."

"It'll take a few days to shake that much loose. Anything else?"

"Get your permits, and any other legal things you might need."

"Okay."

"And get the electricity turned on again, at least a temporary service," Clancy said. "I'll hire an office trailer to be put out behind the hotel. When that comes, I'll need electricity hooked up and a phone line put in, including Internet access. Also a couple privies."

Kenneth was writing it all down.

"Anything else?"

"Be ready to write checks," Clancy said. "The way we get these contractors to jump through hoops is to pay quickly, we might even have to pay for supplies up front. I've worked with these people before, though. They're trustworthy and professional but they need to be paid quickly to keep them moving."

"And when does it all start?" Kenneth asked.

"The physical work probably won't begin until the first of the year. We might get to work on the boiler and some of the demolition, but not much else. The next three months will be spent organizing and getting the contractors and suppliers on board."

"And you think it can be done?"

"Sure enough that as long as you pay my expenses during the work, I'll take my fee only when we succeed."

*

Chapter Fourteen

"Another whole day?"

"The city's got along without us for almost a week," Kenneth said. "Another day won't matter."

"Well, Jesus. This place shuts down at 9 o'clock every night. There's nothing going on here, and you want to stay another day? What is it now?"

"This is going to be our home while we restore the hotel, maybe forever, and I don't want to spend a year in the guest room."

"Way ahead of you," Simon said. He produced a notebook where he'd been making notes ever since their first night. He'd even sketched out another bathroom for the upstairs, a lavatory for the downstairs, and a new kitchen. "We should go through your stuff in the barn, too."

It had been almost forty years since Kenneth and Luther covered it with the plastic sheet but it was all there, just as he'd left it.

The furniture from his folks' kitchen, their bedroom suite, his mother's hand mirror and hair brush, kitchen bowls and utensils, her ironing board were all there. There were old photo albums that he'd long forgotten about. He set them aside to take into the house where he could look through them.

"Wow, a jelly cupboard," Simon said.

"Yeah."

Tom Forbes' lunchbox sat on a shelf inside. It was just an old, scratched, sheet metal lunchbox but Kenneth suddenly felt an overwhelming loss. He sat in one of the kitchen chairs, the lunchbox on his lap.

"I used to watch Amy pack my father's lunch," he said. "It's got this bail to hold the Thermos in the top so it wouldn't rest on the sandwiches. I thought this lunch box was the slickest piece of equipment I'd ever seen. She'd close it up, snap the catches, and he'd be off to work. All these years, I'd forgotten about that." The Thermos was still inside.

"Bring it down," Simon said. "That's the sort of thing we should have around us, little things that say it's your house now, not Fanny's."

Kenneth wanted Amy's kitchen things, too. They could decide later whether to use them or not. His parents' bedroom set wasn't fancy but it could be set up in one of the spare rooms. Amy's iron and laundry basket were there, even her old vacuum cleaner. It was the domestic stuff he'd felt the closest to, things Amy had touched and used every day. Kenneth doubted he'd ever let go of anything that had been Amy's.

He'd also kept back a few things from Fred's collection. The best was an assortment of old records, 78s, some 45s, lots of LPs and a big old tube driven hi-fi set. He'd kept them all, without the faintest idea what the music was. Most of it was popular music, country western, and 40s style dance music by Glenn Miller, Benny Goodman, and Harry James, but there were also a few by Spike Jones, Del Wood, the New Orleans Preservation Hall Jazz Band, and a couple comedy albums by Victor Borge.

"We ought to find a spot in the parlor for the stereo," Kenneth said. "Maybe eliminate one of the chairs. The parlor can be our music room."

"Make it the 'old' music room," Simon said. "Our high-tech CD player doesn't go with an Estey organ. We can make that room with the roll-top desk into a library, put it in there with the TV and wire up some remote speakers to the parlor."

*

They were on their way out of town the next morning when they saw Ellen in front of the empty store.

"You're still here?" she said.

"Just heading back. Your pottery's in the trunk. We're going to do the hotel."

"You really think it's possible?"

"We found an architect from Boston who thinks she can do it."

"A woman with big red hair?"

"That's her. Clancy Matthews. She'll manage the whole project. All we have to do is pay for it. The plans made a big difference."

"Good. I'm glad."

"We'll be back early next month."

"Maybe I'll have a lease on this building by then."

"This building? What for?"

"I've decided I want my own shop and studio."

"Isn't this the old hardware store?" Kenneth asked.

"They closed six or seven years ago."

"This was a great old store," he explained to Simon. "They had everything. When you went in the door it smelled like tools and metal and oil and leather – tons of things. It was almost like a museum. Somewhere in a bin or drawer or tucked away on a shelf in the cellar there was a solution to any problem you might have."

"There's a big cellar and a freight elevator, too," Ellen said. "More room than I can fill in a long time unless I'm better at business than I think I am."

"What brought this on?"

"You taking my work to New York. It got me thinking about a bigger studio, a retail shop, maybe some mail order… When I told Archie he made fun of me." Kenneth recognized the set of her jaw and the determination in her eyes.

"Just your pottery? That seems like a lot of space."

"No, it can be an outlet for local craftspeople, folks who turn out limited amounts of quality goods and want a place where they can always be on display and for sale. I'm going to produce a catalog for mail order and have an internet site, too. With the space in the back I'll have room for classes, either mine or other folks'. There's an apartment upstairs. More room for classes or meetings if I need them."

"And all this happened because we're taking a few pieces back to New York?"

"Yeah. Then Archie took that shot at me and it was pretty much settled."

"I am woman, hear me roar," Simon said.

"What?"

"Nothing. Just a song."

"Will you be gone long?

"Long enough to settle our affairs and arrange to get things moved. Three weeks, maybe a month."

"But you're coming back, right?"

"We're coming back," Simon said. "I'll see to it."

They said their good-byes and Kenneth pointed the Beemer out of town.

"A craft-slash-gift shop in Grants Ferry?" Simon asked. "I mean, what the hell?"

"She's the first one to sense a change in the air," Kenneth said. "And she's finally begun to look beyond Grants Ferry. I remember that determined look of hers. Don't underestimate her."

*

"You leased the old HR Wright block?"

"That's right," Ellen said. "Five years with an option to buy it."

"What the hell for?"

"I'm moving my studio down there and I'm going to have a retail shop in the front."

"What a harebrained idea. You don't need all that space."

"I will."

"…and it's gotta be all fixed up, you know. Who's gonna do that?"

"I've called Earl Stebbins."

"Well, good. Earl's good. Little on the expensive side, but good man. I just hope it ain't for nothin'."

Ellen didn't respond.

"When you think you might open?" he asked after a rather long silence.

"I'm not in a hurry. Sometime after the first of the year. I'll take care of my Christmas orders from here."

"Good. Good," Archie said. "Best not to rush it." If he kept his mouth shut she might see the light in another month or so and forget the whole thing.

*

By the first of November, their antique business was appraised, they'd taken inventory, and their employees were offered the whole package with a 10% discount if they could get it together with a signed sales agreement by January 1.

At their condo, they tagged the items they wanted shipped to Vermont and listed the balance of the contents and the condo itself for sale through the condo association.

"You think we should keep a small pad so we can come visit?" Simon asked.

"I think we're going to need all the cash we can get."

"Yeah, but still. Long nights with nothing to do except play with our Barbi collections…"

"No. We can't leave ourselves an out," Kenneth said. "It would be too easy to cut our losses and walk away. Either we're committed or we're not."

Kenneth called their stockbroker and told him to sell everything.

"Everything? Are you sure you don't want to – "

"All of it" Kenneth said. "Now."
"We're on our way," Simon said.
"Yeah," Kenneth said, "but I don't want to be an innkeeper."
"Who's going to do it, then?"
"How about Diane? She can run anything."

*

"A hotel?" Diane liked these guys but sometimes they reached way beyond their limits.

"Right. A small hotel," Kenneth said. "A nice dining room, a tavern, and a garden where people could sit with a drink or eat dinner in the summertime, all in a quaint little Vermont river town."

"I don't know the first thing about running a hotel. Why me?"

"You've run our events, you've stage-managed plays. They all require a sense of orderliness and an attention to detail. That's what we want, good service and a smooth operation."

"You're kidding about this, right?"

"Not at all," Kenneth said. "We're going to restore the building and we want it to be a class act. You can pick the chef, you can hire and train the help, you can run it and have 49% of the business."

"…and…"

"…and that's it," Kenneth said.

"We're talking classy, not snooty," Simon jumped in. "A mix of offerings – down-home stuff as well as some high-end choices, maybe game when it's in season. Fresh, clean, a variety of things from week to week, not to mention some decadent desserts. It's about making it interesting and fun and comfortable but well done. It's got to be attractive enough to lure people out of the city for a weekend but comfortable and affordable enough that the locals will use it, too."

"Well…"

"You'll work with Clancy Matthews, our architect and project manager to get it ready."

Diane sipped her wine.

"Salary?"

"Negotiable. Fair but negotiable."

"The hotel was built in the mid-1800s," Kenneth said, trying to make it more attractive. "We're going to make it as retro as we can but technically up to date."

"Can I get back to you?" she asked.

"Of course. You should come up to see the place and meet with Clancy so she can include your ideas in the work."

Diane just smiled and shook her head.

"You guys ..."

*

"So," Simon said as they unpacked the car in Grants Ferry later that night, "are we Vermonters now?"

"I am," Kenneth said, "but I was born here. Some people make it after three or four generations. Some never do."

"Well, damn."

"I don't make the rules," Kenneth said. "People keep track. You think you're home free and then one day you'll hear a remark that lets you know they haven't forgotten. The only people who won't care will be other people from someplace else."

"What's the point?"

"I don't know. Sometimes I think they just need to remind you that they have something you can never have, the right to be called a Vermonter. You can mix and play and have a good time and people will like you but everything you do will pass through that window."

"Well, damn," Simon said again.

"You'll be fine. Just don't be surprised when it happens."

*

The truck arrived around noon. Simon's pots and pans and utensils came into the kitchen, the wine went down to the root cellar, their bedroom set went upstairs, and the rest went temporarily to the barn. In less than an hour Kenneth had thanked the moving guys, gave them each a $50 tip, and they were gone.

"Well, that didn't take long, did it?" Simon said. "Probably take more than a week now to sort it out. See if you can find some glasses. I'm going down for a bottle of wine." He returned with a bottle of Merlot. Kenneth had unwrapped a soft cheese they'd brought from New York and was wiping dust from the glasses when Ellen knocked on the back door.

"I saw the moving van."

"Come and gone," Kenneth said. "We were just about to mark the occasion with a glass of wine. Come on in." He wiped a third glass as Simon pulled the cork and sniffed the open bottle.

They set out plates and knives and opened a packet of thin crackers. "We'll just have to make do with Fanny's dishes and cutlery until we get unpacked and settled," Simon said. "So much depends on presentation. This is almost embarrassing. I mean, paper napkins?" He poured the wine.

"Welcome home," Ellen said. She raised her glass to them and then sipped the wine. "Oh…" She took another sip and they watched as she discovered the different levels and flavors. "So this is good wine?"

"It's quite good, yes," Simon said.

"I've never understood what all the fuss was about but – and this is just from grapes?"

"All from grapes," Kenneth said. "Different varieties are often blended together, but, yes, all grapes."

"But it tastes a bit like – well, like blackberry or plums…"

"I know," Kenneth said. "I've never heard anyone say it tastes like grapes."

"…and the cheese, what is that?

"Brie. Cheese and wine," Simon said, "a classic combination."

"Very nice," she said. She read the label on the wine bottle and then found the wrapper for the cheese to note the names.

"You won't find these at Paul's," Simon said.

"No kidding. I'll want to remember them, though. One day…"

"We'll be going back and forth," Simon said. "We can keep you supplied. Oh, Ben loved your pottery. He said he could get three times what you're selling them for. He'll take anything you can send down before Christmas."

"Wow. I have a few more things. I'll be able to do a lot for next season, though."

"He'll be waiting."

"Who could we get to do some carpentry and plumbing here at the house?" Kenneth asked.

"I've just hired Earl Stebbins from up in Windsor to help with the shop. He's very good. Even Archie says so. What are you going to do?"

"Bathrooms and kitchen, mostly. Move a couple doorways, some plumbing. I can do the decorating but not the construction."

"Earl's at the store most every day. Stop by and talk to him."

"Thanks."

"Oh, a trailer showed up behind the hotel the other day. Have they started?"

"Not until the first of the year. Seems like a long time but Clancy says it's realistic. She's managed successful projects before, much more complicated than this one. How's the store coming? Archie must know about it by now."

"Oh, he knows. He was a little annoyed that I'd hired Earl. Archie's crew probably could have done it cheaper, but I wasn't going to hire his guys anyway."

"Good for you."

"I'll put a few things in the windows by Thanksgiving." She finished her wine. "Now what is that again?"

"Merlot," Simon said. "Round and soft. Think Marilyn Merlot."

*

"You suggested we might form a corporation."

They were in Increase's office.

"Oh, yes. It's mostly just filing some papers."

"Good. We want to call it K&S Enterprises, vague enough to cover all eventualities without committing to anything in particular."

"Very well."

"Now, will K&S Enterprises be a vehicle to manage the trust and the properties?"

"As soon as the conditions in the will have been met."

"But as a management tool…"

"Yes, as a management tool, it would be a good thing."

"And after the first of the year, we want to put Luther on full time.

"Full time?"

"That's right. If we don't go into this as if we're going to win, we'll lose. There's really no other way to do it."

*

"I just don't have the time, Kenny."

"It's not on top of your other work. We want you to work for us full time. One job, one paycheck to take care of Fanny's places so we don't have to worry about them."

"Well, I – Archie – "

"This isn't about Archie, Luther," Simon told him.

"Well, I – "

"We'll get you a truck and some equipment," Kenneth said. "You can give your notice and start the New Year with a new job."

"And work clothes," Simon said. "We'll set you up with a uniform company, too. A fresh outfit every morning, haircut every two or three weeks, clean shave every day. What do you think?"

"How about it, Luther? Sound like a deal?"

"Well, I – "

"And medical and dental," Simon said. "We'll have insurance for both you and your wife. Does Archie do that for you?"

"No, but…"

"Then it's time you had it."

If it were anyone but Kenny making this offer he'd be extremely suspicious.

"But there just ain't that much work."

"There will be and we want you set up and ready."

"Well, I appreciate it, but it seems like too much for – "

"Look," Kenneth said, "when my parents were killed I had nobody. Their stuff would have all been sold or thrown out if you hadn't helped me keep it and you never treated me like a kid. You've had this coming for a long time. I'm only sorry it took so long."

"But – "

"Simon and I need someone we can depend on. We take care of the people who work for us. We always have. And part of that is to make sure you don't worry about things like teeth or glasses or your health. You get whatever you need. You take care of yourself and then you can take care of us."

*

Kenneth and Simon made the rounds to introduce themselves to the tenants in the rest of Fanny's properties. Kenneth tried to assure them that broken things would get fixed, maintenance would be done, and everything would remain pretty much as it had been before Fanny died. Not everyone was convinced.

"You gonna put us out?" Annabelle Sweeney spoke as if she were calling to you from the next room. "We been here since we were married, you know."

"I didn't know that," Kenneth said.

"Douglas bought the house in the fall of 1951," she said. "We was married the next spring. We always lived here. Fanny said we could stay."

"There's nothing to worry about, Annabelle. Simon and I might want to paint the outside or tidy up the yard, though. Would that be all right?"

"Don't upset my lilies," Annabelle warned. "I got my lilies. I don't want my lilies upset."

"Luther's going to look after things for us. We'll be sure to tell him."

"Good man," Douglas Sweeney said, this being the first time he'd spoken.

"You gonna put us out?" Annabelle asked again. "Fanny said we could stay."

"I know."

"I don't want my lilies upset. You tell Luther."

"You don't have to worry about the lilies."

"Good man, Luther," Douglas Sweeney said again as they left.

Back in the car Simon asked, "What are we going to do with those two?"

"We'll work around them as long as we can. Just mind the lilies."

"That place would make a great B&B."

"I know. Those two must both be in their eighties by now. In the grand scheme of things, it shouldn't be a long wait."

"Jesus, that's sick."

"We could send Dennis around to measure them up, drop a few hints…"

"Christ, what is that, some kind of rustic humor?"

"Vermont 'pre-need'," Kenneth said.

They had similar visits to the other properties. All seemed to be in sound shape and everyone appreciated that Luther would clean their driveways following a snowstorm and mow the grass in the summer. Nothing comes without a price, however, and the inevitable scent of change lingered long after Kenneth and Simon had gone.

*

"You invited them for Thanksgiving?"

"Yes, I did, and don't raise your voice."

"Christ, it's a family day," Archie said. "Why're you invitin' those two?"

"In the first place, Janet's not coming this year because they're going to Harry's folks instead. In the second place, Kenneth and Simon have no family here and they'd be alone. In the third place, I want to."

"Huh," Archie snorted.

"I invited them, they're coming, and you're going to behave as if it was your idea."

*

"Thanksgiving dinner with Archie Whitaker? Isn't that an oxymoron?"

"Oh, stop it." Simon said. "Ellen said their son and his family are going to be there. We're taking wine and pie."

"You made pie?"

"I don't want to talk about it."

"Apple?"

"It was going to be…"

"Mince?"

"I don't want to talk about it."

"What are we taking for wine?"

"The Pinot."

"The Russian River Pinot? For Archie Whitaker? Jesus."

"He may gargle with it for all I care, but I promised Ellen some good stuff and we're taking the Pinot. Get over it."

*

The day began in the low twenties and had not warmed by the time they arrived. A stiff wind came up the hill from the river and took their breath away when they got out of the car. At the door Archie behaved as if Kenneth and Simon were some of the best friends he'd seen in a while. Hank sniffed their shoes. The house was filled with aromas of roasting turkey and onions.

Archie put the pie on the buffet with the other desserts, took the wine and their coats, and then led them straight to an assortment of liquors he'd set out on the sideboard.

"I go straight for the Jack Daniels, myself," he said. There was a glass on the sideboard with some in it already. Archie slopped in a bit more. "Just help yourselves. If you'd rather have beer it's in the refrigerator." He added the Pinot Noir to the collection.

Kenneth and Simon declined the drinks but Archie retrieved his and led them into the living room where his son, Mark, was watching a football game. Mark got up and shook hands during the introductions but his interest was clearly on the TV.

"And this is Hannah," Archie said. "Isn't she just about the cutest thing you ever saw?" A small blonde girl about 6 or 7 was busy with a coloring book on the floor. She looked up when she heard the voices but went straight back to work. "Takes after her mom," Archie said, "but sometimes I see a little of Ellen in there. My side seemed to take a back seat in that one." He seemed to find that quite funny as he took their coats to the tree in the front hall.

"And Kristen, Mark's wife," he said when he came back. "She's out in the kitchen with Ellen gettin' the last of the meal together. Let's see how they're doin'."

The kitchen was hot and steamy. Both women wore aprons. Kristen was mashing potatoes. Ellen was happy and glowing.

"Hi, guys. Almost ready."

Archie called out introductions to Kristen from the door and then turned back to Kenneth and Simon.

"Eighteen-pounder this year," he said, meaning the roasted turkey that was resting on the counter. "I'll have to carve that sucker up in a few minutes. Whyn't you fellas go in and sit? Put your feet up."

"Actually," Simon said, "I'd like to see if I can help in there." He went on into the kitchen.

"I guess they're all alike, aren't they?" Archie said to Kenneth, meaning the women, which in this case included Simon.

"They seem to be," Kenneth agreed. It seemed an odd observation, but strangely accurate. "Comes in handy, though, don't you think?"

"Hah! You're right about that," Archie said. "Sure I can't get you somethin' to drink?"

"On second thought," Kenneth said as he found himself alone with Archie, "I haven't had bourbon in a while."

"Good man," Archie said. "Bourbon. A drink with balls. Help yourself."

As soon as Kenneth had a glass in his hand, Archie felt that at least 90% of his hosting duties were complete and he was able to relax. The chatter came at a slower pace and a lower pitch. No matter what he was talking about – he never asked questions – Kenneth could respond with occasional nods and agreements without actually listening. After a few minutes Ellen called Archie to carve the turkey.

"Just make yourself to home," Archie said.

Left to himself, Kenneth decided to investigate the photos on the walls. Most were of the children and grandchildren through various ages. The ancestor wall was in the hallway. Parents, grandparents, and old photos of people in what were probably their best clothes. They stood in front of their houses or their cars. There was a wonderful photo of Ellen's parents standing beside what Kenneth thought might be a pre-war roadster with the top down. Her father had his foot on the running board. It was a trip back to the 30s, the 40s, and even the early 50s. Other photos going up the stairway seemed to be a record of past events that Ellen, and occasionally Archie, had participated in as young people.

There was a snapshot of Ellen and himself, taken at some sort of picnic when they were in high school. They were on a blanket and Ellen was holding a half-eaten ear of corn. She was smiling, happy. Kenneth couldn't remember the event.

The photo was in a grouping of others with him in them. Sometimes he was alone, sometimes with Ellen, occasionally in a group of other kids. He'd not even known those moments had been recorded but Ellen had somehow found the photos and framed them. He dragged his finger across the top of one of the frames and brought away a thin ring of dust. They'd not gone up recently.

"There you are," Ellen said. "We're about to sit down."

"These pictures…"

"Nice, huh? Come. Sit. We'll talk later."

Ellen asked Kenneth and Hannah to sit at her end of the table. Archie was at the far end where he could put pieces of turkey on the plates as they were passed. Hank had been given a small meal of his own and was content to catch a few Zs on his bed in the kitchen.

Archie's hosting skills were commendable, if limited. He talked easily about things with which he was familiar and often had strong opinions about things of which he knew nothing. Mostly, though, he told stories of events that happened during the thirty years Kenneth had been away, the people who had moved, the ones who'd died, who married who, the increasing competition and the lower profit margins in the lumber business, the scant carpentry and repair work for his small construction crew, the difficulties of highway maintenance with a small budget, and the endless problems of trying to keep it all afloat as first selectman. Kristen enjoyed Archie's stories but Mark had heard them all before and decided to get his share of the wine and concentrate on his meal so he could get back to the TV and the ball game.

Archie not only agreed to a glass of the wine but declared it to be quite tasty.

"'Member Charlie Perkins?" Archie said, as he spooned up another helping of mashed potato and stuffing.

"Vaguely."

"Had that gimpy finger on his left hand."

"Oh, yeah," Kenneth said. No idea who Archie was talking about.

"Cornered a bear half way up the mountain, oh, ten, maybe eleven years ago now."

"A bear?" Simon said. "Here?"

"Oh, they're around," Archie said. "We just don't see 'em much."

"You never mentioned bears," Simon said to Kenneth.

"I've never seen a bear, here or anyplace else."

"Oh, they're around," Archie said again. "So anyway, Charlie corners this bear. He was after a big buck people had seen up there that year but it was bear season, too. Usually, you know, bears run off to avoid you, but this one was up against some rocks and had no place to go and bears hate that. Meanwhile, Charlie figures baggin' a bear is as good as gettin' that big buck so he raises his gun and it jams. Not even a click when he pulls the trigger. Now bears don't like things pointed at them, either, so the bear charges over to explain this to Charlie, see, in that nasty way bears have, and all Charlie's got for his defense now is this jammed gun. So he grabs the gun by the barrel and when the bear jumps at him Charlie brings the rifle around like a club and conks the bear over the head with it. 'Course that shakes the jam loose and the gun goes off and shoots Charlie in the stomach."

"Jesus," Simon said and put his fork down.

"Made an awful mess of him, bein' that close and everything. Burnt him, too."

Simon looked across the table at Kenneth. Kenneth just shrugged and smiled as he wiped a piece of turkey through a puddle of gravy.

"Eddie Harris was up there and heard the shot," Archie continued, "and then he hears Charlie yelling. Eddie's about a quarter of a mile away but he runs over and finds Charlie on the ground with a big hole in him. Blood all over. Eddie ripped up jackets and stuff so he could wrap Charlie up with a kind of pressure bandage he learned about in Vietnam and then he dragged Charlie out of the woods, loaded him into the car and drove him to the hospital down to Springfield. Eddie said later he never saw no sign of the bear. 'Course we only had Charlie's word for that," Archie said as he ladled gravy over the potatoes and stuffing, "so it could be he just made up that part."

"Is Charlie still hunting, then?" Simon asked as if he were really interested.

"No, no. Walks all bent over – hard to look up, you know," Archie said. "Don't go into the woods anymore."

"Fascinating," Simon said.

Thanks to the bourbon Kenneth just let the scene play out. He and Archie were thrown together now by circumstance and their connection to Ellen. The years had worn their edges away and each seemed willing, in spite of their mutual distrust, to maintain a level of cordiality that allowed Ellen to relax. The Charlie Perkins story aside, it had been a rather pleasant afternoon.

Coffee was served with three choices of pie, chocolate cake, a bread pudding, and a plate of sharp cheese.

"What kind of pie is this?" Kristen asked.

"I don't want to talk about it," Simon said.

Finally they could do no more. Archie stood and stretched.

"Well, whadya say we head on into the living room while the women take care of all this?" he said to the men.

"Good idea," Kenneth said. He and Simon both helped carry things to the kitchen where Kenneth rolled up his sleeves and went to work at the sink.

Ellen and Kristen and Simon put the food away. Ellen had a dishwasher but Kenneth washed and rinsed everything. Simon and Kristen wiped them dry and Ellen put them away. Kenneth was bent over the sink to scrub the corners of the roasting pan when Ellen put her arms around him, pressed against his back, and lay her cheek on his shoulder. It was a full minute before she spoke.

"I've missed you terribly," she whispered.

"I know."

"This is the nicest Thanksgiving I've had in a long, long time."

Meanwhile, in the living room, Archie had cornered Mark and delivered a detailed account of the bazaar just past. To Mark it sounded the same as all the years before except for the addition of Fanny's funeral which he thought should be an annual feature. It always seemed as if the festival ran their lives for at least nine months of the year. Archie had just begun to run through the winners of the raffle when the kitchen crew arrived, still damp from the cleanup.

"Well," Archie said as they came in, "'course we got some new blood now. Kenny just moved back. Left long before you were born, you know."

Something in that remark caused the penny to drop and Mark took a longer look at Kenneth. He now recognized the kid in the photos.

"Kenny? You're in the pictures out in the hall."

"Afraid so."

"Huh." *So this is the guy*, Mark thought. "Mom used to tell us about when you were kids."

"Well, that was a long time ago."

"Fanny Forbes left all her property to him," Archie said.

"Really?"

"Quite a haul, I'd say," Archie said.

"Well, if you knew Fanny at all," Kenneth said, "you'll appreciate that she attached some strings."

"Strings?" Kristen hadn't spent much time in Grants Ferry and wouldn't know about Fanny.

"Basically, in order to inherit the estate, I have to restore and open The Intercourse House within a year."

"Whoa," Mark said. "In a year?"

"That's right."

"Can you do it?"

"We think so," Kenneth said

"And if you don't get it done on time?"

"I lose everything, including any money I've put into it."

"Jesus," Mark said, "and you're willing to risk everything for The Intercourse House? In Grants Ferry?"

"Well, if I don't do it or if I fail, the entire estate, the hotel, all Fanny's houses and the Rogers farm, goes to Jerry Falwell and T*he Old Time Gospel Hour*."

"Oh, that's awful," Kristen said.

Archie covered his smile with his hand.

"No," Kenneth explained. "That's Fanny."

*

Chapter Fifteen

The temperature dropped, the wind blew, and the ground froze solid after Thanksgiving.

"What is it with this cold?" Simon said.

"We've only had a few cold nights," Kenneth explained. "Wait until it gets down to minus 30 or so and doesn't get above freezing all day."

"What do people do here, hibernate?"

"No, we just get on with it. Builds character."

"Horse shit."

"It tests our mettle. I know people who like to claim the lowest overnight temperature. It proves they've suffered just a bit more than anyone else."

"And that's how they entertain themselves? Jesus, there's nothing going on here. What do people do, anyway?"

"Now there's TV I suspect the birth rate has dropped…"

Luther had brought a load of firewood and Kenneth had reacquainted himself with the wood stove in the living room. They made an occasional foray to Springfield or Windsor to get groceries but spent most of their time stripping wallpaper, patching and priming to be ready for the final re-decorating they would do when the carpentry was finished in the spring. Earl Stebbins had agreed to begin when he'd finished with Ellen's shop sometime after the new year.

Clancy had been absent and silent all through November. Kenneth finally gave her a call the first week in December.

"Hey, Kenneth. I'll have the plans finished next week, maybe Wednesday." she said. "I'll drive up so you can give the final okay."

"Good. Any problems?"

"Not really. I think it all works quite well. Wednesday, then?"

"That's fine."

Despite Clancy's cheerful confidence Kenneth was anxious. Two full months were nearly gone from his one year window and it would be another month before the real work would start. Losing those three months seemed like a huge handicap.

He called Diane.

"Clancy's going to be here next Wednesday. Come on up and get a look at the hotel, check out the town."

"Does it ever occur to you two that I might have a life here?"

"Of course," Kenneth said. "But Clancy's got the plans and the work schedule. We can put you up overnight so – "

"All right, all right. Jesus. You got decent wine?"

"We brought our stash from New York."

"Do I get to pick?"

"You get to pick. We don't have any decent cheese, though."

She arrived the following Tuesday afternoon with an overnight bag, a basket full of cheese and crackers, and a couple of baguettes from a bakery they all liked.

"Could you guys find a place any further out of the way?"

"You haven't seen some of the places in the top of the state," Kenneth said. "I think that's one of the potential attractions of Grants Ferry. It seems like it's more remote than it really is. I think we could play on that. It's like stepping back in time."

"It may be at that. Let me see the wines." Kenneth took her to the cellar while Simon set out a selection of cheese and crackers. Diane brought a bottle of Dry Creek Old Vine Zinfandel upstairs and handed it to Simon to open. "You both realize, don't you, that I haven't agreed to anything?"

"Oh, of course, of course," Kenneth and Simon said in unison.

"I just wanted to see what sort of a fix you'd found yourself in, that's all."

"Of course, of course," they said again as Simon poured the wine.

"Everybody back home thinks you guys are out of your minds."

"Of course, of course."

"Well. Cheers. Nice wine. What I want to know is, how the hell did you end up with all this?"

Kenneth told the story. He told it while they worked their way through the Zinfandel. He told it while he showed her to her room. He told it as he gave her a tour of the house while Simon put supper together. He told it while they sat in the living room soaking up the heat being thrown off the wood stove.

"And you actually think this will work. I mean, even assuming you get it done on time? I mean, and then what?"

"We've got to work on that. I think with enough promotion the tavern and the dining room can pay the bills but long term we'll need visitors and new businesses in town." He described the other properties in the estate, the applications for historic buildings and districts, and the potential at the Ellis Rogers farm. They opened another bottle of wine to go with supper and the evening finally wound down around 10:30. Diane hugged them both before she went upstairs.

"I don't know whether you've lost your minds or not," she said, "but it's good to see you again."

Kenneth washed up the last of the dishes.

"I think she'll come around," he said.

"What makes you think that?"

"She dropped everything to come up here, didn't she?"

*

Clancy burned into town Wednesday morning. Kenneth introduced Diane as their hotel manager.

"What do you mean, hotel manager?" Diane said. "I haven't agreed to anything.

"The day's young. You haven't seen the plans or the hotel."

Clancy had two rolls of drawings, spreadsheets, bar charts, and a list of expenses so far which included some financial requirements to get the contractors committed.

"But they haven't even begun," Kenneth said.

"That's true," Clancy said, "but they're on retainer. Once you've paid them they're obligated. I've worked with these people before. They're good, they're reliable, they're flexible, and if we're going to bet the farm, these are people we want on our side. You have all the permits?"

"Increase sent them over the other day."

"Good."

Clancy unrolled the plans for the construction of the new second floor bathrooms. On paper, at least, it looked simple enough.

"All totally modern in function," she said, "but the fixtures are either authentic period pieces or are as close as we can get. It will have the feel of an old, elegant hotel from about 1900 with the convenience and creature comforts of most new ones." She'd included some interior sketches. Each bathroom had a clawfoot tub, a large pedestal sink, and an antique mirror. There was wainscoting all around, marble flooring, and generous shower stalls hidden behind partitions so they didn't take away from the old time feel of the rooms. "The wiring and plumbing will be a bit tricky but it's all possible with, I think, a minimum of demolition. We can even reproduce some of the original wood trim around the new doorways if we can't salvage enough from the ones we remove."

Simon was impressed. "Nice," he said. "Very retro."

"And it can be done in time?" Kenneth asked for the eighth or ninth time. He was more interested in time frame than the artistic merits of the bathroom plans.

"If everything goes perfectly," Clancy said, "we should have you ready to open by mid-September, three weeks before the place turns into a pumpkin."

"Does it ever go perfectly?"

"Well, no, but that's the schedule. I've blocked it out with extra time for unforeseen complications or delays. There's always something that we can't control but I don't think anything will hold us up for long. The contractors know the situation and they're all sympathetic. They'll rise to the challenge."

"Okay," Kenneth said, although he didn't share her confidence.

"Get checks out to these people in the next day or two. I've got verbal agreements from them because they know me but the cash locks them in."

The business talk wound down. Diane had been silent through the entire presentation and discussion.

"So you think this project is viable when it's completed?" she asked.

"Well, that's really not my department," Clancy said. "The building itself can be brought to life again, modernized to current safety standards, etc., but that's really the end of my role here."

"But you've seen the success of other projects, right?"

"Well, yes," Clancy said, "but none of them, frankly, was as isolated as this from other points of interest that would support the facility when it was finally in use."

"I see."

"The hotel needs to be part of a bigger destination. From a project manager's perspective, those plans should be in development now."

"I agree," Diane said.

"I'm sure we can have the physical work done on time. That's my job. But I can tell you that in my work the most important and frequent question I ask is, '...and then what?' Those are the answers you need."

Kenneth watched Diane carefully. He knew her mind was working furiously as she tried to get a sense of it all.

"I think we ought to pay a visit to the hotel and show Diane around," he said.

"Okay," Clancy agreed, "but then I've got to head back and get ready to move here for the duration. Do you have a spare room?"

"Of course," Kenneth said. "We're having some work done this spring, though. It may be a bit rough and dusty for a while."

"No problem. I can chip in toward food."

"Don't worry about food," Simon said. "Just get that damned hotel finished."

"Once it's started, you'll be amazed," she said.

They gave Diane the tour of the hotel. Simon tried again to get Clancy to stay. He'd have felt much better if they could all just hang out together for a while – lunch at Dot's Diner or anything social and not about business – but Clancy was set in her plans. Once they were done at the hotel she got in her car and drove away.

"Sold yet?" Kenneth asked Diane.

"Not yet. Show me the rest of the town."

The common was colorless, not a good time to sell a dream. A few inches of snow would give it some New England charm but it was spare and bleak in the winter sun. The Valiant chugged around the common, and then down the main street. They drove by each of the other of Fanny's properties and then finally out to the farmland where they led Diane out to the hilltop to look east over the river valley.

"There's something like 650 acres here altogether," Kenneth said. "It's not available until Ellis Rogers dies or retires, but there's nothing to say we can't make plans."

"What do you have in mind?"

"Oh, a golf course, maybe a marina and restaurant down by the river, cross-country ski and hiking trails through the woods, maybe turn the farm buildings into some sort of retreat or small conference center…"

"And the hotel?"

"Without the hotel restored and open by the second week of October next year none of the rest matters."

Diane shook her head slowly as she tried to imagine what they'd taken on.

"You guys," she said.

"Are you on board, then?"

"It would be fun, wouldn't it? Still…"

"If you move up shortly after the work begins on the hotel, you can co-ordinate with Clancy, get the details and fittings you want. Get some basic training about the hospitality business, and do it."

"Oh, sure. Easy for you to say."

"You can have the final say over the interior decorating, the menus, the training of the help, all of it."

"Okay, okay. I got the picture. I need some time."

"Clancy will be here right after the holidays."

"Okay, okay. I just don't want to wake up in a nightmare."

"I think I'm finally getting a sense of what a risk this really is," Kenneth said after she'd gone.

"Finally?"

"You saw the place. They're not even starting until January. I mean, that's three months gone."

"I know."

"Couldn't they have been doing something? Tearing out, cleaning up – something?"

"Well, she's got all those plans and the schedule's blocked out, she's got builders lined up. They haven't exactly been idle."

"Yeah, but the ticking clock hasn't been idle, either."

*

"Whadya mean you're goin' to work for Kenny?" Archie yelled. Luther knew this would happen. "What about the three jobs you've got? Don't they keep you busy enough?" Archie sometimes pretended to be dense in order to get his way. "Those two are only here temporary, you know," Archie said, meaning Kenneth and Simon. "They'll spend a bunch of money try'n to fix that old hotel and they'll fail and then they'll be gone and you'll be left with nothing because somebody else will have those jobs you got now."

"Could be," Luther said, although Archie was making a good point, one that had crossed Luther's mind several times.

"And whoever tries to salvage the mess they've made – don't expect them to keep you on. You got somethin' steady here with the town, long as you want it. You know that."

"That's right," Luther said. "And I don't want it anymore. I'll work through the holidays, then I'm working for Kenny."

"He's got a way of disappearing in the middle of the night, you know. Thirty years at a time."

"I know that," Luther said. "I trust Kenny."

"Well, you're a damn fool, then."

Now Luther was pissed. Archie had no cause to say that about Kenny.

"The way I see it," he said, "I've only got a few years left." He took a couple breaths. "I'd like to have one good job in my life where I'm not putting in sixty or more hours a week."

"Sixty hours? You don't put in no sixty hours."

"How do you know? I get paid flat rate."

"I know it's not no sixty hours' worth, what you do."

"Well, you'll find out when you hire somebody else," Luther said. "I'm done come January."

*

"What the hell are you two doin', hirin' Luther away?"

"We need the help," Kenneth said. He and Simon stood in the side doorway and had no intention of letting Archie inside.

"He's been helpin' you, just like he helped Fanny," Archie said. "That always seemed to work out all right. Who the hell's gonna take care of the town hall and the church? And the school?"

"The Lord will provide," Simon said "He's provided for us, after all, and I'm sure he'll provide for you if you just open your heart a teeny bit."

"Just what are you two up to?"

"I think it could be described as protecting Fanny's investments," Kenneth said.

"Glad to hear it. Why in hell can't you do it without Luther?"

"We probably could, but Luther's who I want."

"Everything was going fine until you guys showed up. I never thought I'd see the day I'd miss Fanny," Archie grumbled.

"Well, there you go."

Simon crowded through the doorway to get between Archie and Kenneth. Archie stepped back. He wasn't going to let Simon grab his arm again.

"Will there be anything else, sir?"

"No," Archie said. "No, I guess not."

"We should all get to work, then."

"And I appreciate that," Archie said. "That's good."

Kenneth pushed through the doorway again as Archie walked to his truck.

"Merry Christmas, Archie."

*

"Archie was upset," Luther said.

"Yeah, well, he'll get over it," Kenneth said. "It's time we got you some equipment."

The three of them squeezed into the Kitchen Blue Valiant and drove to Keene, where, following Luther's advice about brands, sizes, and features, they bought a Chevrolet 1500 pickup with a plow and frame, a two-stage snow-blower, some shovels, brooms, and a low bed trailer to haul things around.

"In the spring we'll get you a lawn mower, a weed eater, a leaf blower and – you know – summer stuff, but this will be a start."

"Seems like a lot, Kenny," Luther said. "I mean, I got along for years without – "

"These things make you more efficient," Kenneth said. "and you won't have to work as hard. We want to set a new standard. Raise the bar, you know what I mean?"

"But you don't even own these places yet."

"That's right."

"And you might not?"

"That's true."

"Well, I mean you're spendin' all this money when – "

"We have to behave as if we're going to win," Kenneth said.

"You think you will?"

"We haven't got a worry in the world, okay?"

"Yeah, I guess so."

"We've got big plans."

"You do?"

"Doesn't matter."

*

"This dark and quiet is getting on my nerves," Simon said one night.

"I find it rather peaceful."

"It's not peaceful. Rigor mortis has set in. Everything shuts down after supper. Nobody's out after nine o'clock. What do people do here?"

"Relax. Go to bed early."

"Well part of our plan is going to be a satellite dish, I can tell you that. I've had enough Vermont Public Radio, I'm sick of our CDs, and it's too cold to go outside. I can see why you left."

"That wasn't the reason at all."

"Well, it's reason enough. I can't do a whole year of this."

*

"Ellen called," Kenneth said. "She wants to know if we'll go to the Christmas Eve service. As a student of native customs I thought you might be interested."

"Will it be as lively as Fanny's funeral?"

"Carols, candles, a pageant performed by little kids. Ellen and I played Mary and Joseph when we were in the fourth grade."

"Awww…"

"Ellen says they still use the same script."

"Awww… Of course we have to go."

Ellen had saved a place for them. Archie didn't attend church services. Carols played softly as people filed in. The pageant began and the lights dimmed save for the platform in front where the story would play out, told through alternating carols and scriptures. The children had no speaking parts. If there were any changes from the time he played Joseph all those years ago, Kenneth couldn't identify them, but the costumes had been upgraded and the animals now had paper mache heads. Mary, heavy with child, arrived with Joseph. They're turned away from the inn, of course, and end up in the stable. Ellen took Kenneth's hand.

"This is where you comforted me," she whispered. "It was so real and I loved you so much I almost cried. Damn it, I'm going to cry now," she said, and dug into her pocket for a tissue.

The story finally came to an end and the congregation was hushed.

"Watch this," Kenneth whispered to Simon.

The lights were turned all the way off. A single candle burned at the front of the sanctuary. The Rev. Peter Rodman explained about the passing of the light and the organist began playing *Silent Night*. The congregation sang and the ushers came to the front to have the light passed to their candles. Each went up the aisle passing the light to the first person in each row who in turn passed it to the next. When everyone's candle was lit the choir, with their candles, began the procession to the back of the sanctuary, out the door, and into the night. The congregation followed, one row after the other. Outside a final verse was sung and then it was quiet.

"Peace be with you," the Rev. Rodman called, "and Merry Christmas!"

The candles were blown out and they all stood then, in the dark and cold and the peace of a winter night in Vermont.

Kenneth's arm was around Ellen's waist, holding her close.

"Wow," Simon said. "That was quite a moment."

"I cry every year," Ellen said, "even though I really don't believe it anymore."

*

The weather was cold and the ground had frozen but there had been very little snow, a disappointment for those who long for a white Christmas.

"Where the hell's all the snow?" Simon said. "I thought we'd be up to our asses by now, something different to make it interesting."

"It's not over yet," Kenneth told him. "I remember one year when we had more trouble with mud than snow at Christmas. Christmas Day was in the mid-forties."

As if the weather gods heard Simon bitch, snow came on New Year's Eve and the storm continued for three days. It was dry snow. It didn't accumulate fast but the wind blew it into drifts and when it finally stopped there was a solid eighteen official inches on the ground. Luther barely got the driveway cleared for the final time on the afternoon of the third day when Clancy arrived.

Kenneth's old room had been emptied of Kenneth's childhood things, scrubbed down, and an assortment of Fanny's nostalgic photos and paintings were now on the walls. They'd brought in Kenneth's parents' bedroom set. It wasn't fancy by any means but it was clean and comfortable with a new mattress.

"Not much, I'm afraid," Simon apologized. "We're waiting to do the real decorating when Earl finishes and the dust settles."

"This is fine," Clancy said. "Very nice. Thank you."

"All you'll have for heat," Kenneth said, "is what comes up through that vent in the floor from the kitchen. It works best if you leave your door open. There are more blankets in the closet."

"I'll be fine."

"It's one thing to be cool and another when you can see your breath in the morning," Kenneth said. "However, Earl's assured us that we'll have a working bathroom and hot water every night."

A short time later, over a cup of coffee and some pastries Clancy had brought up from Boston, Kenneth finally asked about work on the hotel.

"The first crew is coming day after tomorrow. I'll get the last of my things in place, get some temporary heaters inside, get a dumpster on site, that sort of prep work. Has the snow been cleared?"

"Luther took care of it. If you need more, let us know."

"Good. I don't want my guys slowed down because they have to clear snow."

"Luther's available whenever you need him," Kenneth said.

"Perfect. This is going to be fun."

"Fun?" Kenneth asked.

"The challenge, the puzzle, the choreography, keeping people happy and productive, keeping everyone focused on the common goal. My chosen work. I love it."

*

Earl Stebbins stopped by several times to finalize the details of the work he and his crew would be doing. He arrived one morning just as Clancy was leaving.

"Earl," Kenneth said. "This is Clancy Matthews. She's overseeing the renovations of the hotel."

"That so?"

"Hi, Earl," Clancy said.

"Hi," he said. "You a contractor?"

"Architect. And I'm doubling up as project manager."

"Project manager?" To Earl work meant hands on, creating a product. Managers had found a way to get paid without producing anything.

"I keep things moving. I schedule the work, make the calls, coordinate the different trades to get the work done efficiently and on time. It's all about timing and keeping people on schedule. You do it on a smaller scale. Fewer players, but it's the same thing."

Earl wasn't convinced. There was something unsettling about a woman doing what he'd always assumed was a man's work.

"I got another week or so at Ellen's," he told Kenneth. "Then we'll get started over here. The more stuff you have out of the way the better."

"And we'll have a toilet and a tub or shower and hot water every night?"

"We'll build the new bathroom first, then the old one. Shouldn't be a problem."

"There, you see?" Clancy said. "Project management."

"I'll be damned," Earl said. He pulled a sheet of graph paper out of his clip board. "I was thinkin' it over and I sketched up another way to lay the bathrooms out."

"Wouldn't it work the way I had them?" Simon asked.

"Oh, your plan would work okay but I think this is just as good and it will be easier to connect to the old cast iron waste line so we won't have to upset so much downstairs," Earl explained.

"Wow," Simon said. "How'd you know that?"

"Well, when you been inside these places as much as I have you sort of develop a feel for it."

"Earl doesn't realize the value of his skills," Clancy said that night at supper. "He's a builder in the truest sense. He doesn't just see his job, he looks for ways to make it better. If I pay attention I might even learn something."

Luther helped move everything but essentials out to the barn for the duration. They sealed doorways to unaffected rooms to control the inevitable dust, and worked out how they would "live" while the house was torn up. Simon bought an industrial vacuum. Plaster dust, rat shit, and splinters would fill the air for weeks. No matter how careful and how fussy they were dust and dirt seeped everywhere as the work progressed. Walls were opened up and reframed, pipes were roughed in, the wiring done, and the walls closed up again. Simon spent over an hour with the industrial vacuum each evening in a futile attempt to stay ahead of it but there was always another fine coating on everything in the morning.

"Jesus. Maybe we should have rented a room someplace," Simon grumbled as his finger left a faint trail on what he'd thought was a clean plate.

"Oh, no," Kenneth said. Dust had settled on his juice, just in the short time since he'd poured it. "This is part of the fun."

*

Dot's place suddenly filled with a dozen strangers one morning around 9:30. The new people were big, loud, and covered in plaster dust. Dot rushed frantically to fill all the orders for pancakes, eggs, sausages, and cup after cup of coffee.

"Second breakfast for you fellas?"

"Naw, we don't really like to eat 'til we've woke up," one of them said.

"I don't usually get a crowd like this all at once. You gonna be around for a while?"

"Three. four weeks prob'ly. We get our piece done, another crew comes for the next step. You do lunch?"

"Oh, sure. Special today's beef stew and biscuits."

"Sounds good. We'll be back." They paid, left tips, squeezed out the door, and ambled back to the hotel.

"Well, wasn't that a surprise?" Dot said when she came by to top up Archie's coffee. She set the carafe on the table and wiped her forehead with her apron.

"Looks like work's started on the hotel."

"Sorry I let this go cold but I was running in circles for a while."

"S'okay," Archie said. "You're gonna want some help when they come back for lunch. Want me to make a couple calls?"

"That would be real sweet, Archie. See if Emily Squires and Helen Roberts can come in. I'll have to run over to Paul's for some beef and potatoes to bulk up the stew."

When the crew came back for lunch Dot was ready. These men were big and rough and loud and their eastern Massachusetts accents sounded crude and their voices were coarse, but they liked Dot's food, they appreciated the service, they tipped well, and they called out to thank everybody as they went back to work.

As much as Archie appreciated Dot's good fortune, he'd lost an important part of his day, the hour or so when he could quietly read his paper, drink his coffee, and sort through whatever was on his mind. This would continue through most of the summer, too, and it wasn't as if there were someplace else to grab a cup of coffee. Dot's was it. As long as the hotel was under construction, Dot and her diner would prosper. Archie wondered why he couldn't feel good about that.

*

Chapter Sixteen

"Town Meeting?"

"The purest form of government," Kenneth explained. "Anyone gets to speak and nearly everyone gets to vote."

"Even me?"

"You're a resident and you're registered. The town and the school budgets are discussed and voted on separately. There are also special items. Years ago, for instance, the decision to put the cannon on the common facing New Hampshire was decided at a town meeting."

"This is going to be great. This place is driving me crazy. It's time for a little excitement."

"Don't go in there and make a scene," Kenneth said.

"I can't imagine what you're talking about."

The large wood stove in the corner pumped out heat that would soon be unnecessary. In came the citizenry with baskets and dishes of food, ready to make a day of it.

"They're bringing food?" Simon said. "You didn't tell me we should bring food."

"I forgot. We all get potluck when we break for lunch."

"I should have fixed something."

"There's going to be more than enough and besides, we have no kitchen. Next year you can bring two."

Copies of the warning for the meeting with a list of all the articles that would be considered were available at the clerk's desk. A few people pored over it and made notes. For others it was just a day out. Women settled into their chairs with knitting or needlework. Two young mothers nursed their babies.

The selectmen huddled off to the side for some last-minute discussion and Ellen slipped into a chair beside Kenneth.

"Well, it's been a few years since we did one of these together."

"Quite a while," Kenneth agreed. "Doesn't look like much has changed."

"Same people, same issues, same complaints," she said.

"This is Simon's introduction to democracy."

"Really?"

"First time," Simon said. "Where I come from it's all done for us."

The church clock struck nine, Increase rapped the gavel, and another Vermont Town Meeting had begun.

"Go, Increase," Simon said.

"He's been moderator for years," Kenneth said, "probably the only person in town with any sense of Robert's Rules."

When the room was in order, Increase asked everyone to stand for the Pledge of Allegiance.

"I can't remember when I did this last," Simon said.

"Me either."

"I don't even remember the words."

"It'll come back."

Ellen recited it all with a clear voice and no hesitation.

"God, I feel like such a patriot," Simon said as they sat back down.

Ellen brought some knitting out of a bag, trailed by two strands of yarn. She pulled several arm lengths of yarn loose from the bag, counted some stitches, and the needles began to click as she added yet another row to what would become a small sweater.

Anna Gardner, the town clerk, read the minutes from last year's meeting. Increase asked for comments. A hand went up.

"Jesus. He's still at it," Kenneth said.

"Every year," Ellen said.

"Who's that?" Simon wanted to know.

"Bill Grover. Even when I was here he'd take time from every meeting to make some pissy correction. It shows he paid attention last year and he remembers details."

"I think Anna leaves deliberate mistakes so Bill can have his moment," Ellen said. "It's become a bit of a contest to see if he can find them all. I don't know who'll take that on when he's gone."

"That sounds like a job I'd like," Simon said.

"I'll put your name in," said Kenneth. "Meanwhile you might consider Inspector of Wood and Shingles and Weigher of Coal."

"Those are real jobs?"

“Still on the books and filled every year. Another interesting job is High Bailiff whose sole legal function is to arrest the sheriff if and when it becomes necessary and to then assume the sheriff's duties.”

“Damn. What a power play that would be.”

“I don’t know if we’ve ever needed the High Bailiff, do you Ellen?”

“I don’t think so.”

The minutes were approved as amended, and the meeting proceeded. Several housekeeping matters were presented, seconded, and passed without discussion.

Increase began to announce the next article in the warning when Homer Dalrymple stood to be recognized.

“Who’s that?” Kenneth asked.

“Homer Dalrymple,” Ellen said. “He’s an accountant, came to town a few years ago. Keeps people’s books, does taxes…”

“Mr. Moderator, it seems to me before we get to the other articles in the warning we should discuss the work being done to the hotel.”

Murmurs rolled around the room.

“I believe that falls under other business,” Increase said.

“Yes, I agree it’s other business,” Homer said, “but whatever’s going on at the hotel may well affect any or all of the other items. Only enlightened can we then act with full knowledge and confidence.”

“What’s going on?” Simon whispered.

“I’m not sure,” Kenneth said. He saw Archie smiling. “An accountant?” he asked Ellen.

“He’s also pastor to a small independent church he started down in the old Moose Lodge.”

“Oh, great.”

“Maybe a couple dozen people altogether.”

“Mr. Moderator,” Homer went on. “I think it’s obvious that the reopening of the hotel will bring changes to our quiet life in Grants Ferry. These changes may well affect us all. I only ask that we be advised as to the plans that we might act accordingly.”

“The chair will entertain a motion to take this discussion now instead of its proper place under other business.”

“So moved.”

“Second.”

“All in favor?”

“Aye.”

“Those opposed?”

“ _ ”

"Very well," Increase said. "The matter is open to discussion."

"Is Archie behind this?" Kenneth asked Ellen.

"He's not said anything but it sounds like him."

"...what the extent of these plans are." Homer Dalrymple was saying.

Kenneth stood.

"The chair recognizes Mr. Forbes."

"Very briefly," Kenneth said, "my Aunt Fanny died and her entire estate was left to me under several conditions." Murmurs in the hall. "The greatest of the conditions is that I must restore and reopen the Intercourse House within a year."

More murmurs.

"And that is your plan?" Homer asked.

"It is," Kenneth said.

"And should you fail to reopen the hotel within the specified time?"

"The entire estate, land and buildings, including the hotel, will then fall into the hands of Jerry Falwell and *The Old Time Gospel Hour*."

A loud buzz rose up and Increase banged it down with his gavel.

"Does that answer your concerns, then, Mr. Dalrymple?" Increase asked.

"Well, Mr. Moderator, it seems to me that we as a community are now faced with a dilemma, one we should consider carefully. If the hotel is indeed renovated and reopened, we might ask who will bring a greater benefit to this community, a great and powerful Christian organization led by a gifted Man of God or two sodomites who – "

Increase banged his gavel. "That's enough, Homer."

"We're at a moral crossroads, Mr. Moderator," Homer said, now solidly in his fire and brimstone preaching voice, "and as a community we must choose a path – "

"Sit down, you god damned fool!" a voice roared from the back of the hall. Kenneth turned to see who had shouted. It was not a voice he recognized and no one was standing. Increase banged on his gavel, ruled Homer Dalrymple out of order and declared the discussion closed.

"Wow," Simon said. "Who are the sodomites?"

"Quiet," Kenneth said.

Ellen giggled.

Archie continued to smile. True to his nature, he'd managed to get someone else to do the work while his hands remained clean.

Order had been restored, though, and Increase moved them through the warning, mostly special items that involved small amounts of money or agreements that would affect the final numbers in the town budget by the end of the day. One of these routine items was to award the road maintenance contract to Whitaker Bros. Trucking.

"What's that about?" Simon asked.

"Apparently there is no longer a highway department and they hire it out."

"To Archie?"

"That's right," Ellen said. "About twelve years ago."

"But Archie's a selectman, right?" Simon asked.

"Right," Kenneth said.

"And the selectmen voted to approve this and put it on the agenda?"

"I suppose so."

"So Archie's voting to give himself work? That sounds like conflict of interest." Kenneth shifted in his seat. This was not a conversation he cared to have while he was sitting next to Archie's wife. "I think we should ask about it," Simon said. His hand shot up.

"The chair recognizes Mr. Hirsh," Increase said before Kenneth could pull Simon's hand back down.

"Thank you, Mr. Moderator."

"Welcome to our small exercise in democracy, Mr. Hirsh."

"Yes, thank you. About the highway contract." Kenneth grabbed him again. "Stop grabbing my arm," Simon snapped. There was general laughter around the room. "I don't understand how these things work, but this contract, is that put forward by the selectmen?"

"Mr. Chairman," Increase said, addressing Archie.

Archie stood up. "That's correct," he said.

"And the highway contract is let to the Whitaker Brothers. Is that your construction company?"

"Me and my brother. That's right," Archie said.

"Is the contract put out to bid?"

"I can't recall that it was."

"And the entire board approves and recommends this contract with your company, Whitaker Brothers, including yourself?"

"That's right."

"Thank you." Simon sat back down.

"You should have let it go," Kenneth said.

"But – "

Kenneth nodded toward Ellen. "We're the new guys in town. This year we sit and listen."

Archie was still on his feet, his face was red.

"Mr. Moderator."

"Mr. Whitaker."

"The tone of those last questions suggests somethin's a little shady. I want to remind folks that twelve years ago this meeting decided to put the road work out to a private company. The selectmen offered it out and got no takers. That was when me and Arthur bought a couple new trucks, hired the fellas who had worked for the town, and took it on. We never made any money from it – ever. We bill for the time we work and we've always done it better and cheaper than it was done before. So I resent somebody suggestin' there's anything shady goin' on."

"Jesus," Kenneth muttered. "Why didn't you just poke him with a sharp stick?"

Archie sat back down, furious that his integrity had been questioned. And it hadn't come from somebody local, either. Outsider. Goddamned busybody. He sensed a change in the room. He'd risen to the bait, and defended something that shouldn't need defending. It would be at least another hour and twenty minutes before Increase would break for lunch. He wanted to get outside but instead he shuffled the papers in front of him, missed most of the discussion, and nearly missed the vote to approve the budget for next year.

They broke for lunch and Simon pulled Kenneth across the room to Increase.

"Simon, Kenneth," Increase smiled.

"Very interesting morning," Simon said. "I admire the way you control the room, Increase. You're very good."

"Well, It's the same tune every year. They just change the words a little."

"This Homer Dalrymple's an interesting man, isn't he?"

"I don't know that anyone takes Homer too seriously."

"...and his followers?"

"A few folks who appear to have found Jesus through Homer Dalrymple."

"Is he actually a minister?"

"Not mainstream. I can't say they've ever gone public until this morning."

"And about the highway contract," Simon said.

"Yes?"

"If Archie votes on a contract that goes to his own company isn't that conflict of interest?"

"In the purest sense, it might be," Increase said. He took a moment to choose his words. "But I've always taken the position that since the town as a whole votes in an article separate from the general budget as to whether we take them on again, even though he may have voted to put it on the warning, it was too fine a point."

"But, I – "

"You see, Simon, sometimes, in small towns with limited means, it's more important to get things done than it is to follow the letter of the law. In this case, the town was having trouble running the highway department after Morris Gibson died. Archie and his brother hired the crew and got the work done faster and better and cheaper than it had ever been done before. It works, so we haven't tried to fix it."

"Okay. Thanks, Increase."

"Anytime."

Kenneth and Simon got into the food line.

"What the hell are you doin'?" Archie loomed over both of them but he was glaring at Simon. Hank was at Archie's side.

"I just want to understand how it works, Archie, that's all."

"You suggestin' I'm doin' somethin' crooked?"

"No, no. Just wondering how things work in a small town."

"We all contribute is how it works," Archie said. "I put in hours and hours for this town. Unpaid. And all that highway work gets billed at cost. I've never taken money 'cept for expenses. You can check back as far as you want."

"No need for that. I'm fine."

"Just what we need," Archie said. "You guys comin' to town stirrin' things up."

"What about your Bible-thumping friend?" Simon asked.

"You mean Homer?"

"Yes. What's he got against the sodomites?"

"I – I guess you'll have to ask him about that," Archie said. People were watching him again. He and Hank pushed through the crowd and went outside to get some fresh air.

"Happy now?" Kenneth said.

"Yeah. Democracy in action." Simon poked at a casserole on the table. "What do you suppose this is?"

*

"Good afternoon, Mr. Hirsh." It was Judith Houghton. "Hello, Kenneth."

"Mrs. Houghton," Simon said. "What a delight."

"Have you enjoyed our town meeting?"

"Very interesting."

"And how do you find it interesting, Mr. Hirsh?"

"Well, aside from the brief diversion by Grants Ferry's moral compass, people appear to assemble as equals."

"I think you've grasped the concept rather well, Mr. Hirsh." She turned to Kenneth. "And you, Kenneth, are you comfortably back?"

"Quite comfortably. Thank you. We've not gone unnoticed, apparently, but it's been easier than I expected."

"And Fanny's house – I understand you're having some work done."

"Some upgrading and modernizing and decorating, yes."

"I think that's commendable. I'd like to see the result, if I might be so bold as to invite myself."

"Oh, yes," Simon jumped in. "We'll have a tea, High Tea, when everything is finished. You should come, too, Ellen. Won't this be fun, Kenneth? High Tea in the parlor with two of Grants Ferry's most elegant women."

Judith Houghton and Ellen were both blushing. Such open compliments were a rare thing in Grants Ferry. Increase treated Judith very well, but even he was frugal in this department. Archie, of course, had no clue.

"Shall we wear hats?" Judith Houghton was not above a bit of drama herself.

"Oh, yes. Big hats and gloves. One can't overdo High Tea."

Increase pounded the gavel to bring the meeting back to order.

"We'll send cards," Simon said. "Later in the spring or early summer. Watch for them."

"High Tea?" Kenneth said as he settled down again.

"With cucumber and watercress sandwiches, cakes, and clotted cream if we can find any. If we can't have fun with that parlor there's no point to any of this, is there?"

"Certainly not," Ellen smiled as she pulled the knitting out again.

"Did we bring Miss Manners?" Simon asked.

"She's around someplace," Kenneth said, "probably out in the barn. This seems like a lot of fuss."

"Of course it's a lot of fuss. You just paint and paper. I'll take care of High Tea."

"I'm not dressing up."

"You certainly are."

"In Grants Ferry, for Christ's sake?"

"Especially in Grants Ferry. Someone has to."

Ellen's knitting needles continued to click, one loop at a time. She was happier in this moment than she'd been in years.

*

"Well, that was a fascinating exercise in town government," Simon said the following Friday, "but I've had enough of the dark and the cold and rustic humor and the limited selection of groceries and eaten enough rat shit and plaster dust for a lifetime. It's time for a trip to the city."

"We've still got work to do on the house."

"Oh, this has been great fun and everything, but I've got to get back to civilization or I'm going to inflict harm on someone."

"I thought we went into this together."

"We're in the situation together, but it's your house, your hotel, your town, and your people. I need a break. I'm taking the Beemer. I'll do some shopping to restock the cupboards while I'm there."

"How long you gonna be gone?"

"I don't know, a week or two. Where are the keys?"

*

By Easter, workmen had tramped through the house for nine weeks. Simon had only succumbed to hysterics twice, once before he went to the city when a carpenter accidentally drove a nail into a water pipe that caused some water damage downstairs and again when the corner of a sheet of plywood had punched the wall going up the stairs the day after he got back. Neither episode was worthy of a tantrum but along with all the stress and dust and total lack of order through a Vermont winter, Simon had snapped and raged at anyone he saw.

"I'm not putting up with this shit," Earl Stebbins said. He and his crew picked up their tools and drove away. Kenneth came home from an errand, found them gone and called to see what was going on. When he put down the phone he was furious.

"You and your fucking tantrums," he yelled at Simon. "Get in the car right now, drive over to his house, apologize, and don't come back until you've cleaned this up."

"Clean what up?" Simon yelled back. "He's a carpenter, for Christ's sake. A hired gun. I'm not apologizing for his clumsy helpers."

"Get this straight," Kenneth said. "Earl's lived here all his life and you haven't. We need him to finish this place up a hell of a lot more than he needs the work. You find out where he lives, you go over there, and you kiss his ring and wash his feet if you have to, but clean it up and get him back here."

"All right. Jesus."

They'd not had a row like that in ten years and Simon had never seen Kenneth so angry. He called Ellen, got Earl's home address and drove to Walpole. When Edna Stebbins answered the door Simon had a bottle of red wine in one hand and a loaf of fresh baked bread in the other. Earl was in the living room with his slippers on, reading the paper. Simon offered profuse apologies, praised Earl up and down for his craftsmanship in front of Edna, invited her over to see what great work he'd done when it was finished, and promised to behave from now on.

"I really don't know what we would have done without him," he told Edna, making sure Earl heard it all. "Kenneth and I have no skill for that kind of work. Earl's a true craftsman. You should be very proud."

Edna Stebbins glowed but Earl was not an easy sell.

"Don't know much about wine," he said, making it clear this was not a gift he would have picked if he'd been given a choice. "Never cared for it much."

"This is a Petit Sirah," Simon explained, "from California. It's best with a meal, a roast beef dinner, for instance, or maybe venison." He was talking to Edna now. "A roast, root vegetables, and gravy. Wine like this can make a good meal even better."

Earl finally agreed to come back.

"But no more hissy fits," he said.

"No more hissies."

"Don't know what it is. I just don't like people yellin' at me."

"No more hissies," Simon said again. "I'll be good. Promise."

Earl and his crew arrived on the stroke of eight the next morning.

*

"Sugar supper?" Simon said. "What the hell is that?"

"A great tradition in Vermont, a spring ritual."

They settled in across the table from Warren Thurber and his family. Warren, about ten years younger than Kenneth, was a wide man, a physical trait that made his arms seem unusually short. Pearl, his wife, was also wide.

She rocked constantly in her chair. Their two red-faced kids shared their parents' features, a strange, genetically challenged family. Their bulk was on their sides while front to back they were only a bit chunky.

"Kenny," Warren said. "How you been?"

"Fine." Kenneth recognized the voice that yelled at Homer Dalrymple during the town meeting. The Thurbers, Kenneth remembered, had limited social boundaries. There was nothing mean-spirited about them, but neither was there embarrassment over anything that might spill from their mouths. A Thurber might launch into the finer points of lancing boils or castrating pigs in the middle of dinner.

"Who's this young fella here?" Warren asked.

"My partner, Simon."

"Good t'meetcha," Warren said. He reached across the table and Simon's hand disappeared inside Warren's paw. "Little bit of a thing, ain't he?" Warren said to Kenneth. "Kinda pretty." Then back to Simon. "You gotta get out to more of these suppers," he said, patting his stomach. "This is my favorite, though. I always like a good pan of sugar."

Simon looked at Kenneth.

"Just wait."

"So, you doin' up the Intercourse House?" Warren said. "S'great. Long overdue. Be nice to have it open again. You gonna serve meals?"

"That's the plan. The Tavern, too."

"My folks took me there once some years ago. Food not as good as what we'll get here. Expensive, too. We just went the one time. Then it closed."

"It happens," Kenneth said. He wanted to get away from talk about the hotel. "What're you doing now, Warren?"

"Drive truck for John Morrison. Tanker. Three runs a week. Gasoline, diesel, or Number two. Long days but it pays good."

"One of those big tank trucks?" Simon asked.

"Yup. Used to drive a big box for Perry Brothers but sometimes I had to load and unload the damn thing. With the tanker I just open a valve and let it run out." He smiled at his cunning.

The serving dishes arrived. Warren and his family cleaned them out in seconds. No one else had a chance.

"Gotta move fast," Warren said around a mouthful of mashed potato. "Don't worry. They'll bring more."

Kenneth and Simon's side of the table got first chance at the refills but only because Warren and his family were still using both hands to Hoover up their first round. When others had plated up the Thurbers grabbed the dishes and cleaned them out again. Simon had never seen people eat with such efficiency.

"How do they do that?" he asked, close to Kenneth's ear.

"Some combination of genetics and social modeling," Kenneth explained, leaning close. "They're conditioned from birth that when this is gone there might not be any more."

As if to confirm this theory, Warren called for another round of beans and ham. Everyone else had finished but the Thurbers were still at it. Finally, the tables were cleared and platters of doughnuts and dishes of sour pickles were brought out.

Warren let fly a long, rumbling belch. "You fellas get enough?"

"I'm good," Simon said.

"Not much to you, is there?" Warren said. "Ever had sugar on snow?

"No, I haven't."

"Well, to a Vermonter, it's like nectar. Ain't that right, Pearl?" Pearl grinned and swayed back and forth. "Like a spring tonic, you know?"

The servers, some bearing as many as seven pans of packed snow, streamed into the room and placed the pans in front of each diner. Simon was baffled.

"Ahhh.... Here it comes," Warren said.

The syrup was distributed in pint-sized pitchers, heavy crockery to hold the heat and keep the syrup liquid and smooth. Each pitcher sat on a saucer to catch drips. Warren snatched one up as soon as it hit the table.

"You got your different styles," Warren explained. "Some people like dollops. Some like lacy threads all over the top of the snow. Myself, I like thick trails, two or three of them." He poured generous amounts of the hot amber syrup with a practiced hand. For all his bulk, Warren approached this event with all the delicacy and precision of a Japanese tea service.

Boiled down to the soft ball stage, the syrup quickly became thick and taffy-like when it settled on the snow. Satisfied with his pour, Warren handed the pitcher to Pearl who poured a thin stream to write her name. The kids shared another pitcher and simply dumped a big puddle in the center of the snow where they could play with it.

"Now here's what you do," Warren said. He stuck his fork into one of the strips of syrup he'd poured. It lifted off the snow, stiff, but still soft enough for Warren to wind it around the fork. He tapped it several times against the snow until he'd created a gob of maple sugar the size of a golf ball.

"Now there," he said, "is a treat."

Warren shoved the whole ball of syrup into his mouth and a look of pure pleasure spread over his face as he savored the rich, delicate sweetness.

At this point, the custom is to pull the syrup off the fork and let it dissolve slowly in your mouth but this syrup had cooled quickly and set firm. Warren pulled but the syrup resisted. Like a bulldog, Warren would not give up his prize. His jaw set and the cords in his thick neck became visible as he pulled at the fork. His face grew red from the effort. He grabbed the fork handle with both hands, gave a mighty yank, and there was a great smack of releasing suction. Not only was the syrup still securely on the fork but it had captured both sets of Warren's false teeth which now grinned at Kenneth and Simon across the table.

"Well, thunofabitth," Warren said. Pearl had been working backwards through the letters of her name but put the R back down on the snow. She glanced around the room to see if anyone was watching. Warren's kids thought this was the funniest thing they'd ever seen, and laughed until they could no longer breathe. The younger even tried to duplicate it.

"Great trick, Warren," Simon said. "Can it be done without the teeth?"

Warren put the fork down and tried to extract his teeth from the gob of syrup with his hands but they were stuck tight. "Well, thunofabitth," he said again.

"Hot water," Kenneth said. "Run some hot water on them."

Warren pushed back from the table and plowed off to the kitchen with the fork and his teeth held high over the other diners as he passed.

"I think I'll try the lacy version," Simon said. He poured a thin stream into a pattern of random swirls and took up a bit on his fork. "God, that's sweet."

"That's what the sour pickles are for. The acid cuts the sweet so you can eat more sugar."

"You're serious, right?"

"That's the way it works. And if the sugar hit doesn't leave you jangly enough, they'll bring coffee along in a few minutes." Kenneth helped himself to another serving of syrup. Simon struggled to finish his first.

"Maybe you have to be born to it," Kenneth suggested. "Try a pickle." The pickles were dark and wizened up, not that shiny, firm green that's so familiar with commercial pickles. "These are old fashioned crock pickles," he said. "The recipe's been handed down for generations. Lots of vinegar, pepper, and dried mustard."

"Jesus," Simon said when he'd taken a bite. "You people don't do subtle, do you?" He began to sweat around his eyes.

"Great pickles," Kenneth said.

Warren came back to the table and sat down. "Well, now. I think I ought to just try that again," he chuckled. "Damnedest thing, wan't it?" In typical Thurber fashion there had been no apology. Warren was determined to have his sugar, though, and called for another pitcher of syrup. Kenneth and Simon stood to leave.

"Good to see you folks," Warren said as he poured another thick strip of syrup on his snow. "Come again."

"Count on it," Simon said, as he stuck a finger into Kenneth's ribs to move him toward the door.

"Good luck on the hotel," Warren called as they were leaving. "Be a great thing for the town."

The wait staff needed the Thurbers' seats for the next sitting but Warren was going to get his full value and the help had to work around him. In a few minutes everything else was set and eight waiters stood by while Warren finished up. Four had place settings and four were ready to scoop up the empty dishes left by the Thurbers as soon as they left. Warren enjoyed his sugar, ate a few pickles, was finally satisfied, and pushed back his chair. The wait staff swooped in and changed the settings in seven seconds flat.

*

Increase and Judith Houghton were on their way in for the seven o'clock.

"Well," Increase said. "I see you've introduced Simon to another fine Vermont tradition."

"I hadn't had sugar on snow for years," Kenneth said, "hadn't thought about it, but then I heard about the supper…"

"And how did *you* find it, Mr. Hirsh?" Judith asked.

"We shared a table with a Warren Thurber and his family," Simon said.

Judith Houghton knew the Thurbers. "And was it instructive?"

"Oh, I'll never forget it," Simon said.

"And how is your house coming along?"

"I've got a couple more rooms to finish," Kenneth said, "maybe a month."

"And the hotel?"

"Clancy, our architect and project manager, says we're well ahead of schedule. Seems hard to believe, but she knows what she's doing."

"That's wonderful. What a nice change that will be."

The Houghtons went inside as Archie and Ellen arrived in Archie's truck.

"No, you stay here," Archie said to Hank. "We'll be back in a while."

"Hi," Ellen said. "You eat already?"

"Oh, yes," Simon said. "Warren Thurber pulled his teeth clear out of his head."

"Sorry I missed that," Archie said. "It's always something with them. One year he dropped a pitcher of hot syrup in his lap."

"I'm sure the table is mopped up by now," Kenneth said. "Enjoy."

There was a chill in the air but not enough to bring a hard frost. The sky was clear and a three-quarter moon peeked through the still bare trees as they walked home.

"Are we going to do this every year?"

"Absolutely," Kenneth said.

"You people are really into this maple thing, aren't you?" Simon said.

Kenneth smiled. It wasn't just the maple thing. Over the winter he'd become comfortable in Grants Ferry. Reconnecting with Ellen again had been good, even if she had married Archie Whitaker. The physical work on Fanny's house and the slower pace seemed to produce a therapeutic calm, a calm he'd not known in the city. Even with the potential for everything to go wrong with the hotel, Kenneth was more relaxed than he'd been in years. The familiar things like the town meeting, the church suppers, the gentle nature of small town life, the quiet and almost total darkness at night, and the sweet spring air that he'd long forgotten, even the people, all these years later, seemed to accept him and he found unexpected comfort in that.

*

Chapter Seventeen

Simon, on the other hand, had grown increasingly restless during the winter and into spring. The silence and the dark nights with nothing to do and no place to go except an occasional church supper were beginning to get on his nerves. Any form of actual night life was over an hour or more away. He might as well have moved to a different country.

"This place was okay for a while," he said, "but Jesus. There's nothing here."

"Isn't that the point, though?"

"Not for me, it's not, and I'm not the one who needs to reside here."

"You've got money tied up here, too, you know. We're in this together."

"That's true and I may have even talked us into it but there's nothing says I have to live here and eat baked beans across the table from a family of Hoovers. Besides, we need to think about how we're going to protect our investment."

"What do you mean?"

"We've got to begin selling this place. We'll be out of money by the time the hotel is done and we're going to need help, new people, new money, investors in the town to keep this thing alive."

"True enough."

"So I'm going to spend more time in the city. You keep the renovations going and I'll be in the city talking this place up. Without more people bringing in money and ideas we're going to be in big trouble. I'll come up weekends."

"Jesus, when did this start?"

"It's been building," Simon said. "You know these people. I've got no connection at all here. I think the false teeth were the final straw. That may count for 'normal' here, but it was too organic for me. I want to go home."

"Can we finish the house first?"

"Fine. But then I'm moving on."

"Well..."

"I'll come up every now and then – weekends, unless I put a party together to get people interested – but I can't live here. I'm going to work up a marketing plan, some combination of history, renaissance, and opportunity. Then I'll get the word out to every gay, lesbian, bisexual, transvestite we know. I might even throw Jerry Falwell into the mix. That alone should catch a few people."

*

"Okay," Diane said when she called. "I've spent the past three months trying to talk myself out of this. If you still want me, I'm in."

"Great," Kenneth said.

"You got a place for me to stay?"

"You can crash at our house until we work something out."

"You do have some sense of what I'm leaving here, don't you?"

"Of course. We just have to make it work."

*

Kenneth continued to wake energized every morning, doing this work because he could, not because he was scrambling to survive. The challenge of the hotel was a risk they had chosen together, no mistake, and there were considerations, but in the end he knew now he would be here because he chose to be here, not because he was trapped. Even taking a meal across the table from Warren Thurber and his bizarre family brought a familiar comfort.

He limited his visits to the hotel to once a week. It was rough and dirty and noisy but was nevertheless moving apace. Clancy and her assistant, a big black man named Frank, kept everything on schedule. Kenneth couldn't imagine attempting that job himself. Whatever it eventually cost, it would be fair. Clancy Matthews was a wizard.

Simon stuck around until Earl finished his work on Fanny's house save for the last of the papering and painting. On Earl's last day, Simon gave him another bottle of wine.

"Thanks," Earl smiled. "You were right. It goes real well with a venison roast. Kinda softened Edna up a bit, too," his eyes twinkled, "handy thing to remember."

"Good job," Kenneth said as Earl drove away. "He'll be back now whenever we need him."

A satellite dish was installed behind the barn, out of sight from the street. They'd connected to the Internet, a slow dial-up connection, but at least they were online again. The days were longer, most of the spring rain had passed, and as the ground warmed the perennials made themselves known. Crocus, daffodils, narcissus, several forsythias – great balls of yellow – had come and gone, buds on the lilacs began to swell and the renewal of spring was upon them. Each morning while Simon fixed breakfast Kenneth toured the grounds to see what had changed during the previous twenty-four hours.

The familiar things from his childhood brought a new and solid sense of place, something he'd not felt since the night his parents died.

Simon packed his bags in the Beemer.

"You gonna be all right in this house by yourself?"

"No problem. I'll be busy. There's plenty of work to do yet and I haven't even begun on the garden."

"The garden?"

"Well, there's all that space that Fanny worked every year. I'll have the time. Seemed too good to pass up."

"You told me you hated gardening."

"Ah, yes. But now I choose to garden."

*

Kenneth had sent Luther to a dentist in Springfield to get his teeth fixed shortly after he came to work for them. When he later insisted that Luther should take Yvonne in as well Luther turned away so Kenneth wouldn't see the tears.

"You sure you want to do all this?" Luther asked some time later.

"Simon and I take care of the people who work for us," Kenneth reminded him. "We take care of you so you can take care of us."

Only because it was coming from Kenneth was Luther able to trust and accept his good fortune. His work was relatively light and much of it had become power-assisted. He'd cleared snow in the winter, made dump runs for the tenants, helped Kenneth and Simon move stuff back and forth during the construction at Fanny's house, and now the snow was gone he'd been cleaning up the yards around all the properties. By April he had them in good shape.

Jerry Martin, who lived in the Allen Place, called to say he'd found work in Connecticut and they'd be moving the first of May. When they'd gone, Luther and Kenneth gave the place a quick clean, made a few necessary repairs and then offered it to Diane.

"Perfect," she said. "Clancy could come, too. Get the women out of your hair."

*

"So I was thinking," Kenneth told Luther when he'd stopped by one day, "we ought to have you and Yvonne over for supper one night when Simon's up for the weekend. Now that the weather's warmer we could do a cookout or something. What do you think?"

"Oh, I don't know, Kenny. Yvonne don't like to go out much."

"Just the four of us. Nothing fancy. The women are gone now. No pressure. Very simple. No crowds. Tell Yvonne we'll fix whatever she wants."

"Okay. I'll see."

"Yvonne says she thought a cookout would be good if it's warm enough," Luther said the following Monday.

"Really? Great. She have anything in particular she'd like to eat?"

"Well, it's funny. Usually she don't care one way or another but without takin' a breath she said she'd like barbecue chicken, potato salad, watermelon if you can get it this early, and ice cream."

"Got it," Kenneth said. "Does she like spicy?"

"Spicy's good. Lots of flavor but not too hot. Sometimes I think she's not able to taste much. She salts stuff to bring up the flavor, even salts watermelon."

"Beer? Wine?"

"She takes beer sometimes but I keep her away from the hard stuff."

"No problem. How about the third Saturday in May?"

*

Archie had come to more fully appreciate Luther when he'd needed to hire three people to do the work Luther had done by himself. Luther never said anything but he noticed dust on the windowsills in the church, untrimmed grass on the common, litter in the school yard, even the entrance into the town hall was dirty. These new guys didn't apply themselves.

Another person who noticed the substandard janitorial services was Mary Louise Turner, the principal at the elementary school. Being a stern taskmaster (or taskmistress) she'd always appreciated Luther's industry and attention to detail. It was entirely due to her determination and high standards – and Luther's dependability – that the school had eventually been dragged into acceptable condition over the weeks and months since she'd been put in charge the previous summer. The new man, however, a Mr. Jeffors, needed prodding at every step. He never seemed to learn a routine, his performance never improved, and the school property had once again begun a slow decline which was annoying, frustrating, and unacceptable. Mr. Jeffors was also lax in his personal hygiene.

Mary Louise Turner missed Luther. She'd found his reticence and mumbling quaintly charming – a bit rustic, perhaps, but charming nonetheless – and his employment with that gay couple had been a good move for him personally. He'd cleaned up rather well, she thought, not that he was ever dirty, you understand.

Luther seemed happier, too. She'd even seen him smile from time to time. He'd never smiled at the school but she found it to be a nice smile. Their meetings, usually at the store or the post office, were always the same. She'd speak, he'd mumble some unintelligible response, and they'd go their separate ways. He never smiled at Mary Louise Turner, however, and she found that disappointing.

While she demanded perfection at work, Mary Louise Turner's home was a sorry affair. She'd hired Archie Whitaker's crew to make a few repairs and put a coat of paint on the outside shortly after she bought the house, but that was it. To passersby, her house was presentable, but Mary Louise Turner was not a housekeeper. The inside had become strewn from one room to the next. The kitchen was a shambles and she often had to wash dishes and utensils before she could cook a meal. Some nights she ate straight out of the pan.

Her back yard was a mass of patchy grass, weeds, and overgrown bushes. Several small maples had self-seeded from the tree next door.

Before coming to Grants Ferry Mary Louise Turner had always lived in apartments. Now she was here in the country in her own house it seemed as if she should have a vegetable garden. She remembered how her grandfather had grown tomatoes. He'd find the one among hundreds that was perfectly ripe, pick it, rub it on his shirt, and then let her eat it right there in the garden so she would know and never forget the taste of a perfect tomato. This was her fantasy: fresh, home-grown tomatoes from her own garden.

She drove to a hardware store in Windsor and bought shovels, forks, rakes, loppers and pruners. She would have a garden and she would have fresh tomatoes and basil and oregano and thyme and chives and mint and parsley. Back home again she clipped and lopped and sawed about five feet down one side of the yard and stopped, exhausted, soaked in perspiration and, as she realized the scope of the work to be done, hopeless. Broken-hearted, she went inside, rinsed out a cup from the pile in the sink, and fixed a cup of tea. She took the tea to the back porch and sank into the glider. The chains that suspended it from the ceiling groaned in protest.

If the heavy work were done, she thought, she could then plant and nurture and harvest on her own. This would be light work, enjoyable work, work that would bring her in touch first-hand with Mother Earth. The yard would not only be restored and productive, but Mary Louise Turner would remain fresh, pleasantly scented, and feminine well into a warm summer day.

*

"Oh, Mr. Pike!" Mary Louise Turner had "stumbled onto" Luther as he came out of Paul's Grocery. He seemed to not hear her. "Oh, Mr. Pike!" she called again. Luther hesitated but kept walking toward the K&S pickup. She rushed across the street then and caught him as he reached for the door.

"Oh, Mr. Pike!" Luther supposed he was rid of this woman when he took the job with Kenny and Simon but here she was and she was close. He caught a light floral scent. "What a nice surprise," Mary Louise Turner said as she positioned herself so he couldn't open the door. "I must say we all miss you at the school, Mr. Pike. The new man doesn't keep the building and grounds nearly as well as you did." She paused for some sort of response but Luther avoided her eyes and said nothing. "Is your new position to your liking?"

"Yup."

"That's wonderful," Mary Louise Turner said as she touched his arm, "I'm so happy for you."

At her touch, Luther felt that tingling in his loins again, a strange, unsettling, and unbidden tingling. His breathing turned shallow and the muscles in his abdomen contracted slightly as if being lightly tickled.

"I expect you're terribly busy with all your new responsibilities," she went on, "but I have a few things that need tending around my house. You always did such excellent work at the school and I wondered if you might have time to fit me into an hour or two now and then?"

The truth was, Luther had more time on his hands now than he'd had in years.

"I – I don't know," he said, looking anywhere but at Mary Louise Turner.

"My back yard has been terribly let go and now we have this lovely spring weather, well, I tried to tidy it up myself but I must say it's not suitable work for a lady." She seemed able to speak without taking a breath. "Young people just don't have the experience or the ambition, I'm afraid, and I thought someone with a sound sense of what needs to be done would be the solution. And then I saw you this morning and I thought I'd ask. And naturally I'm happy to pay you whatever you want."

Luther didn't need more money and he'd come to enjoy having entire weekends free although it felt as if he should be doing something productive instead of hanging around the house. As much as he enjoyed his new freedom, he suddenly heard himself say, "Weekends?" The word had actually come from his own mouth. What the hell was going on? He hated this woman.

"Why, yes, the weekend would be fine," she said. When she smiled the corners of her mouth sunk back into her round cheeks. "Saturday morning?"

"Lemme see." He couldn't stop himself. "Maybe next week…"

"Oh, that would be marvelous!" She touched his arm again, this time with an intimate little squeeze, and the tingling came again. "That would be wonderful. Thank you, Luther."

Son of a bitch, Luther thought. *God DAMN it.* And for the first time she'd called him Luther, instead of Mr. Pike. *Jesus!*

"Thank you, Luther," she said again. "Next Saturday, then. About nine?" And before he could take back everything he'd just said she swept off across the street. Luther noticed a particular lightness in her step, something unusual in a woman as large as Mary Louise Turner. In spite of her bulk she slid easily into her Volkswagen, smiled, and waved as she drove away.

Luther sat for several minutes without starting the truck. He needed to let his head clear and sort out what had just happened. Somehow, he'd agreed to go to this woman's house and do some work for her. Why in the name of Christ would he agree to that? He hated Mary Louise Turner and that way she had of making him feel so stupid, even while she praised him. He shuddered as he remembered again the sight of her thick legs the day she'd reached into her car that morning last fall – and yet, he'd agreed to go to her house, her *house*.

And, having agreed, Luther knew as well as he knew anything that he would be there at nine o'clock a week from Saturday morning because he'd given his word, even if it seemed as if someone else had made the agreement for him.

But it was done. He would apply himself, he decided. He'd show up, work for a couple hours, maybe until noon, and then he'd pick up and leave. He might not even wait to get paid. But then she'd have reason to come after him, maybe even come to his house.

That was the last thing he wanted.

Shit.

Prob'ly have to go to her door.

God damn it.

*

"A Colorist?"

"That's right," Clancy said. "He's amazing."

Brian Coleman was a small man. He wore faded jeans, cowboy boots, a leather jacket, and a Red Sox baseball cap. He opened his laptop, dragged the mouse around, gave it a couple clicks, and a generic Victorian house appeared on the screen.

"Kind of the same style. You have to make some decisions with the actual building but this will give you the overall effect." He went to the color palette and scrolled through the colors. "Okay," he said. "Pick out a color you want for the body of the house."

"Arabian Sunset," Simon said. "I like that one."

"Okay. So I plug it into the house body color, and bingo!"

In a flash the Victorian house was Arabian Sunset. The trim and details were highlighted with suggested complimentary colors. When Brian dragged the mouse over the different colors the name of the color came up in a little balloon.

"Wow. Just like that? Do it with some sort of antique gold."

Brian dragged through the palette again, clicked the mouse, and the image was immediately transformed to the new color scheme.

"You're not limited to these suggestions," Brian said. "You can tweak the trim colors one at a time, for instance, and it will shift the others accordingly. Or you can override it entirely and put your own color choices into the mix."

"Okay," Kenneth said. "This house, for instance. There are lilacs on either end of the porch and more along the sides of the yard. What happens when we make lilac the base color?"

A couple clicks gave him his answer. It was called "New England Lilac".

"I like that," Kenneth said. "Can you do detail highlights like red or gold bands on the porch posts?"

"Actually, there's another level of the program that adds bling," Brian said. He dropped down a menu, clicked on options, and chose Level 3. Going back to the house image again, there were now more detailed highlights.

"Perfect," Kenneth said. "That's what I want."

"Good," Brian said. "Just let me give it a name and save it."

"Call it the Deacon Hitchcock House."

A few minutes later Diane and Clancy joined them on the common. Brian sat on the bench by the cannon. The image on his computer screen was a wooden Victorian business block which could easily be a hotel or a bank. Brian played with a few colors but nothing seemed to work.

"I don't want it to be the same," Kenneth said, "but what if we tried the lilac again?"

The lilac combination came up but it was too dark for a building so large and close to the street.

"I think,' Brian said, "if I can just lighten it a bit, maybe a gentle lavender..." A couple clicks and the image that had been over-powering and gloomy was now light and fresh. He put in the Level Three option which added red highlights and some deeper violet shades for the trim. The image suggested whispering breezes, blousy peonies, a basket of fresh-cut flowers, big hats, and parasols.

"I think that's it," Simon said. Kenneth agreed.

"Gorgeous," Diane said. "What's that color?"

"Lavender Lip Gloss," Brian said. He saved the file. "Anything else?"

"Well, there are some other houses, all part of the same collection. Maybe we could do them all as long as you're here."

Each color scheme, although uniquely individual, contained a bit of lilac or lavender, just enough of something purplish to symbolically link the properties. Back at the house, Brian brought a printer in from his truck and produced colored images and spec sheets for each property. Ten minutes later he was on his way back to Boston.

*

The staging arrived, two trailer trucks full of sections and braces, another loaded with planks, and still another with a box trailer. A van with at least ten guys showed up a bit later and the whole gang came into the diner for coffee. They were loud and oblivious to anyone else in the diner.

Archie thought they spoke French. He'd heard there were crews closer to Boston and Nashua, New Hampshire, huge pools of French Canadians who specialized in certain trades. Drywall was one. Painting was another. Staging and scaffolding seemed to be yet another. Archie parked where he could watch as the scaffolding took shape down the two street sides of the hotel. By noon, the crew had moved to the back sides and out of sight.

"Ain't that somethin' though?" he said to Hank. Archie had an admiration for a crew that knew its job and worked well together. The scaffolding had gone up faster than he could have imagined and he respected that, even if it was on a project he opposed.

When he drove past again later that afternoon the hotel was entirely hidden behind translucent tarps.

"Well, son of a bitch," he said.

*

Yvonne was a small, solid woman who wore her pants high with the cuffs turned up around heavy boots. Her hair was in a severe, blunt cut lightly streaked with gray. Her hands were thick and callused, a woman formed from years of labor around the house and the homestead.

"Tamed them cats," she said, before they'd even said hello.

"How'd you do that?" Kenneth asked.

"Didn't feed'em. Just put out water. They was too dumb to hunt so they got pretty hungry after a couple days. Soon's they knew who put the food out, they changed their attitude."

"That sounds too easy," Simon said.

"They was too soft and fat. Now they follow me around. One day I might even let'em in the house."

"Told you," Luther beamed. "She's got a way with'em."

"You like animals, then?" Simon said.

"When they're useful. Those two don't know nothing."

"I see. Well, I'm about to cook up the chicken. Kenneth, why don't you show Yvonne the house?"

"These're my good boots. I ain't tracked in anything."

"Boots are fine," Kenneth said. He took Yvonne and Luther inside while Simon got a pan of marinated chicken pieces from the refrigerator and took them out back to the grill and the picnic table which were set up behind the house where they could look down over Fanny's fruit trees and the beginnings of the vegetable garden.

Simon was taking the chicken off the grill as the others came outside.

"Nice house," Yvonne said. "Little fussy, though, ain't it?"

"You think so?" Simon said. "Is it too much?"

"Too much to take care of," Yvonne said.

"Right. Well, let me get the salad and we can start. Kenneth, you want to bring out the iced tea?"

Inside, Simon was clearly irritated. "I didn't realize we were having the Clampetts over," he sputtered.

"Take it easy. She's doing the best she can."

"This is her best?"

Yvonne stopped talking while she worked her way through a substantial pile of chicken and several helpings of potato salad.

"Beer, Yvonne?"

"That'd be good, thanks." She stopped eating long enough to chug down half a bottle without taking a breath. Simon rolled his eyes.

Kenneth relaxed and looked out over the garden remembering the hours he'd had to spend weeding carrots and beets and tying up tomato plants. Harvesting always came at inconvenient times and he'd need to drop everything to pick beans or corn or tomatoes. Not to mention the canning all the years before Fanny bought the freezer, jars and jars and jars of string beans, tomatoes, pickles, peaches, applesauce, blueberries, and jams and jellies. It all came back now, the hours and the tedium, and even the slight satisfaction later on in the winter when they ate the product of their labors.

He snapped back to present time when he realized Yvonne had spoken.

"What's that?" he said.

"You got woodchucks?"

"I haven't seen any."

"Fanny had'em."

"Woodchucks?" Simon said.

"Big rodents that burrow underground," Kenneth explained.

"Oh, wonderful."

"They can clean you out," Yvonne said.

"Yup. Fanny had'em bad one year," Luther said. "Brought Yvonne over for a little pest control. Yvonne's probably the best shot in town."

"Shot? Like with a gun?" Simon asked.

"She's better with iron sights than most people are with scopes," Luther said.

"So she shoots them? Isn't there some other way?"

"Oh, sure. You could hit'em with a hammer," Luther explained, "but it's harder and takes longer."

"I see," Simon said. Kenneth got the old joke right away but Simon got back to what he did best which was the food. He lifted a large watermelon out of a cooler where it had been sitting in cold water and set it on the table near a long knife. "Here," he said to Kenneth. "Cut this open while I go get the ice cream."

Kenneth cut several pieces and put them on a tray where Yvonne could go to work on them. She salted each piece, sucked in the soft, cool flesh and then stood up to see how far she could spit the seeds.

Simon returned with the ice cream maker, a wooden tub with a crank that he'd found in the shed. A second trip produced a big bag of ice and a small bag of rock salt. He put the ice in the tub around the ice cream container, poured in some rock salt, and stood back.

"There," he said. "I think one of the old timers ought to crank this thing." Kenneth started to get up but Luther waved him down. Yvonne took a deep breath and spit another seed.

"'I can do better'n that," she said. "Just gotta get warmed up." One by one she fired the rest of the seeds off into the tall grass toward the garden. Each time she took a deep breath, leaned back, and used a combination of whipping her torso forward and spitting at the same time. Simon just shook his head. *The things that entertain these people.*

He was now referring to them as "these people." As much as he would be offended if the situation was reversed, he was growing more distant. He sat at the end of the table, his mind wandering to good times in the city.

"Feels like it's done," Luther said. Kenneth opened the canister. The ice cream was smooth and stiff and clung to the dasher. Slowly, while Simon held the canister down, Kenneth pulled the dasher, cleaning it off with a rubber spatula. Simon quickly dished up four generous servings.

"Here you go, Yvonne," he said. Yvonne let go a spurt of seeds with a burp like a machine gun then gave her attention to the ice cream.

"Might have had one at twenty-one feet," she said. "One day maybe I'll do twenty-five. That would be a record."

"A record?" Simon asked.

"The Firemen's Field Days," Luther said. "They's always a seed spittin' contest."

"Really? Who's the current champ?"

"I think it's Archie. 'Course, he's got the height advantage. Don't seem exactly fair somehow."

"I see what you mean. Maybe they should handicap him."

"Good idea," Luther said. "I think I'll bring that up this year."

"Glad to help," Simon said.

After a while Luther said they had to get back and tend the animals.

"Wicked good chicken," Yvonne said to Simon. "Can you write it down?"

"I sure can."

"The potato salad, too?"

"Of course."

"You see any woodchucks around, you let me know."

"I'll do that." Simon said as they climbed into the K&S pickup.

"You get a couple fattened up, though, they make up into a decent stew."

"I'll keep that in mind."

Luther backed the truck out of the driveway.

Kenneth chuckled. "Piece of work, isn't she?"

"Woodchuck stew?"

"Well, woodchucks are vegetarians, after all. Not gamey like carnivores can be."

"You ever eat woodchuck?"

"I can't remember. The fire department used to have game suppers from time to time. You're apt to get anything at one of those."

"Oh, boy. Sign me up."

"This is who these people are. Stop bitching."

"Okay, okay," Simon said. They brought the dishes and trays and leftover food back into the house. "Tell me," he said, "do you think this house is fussy?"

"I think it suits the people who live here," Kenneth said.

*

Luther came by Monday morning to thank them again for the cookout.

"I thought you said Yvonne doesn't talk much," Kenneth said.

"She don't usually. Couldn't stop talkin' about your house, though. I might need to have you guys help fussy ours up a bit."

"I didn't think she liked it," Simon said.

"It's too big, too much stuff. Our place is small but – well, Yvonne's not very girlish, you know. A little fussy stuff and some colors might make her happy."

"I'll see what we can do," Kenneth said.

*

"So," Diane said, "what would your perfect job look like? What would you like to do if it were possible?" She'd gone back to New York in search of a chef. Jonathan Holbrook was head chef at Sparrows, a trendy, upscale bistro that was one of the current places to eat.

"My ideal job?"

"That's right. Your perfect job."

"Well." He'd never been asked this question in an interview. Most places knew what they wanted and expected him to fall into line. "I think – well, I'd have a small place, might seat 30-40 people tops. Smaller would be okay. I'd like it to be classy, but not overdone, a sort of casual elegance. I'd source food locally when possible, I'd cook things that were in season, there would be a few items that were always on the menu – the usual meat and potatoes stuff because people expect them but there would always be surprise specials when something unusual was available. Reasonable prices, generous servings, good service."

"That's it?"

"Well…"

"Come on, I want to hear it all."

"Well, if it were my place, I'd come out of the kitchen and meet people from time to time, see how they liked the meal, take suggestions, find out if it's what they expected when they ordered it, see if there were any surprises. I don't know, I always thought people might like to meet the folks who put it all together for them, you know, develop a relationship. I've never been allowed to do that."

"How would you feel about running a kitchen in a hotel?"

"Oh, Jesus. A hotel?"

"A small one, an inn. I've got these friends in Vermont – "

"Vermont?"

"Yeah. Little town. A couple of my friends are restoring a hotel. I'm the manager and I need someone to run the kitchen, the dining room, and the tavern."

"Where is this place?"

"A place you never heard of, Grants Ferry," she said. "Take a couple days off and come up to look it over. It won't open until fall. If you get on board early you can design the kitchen."

"Is there a catch?"

"Yes."

Of course. There was always something.

Diane explained the will and the conditions. She also told him about Clancy and the skill with which she managed the restoration.

"You really ought to see the place," she said.

*

Jonathan drove to Grants Ferry on his next days off and got a tour of the hotel. Diane saturated him with vivid descriptions of the finished dining room and the Tavern. Not too pricy, but varied and well presented. Jonathan could customize the kitchen to his own style. He was encouraged to seek out and train local people since Diane and Kenneth were determined to hire as many local folks as possible.

But…

"There's nothing else here, though, is there?" he said.

"What do you mean?"

"Well, it's just a tired little town. Who's going to patronize the place?"

"We expect it to be a rather slow start," Diane said. "We'll advertise up and down the river valley at first and hope to get some interest here in town but Kenneth and Simon are developing a campaign to draw people up from the city. The hotel is only the beginning. We see a sort of renaissance here in Grants Ferry. If we can sell the vision, others will come and invest."

"I've spent my entire professional life going from one flash in the pan to another. Is this going to be the next one?"

"It will take some time, but I think it can work, especially when other people come and start their own businesses."

"And you? Have you invested?"

"I've not bought property yet, if that's what you mean but I've put money into the business side of the hotel. I'll own a big share of it. Kenneth and Simon have given me a house to stay in, a big place. There's room for you, too."

"And pay?"

"Anything that's fair."

"And if these guys fail?"

"That's not a conversation we've had. Clancy says the construction work is a bit ahead of schedule and she doesn't see why it shouldn't be done in plenty of time."

"...and if it's not?" Jonathan persisted.

"Then we lose. Kenneth and Simon lose a small fortune. I pack up and try to jump start a career in New York. You look for another flash in the pan restaurant someplace."

On the one hand it could be the kind of place Jonathan had dreamed of. On the other it was in a town with nothing to recommend it. Still, the others were risking far more than he would be. And he could always find work someplace... He realized Diane was speaking.

"– think you might give me an answer?"

"What?"

"I said when can you give me an answer."

"Let me work Sparrows through the end of the month," he said, "then you give me a place to stay and feed me, I'm in."

*

So how's it coming?"

Kenneth, Clancy, and Diane were in Clancy's trailer.

"All on schedule," Clancy said. "Look." She pulled up some bar graphs on the computer. "Each bar shows the progress of different pieces of the job that are underway. The base color for a particular job is yellow and the color changes when I tick the completion markers. Green means it's ahead of schedule, red means it's behind."

"So what's that big red bar, then?"

"Oh, there was more work on the outside repairs than I thought. I brought in a couple more guys to deal with that. We'll be caught up in a week or so and ready to start painting."

"Isn't that amazing?" Diane said. "She stays on top of everything."

"And the inside, how's that coming?"

"It's taking shape. Diane has been looking at paint and wallpaper."

"I've found some reproduction prints that will be quite nice," Diane said. "I'm getting the order together so it will be here when the walls are ready."

"And the kitchen?"

"Jonathan worked it out with the equipment people and they'll begin installation in a week or so. He's also begun advertising for local help."

"So we're okay, then?"

"We're okay. Just keep writing the checks."

*

Luther planned to put in a couple hours that first Saturday and be done but Mary Louise Turner had a long list of projects. Around 10:30 she insisted he stop for a break and brought him a cup of coffee and a doughnut. By the end of the month the doughnut had become a piece of pie and then she'd "put together a little lunch as long as it's noontime." They ate together at a table on the back porch.

Luther knew this was crazy. Every Saturday he vowed he was done and every Saturday she added another project or two. Whenever he was still for a second she began to chatter. He decided the reason for the coffee and the lunch was as much about the chattering as anything. She just couldn't seem to shut up. Luther knew he should tell her he wasn't coming back again but even when he'd had a chance to speak he couldn't make the words come. He was always there at 9 am the next Saturday.

He pruned her old fruit trees that had been let go for several years, built an arbor for the climbing roses she'd bought, prepared a vegetable patch and set out all the cabbage and tomatoes and cucumbers and squash plants. He planted her string beans and radishes and carrots and each week she marveled at how nice it looked and what a nice job he'd done, and meanwhile she'd been thinking, and then there would be another project ahead of him.

*

"Hey, Luther," Kenneth said. "I hear you been doing some work for the teacher."

"Yeah, you shoulda seen the place," Luther said. "God damn disgrace."

"Really?"

"A shithouse. Those people before her, the Mortons – remember them?"

"No, I don't."

"Never took care of the place. Used to be nice years ago. I suppose she thought she'd fix it up."

"Good for her."

"'Cept it just got worse. She's hopeless. Inside's not much better."

"You've been inside?"

"Just the kitchen. She makes coffee. Sometimes there's pie." He wasn't going to tell Kenneth she also gave him lunch.

"You better be careful, there," Kenneth teased. "It all starts with pie and coffee."

"Aw, shit, Kenny. You seen her. Enough to make you sick."

"Pie and coffee and lots of chores. All the signs of a lonely woman."

All Luther had even seen was a hopeless fat lady who was driven to talk and order people around. It never occurred to him that she might be lonely.

"Well, shit," Luther said.

Kenneth's observation, whether kidding or not, left Luther unsettled. He didn't care about Mary Louise Turner's house or her yard. That was just a reason he'd given to Kenny. He didn't like this woman at all. And yet, every week she'd thank him and say, "Next week, I think we could…" and she'd list off three or four things that would keep him busy for at least three hours and Luther knew he would be there simply because he'd not been able to tell her he wouldn't. She did the talking; he did the work.

A couple times she'd had him come inside to move a piece of heavy furniture. He didn't like being in the house alone with her and he always got back outside again as quickly as he could. Going into the kitchen to wash up at the sink was okay, though, and the coffee and pie were always good. Mary Louise Turner didn't know shit about gardening but she sure knew how to bake pies. Besides, the kitchen had been picked up now. She'd probably hired someone to come and hoe the place out.

It was three hours a week for $60, a cup of coffee and a piece of pie and lunch.

And it was cash. Luther had always liked cash.

*

Renovations to Fanny's house were complete. The bedrooms were scrubbed and painted and papered and decorated. The floors were sanded and finished and furnishings from the collection of furniture in the barn were selected and brought inside. Old wooden pieces, some with polished marble tops, were cleaned and oiled, curtains which were still serviceable had been salvaged, cleaned, starched and hung, and the rooms were fitted with cozy fixtures, both old and new. The master bedroom now had direct access to the bathroom and a second bathroom was available for the guest rooms. Kenneth's old room became the office for K&S Enterprises and would serve until they needed real office space. Except for the cellar, which harbored a constant damp now that the furnace wasn't running all the time, the house had been cleared of any remaining trace of cat.

The kitchen, of course, had become a command center where Simon could cook and create in comfort when he was in town. One side was totally fitted out with work space and new appliances and power strips and lighting. Amy's kitchen table and chairs were by the windows that looked out over the driveway. The pantry and shed, save for some cleaning out, painting, and organizing, had been left as they were.

The dining room was decorated with mural type wallpaper that depicted a panoramic park-like scene with carriages, women with parasols, and children rolling hoops, all under a high canopy of towering elms, soothing pale greens and browns which romanticized a happier, simpler time. Even with the sideboard against the inside wall, there was now room to open the table and comfortably seat ten – twelve in a pinch.

The living room wallpaper was large blowsy roses and peonies and wisteria. The chairs were functional but stylish and meant to be used. The parlor, on the other hand, with the option of being hidden behind the two sliding doors, had been done over with deep red walls and a cream trim. Heavy curtains with a red on red weave now hung in the windows, and behind them to filter the incoming light were cream colored sheers. A large oriental rug covered the center of the floor. Small walnut or cherry tables stood beside each of the chairs to take cups and plates, and lamps with tasseled shades stood discreetly behind each chair. The Estey organ was oiled and glistening in its corner by the door and Fred's stereo sat on the other side. The best furniture pieces had been saved for this room, graceful settees with heavily starched antimacassars on the backs and arms. The walls were hung with a mix of large dramatic landscapes and small photos of nameless people from years ago that they'd found in the attic. The glittering multi-bulb ceiling light had been wired through a dimmer and could be set to cast a soft glow over the entire room. In short, it was totally overdone and absolutely perfect for High Tea, as promised, with Ellen and Mrs. Houghton.

After consulting Miss Manners on the proper form, Simon bought cream colored cards and matching envelopes from a stationer in the city. Proper invitations are to be hand-written, Miss Manners instructed, so Simon also bought a medium/fine calligraphy pen and some black ink. He made seventeen attempts before he'd created two that satisfied him.

Mr. Kenneth Forbes
and
Mr. Simon Hirsh
Will be At Home
At three o'clock

On the afternoon of 11th June
And request the pleasure of your company
For tea, conversation,
And a bit of music.

It took nearly as long to address the two envelopes.

*

The bell over the shop door jangled and Ellen came out from the back to find Judith Houghton.

"I just had to come by," Judith Houghton said. "I got my invitation to tea this morning."

"Me, too. Come in, come in. Have a look around."

"Oh, my, I had no idea," Judith said as she looked over the crafts on display. "We've driven by, but – oh, my, I should have come sooner." There were luxurious shawls from a local weaver, some intricately knit sweaters and hats, oil paintings, watercolors, a few whimsical sculptures made from found materials, and, of course, Ellen's pottery was on display.

"Have you been busy?"

"Not especially. A few curious people and Kenny stops by now and then, but that will change."

Judith Houghton held the sleeve of a soft mohair sweater against her cheek.

"It will change," Ellen said again. "Kenny and Simon and the hotel will make the difference, I think. They were my inspiration to create the store in the first place. Then one thing led to another. All of us in the shop are now filling orders to stores in New York through connections Simon made for us. I'm putting together a mail order catalog, too, and before long we'll have a website on the Internet."

"My goodness. I didn't realize you were such a clever business woman."

"Nor did I. Sometimes all we need is a chance. I have a sitting room upstairs. Come up and I'll put the water on."

The following Monday they went for a day in Boston where they found similar off-white flowing summer dresses with matching shoes, gloves, handbags, parasols, and wide-brimmed hats and spent far more than either of them considered decent. Later, bags in hand, they sat in a small tea room where they refreshed themselves over cakes and exotic tea accompanied by light dabs at the corners of their mouths with crisp linen napkins. It was fun and exhausting and they arrived back home long after suppertime, happy and confident.

*

Ellen wore her new outfit from the time she got up that morning so she could get used to the long flowing skirt. At noontime she called Judith Houghton.

"It's such a nice day I thought I might come by and we could walk from your house."

"Oh, what fun," Judith Houghton said. "Yes, let's do that."

Their skirts swayed in the light breeze, their hats and parasols protected them from the sun, and they arrived with a glow in their cheeks.

Simon met them at the door, delighted that they'd taken up the spirit of the occasion. He'd carefully pressed a shimmering royal purple silk shirt with blousy sleeves, put on his black leather pants with the red stitching up the outsides of the legs, pulled on his authentic tooled black cowboy boots, and tied a cream colored bandana loosely around his neck. The ends of the bandana were tossed over his left shoulder. He'd also applied makeup.

"My dears, my dears, come in, come in," Simon said. It was cooler inside. A string quartet played softly from somewhere. Air kisses for each of them. "Aren't you just perfect," he said. They blushed as he stepped back to admire their costumes. "Absolutely perfect. Come in. We'll be in the parlor."

The sheer curtains in the windows softened the sunlight and the deep red from the walls created a warm, rosy hue.

"What a gorgeous room." Ellen said, bowled over by the change from when she'd seen it last.

"I must say, Mr. Hirsh," Judith Houghton said when she had taken it in, "this is quite more than I anticipated."

"Oh, dear, is it too much?"

"Not at all," she said. "I think it's wonderful. I've never had the confidence to be so bold with colors."

"Well, the paint company says just buy the paint, the color is free."

"I think it's absolutely charming."

"I don't know where Kenneth is," Simon said, "I swear the man has no sense of time at all." He left and called up the stairs. "Kenneth. The guests are here."

"All right. Be down in a minute."

Simon turned back into the room and shook his head. "I do apologize. Raised voices have no place at Tea, but the man is chronically last minute. I suppose he wants to make an entrance."

Ellen smiled. When they were young Kenny had to be fifteen minutes early for everything.

"I'll just run out to the kitchen and fetch the refreshments," Simon said. "Feel free to look around if you'd like. I'm sure himself will be down shortly." He bustled off to the kitchen.

"Don't you just love him?" Ellen said.

"Very energetic," Mrs. Houghton agreed, "and so creative – both of them."

"Both of them?" That was Kenneth. He wore a double breasted dark blue blazer, crisp linen trousers, and white bucks. A lavender ascot was tucked into an open collared white shirt. Simon was cute but Kenneth was stunning.

"We were discussing colors," Mrs. Houghton said, "and how they affect us."

"Ah, yes. The energy of colors."

"Toot, toot, toot. Here we come." Simon pushed a tea trolley into the room. The top was laid out with a tea service for four and a three-tiered server with plates of tiny cucumber sandwiches with the crusts trimmed off, small yellow cakes with flecks of orange peel in the frosting, and a selection of English biscuits along with raspberry jam from Fanny's larder and a dish of clotted cream that Simon had brought from New York.

"Shall I be mum?" Simon asked. Before anyone could answer he began the process of pouring and serving. Kenneth had never developed enough fussiness to satisfy Simon and was content to sit and be served. Besides, with nothing else to do, he could take a good look at Ellen. Her hat and her hair framed her face perfectly. She watched Simon pour the tea and prepare the plates, so focused that the world around her seemed to disappear. It was almost flow-like. Kenneth hadn't seen her as relaxed and happy since he'd come back.

Tea was served and they sipped and made small talk about the town, the weather, and the plans Kenneth and Simon had for the hotel and the rest of Fanny's properties. When they'd finished Simon gathered up the dishes and wheeled the cart out to the front hall.

"A delightful treat, I must say," Mrs. Houghton said. "I might even attempt a tea myself one day."

The string quintet music faded and then stopped.

"It's not over yet," Simon said as he returned to the parlor. "Kenneth?"

Kenneth produced a polished brass music stand from beside the organ.

"This afternoon," Simon began, "we offer a few selections from the sheet music collection of the late Fanny Forbes. I will preside at the Estey Renaissance and Mr. Kenneth Forbes, who has suddenly remembered to clean his glasses, will present a sampling of the old favorites, occasionally joined by myself on the choruses. Our first selection is *Beautiful Dreamer* by Mr. Stephen Foster."

Simon's leather pants squeaked as he slid onto the wooden bench. He played a brief introduction and then Kenneth sang in a clear and easy tenor that complemented the lyrics. Ellen and Mrs. Houghton applauded with gloved hands when it ended while Kenneth and Simon took deep bows. Ellen had never heard Kenneth sing. She dabbed at her eyes with her napkin.

"Next on our program," Simon said "we bring you a classic from Mr. George M. Cohan, *Mary is a Grand Old Name*." Again, Kenneth eased through the song, milking it in all the right places.

"*After the Ball* by Mr. Charles K. Harris, King of the Tearjerkers," Simon announced. Kenneth plied them with all three verses, a sad tale of misunderstanding and lost love. Simon joined in the choruses.

"*I Don't Want To Play in Your Yard*," Simon said, "a bit of whimsy from Mr. H.W. Petrie and Mr. Philip Wingate."

"And finally, *I Wonder Who's Kissing Her Now*. The lyrics are by Mr. Will Hough and Mr. Frank Adams; the music by Mr. Joseph E. Howard and Mr. Harold Orlob. Mr. Forbes and I invite you to join in the chorus."

Kenneth provided cards with the lyrics, Ellen and Judith Houghton stood, and they all finished with a great flourish. Ellen was in tears.

"Well done. Well done," Judith Houghton told them. "Well done. What a fine voice you have, Kenneth."

"Thank you."

"Absolutely marvelous. Thank you so much."

"Glad you enjoyed it," Kenneth said.

"And the organ. I'd heard about Fanny's organ for years but I'd never seen it. What can you tell me about it, Mr. Hirsh?" Simon led her to the Estey where he could explain its finer points.

"That was beautiful," Ellen dabbed her eyes again. "I never heard you sing when we were kids. I had no idea. "

"Yeah, well… Amy and I used to sing together. I stopped when she died."

"So what got you started again?"

"Oh, it was maybe twelve or fifteen years ago. I heard about a glee club not far from where I lived in the city. They sang a lot of the old timey songs that Amy liked so I went by one night and they invited me to sit in."

"Was it fun?"

"Well, yeah. It was just singing those old songs and having a good time, doing some simple harmony. It's where I met Simon."

"That's right," Simon said. "He wasn't going to come back but I kept after him all week. The glee club gained a tenor who even performed a solo from time to time when we did concerts."

Ellen looked as if she was seeing Kenneth for the first time.

"Well, it was just lovely," Judith Houghton said. "We need more music in Grants Ferry. I shan't forget this, Kenneth."

"Nor will I," Ellen said.

"I was afraid of that."

"Thank you so much for the tea, Mr. Hirsh," Mrs. Houghton said. "It's been an absolutely delightful afternoon. I shall reciprocate."

"I look forward to it," Simon said.

"I'm afraid I can offer nothing in the way of the entertainment we had this afternoon."

"It's not required. This was a sort of celebration."

"And well done," Judith Houghton said again. They were in the hallway and the women took up their parasols. "Thank you again. It's been a delightful afternoon."

"I really don't know why I was so surprised," Ellen said to Kenneth. "I always thought you could do just about anything but it was wonderful to hear you sing and so well. Thank you."

"Yeah, well…."

"Oh, don't give me that 'aw, shucks' routine. You're good and you know it."

"Thank you."

Ellen and Mrs. Houghton made their way down the front steps and Simon closed the door.

"I think it went rather well, don't you?" Simon said.

"I could have done without the music."

"Oh, poo. Don't keep your light under a bushel."

"You never stop, do you?"

"No. And lucky for you I don't," Simon said. "Bring the cart to the kitchen," he called as he walked away. "And mind the thresholds," he called back. "We don't want to break Fanny's crockery."

*

Mary Louise Turner admired Luther's consistency and industry. He showed up on time, set about whatever tasks she'd laid out, and didn't shirk. She even had to insist that he stop for coffee. When the weather got warm he'd work in his T shirt which grew wet in great patches. His thick, sinewy arms glistened with moisture and grew darker each week from exposure to the sun. Luther's muscles had come from years of manual labor. There was sturdiness to his frame and she could see the muscles in his back move under the damp shirt as he worked. This, she thought, was a man as man was meant to be, a creation of honest work, not honed and buffed from hours strapped into a machine at a gym. Mary Louise Turner saw honesty – a basic, primal honesty – in Luther Pike.

Mary Louise did not take the heat well and she powdered herself several times a day and the powder had a gentle aroma of spice and flowers – very light. She didn't want people to find the scents heavy. Heaviness in a scent might call attention away from her delicate feminine nature.

Her summer frocks were loose, billowy things that could catch even the smallest breeze to bring a puff of fresh, cool air inside. She liked bright colors, too – springtime and summery colors – often splashed with huge printed blossoms.

No matter where he was or what he was doing, Luther would see this huge flowery cloud setting out the coffee cups and pie. Even with the over-size cut of the frock, Luther saw her flesh roll around underneath. Her massive biceps were exposed, great slabs of soft flesh. Every Saturday Mary Louise would settled into one of the Adirondack chairs on the back porch and apply a layer of sunscreen, first to her arms and then to her trunk-like legs. She'd rub them and rub them and pull up the hem of her skirt while she applied the lotion to her knees and the lower part of her thighs. She was slow and thorough and Luther couldn't miss it, all that soft flesh being manipulated under those fat, pink fingers… He wondered idly whether she bought her sunscreen by the quart.

The lunches grew longer and more elaborate. Mary Louise introduced Luther to cold soups and salads with mushrooms and sprouts and several versions of thick creamy dressings. And she talked. Her chatter had moved on to personal stories about her life before Grants Ferry, the years of Massachusetts classrooms where her innovation and drive were never appreciated. She'd never been popular with the fellas, she said, so she cooked and embroidered, and she often knit things for charity, filling her life with hobbies and volunteer work.

"I've always been extremely feminine," she said as a fat finger pulled a wisp of hair away from her eyes. She'd painted her nails a fiery red and they flashed in front of Luther like a cluster of crimson fireflies. "I know there are truly good men who appreciate women of size," she said, "but none have come my way so far..." She took a bite of sandwich, chewed it, and swallowed. "So here I am in Grants Ferry, almost a year into a new job, a new challenge, a house of my own, building a new life."

Lunch was a stack of chicken salad sandwiches, a dish of dill pickles, and beer. She'd bought beer, she said, "because of the heat."

"I'm a passionate woman, Luther," she said a little later, "with strong emotions, but in my authoritative role at the school I'm forced to keep my emotions in check. School must be about order and discipline and meeting academic standards. I'm sure you understand that very well. You have a discipline I admire, Luther, I really do. And so, as my role at the school requires it, that's who I am there, but at the end of the day it's a sad and lonely existence for a woman with strong passions."

She kept on in that constant sawmill whine of hers. Luther kept his head down and focused on his lunch. Mary Louise Turner could fix a good meal.

"Luther?" He started at the sound of his name. "Land sakes, you must have been a thousand miles away. Can I get you another beer, Luther?"

"No," he said. "No, thanks."

"You're sure? It's so awfully hot…"

"Well…" Had he ever told her no and stuck to it? "Sure," he said.

She went off in a great swirl of flowers and colors and returned shortly with a bottle already sweating in the heat. She picked up his glass and poured the beer slowly down the side.

"I should have mentioned it earlier," she said, as she put his glass back on the table "but I do have one more little chore, if you have time."

"Sure…"

"I just can't sleep in this hot weather and I'm simply a wreck without my eight hours so I ordered an air conditioner from Sears. It was delivered yesterday. Do you suppose you could take it upstairs and put it in the window for me?"

"Sure," he said. Why not? It was just one more thing…

He picked up the heavy carton, got it balanced, and followed Mary Louise up the stairs and into her bedroom

"I think it will go in that window," she said, "and there's an outlet right there."

Luther opened his jackknife and cut the box away. The air conditioner was the kind that is held in place by its own weight when the sash is drawn down behind a metal collar. Luther got the machine secured and opened the bellows on either side that sealed the rest of the window opening. When he was satisfied it was secure, he plugged it in and turned it on. Almost immediately cooled air was pushed into the room.

Luther folded his knife, put it away, and gathered up the box pieces and the wrappings.

"Oh, it's cooler already," Mary Louise said. "Thank you so much, Luther."

The bed springs squeaked and Luther turned around to find Mary Louise on the bed, naked.

"Holy fuck." The cardboard pieces slid out of his hands. "Oh, Jesus."

Mary Louise was smiling.

The cool air was filling the room.

"You ever make it with a fat girl, Luther?"

"H-holy fuck," Luther said again, this time a bit louder.

Mary Louise Turner lifted a large breast and pointed it at him. When she took her hand away it dropped and slapped against the other one.

"It's just so nice and cool now, isn't it?"

Luther's T shirt was still damp and the cool, dry air from the air conditioner caused a shiver to overtake him. Mary Louise Turner mistook the shiver for excitement. She giggled with an excitement of her own.

Luther began to sweat again, even in the coolness of the bedroom, as he struggled to deal with his situation. His field of vision closed in, as if the light had gone out all around and he could see only a narrow path in front of him and this narrow path led to a sagging bed and a naked fat woman who stroked her leg and drew her hand up over her massive belly to her breast again.

As far as Luther was concerned, this woman was and had always been in a position of authority. She gave him orders when he worked at the school, although she was always very polite when she did so. And she always had a list of chores and instructions for him when he came by on Saturday, although here at her home the orders had come in the form of requests.

"Come over here, Luther," Mary Louise purred. "See what it's like to play with a fat girl." She bounced a breast in her hand again, beckoning. Was this an order or a request? Or, in some bizarre way, was it an invitation?

No, this is totally fucked up, Luther thought. *This is wrong. What the hell am I doing here?* He pulled himself together and picked up the box pieces.

"Put down that silly cardboard, Luther."

The cardboard slid out of his hands again.

"I'm a passionate woman, Luther. Let me show you." She rubbed her massive thigh again. "Come. Share my passion. Come."

Luther's better sense was screaming inside his head, urging him to run, run down the stairs, drive away, never come back. Run! Run! Run! Run!

And yet, as in a trance, he stepped over the cardboard and walked slowly toward the bed.

*

Chapter Eighteen

Ellen's vision of her store as a cooperative where each of the crafts-people would take shifts in the shop never worked. No one wanted give up a day to clerk in a store when they could be home producing goods. Ellen, too, had found that part frustrating. The solution was Blanche Peterson.

Blanche was a quiet woman in her seventies. She'd produced boxes of needlework over the years until arthritis put an end to it. She stopped by one day to see if Ellen might like some of her collection in the store. Blanche had an appreciation for detail and spoke easily and freely about both her work and the qualities she could see in the other products in the store. Since she was no longer creating work herself, Ellen wondered if she might be interested in managing the shop for the four days they were open, Thursday through Sunday.

Blanche Peterson was a natural host, welcoming to everyone, and able to describe the items in the shop, including the special patience and skills needed to create them. Ellen invited Blanche to write the copy for her catalogs, brochures, and even for the website.

With time to get back to her studio, Ellen experimented with some new lines for her table settings. She created a more traditional and less expensive pattern that could be easily produced by trained staff. Then, more as a bit of whimsy than anything, she'd come up with a set of four mugs. These were basic mugs, a bit taller and more slender than her others and with a traditional glaze, but to each of the four mugs she'd added the figure of buxom young women on the far side of the cup. Each wore an off the shoulder peasant blouse. Their arms wrapped around the mug as if they were holding a large basket and the tops of their breasts squeezed up against and even a bit over the rim of the cup and each of these young women appeared to be reaching for a kiss.

They were made from complex molds, carefully hand painted before firing, and were not cheap. One of the four, just for something different, had a peek of nipple showing above the lip of the cup – just a touch of naughty. After all, Ellen reasoned, if she couldn't have fun with this stuff, there was no point.

*

Homer Dalrymple was frustrated. No matter when he passed the hotel, the tarps were always lashed tight and the building hidden. If this undertaking were honorable, he reasoned, there would be no cause to hide its progress. Following an errand at the bank one morning, he walked to the trailer behind the hotel and asked to be given a tour of the work. Clancy refused.

"And what's the reason for your refusal?" he asked.

"It's not my property and not for me to say who goes inside." she said.

Homer's interpretation of a Bible-guided society had women's roles well defined and this woman was defiant and territorial and had clearly forgotten her place. He produced a small notebook and tried to ignore the big red hair, the form-fitting jeans, and the work boots.

"What's your name?" he said.

"You first."

Again, an unacceptable and truculent response. Homer's indignation rose up but the strength and wisdom of the Lord gave him the grace to respond calmly in the face of this brazen behavior from a woman who had assumed a role normally reserved for men.

"I'm the Reverend Homer Dalrymple…"

"Oh, my," she said. "The *Reverend* Dalrymple."

"Yes, and my congregation and I have deep concerns about this project."

"Your congregation?"

"I've come on their behalf."

"Really? Well, I'm Clancy Matthews and my job at the moment is to restore the hotel and it doesn't include escorted tours during the work."

Homer wrote her name in his notebook. Clancy saw this and tapped Homer's name into her computer, each making a show for the benefit of the other.

"I'd like to be given a tour of the project," Homer said again.

"'Fraid not, Homer. If you want a tour you'll have to ask Kenneth."

"The sodomite?"

"That's the one."

"I see," Homer said, making another note. "Clancy – is that your given name or some sort of chosen non-gender transsexual name?"

Clancy was off her stool to engage in a bit of physical confrontation when the light coming through the open trailer door was blocked out by Frank, a burly black man wearing coveralls and a yellow hard hat.

"Oh, sorry," he said. "When you got a minute, Clancy."

"Give me about five, Frank," she said. Frank's intuition often bought him around in times when Clancy might soon find herself in trouble. "The Rev. Homer Dalrymple is just leaving. Could you see him safely to the street?"

"Sure thing," Frank said. "This way, sport." Frank reached out a dusty black hand to take Homer's arm,

"Don't touch me," Homer said, pulling away.

"He givin' you trouble, Clancy?"

"Just see him to the street."

Frank backed down the trailer steps. Homer kept a careful distance. When they reached the sidewalk Frank put out his hand and stood close. Homer held his breath.

"Clancy's troubles are my troubles," Frank rumbled. "You unnerstan'?"

"Completely," Homer said.

Frank glared at him for several seconds before he stood aside so Homer could scurry off down the street where he passed Ellen's front window. He'd watched the transformation of the old hardware store with a mild curiosity through the springtime and into summer but had never stopped to look inside. He had little personal use for hand crafts, but in his mission to implement God's will in this beleaguered community he was naturally interested. Only through constant vigilance and frequent prayer could God's vision for mankind be revealed and accomplished.

Homer approved of Ellen's contribution. After all, what could be more rewarding than an outlet for the handiwork of the local citizenry? He surveyed the shop windows, a pleasant mix of woven scarves and shawls, a few small sculptures, some created from found items (i.e., junk), paintings in several styles and mediums, and, of course, Ellen's pottery. He recognized her trademark place settings and planters with the various family members, amusing to be sure, but not to his taste. He then noticed a small set with what looked to be young women holding the mugs in their arms while reaching for a kiss. Clever, he thought, but then…

There it was, a peek of nipple pressed against the lip of the cup.

"Disgusting," he muttered.

And then the beginnings of interest made itself known in his loins. Horrified, he hurried off before this interest would affect his gait.

*

Archie had become accustomed to the construction crews as they crowded into the diner each day. He had his papers and his coffee and his window and the construction guys were soon gone, leaving the diner quiet again. Dot would then come to top up his coffee so he was surprised when Homer Dalrymple appeared instead.

"Homer? What brings you out this time of day? Saw you over by the hotel."

"Yes, I asked to survey the progress but that red-haired woman refused."

"Clancy? Feisty, ain't she?"

"Some ruffian, a black man named Frank, actually put me off the site."

"I expect she's just doin' her job, Homer. Just like we all are."

Homer watched the construction crowd walk back up the street. "I – I wonder if I might sit for a minute," he said, glancing at Hank.

"'Course. Move over, Hank." Archie slid Hank's plate closer to the window and Hank followed it. Homer inspected the bench for dog hair before he sat down. "Coffee?" Archie asked.

"I don't take caffeine. Thank you, though."

Dot appeared with the carafe and another cup.

"Homer," she said. "What'll you have?"

"Homer doesn't take caffeine," Archie said before Homer could answer. "You got anything else?"

"Herbal tea. Be right back."

"What's on your mind, Homer?"

"Well, I – I passed Ellen's store. It's a fine contribution to Grants Ferry."

"Here you go." Dot came back with a pot of hot water and a small basket with a variety of herbal teas. "Help yourself. doughnut?"

"No, thank you. This will be fine. Well, perhaps a spot of honey…"

"You got it."

Homer selected something from the basket that turned his hot water green. Archie shook his head. *Might as well eat weeds as drink herbal tea.* As for Ellen's store, Archie also admired what Ellen had accomplished. She was happy and busy and Archie liked that. What he didn't appreciate was that she seldom had time to mind the house and fix his supper. She seemed to spend a lot of time with Kenny Forbes, too, but that was another conversation.

"Yup, she's done a good job," Archie said. "Can't argue with that."

Dot put a little bear-shaped plastic squeeze bottle of honey on the table.

"And I – I – I'm not sure how to say this, but – "

"What do you suppose the connection is between bears and honey?" Archie said.

"What?"

"You'd think it would come in a bottle shaped like a bee, wouldn't you? Or one of those cone-kinda straw bee hives."

"I – I guess so. I really – "

"I think it's because of Winnie the Pooh, myself."

"Winnie the Pooh?"

"Yeah, he was always after honey, wasn't he?"

"I – I don't know. I suppose so… I'd never thought about it, frankly."

"Makes you wonder, though."

"Yes. Well." Homer had experienced Archie's method of avoiding conversations before. He tried again. "About Ellen's shop, were you aware that she has pornography in her front window?"

"Porn? Ellen?" *Well, that would be something*, Archie thought. Ellen was certainly no prude, but porn? "No. No, I didn't know that. Porn, you say?"

"I'm sure it's some of her work – maybe someone else's – but one of the mugs – there are several – but the mugs, the ones that have young women with their arms around the mug?"

"Yeah. Pretty clever, aren't they? She brought a couple of the early models home. What about'em?"

"Well, one of them – one of them has –" he looked around the room be sure they were alone. "One of them has a nipple showing," he whispered.

"A nipple?" Archie said, whispering back. "On one of Ellen's mugs?"

"Well, it's in her window."

"Right…"

"Children might see it."

"Oh, for Christ's sake, Homer," Archie said at normal volume. "We should pretend women don't have nipples?"

"Well, no. I mean, that's not the point, but in the interest of decency…"

"Is it just the one nipple or two?"

"Well, I only saw just the one."

"All of it? Big and pink and – "

"No, no, no. Just a bit of the top…"

"Oh, well," Archie said, "if it's only a bit of the top…."

"Well, I thought you should know," Homer said, "in the interest of decency and the children."

"Right," Archie said. "Decency and children. I'll get right on it." Pretending to agree with Homer was the easiest way to get rid of him.

"Ellen will listen to you, Archie. I just want to avoid trouble in the long run."

"Trouble?"

"Well, public outcry. I thought we might be able to deal with it quietly, you know. Catch it early. People needn't know…"

"Oh. Right."

"I know you can take care of things. You've always had a way of taking care of things." Praise can be a powerful tool. "Grants Ferry has been very lucky to have you."

"I appreciate that," Archie said. "Drink your tea while it's still hot."

Archie wasn't about to get in the middle of this one.

Besides, Homer was a moron.

*

"What do you mean you're not having stalls at the fair? Any of you?"

"We've got the store," Ellen said. "Everything's inside where it's clean and dry and displayed well and we're just down the street. We'll put out a sign."

"A sign? I don't think so."

"And why not? We're going to give you fifteen percent of whatever we sell those two days."

"We gotta keep people on the common, keep'em focused, that's why not. Now I've got to fill five empty stalls."

"I think it's time you started thinking beyond the common and the raffle and the bean supper."

"I been doin' this long enough to know what works," Archie said, his volume increased with each degree of agitation. "And what works is keepin' customers focused on the common until they spend some money. I'm damned if you're puttin' up a sign to draw people down the street."

Ellen willingly discussed anything but refused to argue. She walked out the door and drove over to Kenneth and Simon's house.

"I'm going down to Springfield and Keene to look for a van," she said. "Want to come?"

"A van?"

"For the store. I'm done depending on Archie and his truck when I need to move product."

"What about Archie?"

"I've never taken him when I bought a car and I don't intend to start now. Besides, I want to spend the afternoon with someone I like. Simon can come, too."

"He's in the city."

"All the more time for us, then."

"Whoa. Something going on with you and Archie?"

"Maybe. Not ready to talk about it yet."

This was an agreement they'd always had. The conversation would continue but not now. When she was ready, they'd talk.

"So the store's doing well enough to buy a van?"

"Probably not but you-know-who needs to think I'm thriving." Kenneth knew she was steamed about something. "He got on my case because I want to put out a sign during the Harvest Festival to bring people to the store."

"What's the harm in that?"

"None than I can see. We're going to give the festival fifteen percent of whatever we make those days. They can't lose."

"What is it then, because it's something new?"

"I see you haven't forgotten what it's like. You coming or not?"

*

"I seen Ellen and Kenny headin' out'a town yestiddy," Benny grinned.

Archie was getting the latest gossip along with his gasoline.

"That so?"

"Seems like they see a lot of each other, don't it?"

"Christ, they've been tight since kindergarten. What d'you expect?"

"Well, she ain't married to him. Just seems funny, that's all, seein' your wife out with another man," Benny said. The pump snapped off and Benny hooked the nozzle back in its cradle. "Looks like the better part of $18 there."

"Put it on the tab," Archie said. "And make a note someplace that you told me about Kenny and Ellen so I don't have to hear about it again."

*

"You're spendin' enough time with Kenny Forbes that people are beginning to notice," Archie told her that night when she came home.

"Really?"

"Don't look good. You ought'a be careful."

"Careful of what? Kenny's been my friend as long as I can remember. I don't care what people say."

"Well, I do. You ought'a be more discreet."

"Right, and you ought to think about all the time you spend at Dot's."

*

"How do you feel about going on a picnic?" It was Tuesday afternoon, a week later. Kenneth was in the vegetable garden with a cordless phone.

"A picnic? Now?"

"Yes," Ellen said. "I'll pack a hamper, grab a blanket or two, and we can enjoy this gorgeous day together unless you've got something more important to do."

"No, no. Just out in the garden. Give me half an hour to get cleaned up."

Ellen arrived in her new van, got out, and pushed her sunglasses up on her head. She was dressed in a sleeveless top, denim shorts, and sturdy shoes.

"Whoa. You look better than you did in high school."

"Thank you, sir," she smiled. "Grab your walking shoes."

Kenneth found his hiking boots, handed her the wine he'd retrieved from the cellar and put in the freezer when she'd called, then brought out a couple foam roll-up exercise mats. When he got in the van Ellen pulled him close enough to give him a kiss.

"Thanks for coming on the spur of the moment. I've been waiting for a day like this all summer and there's no one else I want to spend it with." She drove west toward the Interstate.

"So how're you doing?" she asked.

"Well, Clancy's got the hotel on schedule, I don't think we'll run out of money before it's finished, and it looks good."

"I wasn't asking about the hotel."

"I know."

"What's going on with Simon? He never seems to be around anymore."

"Yeah, well, he was restless here. Small town life just wore him down. He was moody…grumpy most of the time. I don't think he ever understood what living in a small town meant. He needs the stimulation of city lights and noise."

"And you?"

"Well, I never completely adapted while I was there. I was reasonably happy, I think. Looking back, though, I was never 'at home', if you know what I mean. I liked it, and it excited me but I don't think I ever pondered the concept of 'home'."

Ellen turned onto a narrow road that took them north.

"You going up to Old Baldy?"

"Seemed like the perfect place for a picnic on a day like this."

"I agree."

"And now? How do you define 'home' now?"

"It's funny," Kenneth said as they bounced along the narrow dirt road. "I resented every minute Fanny made me spend in her garden, but this year they're my beans and my carrots and cucumbers and tomatoes… Simon can't imagine why I'd waste time growing my own food. We used to argue about exploiting the Mexicans in California to keep our food cheap but the reality of the way humans treat each other is bigger than any of us. He used to say that if we didn't buy the produce they wouldn't have any work at all, which I suppose is true enough. Still…"

The road narrowed and a branch scraped along the side of the van.

"He's gone, then?"

"Yeah, pretty much. He'd stay if I insisted but I know he's happier in the city. And besides, what he's doing down there is just as important to our success here as what I'm doing on this end. I can't complain."

"Do you miss him?"

"Sometimes, but not as much as I thought I would. When he comes up for a weekend now it actually feels like an interruption and I'm a little annoyed."

Ellen parked at the end of the road. They took the food and the gear out of the van and began the walk up the rocky path to the summit.

"I'm not sure it's any of my business," Ellen said, "but are you still a couple?"

"We're still business partners. I'm not sure about the rest."

"Oh, wow."

"Simon and I have always agreed that if one of us was ready to move on, the other would let it happen. We've not talked about it, but I think that's where we are."

"And you're okay with that?"

"What would change if I wasn't? Yes, I'm okay. It's no fun hanging on to someone who's ready to leave."

The path still contained rough spots and large stones. Ferns obscured the ground making it very easy to lose one's footing.

"The minister who came after the Nelsons was an outdoor type," Ellen said. "Clarence Chesterfield. He was forever arranging hikes and camping trips. He'd hiked up here several times and thought it would be a perfect spot for the Easter Sunrise service.

"I always thought it was a chore to get up and drive out to Ellis Rogers' place," Kenneth said. "I can't imagine hiking up here in the dark."

"Well, this guy was a fitness freak. We were running a little late and Elsie Palmer stumbled in the dark and broke her ankle. It took four men to carry her back to the car."

"Sorry I missed that."

They broke through the trees and climbed the last 100 yards to the top. The name Old Baldy came from the bare rocks, scraped clean and left smooth by the glaciers. Nothing save for bits of moss and grass in some of the cracks had ever taken root and the top had remained clean for centuries with only a wooded fringe around the edge.

The view extended 360°. To the north the river veered west for several miles and then north again. To the west there was an occasional glint off a vehicle on the Interstate. South was the village itself, with the church steeple, the shrouded hotel, the common, the school, and all the buildings that made up the town center. Further to the south was the Whitaker Brothers sawmill and lumber yard, and then, more to the east, was Ellis Rogers' farm with the large pasture near the river. It was a sweeping panorama that no photograph could capture. It was too big, too dramatic.

"Long time since I've been up here." Kenneth said.

"Me, too."

Kenneth remembered the one level spot, found it, rolled out the foam mats, and spread the blankets over them. Ellen unpacked the hamper and set out the plates and utensils.

"The sandwiches are ham and cheese, egg salad, and roast beef," Ellen said. "Potato salad in here, some sliced cucumbers and carrots, and blueberry pie for dessert. A couple kinds of cheese, too."

Kenneth handed her a glass of wine.

"Here's to tomorrow," he said.

"To tomorrow," she smiled. "Oh, my. That's nice. What is it?"

"Gewürztraminer."

"Ga –what?"

"Ga-*vertz*-tra-mee-ner. A cool climate grape. It's almost always bright and fresh. A nice picnic wine."

"Whoa. That goes down way too easy," she said, and took another sip. And that was another thing she liked about his return. He brought things like the wine from outside, things she would have never known about. "Remember when I used to pack lunches for us when we were out walking after the accident?"

"Sure do."

"That's the way I felt when I put this picnic together. My mom always offered to make the sandwiches for us but I wanted to do it. Funny the things we remember."

They sat, looked out over the valley, and soaked up the sun.

"Are you happy, Kenny? Is it good to be home again?"

"Well, it feels like I'm in some sort of holding pattern, you know? I'm still working on the yard and the garden but at least I don't think of it as Fanny's house any more. I'm just hovering, though, waiting until the hotel is finished and open. I've got good people working on it but until it's over…"

Ellen dished potato salad onto the plates and held out the container with the sandwiches.

"I thought we'd see a lot more of each other once you were back."

"Yeah, well…"

"Fanny's gone. There's nobody to stop us."

"What about Archie? I don't want to cause any trouble."

"If there's trouble, it won't be your fault," Ellen said. "Pour me some more of that whatever you called it."

"Gewürztraminer."

"That's it."

He refilled her glass.

"And you? Are you happy?"

"I don't know," she said. "I feel like I'm on the edge of something and I don't know where it will take me."

"Are you happy, though?"

"I feel good about the store and my studio and my work. It's become real, not just a hobby. I finally see myself as a professional. I'm even signing my work now."

"Good for you."

"Since the first of the year. And I sign it 'Ellen LeClaire'."

"What's Archie think of that?"

"Hasn't even noticed."

*

As far as Archie was concerned, it was just one damn thing after another since she took that lease on the store. Ellen had spent more and more time down there and left Archie with more and more evenings with nothing but TV and beer. He had to hand it to her, though. The place looked good. He'd only seen a few actual customers inside but he knew the UPS truck showed up out back every couple of days and they don't just stop by for a visit. On the other hand, he wasn't getting the support at home that he'd grown accustomed to – like supper and clean underwear. He could always find something to eat, even if he was reduced to one of those frozen god damned microwave meals but he'd never been reduced to doing his own laundry and that had really pissed him off. Truth was, he hadn't really missed her company which was odd since he'd become so used to it. He missed what she provided. Well, she was his wife and that was her job, god damn it. Now he had to compete with a fucking store.

They used to have sex fairly regularly, too, but there hadn't been even a whiff of that since he made the crack about her starting a business. His old bullying nature began to fester and bubble but he knew better than to use it on Ellen. Before he and Ellen were married he'd sometimes go down to the Ferry Slip and pick a fight with some poor bastard but those days were long gone. He really wanted to push someone around, though.

Help for the fair had been elusive and slow to sign up this summer and he knew better than to be too heavy-handed with volunteers. Look at'em cross-eyed and they're gone. He wasn't sure he could rely on these younger folks. Some of them acted as if he didn't know what he was doing. They needed to understand the importance of commitment once they agreed to something. They didn't seem to share the sense of honor in keeping one's word that was hardwired in folks from his own generation.

He hated to do it but Archie finally called Kenneth to see if they could help out.

"I don't think so, Arch," Kenneth said. "Our grand opening for The Intercourse House is that weekend."

"Grand opening? That's gotta be at least two weeks away from your deadline. Can't you hold off a week or so?"

"What for? We thought the tavern and dining room would be a nice choice for folks at the festival, something new. Diane and Jonathan have some great lunch options planned."

"Lunch? What about the food tent? That's where people are supposed to buy lunch."

"We're not going to attract anybody who wants a hot dog or a doughnut and industrial coffee," Kenneth said. "If anything the hotel will complement whatever you have at the fair, a high-end alternative. We'll have tea and cakes and cute little sandwiches from three o'clock to five or so."

"God damn it," he fumed, "you gonna compete with the bean supper, too?"

"Dinner at the hotel will only attract folks who don't want to eat in a mess hall. When the word gets around, the hotel will bring more people. We'll make a donation to the festival when it's all over. It'll be a great contribution to the weekend."

Like hell it would. A restaurant was nothing but competition, to say nothing of the Tavern. Nobody would wander from the common clear down to the Ferry Slip for a beer but the Tavern would be right across the street. A Rite-Aid wouldn't have been competition. He was sure of that. It would have been an attraction, something new to show visitors that Grants Ferry was moving out of the past and into the future but nobody listened to him anymore.

Folks around town seemed excited about the hotel, though, from the day they closed it in behind those tarps. As much as Archie resented Kenneth and Simon and Fanny and the hotel and all the ways he knew this could complicate his life, he didn't care much for the idea that Jerry Falwell might set his hooks in the town, either. Those guys were okay on TV from Virginia or wherever the hell they were but he didn't want them throwing their weight around in Grants Ferry.

And then Homer had his own high moral campaign going. He'd even offered a suggestion that something might "'happen'...if you know what I mean."

"I'm tellin' you Homer, anything with even a suspicion of being illegal 'happens' around that hotel job and I'm coming for your ass, you understand?"

"Oh, of course," Homer said. "I'm surprised you even thought such a thing."

"I think lots of things," Archie said, "and that's just one of'em."

"But what a gift it would be to have the Rev. Falwell and his Christian ministry here in Grants Ferry, Archie. Think of that."

Archie had thought of it and he didn't like the idea of people walking around in Christian lockstep any better than he liked the idea of Kenneth's gay friends prancing into town. Homer'd only shown up a few years ago himself. No more come to town than he set up that little no-name church of his. At the moment he was only a nuisance. If he ever got in with Falwell he'd be a total pain in the ass.

"You just stay away from there," he told Homer again. "Any funny business around that hotel and I'm coming for you, you understand?"

"Of course," Homer said. "I'm a man of peace, a servant of the Lord."

"Just be sure you remember that," Archie said.

In spite of his aversion to religious participation, Archie held a strong notion of what he understood Christian goodness to be, at least when it was convenient. The church, in his eyes, was a generally unorganized group of volunteers headed by poorly paid staff which had no real power to do anything. Archie believed his leadership around fundraising events like the Harvest Festival had been the key to the church's continued existence in Grants Ferry. They'd never have any money otherwise. Besides, the church had been in Grants Ferry from the earliest days. For that reason alone it should continue and be supported. He didn't need to be a card-carrying member to help out.

Homer Dalrymple's little non-brand church, on the other hand, was new. If one could assume anything from the themes on the changeable sign out front, it seemed to preach nothing but fear and distrust, if not outright hatred, in an attempt to make the world right. Occasionally there was an invitation to salvation. Archie wondered where Homer got his material. He certainly wasn't smart enough to think it up by himself.

They were a small group, unsmiling and certain in their faith. They carried their Bibles with them always. They were only a handful, but apparently ignorant enough to be influenced by a dink like Homer Dalrymple… Archie had heard they were stockpiling food.

Sometimes two or three at a time came calling in the manner of Jehovah's Witnesses. The last two that came to Archie's house were a couple of very serious women. One might have been a Crandall, a rough bunch from out on the end of the Pierce Farm road. She had a bit of mustache. She and the other woman railed about something going on far away from Grants Ferry, an issue Archie cared nothing about. They stumbled through their rehearsed script and waved their Bibles as if the words inside would fly out and show him the light, a gesture that seemed decidedly unChristian. Archie was never mean or rude, though. They always got to finish their rant before he thanked them and closed the door. If the Congregational Church ever took up that kind of behavior, he was done.

*

The tarpaulins came off and the staging came down the week after Labor Day and the Intercourse House façade was exposed to sunshine for the first time in months. What had been a weathered gray hulk now glowed with lavender and purple offset with deep red and gold highlights. A magnificent old sleeping matron had come to life again.

Kenneth, Ellen, Diane, and Clancy were across the street on the common.

"It's gorgeous," Ellen said. She'd squeezed Kenneth's arm as the tarps dropped to the ground. "Just gorgeous. I had no idea."

"You like it, then?"

"I love it. I was expecting a fresh coat of the old colors, I guess, whatever they might have been, but this is so fresh and light. It's beautiful."

Archie was disgusted. He'd been up the street in his truck but as soon as the first tarp dropped, he drove away. *Purple? I mean Christ Almighty, purple?* Garish was a word that came to mind, although garish was not a word he'd ever found occasion to use before. Whorehouse was another. And now this purple monstrosity would loom over the Harvest Festival. Just what he needed. Last year it was a funeral. This year it's a purple hotel serving lunch and dinner and drinks at the bar.

"Christ almighty," he said.

By the end of the day most of the town had come by. Most everyone liked it but Homer Dalrymple was appalled. The color scheme only confirmed his worst fears. Purple, in any and all of its variations, was nothing but a beacon to attract people from the gay/lesbian community. The town would soon be overrun. He prayed for guidance, for a plan of action, a sign. When the idea came to him later that night, he believed it had come directly from God.

*

"We unveiled the hotel today," Kenneth said when he called.

"How's it look?"

"It's great. Ellen and Diane love it. I think most of the town came by before supper to have a look."

"It's not too much, is it?"

"I don't think so, but it sure does make a statement."

"Good. Get some good high resolution snapshots, different angles and perspectives, and email them to me. I'll add them to the promotional stuff I'm working on."

"How's that going?"

"Tepid."

"That good, huh?"

"Well, all I've had to work with is a tired old town, an architectural rendering, and promises. A good color photo will make it real. How's the inside coming?"

"Still pretty rough."

"They still on schedule for the fair?"

"Clancy says yes."

"Great, I may be able to convince a few of the potentials to come up for the weekend. Let me know how many rooms will be ready."

*

In a small town it can be the silent things that draw attention, the long, black Cadillac limousine with smoked glass windows that slid into town the following Monday for instance. It whispered across the bridge on the edge of the village, floated past Benny Munson's garage, and coasted to a stop near the common where it idled silently for several minutes. Moving again, it made two slow revolutions around the common before it continued on down the main street. Even though it was virtually silent it might as well have been led by a brass band and a squad of strutting majorettes.

The Boston construction people, carpenters and plumbers and electricians, had taken their breakfast at Dot's and were headed back to work. To them a limo was a common event and they paid little attention. Archie, however, was on full alert.

"What the hell?"

Dot had just brought the coffee to warm his cup.

"Whoa. We don't see many of those around here, do we?" She leaned over to get a better look, and steadied herself once again with a hand on Archie's shoulder.

"We don't see any of'em," Archie said, "I don't have time for coffee, Dot."

"Oh, that's too bad. It just got quiet again." She straightened up and brushed some non-existent lint off his shirt.

"Somethin's up." He heaved himself out of the booth. "Come on, Hank."

"Well, the coffee's always on, you know. Stop by later if you like."

The limo continued on through the town toward the river. Archie followed in his truck at what he assumed was a noninterested distance. At the Ferry Slip the limo was on its way out of the parking lot when he got there, heading back to town. So much for Archie's being able to pretend he was on his way for something else. He dropped all pretense then and followed the limo back to Increase Houghton's office.

"Well, this can't be good news," he said to Hank. The driver got out, opened a rear door, and two large, well-groomed men in dark suits got out. One carried a briefcase. They surveyed the street, went up the walk, and in the front door.

"I'd like to be a fly on the wall in there right now," Archie said. "Where do you supposed those two came from?"

When she heard the front door Irene Bills thought it might be Luther coming to pick up his check for the past week. She still had a bit of a thing for Luther. Instead two strangers in dark suits appeared. Their hair was longish, styled, and blown dry. One carried a black leather briefcase. Both flashed a fine display of perfect teeth.

"Good morning, Ma'm," the one without the briefcase said. His voice was deep and very smooth. "I wondered if we might have a moment with Mr. Houghton." He clearly pronounced the T in Houghton.

"I can find out," Irene said, in full guard dog mode. "Who's calling?"

"I'm Jerome Butler," Jerome Butler said, offering Irene one of his cards, "and this is my associate, Clarence Godwin."

"Right," Irene said. She handled the card as if it might be sticky. "Will Increase know what this is about?"

"Probably not until we speak with him."

"The policy here is I give him a heads up," Irene said.

"And we respect that, miss – "

"Then there shouldn't be any problem, should there? What do you fellas want?"

"This is really a matter for – "

Irene was out from behind her desk and between the two men and the door to Increase's office.

"INCREASE!" Irene's voice sliced through the office. Butler and Godwin winced.

Increase opened his door.

"Increase, I got a couple suits here who won't state their business. Want me to call the sheriff?"

"I don't think that'll be necessary," Increase said. Butler and Godwin leaned around Irene to introduce themselves. "It'll be all right, Irene. Come in, gentlemen." Increase closed the door, gestured for the men to sit, and went to his own chair behind the desk.

"We regret any misunderstanding, Mr. Houghton, but – "

"Irene's been with me a long time. Absolutely dedicated," Increase said, "very protective. She once physically ejected someone."

"Really?"

"She'd probably take on two or three if she was steamed enough. There was a fella in here once, about your size. Raised his voice to me. Irene busted into my office, grabbed the poor cuss, and threw him down the front steps."

"Yes, well…"

"Took me some time to calm things down after that."

Butler and Godwin just smiled.

"Couldn't do without her," Increase said.

"I can assure you there will be no raised voices today."

"Hired her straight out of high school, you know," Increase said, ignoring them. "Ayuh, ayuh… I taught her what she needed to know and she's taught me the rest. Indispensable."

"Yes, well, we represent The Rev. Jerry Falwell…"

"Ah. That your car out front?"

"It was provided…"

"Must be handy, having someone drive you around."

"Yes, it is," Butler said. "Now, we've been given to understand that the Rev. Falwell or his ministry has been named in the will of one of this town's former residents."

"Might be."

"In that regard we were naturally curious as to why we'd not been notified."

"You haven't been notified because the will doesn't require it," Increase said.

The two men exchanged glances. "Can you explain that?"

"Kenneth Forbes, the deceased's nephew, is named as the recipient of the estate."

"Yes, but I don't understand why…"

"He must, however meet certain conditions."

"And has he?"

"So far."

"And if he fails?"

"He loses."

"And there are criteria in that event?"

"Yes, there are."

"Can you tell us what they are?"

"Yes, I can, but I won't."

"And why is that?"

"Those details are not to be made known unless Mr. Forbes fails to meet the conditions set in the will."

"And there are terms and conditions following that failure?" Butler asked.

"There may be."

"I see." Jerome Butler considered this for a moment. "Can you tell us the approximate monetary value of the estate?"

"It's not been audited, but we've estimated in the neighborhood of $1.5 million, mostly in the form of real estate. Could be as much as $2 million."

"Are there conditions attached to the real estate?"

"There may be."

"I see. And Mr. Forbes, if we could return to him for a moment. Is it your understanding that he intends to meet the conditions?"

"Yes, it is."

"Do you suppose we might have a conversation with Mr. Forbes?"

"Kenneth Forbes is free to speak with anyone he chooses."

"Thank you for your help," Butler and Godwin stood.

Irene simmered at her desk while Increase showed them out.

"What a couple of grease balls."

"Now, now…"

*

Kenneth's doorbell had not rung since Judith Houghton and Ellen came to tea. Two men stood on the porch, a limo was at the curb, and Archie sat in his truck about a hundred feet up the street. *Interesting combination,* Kenneth thought. He opened the front door but kept the screen door closed.

"Mr. Kenneth Forbes?" Butler and Godwin were all smiles again.

"That's right. Who are you?"

"I'm Jerome Butler and this is Clarence Godwin. We represent the Rev. Jerry Falwell and *The Old Time Gospel Hour*. Could we have a few moments of your time?"

"I can't imagine what you or Jerry Falwell might say that could possibly be of any interest to me." Kenneth found it hard to believe that humans actually came with that many teeth.

"The conditions of your inheritance have been brought to our attention."

"Have they?" Kenneth said. "How'd that happen?"

"We're not at liberty to say."

"Would it rhyme with Dalrymple?"

Butler and Godwin smiled again but the teeth were now out of sight.

"Do you expect to fulfill the requirements of the will?" Butler asked.

"Yes, I do."

"We've been told the deadline is drawing near…"

"Is it?"

"…and we've come on behalf of the Rev. Falwell to offer you a truly generous settlement to give up your quest, an offer that frankly exceeds what we believe to be the estimated value of the estate."

"And how much is that?"

"I'm sure you're familiar with the estimated value of the estate. We're authorized to offer – "

"And turn it all over to you guys?"

"We're in the will."

"I've heard that rumor, too," Kenneth said.

"We're a powerful ministry, Mr. Forbes."

"So what?"

"Bravado may be unwise at this point. You realize, of course, that you stand to lose everything, including your substantial investment thus far. "

"I can't say that ever occurred to me."

"The Lord works in mysterious ways."

"Interesting cliché."

"In the Rev. Falwell's eyes, your failure would be a direct result of your choosing a life of sin and – "

"What I do with my life is none of your business," Kenneth said. "Get the hell out of here."

"It's within our means," Jerome Butler began, "to – "

"Get the fuck off my porch." Kenneth said and slammed the door.

Butler and Godwin walked back to the comfort of their airconditioned car. The driver got out and smartly opened the door so they could crawl in and hide again. Several minutes later they all slithered up the street and out of town.

"I was just paid a call by a couple of Jerry Falwell's emissaries." Kenneth was on the phone to Simon.

"Anything to do with Homer Dalrymple and his crusade against the Sodomites?"

"That would be my guess."

"What's in it for Homer?"

"Aside from a victory over the Sodomites, I suspect Homer might have visions of a position in the Falwell organization."

"Whoa. You think so?"

"I really can't think of anyone else who would stand to benefit but what do I know?"

"Archie?"

"I doubt it. He's too suspicious of outsiders, especially outsiders who just show up. No, Archie wouldn't want Falwell in town. Besides, you and I are driving him crazy already."

"Well, keep an eye on Homer."

*

Chapter Nineteen

The Harvest Festival Committee thought including Ellen's store in the fair was a wonderful idea. Archie warned them it was a big mistake, but the rest of the committee, god damn them, had seen "the overall advantage" and outvoted him. He was even more upset over Ellen's public betrayal. She'd never got in the middle of his business before. He sat in silence and steamed through the rest of the meeting. When they adjourned he went straight out to his truck and drove home. Ellen stayed behind and chatted for another half hour. When she came home sometime later, Archie was waiting.

"Where do you get off goin' over my head like that?" he roared.

"Like what? Offering a new idea?"

"Sabotage is what it was. Christ, I'm havin' trouble enough this year without my wife showin' up and changin' things."

"All I did was make a suggestion. Turns out they thought it was a good one."

"I know what the good ones are, god damn it, and I decide." He was getting louder.

"And who are you, the Festival Czar?"

"Now, you listen to me – "

But she didn't listen. She left the house, got in her van, and drove to her apartment over the store.

Too late, Archie realized he should have known better. He'd never won an argument with her. Never. And then there was the hotel, that mass of purple looming over the east side of the common. It was just one damn thing after another, and a good time to call on Mr. Jack Daniels.

He was still in a foul mood at Dot's the next morning when the sheriff's cruiser appeared and turned up the street by the hotel. About ten minutes later it came out again and left town.

“Now what do you suppose that was about?” he said to Hank.

“What’s that, Archie?” Dot had arrived with his refill.

“Sheriff turned up the street by the hotel and left a few minutes later. Don’t you find that odd?”

“After this past summer nothing would surprise me,” Dot said. “Warm that up?”

*

Clancy was on the phone to Kenneth before the sheriff got back in his car.

“The sheriff just handed me a stop work order,” she said.”

“A what?”

“A court order. I’ve got to shut everything down. Now.”

“What the hell’s going on?”

“I don’t know. He agreed to let the guys use up the plaster they’d mixed, though, the painters can finish the walls they’re working on, and the tile guy can set the tiles he’s got the cement down for, but then we’ve got to shut it down.”

“God damn. Did he give a reason?”

“No. He delivered, I signed, and that was it. Diane’s come totally unhinged.”

“Okay. Do what you have to do. Tell Diane to pull herself together and meet me over at Increase’s office.”

*

“Got the FAX a few minutes ago,” Increase said. “The Falwell folks have contested the will and convinced the court to stop the work until a ruling is made.”

“Can they do that?”

“Apparently.”

“Well, Jesus,” Kenneth said. “We can’t just stop work. We’ll miss the deadline.”

“I’m sure that’s what they had in mind,” Increase said, “but if they can stop the work, I believe I can stop the clock.”

“And that will help?”

“Well, you’d always have a little over three weeks to finish. We just have to wait and see how it plays out.”

"But we've risked everything," Diane said, barely able to speak. Ordinarily she was a brick. "How long will this last?"

"No way to know, really. They'll string it out as long as they can."

"Oh, God," She was trembling.

"Can we even go inside?" Kenneth asked. "There are things we could be doing there that are not directly connected to the building, like cleaning up the dressers and chairs and bed frames…"

"Afraid not," Increase said. "The only access under the order is for maintenance and security. Beyond that any entrance to the property is in violation of the order."

"The bastards."

"I think for now," Increase counseled, "We should proceed as if we expect a minor delay, ready to resume at a moment's notice."

"And if it's not minor?

"Then we'll be dealing with a longer delay."

"Oh, God," Diane moaned again. Kenneth was furious.

"Am I going to lose to these sons-a-bitches?"

"Not if I can help it," Increase said.

*

"A what?" Simon yelled.

"A court order. Everything's stopped. We can't even go inside."

"I've got half a dozen prospects coming up over Columbus Day weekend. They all want to stay at The Intercourse House and you're telling me it won't be open?"

"Not that weekend. Increase says this could drag on for months."

"Jesus Christ!" Simon shrilled. "This past year has been for nothing, then? We've lost it all?"

"Not yet. Increase has stopped the clock. When it starts again we'll have about three weeks to finish it up but no one has any idea when that will be. Clancy says the biggest problem is that the work crews could all be off on other jobs by then."

"Son of a bitch."

"Diane's in total meltdown. I've never seen her come apart that way."

"Any point in my coming up?"

"I can't see any. Just keep doing what you're doing."

*

Two sheriff's deputies arrived a short while later and wound two bright yellow strips of DO NOT CROSS tape all around the hotel, a harsh insult to the lavender. Archie and Peter Rodman both saw them and arrived in Increase's office at the same time to see what was going on.

"Falwell's people have contested Fanny's will," Increase said. "There's a court order to stop the work until it's resolved."

"You think there's some way the will's in question?" Archie asked.

"I don't think so. I wrote it. But anyone can challenge anything."

"The hotel's created such high anticipation all summer," Peter Rodman said, "and I'm a bit concerned as to the impact this may have on the Harvest Festival. Perhaps we should hold an informational meeting to keep the rumors at bay."

"Can't hurt," Increase said. "Facts, even unpleasant facts, are worth more than rumors."

"As if I didn't have enough going on," Archie grumbled.

*

Ellen came in without knocking.

"What's going on with the hotel?"

"Falwell's people. Court order." Kenneth said. He explained the situation.

"Oh, god, I'm so sorry. You were so close."

Kenneth saw her tears and wrapped her up in a hug. His intent had been to comfort Ellen but in fact it took away some of the tension for both of them. After a few moments Ellen stepped away.

"I can't remember the last time I was held like that."

"Really?" Kenneth thought Ellen was quite huggable. It seemed unlikely that Archie wouldn't.

"Archie has never been what you could call affectionate," she said. "He's a Whitaker, after all. Affection is not something he knows, except maybe with Hank."

Kenneth didn't want to hear about Archie and Hank.

"You know," he said, "when Clancy called to tell me the work had to stop it hit me almost as hard as when Amy died. The life I had known then, content and full of promise, was suddenly taken away, stolen." He set out a plate of muffins and put on water for coffee. They sat, across the kitchen table from each other. "Clancy's shut the job down. Diane is practically catatonic. Simon has people, potential investors, booked to stay at the hotel over the festival weekend so you can imagine how he's taking it."

Ellen stroked the back of his hand. When they were kids this sort of touch had been uncomfortable for him. She was glad that was gone now.

"Remember how we used to work backwards to whatever it was that led us to something in the present?" she asked.

"The source of all that came after?"

"Yes, like that. I was doing that the other day and I realized everything I've done this past year goes straight back to the instant I saw you at the bean supper. It was wonderful to see you again, of course, but it began then. Nothing has looked the same since."

"Really?"

"It lifted me out of the rut I'd been in. I've become more independent. I think that's why Archie's grown more distant. I think he's proud of what I've done on the one hand but resentful on the other. I'm having a wonderful time but in the process he's lost a housewife."

"A housewife?"

"Well, we were never truly partners, were we? We were married. Not the same at all. You've helped me see that as well."

"Interesting distinction. Would you rather be a housewife?"

"No," Ellen said. She stirred her coffee. "No, I wouldn't. I was a good one, though." She split a muffin in two and spread each piece with some of Kenneth's own blueberry jam. "I've begun to think I should leave him."

It was out in the open now with the one person she could trust.

"So," she said. "The hotel. What will you do?"

"Whatever it takes to keep it away from Jerry Falwell."

*

Archie rapped the gavel and brought the room to order.

"All right," he said. "There's been lots of rumors since that yellow tape went up around the hotel, so Increase is gonna explain the situation. Increase?"

Increase, who was at the back of the room, made his unhurried way to the front. It was a long-held practice of his, a gimmick, really, to both calm the crowd and raise expectations.

"I won't bore you with all the history," Increase said, "but the hotel work was ahead of schedule. Jerry Falwell and his organization somehow got the idea that they'll be given Fanny's estate if Kenneth fails to complete the renovations and open for business by Oct 16. They've now filed a challenge to the terms of Fanny's will…" Some angry grumbling. Increase held up his hand to quiet them. "…and a court order has stopped the work, clearly an attempt to prevent Kenneth from meeting his deadline." Angry rumbles. Increase held up his hand again. "In response, as executor, I've stopped the clock and it won't start again until the court order is lifted."

"Good!" someone yelled, followed by a smattering of applause.

"So we dodged the bullet, then?" This was Warren Thurber.

"Well," Increase said, "the deadline will always be at least twenty days and ten hours away until the clock starts again. However, the longer Falwell can hold up the work the harder it will be to complete it."

"Bastards!" That was Benny Munson.

Homer Dalrymple smiled against the back wall.

"So that's the story," Increase said. "It's happened and we just have to see where it takes us."

It wasn't just the building renovations, of course. Jonathan had recruited and begun training his kitchen help and dining room staff. More than a few folks had looked forward to a job or dinner or a drink in the old Tavern. It had been so close and invisible forces from outside had snatched it away.

George Fisher stood up.

"It just ain't right," he said. "My boy, Jimmy, Jonathan hired him, you know. And Jimmy was proud, too. A real job, a clean job, here in town. He can't drive, you know, and we always wondered if he'd ever have a good job, but they – Jonathan and Diane – they give him a chance, a good job." He wiped his eyes. "A good, clean job and Jimmy was proud and happy. He just don't understand where it all went and I can't explain it, neither. It just ain't right."

Kenneth stood up. "Thanks, George. I'm here to tell you, though, that nothing has changed except the day we open." There was general applause. "We're doing everything we can."

Archie, too, felt cheated. Watching Kenneth fail would give him immense satisfaction but Falwell and his bunch were outside the rules. Fanny, god damn her, couldn't have foreseen this turn of events and this back door legal bullshit was a tactic that even Archie the Bully found disturbing.

*

Columbus Day Weekend arrived under thick clouds and steady rain. A slow weather front had crept in Friday evening and was expected to linger until sometime Monday. The ground turned to mud underfoot while the vendors set up Saturday morning and only grew worse with foot traffic. The customers who showed up were surly and in no mood to shop. Even chili and hot soup, traditional cold weather favorites at the food tent, were left bubbling away in their cauldrons.

Visitors who followed the signs down the street to Ellen's store, however, found a dry, warm space, and were offered a mug of mulled cider and a doughnut. Most lingered long enough to purchase something.

Diane had gone to New York for the weekend and Clancy had returned to Boston, but Simon arrived Friday evening with four of his six potential investors.

"Four people?" Kenneth said when Simon told him they were coming anyway. "Where the hell are you going to put them?"

"We've got room at the house. They understand about the glitch with the hotel."

"You call it a glitch?"

"Sure. No sense in letting them think it's a big deal, right? They still wanted to come so I said okay."

"Great. A house full of strangers on top of everything else."

"Not strangers, potential investors. I know it's supposed to rain all weekend but we'll make pizza, drink wine, play scrabble, and if there's a break in the weather we can show them around."

Kenneth resented the intrusion. He'd not invited these people, after all, even if they had expressed an interest in the town. From the moment they arrived it was noisy, crowded, and irritating, and they were camped out in his home.

"I'm going out," he said the next morning.

"Out?"

"Yeah, drive around."

"In the rain?"

"You guys go ahead and party. I need to get out."

He eased the Valiant out of the barn and drove off. The wipers chattered on the windshield and he made a mental note to have Benny replace them. He puttered slowly up and down some of the residential streets, paying no attention to where he was going. His thoughts were as aimless as his drive through the town. As he turned onto Main Street the wipers were suddenly overwhelmed and he pulled over to the curb. Through the downpour he could just see the glow from Ellen's shop windows, the only bright spot on the street. It would be warm and dry inside, and good company. When the rain let up a bit he got out and jogged to her store.

"Well, there you are," Ellen said. "I've been worried."

A half dozen people were in the shop.

"Yeah, well... Simon's back at the house partying with a bunch of people he brought up from New York."

"Friends?"

"Potential investors. They were all supposed to stay at the hotel."

"Oh. Any word on that?"

"Nothing."

"Come on upstairs and we can talk. Blanche and Claire can mind the store."

The front room of the apartment was now a bright and comfortable lounge. A sink/stove/refrigerator unit, a microwave, a drip coffee maker and a kettle for heating water were clustered in one corner. Shelves overhead were filled with plates, cups, saucers, and a few bowls. The room had been freshened up with new wallpaper and paint. Ellen filled the kettle, set it on the burner, ground some beans in an electric coffee mill, and dumped the grounds into a French Press.

"Nine months ago I was drinking the cheapest instant coffee I could find," she said while she put several home baked cookies on a plate. "Now I won't settle for anything but fresh-ground Fair Trade Sumatran coffee beans. What's happening to me?"

"You're just learning about some of the things that exist outside Grants Ferry, that's all." Kenneth spotted all the framed photos of him that he'd seen in her front hall. "You were going to tell me about these."

"That's right. It was after you'd disappeared," she said. "Judy Campbell was the only person who would ever talk with me about the friendship you and I had. Said she always envied us. Anyway I mentioned one day that I wished I had more photos of you. And then – I guess Judy told people – they just started showing up, any photos that people had taken of you. I framed them all. When I married Archie I hung them in the front hall."

"What'd Archie think of that?"

"He's never said a word."

"And now they're all here."

"He's not said anything about that, either." Ellen wiggled the kettle as if moving it would heat the water faster. She wanted to talk about something else. "So you still have no idea how long the work will be on hold?"

"Falwell's people can drag it out for months. Every time Increase responds to one issue, they come back with something else."

"It doesn't seem fair."

"Nobody ever said life is fair," Kenneth said. Another wall held recent photos of Ellen's children and grandchildren. There were no photos of Archie.

"So you're doing okay?" he asked.

"I think so. The orders from New York keep coming, thanks to you two, and my website has brought some more. The rest of the folks in the shop seem happy with their sales as well. I'm going to have to find some production help pretty quick, though, especially for the simpler, less expensive lines. I don't know if I can teach the sort of whimsy I want in the other pieces."

He was really asking about her and Archie but he knew she'd tell him when she was ready. Ellen poured the hot water into the French Press and brought cloth napkins and heavy flatware to the table.

"One day I couldn't stand paper towels and paper napkins either," she said, "so I bought some decent utensils, made some cups and plates for myself, and curtains, and – and I don't know, it was fun. Sometimes I think I care more about this place than my home."

"Maybe you do," he said.

"Whoa. Is it that obvious?"

"All I know is I see a happy woman. I didn't see that a year ago."

Ellen sipped her coffee.

"I am happy," she looked up again. "...when I'm here. I try not to dwell on it because it reminds me of the years I – "

"You can't look back," Kenneth said.

"But – "

"Listen, it happened. Knowing what I know now I probably would have made a lot of different choices twenty-five or thirty years ago."

"But you got away and I stayed here and – "

"It's not right or wrong. It's what happened."

"I know," she said, "but, sometimes... Sometimes it seems like I wasted those years. You and I – we were always different from the other kids but you – you escaped and I've stayed here. I let myself become one of them."

"You may have stayed but you've never been one of them and you never will be. Look what you've done in just one year."

"But ..."

"You think anyone else in this town has the intelligence or the initiative to do anything like this? Just keep doing what you're doing. You're good at it. It makes you happy and it shows. If something else makes you happy, do that."

"But thirty years... "

"They're gone. Forget them. You have a couple children and some grandkids. I'll never have grandkids."

That brought a smile. Yes, she had grandchildren. "We would have had beautiful children, Kenny."

"Oh, don't start that again."

"But I used to dream about that, sometimes even after Mark and Janet were born. I never told anyone."

"I should hope not."

"They were such sweet dreams, Kenny. Oh, Mark and Janet were wonderful children and I remembered all the things you told me about Amy and the kind of mom she was. That's what I tried to be. My mom was wonderful, too. I don't mean to dismiss her, but she was my mom. You and Amy, though – Amy was really your best friend, not a typical mother at all, at least not around Grants Ferry. It just made so much sense. So that's who I tried to be with Mark and Janet."

"How'd it work?"

"Well, there was still the Whitaker influence, of course, but pretty well, I think. We're still friends and they appear to have a good relationship with their own kids, Janet more than Mark, but Kristen's wonderful. I told her everything I could about Amy."

Kenneth liked the idea that Amy's influence was still present all these years later and was glad once again that he'd kept so many of her things.

"It wasn't all fun while I was away," he said after a few moments. Kenneth had never talked about these years. It was an adventure he'd put behind him when he'd finally landed a good job. "I traveled and saw lots of places I'd read about and I saw new and strange people and it was exciting and even a bit dangerous sometimes. I'd got most of it out of my system by the time I met Simon."

"I missed you so much."

"I know. I'm sorry. I wondered for a long time whether I should have taken you with me."

"Really?"

"You wouldn't have liked it. Too big, too noisy, too dirty, too risky, too many people. And there's a seedy underside to the city, any sizeable city, really, that's truly awful."

"It doesn't sound very nice."

"A lot of it's not. But so much of it is exciting and unpredictable and I'd read about such places and that's what I was after." Kenneth finished his coffee.

"More?"

"No, I'm set. Thanks." He looked out at the street again. The rain had become a steady, soft shower. "I've been remembering graduation and the speech that guy made, all about duty to community. Help it grow and thrive, volunteer, contribute, give back..." He folded his napkin and put it beside his plate. "Duty," he chuckled. "It sounds like Gilbert and Sullivan, doesn't it?"

He smiled, remembering.

"I was in a couple G&S productions years ago. Wonderful stuff." He shook his head. "And here I am in Grants Ferry."

"You're not going to leave me again, are you?"

"No, I'm not going to leave you again."

*

Simon was at the kitchen door later when Kenneth got out of the car.

"Where the hell have you been?"

*

They fed and entertained the potential investors all weekend. Simon finally drove them back to New York on Monday leaving Kenneth with piles of laundry and cleaning up. For all the work and the food and wine that was consumed there were no commitments and little evidence of actual interest.

"I'm not going through that again," he told Simon when they talked later in the week. "It's taken me three days to get the house put back together."

"I'm doing all I can, god damn it," Simon shot back. "It's not my fault Jerry Falwell's being such a prick."

"Mine, either, but I'm not having a houseful of strangers camping here again. Find some other way."

*

November came cold, gray, and grim and this did nothing for Kenneth's increasingly dark mood. He searched for ways to keep busy, anything to move his mind away from the hotel. He cleared out some of Fanny's canning that was long past fail-safe. He checked out Fred's tools and bits of hardware and wondered whether he dared to throw any of that out. He inventoried and sorted their wines. Sometimes he watched television. Sometimes he trolled the Internet. His meals were simple. He wasn't up to fussing over anything.

Luther had brought a couple cords of firewood in October and Kenneth spent parts of days for two weeks getting that inside and stacked. He and Ellen got together for coffee a couple times a week and that was nice, but the waiting was wearing him down and he'd become anxious and moody.

"Maybe you should take a few days and go someplace for a change of scene," Ellen suggested.

"No, I don't think so," Kenneth said. "My mind would be back here anyway. When the order's lifted I don't want to waste even the time it would take to drive home."

Diane had grown so jumpy and nervous he couldn't stand to be around her. Jonathan went back to the city to hang with friends there and wait it out, but Diane, like Kenneth, couldn't bring herself to leave, just in case the call came. Then she called one afternoon, surprisingly upbeat. "Hey, Kenneth. Clancy's coming up for the weekend. Come for supper on Saturday."

"What's going on?"

"She wouldn't say, just that she had something to show us."

If whatever it was would pry Diane out of her funk it would be worth it.

"What can I bring?"

"We'll probably do a lasagna and salad. Bring a dessert, but don't fuss."

They were well into the wine when Kenneth arrived Saturday afternoon with a cheesecake and a sauce made from some of Fanny's blueberries.

"This needs to be in the fridge. Is there room?" He needn't have asked. Diane seldom bought ahead and didn't keep leftovers. The refrigerator was almost empty.

"So how've you been?" Clancy asked.

"Been better. I'm thinking I might buy a gun and take up hunting so I can go out and kill something."

"I've got a surprise as soon as we get this in the oven," Clancy said. "Grab some wine."

Kenneth refilled their glasses and poured some for himself from an open bottle. There was already an empty on the counter. Luckily, he felt no need to catch up. Clancy's laptop was open and humming on the dining room table.

"Okay, here's what I've done," she said. "I reviewed progress at the hotel up to the time we shut down. If everything had continued with the professionals on the job we'd have wrapped up with time to spare. You could have opened for the fair with no problem. So I've sorted out three levels: the things that absolutely need to be done to open for business, things that would be nice to have done, and the last few finishing touches. And from those lists, I broke it down to specific jobs, in priority order. It's what I do anyway but this has a couple more layers to it."

"And why are you telling me this?" Kenneth said.

"With this, if you can get enough help, the odds are very good that you can meet the deadline. Very little of this is highly skilled work, after all."

"It can really be done, then? After all this time?"

"I certainly hope so. My fee's hanging on it."

*

Ellen stopped by the next afternoon. Kenneth took her coat to the hook in the shed and when he came back she flung herself into his arms.

"Just –just hold me," Ellen sobbed. "I'll tell you, but just hold me." After a few moments she pulled herself together, wiped her eyes with a tissue, and they sat at the table.

"I've – You know I've been spending more and more time at the store," she said. "With Christmas coming, orders had to be filled and we've been really busy so some nights I've just gone upstairs to the apartment and slept on the day bed I've set up in one of the bedrooms. I got it originally so I could grab a nap now and then, but I've spent a few nights there as well."

Kenneth set a box of Kleenex on the table. She pulled out three.

"So last night I was at the store again. It was late and Mark called. Kristen's folks want them to go there for Thanksgiving this year. Janet and her husband can't come, so that leaves me alone with Archie. That's never happened before. I mean, we always knew the kids would have other obligations one day so it wasn't a total surprise, but then Mark said that Archie called and had obviously been drinking, barely coherent, apparently. So he unloaded on Mark about my not being home and leaving him to fend for himself."

"Oh, God…"

"Then he started on about the time you and I spend together…"

"Great. All we need is to stir that up on top of everything else."

"So Mark gets on my case. They always like to pull that macho crap, doubling up on me."

"You let them get away with it?"

"I can handle both of them, together if I have to." She took a minute to blow and wipe her nose and dab at her eyes. "The thing is, it's been nice to be alone when I've stayed at the store. I do things at my own pace, I can stay up late or get up early and there's no one to care. I'm comfortable there and I'm happy. I'm doing things for me, not someone else."

"And now there's Thanksgiving."

"That's right. It's always been a big day and one of the kids has always made it back, sometimes both of them, but not this year. Frankly, Mark sounded as if he was just as happy to go to Kristen's parents' house. Can't say as I blame him."

Kenneth waited.

"And I realize I don't want to be alone with Archie anymore. We could invite people for dinner, I suppose, but I don't think I'm up to cooking a big meal."

"I could do Thanksgiving here," Kenneth said.

"Here?"

"Why not? Simon's going to be in New York. Clancy and Diane and Jonathan all have families somewhere else, but there's Luther and Yvonne and the Houghtons. Now I think that would be an interesting crowd."

"You want to cook for that many people?"

"I've done it before. I'm not doing turkey, though. Maybe Mexican or Tex-Mex. Tortillas, burritos, enchiladas, chicken mole, salsa, corn chips, fajitas, tamales, and Corona with wedges of limes stuck in the neck and maybe a pitcher of margaritas and fried bananas for dessert.

"Sounds wonderful," Ellen said, her energy suddenly returned.

"Think Archie would come to that?"

"Who knows? Ask him if you want. I'm coming early to help the cook."

*

Kenneth backed slowly out of a parking space at Paul's Grocery when there was a heavy thump from the back of the car. Startled, he looked around to find Archie with a big grin on his face after having pulled one of the favorite high school pranks of forty years ago. Kenneth rolled down his window.

"So you and Ellen been pretty tight lately, haven't you?" Archie said as he leaned over. The grin was gone and the sour smell of beer came in the window.

"Have we?"

"Don't think I ain't noticed."

"Well, you may well have since I've not tried to hide anything."

"Everything was goin' fine until you showed up last year, you know. Did you put her up to that friggin' store?"

"No, I didn't. The store was all her idea. Simon and I were quite skeptical when she told us about it."

"That so?"

"Yes, it is."

Archie thought about that. Whatever he thought of Kenny, he'd never known him to lie, even when it would have been a lot wiser in the moment for him to do so.

"She's all but moved out," Archie said, "stays in that apartment over the store."

"She told me she'd spent occasional nights there…"

"Oh, it's a hell of a lot more than occasional I can tell you."

Kenneth decided he'd redirect the conversation to something less personal.

"I understand your kids won't make it up for Thanksgiving this year."

"Yeah, well. They got their own lives, haven't they?"

"They tend to do that, I guess. I'm going to have a few folks in."

"That so? Fill the house up with a bunch of your lightfooted friends?"

"No. Simon's in the city so I thought I'd invite Luther and Yvonne and the Houghtons. You and Ellen, too, if you want to come."

"Well…" Archie considered what that might look like.

"I'm not doing turkey, though," Kenneth said. "I'm going for Mexican."

"Whoa. Mexican?"

"Simon will ship me some supplies and I'll have Paul order up a few cases of Corona."

"Mexican? *Mexican?*"

"Great food, Mexican."

"For Thanksgiving? Don't sound right to me." Archie pushed himself off the Valiant.

"Well, after all, they harvest most of our food. Seems appropriate somehow."

"Well, I'll get back to you on that one," Archie said, and went into Paul's.

Kenneth hummed *La Cucaracha* all the way home.

*

"Ellen's not doing Thanksgiving this year," Archie said when Dot brought his doughnuts and poured the coffee the next day.

"She's not?"

"Nope. The kids are both gonna be with their inlaws. Says she's too tired from the store to cook, anyway."

"Oh, that's a shame. You always have a big dinner at Thanksgiving, don't you?"

"Used to."

"So what'll you do?"

"I don't know. Kenny's planning some damn thing with Mexican food and Ellen's going over there. He invited me, too, but Mexican? I mean, Jesus. What kind of Thanksgiving is that?"

There was no one else in the diner. "Mind if I sit?"

"Oh, sure. Move over, Hank." Hank shuffled over toward the window.

"Just let me get another cup and I'll join you."

She returned with a fresh pot of coffee and a plate with some more doughnuts. She broke one into pieces on Hank's plate.

"I don't know, Dot, it just seems like everything's fallin' apart, you know?"

"It's been a wild summer, all right. So busy, and then it just stopped, didn't it?"

"Yeah. Throws you off. I'm done with the Harvest Festival, though. I've talked about quittin' for years but this year I'm out. Should'a quit on a high note last year."

"You've been doing it so long, Archie. You deserve a rest."

Archie stared out the window and stirred his coffee, just something to do.

"You know what?" he said, "I looked in the mirror this morning and there was an old man lookin' back at me."

"Oh, stop it."

"First time I noticed. When did that happen?"

"I don't see an old man," Dot said.

"Christ, I'm just so tired, you know? Things change and I just can't seem to adjust. I mean, the kids always come home for Thanksgiving, at least one of'em, and the grandkids… Now nobody's coming and Ellen's got her shop and she's going off to Kenny's place… Mark said I could go with them to Kristen's folks but I hardly know any of those people – father's some big cheese in Hartford or New Haven or someplace, mother's way up on the society ladder… I haven't got anything to say to them…"

"You could still go to Kenny's…"

"Yeah, but I'd have to pack a sandwich or go hungry, wouldn't I? No, I don't think so."

"Well, it's Thanksgiving. There must be something to be thankful for…"

"I'm damned if I can see what it is."

"Well, maybe… I don't how it would look, but… Well, I – I could cook us dinner."

"What?"

"A nice turkey dinner. It's been years. I never bothered after Pete left and I was alone. It would be fun to do it again. Turkey, stuffing, roasted vegetables, pie. I haven't cooked a turkey in years. There's no sense in both of us being alone."

"No, I suppose not." He took a bite of doughnut and considered. Dot had always been good company. A little tired around the eyes and the diner had put a few extra miles on her, but she was hard-working, generous, a decent cook… It never occurred to him that she might enjoy some company. Besides, Ellen would be over at Kenny's and Archie wasn't crazy about spending the better part of the day with either Increase or Luther. What's the harm? "Okay," he said. "Why not?"

Dot was a bit light-headed when she stood up and grasped the back of the booth to steady herself. She'd never asked a man for a date. Well, this wasn't a date, of course, she was very clear about that. Not a date. It was just two friends sharing a meal, wasn't it? He'd agreed, though, and she was delighted.

"But you gotta let me buy the turkey," Archie said. "I always get a fresh one from Carl Johnson."

"All right. Not too big, though. You'll be stuck with leftovers for a month."

*

It was all totally innocent, Archie reminded himself. What with Ellen's attitude lately and her deciding to desecrate Thanksgiving with Mexican food and people who weren't part of the family, it came down to being practical. And besides, this way he could count on a nice traditional dinner.

Still, it was something out of the ordinary, too, and he felt he should acknowledge that somehow. Dot was going to a lot of trouble and it only seemed only right to do something a little special. Down at a big grocery in Springfield he bought a couple bottles of red wine. He'd not paid any attention to what Kenny and Simon had brought the year before so he bought two different reds costing just under $20 each. He thought that was outrageous but he didn't want something trashy, either. He also dropped by the liquor store and got a fresh bottle of Mr. Daniels' best.

He'd got a haircut the first of the week, early enough so it wouldn't look like he'd just had it done, and he brushed Hank for an hour so he wouldn't be dropping hair all over Dot's house. He shaved twice that morning, just to be sure, and then found a bottle of Old Spice aftershave, a Fathers Day gift from one of the kids years ago, and splashed some of that on. He wasn't used to having a cloud of scent follow him around but he understood women liked it. Won't hurt, he thought.

And it didn't. Dot hugged him when he arrived and lingered long enough to take a deep whiff of the Old Spice before she stepped back to get a look at him. She was happy, Archie thought, and she looked good in her own kitchen.

"Don't know much about wine but Kenny and Simon brought some to our house last year," he said. "Hope that's all right."

"Perfect," Dot said.

"Simon said it was important to open it and let it breath. I'll see if I can manage that."

"I don't think I've got a corkscrew," Dot said. "Never had a use for one."

"Well, damn. Shoulda brought my Swiss Army knife. Okay, gimme a small knife or a nut pick and I'll see what I can do." Hank had gone around the kitchen four times and sniffed everything in reach. "Give it a break, Hank. Find a place to lie down."

"He probably smells the cat," Dot said. Hank plopped in the kitchen doorway and continued to sniff the air while Archie dug away at the cork. He got most of it but the last few pieces dropped into the wine. So much for being suave and debonair. He eyed the Jack Daniels but took a couple deep breaths instead. There was no hurry.

"No matter," Dot said. "It's going to be fine. There are some stemmed glasses up on that top shelf. I've just got to finish the gravy and we'll be ready."

They ate slowly, talked about this and that, and laughed while they picked cork pieces out of the wine. They were quite mellow by the end of the meal.

"Don't think I can do pie right now," Archie said. "Need to let this settle first."

Dot stood to clear the dishes. "Whoa. That kind of snuck up on me," she said. She held the table a couple seconds to get her balance and then Archie helped carry dishes to the kitchen, something he never did at home.

"Go find a chair in living room," Dot said. "I'll just cover this up and start coffee."

Archie found a couple small glasses in the cupboard and grabbed the Jack Daniels. In the living room he took the biggest chair, poured some whiskey into each glass, and settled back.

Damn sight better than Mexican, he thought. *Damn sight. And here's to you, Jack.*

Dot came in, poured the coffee, set the cups on the table between the chairs, and sat down.

"Ah, that feels good," she said. She kicked off her shoes.

"Lot of work, eh?"

"It was fun. Thanks for coming. It's nice to have a man across the table for a change."

Archie lifted his glass with the Jack Daniels. Dot took hers up and they clinked the rims.

"Good meal. Good friend," Archie was not one to express sentiment and again he was surprised. He sat and reflected for a minute, full of a good meal, some wine, and now a bit of whiskey.

"What's it look like to you, Dot?"

"What's that?"

"Next year, the year after that. The future. What's it look like? Damned if I can get a grip on it."

"Well, for myself," she said, "I bought a double-wide in Florida."

"Florida?"

"Yeah… My sister and her husband bought one a couple years ago. They go down for the winter and they love it. Quite affordable, too. I found one not far from them."

"Jesus. You goin' to Florida?"

"At least for the winter. It's time to sell the diner and move on. I appreciate all the business the hotel job brought me but it just about wore me out. I'm negotiating with Emily Squires and Helen Roberts."

"What about this place?"

"Oh, I don't know. I probably ought to sell it. The cash would make things easier, something for emergencies; give me a chance to travel a little. I'm just tired, Archie. You know what it's like."

"I sure do." He sipped his whiskey. "So when you goin' down?"

"I don't know. I'd like to see the hotel open again. After that…"

And he'd just begun to enjoy her company.
"Well, damn..." Archie said.

*

Ellen and Kenneth strapped on a couple of Simon's frilly aprons and the two of them chopped and mixed and baked until the house was filled with the aromas of peppers and refried beans and cumin and cilantro and roasted meat.

Luther and Yvonne showed up an hour early. Kenneth glanced at the clock.

"I know, I know," Luther said, "but Yvonne was bouncin' off the walls."

Yvonne held out a white plastic tub with a snap lid. It was frozen solid and frost collected on it in the steamy kitchen.

"Not for today," she said. "Keep it frozen. Then just warm it up."

"Just warm it up?" Kenneth said.

"Woodchuck stew. This year's crop. Makes a nice meal on a winter night."

"Well, thank you."

"And there's this, too," Luther held out a glass gallon jug. "Got a good batch of hard cider this year."

"Oh, wow. Thank you," Kenneth said. "This will help with the cold winter nights." He took them both to the shed. When he returned, Increase and Judith Houghton were handing their coats to Ellen.

"Is Simon not here, then?" Judith Houghton asked. She'd expected to find him at the stove.

"He's with friends in the city."

"Indeed?" She was genuinely disappointed. "And Archie?" she asked Ellen.

"Archie didn't think Mexican food belonged at Thanksgiving. Dot Brookes offered to cook a turkey dinner for him."

"Dot from the diner?"

"That's right."

"I see. Well, I must say this is very unusual and exciting." She wanted to get away from conversation about people who were absent. Everyone else seemed at ease and it wasn't for her to judge. "I'm not at all familiar with Mexican food."

A few minutes later they were in the living room around bowls of salsa, corn chips, and sweating bottles of Corona, each with a wedge of lime stuck in the neck.

"What's the lime for?" Ellen asked.

"I don't know. That's the way they serve it. Someone told me once that you'll never find Corona on tap because it can't be served properly."

Yvonne stuck a corn chip into the spicy salsa.

"Better try it first," Kenneth said. "That one's pretty hot."

She tipped most of it off and tasted what was left.

"Hey, I like that."

"I told you she likes spicy," Luther said. The others all found it too much so Yvonne happily downed the entire bowlful.

Kenneth and Ellen mingled for a while and then went off to the kitchen for the last of the prep. Fifteen minutes later they were ready. Platters of all the different dishes were spread out on the sideboard where people could pick and choose. Increase and Judith eagerly took small portions of everything. Luther and Yvonne were more cautious.

"What's this?" Yvonne said.

"Tamale," Kenneth explained.

"Looks like corn husk."

"It is a corn husk. It's like a wrapper to hold it together while it cooks."

"I'll be jigged," she said.

Kenneth described each dish and what was in it and once explained, Yvonne went after them all.

"Well," Increase said as the meal wound down. "That was very nice. All of it."

The rest agreed.

"I thought Mexican food was real hot," Luther said.

"It can be, like the hot salsa, and some people like it that way, but I think if it's done well, it's just a really nice mix of flavors with a gentle heat."

Increase pushed back his chair and cleared his throat.

"I got a call from the court yesterday afternoon," he said. Increase liked to sit on news until the last minute. "And they, the court, have apparently decided the Falwell crowd is playing games."

"Didn't we know that?"

"Yes, we did, but as a matter of form the court lets it run through a few cycles to establish a pattern, an intent to obstruct, so to speak. In any case, that threshold was crossed yesterday afternoon and the judge will rule in our favor."

Kenneth held his breath, waiting for the hitch.

"Now here's the thing. The court order will be rcmoved and dated on December 3 and your new deadline is midnight, December 31, New Year's Eve. Once the order is removed, you'll have a bit over four weeks to complete and open for business."

"Why not just lift it now?" Kenneth asked.

"There's a good chance the Falwell people will appeal this ruling and take it to a higher court. They'll get a notification by fax at 4:58 Friday afternoon on the third. At 5 pm that same day, the appeals court goes into recess until January 3. By the time an appeal could be filed and heard, the deadline will have come and gone."

There was silence around the table as the sweetness of the plan became clear.

"And there's no way for them to get around this?" Kenneth asked finally.

"Only if they find out in time to file an appeal. Now officially you know nothing but the judge agreed to let me give you a heads up so you can hit the ground running the first thing December four. You can plan based on that date, arrange for deliveries, and be ready to go to work. Just stay under the radar until it's official."

*

Chapter Twenty

"The new deadline is midnight, New Year's Eve," Kenneth said. "We can start work again on December fourth."

"Okay. Got it." The pitch of Clancy's voice increased steadily as the impact of the news sunk in. "Got it. Great."

"Keep it under your hat, though. Falwell's people can't know until it's too late to appeal. Work from home, use FAX and email."

"Okay. Got it. Okay."

*

"You sure this isn't a joke?" Simon said.

"It's no joke."

"Who's going to do the work?"

"No idea. There's no chance of getting the crews back and we're getting into Christmas."

"I'm coming up and I'll bring Roland."

"Roland?"

"One of the guys who wants to invest if we pull it off. He's a decorator. You should see his place. Did it all himself – very handy with fabric swatches and a screw gun."

*

Clancy arrived the next day.

"Can I even go to the trailer?"

"No. Stay out of sight. Go to Diane's, put your car in the garage, and stay in the house. Just be ready to roll when the ball drops."

*

"This is Roland," Simon said when they arrived in a minivan a few days later. "The car's full of his tools. Just point him at something and tell him to fix it."

"You were here in October," Kenneth said.

"That's right. A long wet weekend of wine, pizza, and scrabble."

"The rest of them bailed," Simon said, "but Roland's on board. I'm going to show him what the town looks like in the sunshine. Back in a while."

*

Luther was at the hotel before dawn on the fourth so he could rip down the yellow tape before the others arrived but Clancy showed up in time to help with the last of it. They were warming up in Clancy's trailer when Kenneth and Simon and Roland came in.

"Glad you guys are here," Clancy said. "Grab some coffee."

The hotel was cold, the heat only being run warm enough to prevent pipes from freezing.

"We've got to concentrate on the tavern, the dining room, and the kitchen," she said when they'd gone into the hotel. "A couple of the guest rooms are so close to done I don't think it will be hard to finish them up. Forget the ballroom. It's full of all that furniture from your place anyway. Speaking of which, someone who likes to clean and polish and wax should get to work on that stuff."

"Maybe Yvonne," Luther said. "She should be done with her chores by now."

"She likes to clean?"

"She likes to work. Don't much matter what it is. Show her what you want and that's what you get."

"Great. First, though, we need to clean the place out, I mean really clean it. And it needs to stay clean, every day."

"I'll go back to the house and get my industrial vacuum," Simon said.

"Can I take a few minutes to see the rest of the place?" Roland asked.

"Sure," Clancy said. "Follow me." She led him off to the tavern and Kenneth was left alone in the big, empty dining room. Painters had begun on the ceiling but the walls were untouched and would need serious patching and sanding to get them ready for paint or wallpaper. It would take more than three weeks just to finish this room, he thought. Light fixtures were missing, wires stuck out of boxes, dust was everywhere, the windows were filthy, there were no curtains or curtain rods…

"Okay, where do I start?" Ellen was in the doorway.

"What are you doing here?"

"I'm going to see this place open by the New Year." She had on white duck painter's jeans and a paint spattered sweatshirt. "What's first?"

"Clancy says to clean up."

"Good. Let me find a broom."

"What about your store? It's the Christmas season."

"Blanche and the others can handle the store." She pushed the sleeves of her sweatshirt up over her elbows. "Besides, a few days ago somebody told me I should do whatever makes me happy. Right now, this is it."

*

The kitchen had been completed before the shutdown so with just a bit of wiping up Jonathan was ready to brew coffee and heat water for tea.

Diane went to her office and printed out the orders for food and liquor to review with Jonathan before she called the suppliers.

"Hey, Kenny," Yvonne was still in her chore clothes and a faint smell of barnyard came in with her. "Luther says I can help. Whatdya need?"

"Clancy's the one to ask," Kenneth said. "I think she's in the trailer out back."

"Oh, yeah, the trailer." And she was gone.

"Who's that?" Diane asked.

"Luther's wife, Yvonne. Good worker."

"You have woodchuck problems," Simon said as he returned with the vacuum, "she's the one to call."

"Woodchucks?" Diane said.

"Big rodents. They live underground. You might get them served up in a stew."

"A stew?"

"Well, they're vegetarians, after all. How bad could it be? I need to find an extension cord."

*

"You Clancy?"

"That's right."

"I'm Yvonne. Kenny said to come see you."

"You've come to work?" Clancy asked.

"Yup. Come to help Kenny and Simon. Nice fellas."

"Yes, they are."

"Kenny gave Luther a real good job. Fixed our teeth and everything. Nice fellas. So I come to help."

"Well, good. Yvonne, is it?"

"That's right. Yup. Yvonne."

"Right. Well, we've got a lot of furniture upstairs that needs to be cleaned, polished, and made to look like new again so we can put it in the guest rooms."

"Yup. Yup. I can do that. I'm a good polisher."

"Okay, there's a box over there with some finish restorer, polish, touch up sticks in different colors, lemon oil, marble cleaner, and lots of rags and rubber gloves. Why don't you take it upstairs to the ballroom. I'll be up in a few minutes to show you what we need, okay?"

"Okay. Upstairs?"

"Third floor."

*

"Give me something to do that will keep me away from that damned computer," Diane said.

"You okay on a stepladder?" Clancy asked.

"Sure."

"Good. All that wood paneling and ceiling work in the tavern needs to be scrubbed and oiled. There's a big can of lemon oil around here someplace. Find some rags, steel wool, and rubber gloves. Ceiling and beams first."

*

Jonathan wheeled the coffee urn and tea fixings into the dining room on a large rolling table. Dot Brookes followed with a tray of fresh doughnuts.

"How'd you know we'd started again?" Kenneth asked.

"Saw the tape was down," Dot said.

"You guys are back to work?" Warren Thurber called from the doorway.

"Started this morning," Kenneth said. "We've got until New Year's Eve."

"Damn," Warren said as he looked around.

"Have some coffee and a doughnut."

"Can't stop today, but I'm free the next few weeks 'cept for a short night run now and again. I'll bring Pearl, too."

"Deliveries start the first of next week," Clancy said. "We'll have lots of lifting and carrying. At some point we'll have some things that need to be assembled. You might be able to help Roland with that."

"Anything you need," Warren said. "Goddamn shame they shut you down that way. Pearl thought so, too." He looked around again. "Damn. You gonna get'er done?"

"Goddamn right," Clancy said.

*

Kenneth and Ellen went to work on the walls in the dining room. Simon and Roland decided to concentrate on the entrance and the reception desk area. Diane continued to scrub away at the woodwork in the tavern. Earl Stebbins climbed into Clancy's trailer just after 8:30, followed by Stub Newton, his best carpenter, Bill Wesley, a plumber, and Harvey Gibson, an electrician. Earl made introductions.

"This is great," Clancy said. "A licensed plumber and an electrician. Let me grab my punch lists and I'll show you around."

"I got a couple painters, too, good ones, who can start Monday."

"That's great," Clancy said.

Kenneth saw them them walk through the dining room to the tavern.

"How'd Earl Stebbins know about this?"

"I'm sure I have no idea," Ellen said. "Handy, though, isn't it?"

Clancy laid her lists on the bar.

"I tried to prioritize these jobs but feel free to change the order if it makes sense to you. Just bring me the lists at the end of the day with the items you've completed checked off. I'll give you a clean list every morning."

"This project management?" Earl asked.

"Yeah, sort of," Clancy said, "although this has a distinct anal component. I didn't know what skills I'd have available so I broke it down more to keep track of things."

"Right."

"If you guys see something I've missed just take care of it. Supplies and fixtures are in the cellar and everything should be sorted and labeled."

"Hey, Clancy," a deep voice boomed when she came back to the dining room.

"Frank! You made it." She pulled herself up to plant a kiss on his cheek. "Everybody, this is Frank Adams. Frank's my main man, my eyes on the job. If you need anything, anything at all, you find Frank."

"Who's that?" Yvonne asked Luther.

"Frank. He helps Clancy."

"Big, ain't he?"

"Sure is."

Yvonne stared up at him.

"I'm Yvonne," she said. Frank took her hand and shook it gently.

"Hi, Yvonne. I'm Frank."

"You're really big." She held her hand against his. Fingers and all, her hand hardly reached across his palm.

"I come to polish the furniture," she said. "Upstairs."

"Oh, yeah. All the dressers and tables and mirrors and such. How you doin' with that?"

"I'm a good polisher."

"Well, that's good," Frank said. "We can always use good polishers."

Yvonne rubbed the dark skin on the back of Frank's hand.

"I'm a good polisher," she said again as she released his hand. "I'm way upstairs. You come up and see and you can tell Clancy what a good polisher I am."

"I'll do that," Frank said. "I'll come by later on, okay, Yvonne?"

"Okay," she said. "Okay, Frank."

*

On Sunday morning it was Edna Stebbins who pushed the coffee cart out of the kitchen.

"Hello, Simon."

"Mrs. Stebbins? Oh, wow. Hey Kenneth. C'mere. This is Earl Stebbins' wife." He snapped his fingers a couple times as he struggled to remember her name. "Edna, right?"

"That's right," she smiled.

"And you've come to help?"

"I work here."

"Work here? To help finish the hotel?"

"No, no. I work with Jonathan."

Earl had just come for a cup of coffee.

"The ad said it included training so she came over and interviewed. Jonathan made her assistant chef," he said with obvious pride. "How about that?"

"Yeah. How about that?" Kenneth said.

Jimmy Fisher was on the job, too. He pushed a cart with bowls of fruit and a tray of Dot's doughnuts in from the kitchen. He wore a starched cook's jacket and a cook's hat, very focused on what he was doing, set everything out precisely, and never looked up.

"How's he doing?" Kenneth asked when Jimmy returned to the kitchen.

"Jimmy? He's doing very well," Edna said. "You should have seen him swell up the day Jonathan gave him his chef's jacket and hat. He's a really sweet young man."

Jimmy's parents, George and Mina Fisher, had come in the other end of the dining room in time to see Jimmy at work. Kenneth saw them.

"Jimmy's doing good, George."

"He could of wound up on the highway crew like me," George said. "Hard work. Hot in the summer, cold in the winter. Dirty. Never make enough money. I don't know how you guys managed this," he choked on his words," but I owe you big time for takin' Jimmy on. I never seen him stand so tall. They's lots of people would've wrote him off, you know, but he's a good boy."

"Jonathan says he's a good worker, very conscientious."

"He'll work hard. You'll see. He's responsible, a good boy."

*

That same morning the Rev. Peter Rodman had put out a call to the congregation for sets of extra Christmas lights and during the afternoon he and the folks who brought the lights hung them around the porches on the two street sides of the hotel.

Kenneth and Simon and Ellen and Clancy had been so busy inside they didn't see them until they'd closed up to go home for some rest.

"Wow," Clancy said. "I wish I'd thought of that."

Early the next morning Yvonne gathered several bags of Princess Pine from the woods behind their house and stayed up that night to make two wreaths which she decorated with pine cones, holly, and red bows. Luther hung them on the front doors. With the twinkling lights on, and the soft light coming from inside, the old hotel had come to life once more.

*

Archie hunched over the paper, his coffee untouched for the past half hour.

"How come you're not over there helping out?" Dot said.

He didn't want to be over there helping out, that's why. He wasn't going to help with something he didn't agree with in the first place. He didn't care to be asked about it, either.

"Looks like everybody in town's over there anyway. I'd just be in the way."

"But – "

"Look, Dot," he said, "I don't actually know how to do anything."

"Oh, stop it. You do lots of things." She slid into the booth.

"What I do is I get other people to do things," he said. "Have you ever seen me actually do anything at all? Of course not. I pay somebody else to do it."

"But someone has to do that part."

"Yeah, maybe, but I'd be hard put to place a value on it right now. What they'll be doin' over there is paper and paint and odds and ends of carpentry and electrical work, maybe some plumbing. I don't know any of that stuff." He fussed with his coffee cup. "I see you're takin' them doughnuts."

"Those work crews gave me the best year I've ever had. I just feel I owe Kenny and the rest of them something for that. Fresh doughnuts are a small thing."

"I suppose so." The spoon clinked the side of his cup. "A couple of my guys even asked if they could give'em a hand for a few days. I told'm go ahead. I'm gonna pay'em anyway. What the hell, it's Christmas."

The front door banged open. Homer Dalrymple stormed in, out of breath, and stormed straight over to Archie's table.

"They're working on the hotel again," he said.

"Morning, Homer," Dot said as she got up and went back to the kitchen.

"They been at it since Saturday, Homer," Archie said. "Where you been?"

"But there's a court order."

"Been lifted."

"But – "

Archie didn't want to hear it.

"Lemme tell you somethin', Homer. For somebody who calls himself Christian you got this annoying mean streak."

"What?"

"You stick your nose in where you got no business."

"Why, I – "

"Who are you to come around tellin' me Ellen's producin' porn over in her shop?" Archie puffed up with an anger that had been building for some time. "I seen those mugs. The most they are is a little bit naughty. Nobody but you gives a shit about a peek of ceramic nipple. You just can't stand to see somebody else havin' a good time, can you, you little priss."

"What? I don't – "

"Shut up, Homer. Just shut the hell up."

Homer shut up.

"You got a mouth like a duck's ass," Archie said. "Little greasy turds slide out every time you open it up."

Homer worked his mouth but nothing came out.

"You called those Falwell people, didn't you? No way they'da known otherwise. It's one thing to stir things up a little at town meeting and it's another when you call in outsiders, people like Falwell."

"Why, I – "

Archie took a sip of his coffee. It was cold.

"Christ, that's awful." He put the cup down. "I hear Frank's back, Homer. Why don't you and me go over and say hello?"

"No, I don't think – "

"It's the polite thing to do instead of sneakin' around makin' long distance phone calls."

"Oh, if it's settled I think we should just leave them to it."

"We could just drop by, perhaps there's something you could do to help…"

"Actually, I – I'm running late," Homer stammered. "Some other time perhaps."

"Yeah, some other time," Archie snarled. "Until then, stay out of my sight."

Homer backed all the way to the door before he turned and hurried out. Dot returned with two clean cups and a carafe of fresh coffee.

"What was all that about?"

"Homer's a servant of the Lord," he said as he rubbed his left ear and realized he had just defended Kenneth, Fanny's dream, the hotel, and the whole damned situation. "Asshole…"

Dot had just poured the coffee when Archie saw the long limousine again.

"Oh, for Christ's sake. They're back."

"Who's that?"

"Falwell's people. Sorry about the coffee, Dot. Come on, Hank. We're gonna keep an eye on'em this time."

Archie followed the limo straight to Increase's office, got out of his truck, and followed the two men inside. Irene was on her feet as soon as she saw the suits.

"INCREASE!"

Again, Butler and Godwin flinched. Archie and Hank closed the door, blocking the exit, as Increase appeared from his office.

"Ah, Mr. Houghton," Butler purred. "Might we take a few moments?"

"Certainly," Increase said, and led them to his meeting room. Archie and Hank were right behind them. Increase gestured to Archie to keep quiet.

"Um, I thought we might meet privately," Butler said.

"This is our First Selectman, Archie Whitaker," Increase said. "He's naturally interested in goings-on in town. Oh, and this is Hank. He goes where Archie goes. Inseparable, much like Irene and myself. Have I told you about Irene?"

"Yes, thank you, during our previous visit. It was very interesting."

"Indispensable. Don't know what I'd do without her. In any case, anything you have to say to me you can say to Archie and Hank. Archie is discreet and Hank is mute, except in times of high excitement."

"Very well," Butler said. He cast a glance at Hank. "We, the Falwell organization, recieved notice that the stop work order has been lifted."

"It has."

"We were prepared to appeal but the ruling arrived at our offices on the eve of the appeals court recess."

"Did it?" Increase said.

"We, and by 'we' I mean the Falwell organization, believe there may have been a bit of collusion involved."

"That so? Well, you're welcome to believe whatever you want."

"What are your plans now, if we might ask?"

"Well, I keep the holiday weeks pretty clear these days, keep a low profile at the office, give Irene some well-deserved time off… I don't live a complicated life here in Grants Ferry. Judith and I enjoy each other's company, no other family, so we – "

"And the hotel?"

"The hotel? What about it?"

"We understand," Butler said, showing the first trace of irritation, "that the deadline is now New Year's Eve."

"That's correct."

"And you will then determine whether the conditions of the will have been met?"

"That's right. Judith and I generally make it a point to turn in early on New Year's Eve but I expect we'll stay up this year, just to see what happens."

"You've not been very cooperative, Mr. Houghton."

Increase didn't respond. The room was silent, the conversation obviously at an end. Except that Godwin seemed to have no ability to speak, he and Butler could be twins. Together they turned to look at Archie. Archie smiled. They then looked at Hank who in turn looked at them.

"Unusual dog," Butler said. That served as a farewell gesture. He and Godwin turned together and left the room, left the reception area, and left the office.

"God damned outsiders," Archie said. "You think they're gonna be trouble?"

"They won't be visible but don't rule'em out until it's over," Increase said.

*

Increase called Clancy.

"I think you should leave lights burning in and around the hotel at night."

"Something going on?"

"Cheap insurance," Increase said.

*

Delivery trucks began to arrive and the center of the dining room soon filled with mattresses and box springs, TV sets, tables and chairs, glassware, cutlery, china copied from the original pieces at the historical society, napkins, tablecloths, towels. Diane identified each box and each item and labeled them so Luther and Warren could take them to the rooms where they would ultimately reside. A commercial washer and drier were delivered to the cellar where Earl Stebbins' guys had them hooked up and running in less than an hour.

Frank climbed to the ballroom several times a day to tell Yvonne what a good polisher she was. Irene Bills donned rubber gloves and washed years of grime off the tall windows. Dennis Coombs offered to run to Springfield or Windsor if something was needed. People Kenneth had long forgotten came to help. Some were young people he'd never known. Some came for a day, some came for a few hours, but they came, they worked, they laughed, personal differences were forgotten, and the work progressed.

The Thurbers were there every day. Warren and Roland assembled the tables for the dining room and the tavern and carefully took the factory protective wrapping off each of the chairs. Pearl Thurber washed and sorted and ironed all the linens from napkins to bedspreads and tablecloths. Increase and Judith Houghton carefully unpacked, washed, and wiped each piece of china and glassware and put them away.

Each day the table was set with food and drink and each day the people came and set themselves to whatever needed doing. It was cheerful, serious fun and provided an opportunity to share in the completion of a project they'd watched for a year.

*

"I seen the lights on at the hotel last night," Benny said after he'd set the nozzle in Archie's truck. "They working through the night?"

"No, I don't think so. Just security. How'd you happen to see'em?"

"I'm up a lot at night. Always been that way. More lately. Somethin' to do with age, I think. Can't sleep so sometimes I just sit at the front window and look out at the common, you know, and it relaxes me."

"That so?"

"Yup. Interesting the way it changes through the seasons. Always the same but always different, you know? It was nice to see the Christmas lights they put up but they went out around 10. Last night, though, everything was lit, inside and out."

"Just security. You see anything unusual, though, let somebody know."

"You think it's anything to do with that limo that slid into town a few days ago?"

"You mean Falwell's people?"

"That who that was? Bastards that shut Kenny down?"

"They came by to see Increase."

"Bastards," Benny said again.

"Increase thought leavin' the lights on was a good idea."

"Damn right." The nozzle clicked off and Benny returned it to its cradle. "Just over twenty bucks."

"Put it on the tab."

"Bastards," Benny said.

*

Aside from his tendency to spread gossip, Benny had little to do with town affairs. He ran his garage, pumped gas, and except for shutting down during hunting season and an occasional day to fish the brook along the road out of town, that was his life. His sleep came in snatches, never more than a couple hours at a time.

He was at his window again two nights after his conversation with Archie when a pickup without its lights on crept up Main Street just after 2 am. It turned and parked in the shadows on the side of the common away from the hotel.

The pickup's inside light went on and then off as the driver got out. Whoever it was retrieved something from the open back of the pickup and set out across the common toward the hotel.

"Bastards," Benny said. He quickly got dressed, grabbed his shotgun and a pocket full of cartridges. Downstairs he stopped at the garage for the tool he'd need and then trotted across the street to the pickup. Satisfied the driver was nowhere in sight, Benny dropped to the ground, quickly unscrewed the valve stems from all four tires and put them in his pocket.

The air hissed out of the pickup's tires as he took up the shotgun again and ran across the common to the rear of the hotel. Even with the lights, it was darkest there, and out of sight of the street. If someone was going to cause mischief, this is where it would be. He crept behind Clancy's trailer. He saw a small figure moving about in the shadows.

"What the hell are you doing?" Benny yelled. Before the figure could answer Benny pumped the shotgun and blasted two shots into the night.

The figure, clothed in black, wearing a black knitted watch cap, streaked out from behind the hotel and tore across the common to the pickup truck. Benny let loose two more blasts. The truck engine roared to life and the truck jerked forward. In less than 20 yards it stopped again. The driver jumped out and discovered the flat tires. Benny chuckled at the string of cursing as the figure got back into the pickup. The headlights came on, it turned around, and flopped back down Main Street.

Benny was on his way home again when Warren Thurber drove in from an evening run.

"Hey, Benny. What you huntin' this time a night?"

"Somebody out to mess with the hotel," he said. "Found these bolt cutters by the electric meter."

"Dayum. Who was it? You know?

"Not sure. Shouldn't be hard to find'em, though." He showed Warren the valve stems. "Drove off on his rims."

*

"Drove off on his rims?" the sheriff said.

"Yup. Off down Main Street," Benny said.

"How'd that happen?"

"Somebody had his valve stems." Benny held out his hand. "Forgive me for I have sinned."

"Any idea who it was?"

"Well, they's been some Jesus people around lately."

"Jesus people?"

"Yeah. Archie knows who they are."

*

"Benny says somebody was about to vandalize the hotel last night."

"I warned that little peckerhead," Archie said.

"What peckerhead is that?"

"I doubt he did it himself, but you might check in with Homer Dalrymple and his followers."

"You want to come along?"

"No. Probably safer for everybody if I stay away from that crowd."

*

"Anybody in your group who might want to vandalize that hotel?"

"Why, we're a Christian community." Homer was shocked. "No. No. That's not what we do."

"Glad to hear that," the Sheriff said. "Any of your members drive pickups?"

"A few, I suppose. I don't pay that much attention."

"Good. Gimme a couple names and then we'll go see'em."

*

"Found'im," the Sheriff said. "You want to press charges?"

"Let's talk with Increase and Kenny," Archie said. "So far it's only between you and me and Benny."

After a couple phone calls they were all in Clancy's trailer.

"Vandals?"

"Just the one," the Sheriff said. "And he didn't get a chance to do any damage."

"And what would be the advantage, since there was no damage," Kenneth asked.

"Well, he might have quite a time explaining just what he had in mind back by your electric meter with a pair bolt cutters and he might have quite a time explaining his four ruined tires and rims. But other than its entertainment value, there may be none."

"And you think you issued enough of a warning to keep them from another attempt?"

"I'm not sure he needed it. From the looks of the pickup seat he had an issue with bowel control on the way home, but the question is whether you want to make an issue of it."

"I'm inclined to let it go," Kenneth said.

"Really?" Archie said. He would have extracted some major revenge, something like the stocks where the sneaky bastard could be locked up and people could throw garbage at him.

"I think he's been sufficiently warned," Kenneth said. "Even Homer can grasp the concept of turning the other cheek. No need to stir them up any more."

"Probably a good move," the Sheriff said. "But having Benny on guard is about as safe as you can get without locking them all up."

*

Except for some last papering and painting, installing curtain rods, hanging drapes, and a lot of little finishing touches, the bulk of the work was done by Christmas Eve. The fire inspector, the health inspector, and the guy from the liquor licensing board all came, inspected, and left signed certificates on Friday afternoon. Ed Jenkins, the regional state official who would issue the final Certificate of Occupancy, was satisfied and ready to sign the certificate late Friday afternoon. Kenneth, Simon, Diane, and Clancy were all in the trailer with him.

He pawed through the contents of his briefcase for several minutes. "I don't seem to have a blank certificate," he said. "Must have used the last one over in Chester this morning. No problem. I'll go back to the office, complete one, and put it in the mail. Should be here the first of the week."

"Can't you just bring it back?" Kenneth said.

"No time. Family's leaving on a two-week vacation as soon as I get back to Springfield. I'll fill it out and pop it in the mail. Be here in plenty of time. No worries."

*

The work on the hotel stopped for Christmas Eve and Ellen had rushed back to her apartment to grab something to eat, get cleaned up, and changed so she could join Kenneth and Simon and Roland for the Christmas Eve service. The phone rang just as she stepped out of the shower. She let the machine get it.

"Ellen, it's me," Archie said. "If you're there I'd like to – "

"Hi, Archie."

"You got a couple minutes?"

"Just about. I'm going to the Christmas Eve service."

"Oh. Yeah. Right. Well. Listen, I – uh – I see you're helpin' Kenny with the hotel."

"Yes, I am. It's going to be lovely."

"I suppose so. It used to be pretty swanky in its day…" Awkward pause. "How've you been?" he said.

"Busy. Business at the store has been better than we'd hoped, actually."

"Good. Good. Glad to hear it."

Another pause

"I – You and me. It feels like you've sorta moved on," he said.

"Yes, I think I have."

"Yeah, well… Listen. I'm just tired of fightin' everything, pushin' the river, you know?" Another pause while she waited for him to go on. "And I'm thinkin' it might be best all around if we just end it, make a clean break."

Ellen had avoided speaking the word no matter how many times she'd thought it.

"Are you suggesting divorce?" There. She'd said it.

"That's right."

Ellen waited.

"Look I'm tired of bein' on edge all the time, " Archie said. "I don't want to be difficult. Take whatever you want from the house. We each get the place appraised, split the difference between the two appraisals, if there is any, and I'll buy it back, clean and simple."

"And you're sure? That's all?"

"Look," Archie said. "You're as good as gone anyway and I don't want to hold you back. Let's just get it over with and move on. Call it a Christmas present."

Christmas Eve fell on a Friday. Despite the disappointing return from the Harvest Festival in October a holiday spirit was in the air. The children performed the pageant and the congregation once again sang *Silent Night* as they filed out of the church and into the night with their lit candles. Ice crystals on the tree branches caught the lights from the hotel and the colors danced from one branch to another. Ellen held tight to Kenneth's arm as they sang the last verse. Simon and Roland were with them.

When the singing stopped, the crowd, as if by some magical, silent command, stood in stillness for a full minute. The candles flickered, the lights twinkled, and puffs of breath were visible in the cold night air, but no one spoke. Peter Rodman finally broke the spell as he bade them all peace, farewell, and Merry Christmas. It was then they blew out the candles and went off into the night.

"I don't want to be alone just yet," Ellen said, still holding Kenneth's arm.

"Come on back to the house, then, Simon's made up some eggnog and cake. You mind walking?"

"No. A walk tonight would be nice."

"Well, I liked that," Roland said, talking about the pageant. "Even as a hard-core, card-carrying atheist I still have to admit the story, the legend, the myth, has a certain charm. It's a nice local custom. Been going on long?"

"They used the same script when Ellen and I were in it about fifty years ago," Kenneth said.

"Really? Well, it's a great story. Almost makes you want to believe it."

Kenneth had put up a Christmas tree in the parlor bay window and decorated it entirely with Amy's lights and ornaments, the first time they'd been used in over forty years. The lights didn't blink and the ornaments were simple compared to the newer models, but it was as close to the trees Amy used to decorate as Kenneth could manage. He'd spent two hours draping individual strands of tinsel over the branches the way Amy used to. Ellen settled in a chair near the tree while Simon served up the eggnog and cake from the tea cart.

"Careful with the nog," Simon said. "Lots of rum. Very sneaky."

The light from the tree gave Ellen's face a warm glow. She was clearly happy and as lovely as Kenneth had ever seen her.

"So you've done it," she said.

"The hotel? Looks like it."

"Now what?"

"We're going to throw a New Year's Eve party for everyone who came to help. We'd have been screwed without them. It's little enough."

"And after that?"

"I need to get investors up here," Simon said, "get them interested. Once they can see the possibilities…"

"There's potential here," Roland agreed. "It could be a great place for folks to come and unwind. The hotel's a gem and with some of the larger old houses as B&Bs, hiking trails and a golf course, maybe the marina on the river, it could be quite the place. Not big and splashy and commercial but comfortable, a good place to relax for a week or so. Anyone with an imagination will see the potential if they take time to get familiar with the area."

"Well, that's next year," Simon said. He topped up Kenneth and Ellen's cups. "We've still got a week's work to get the last details in the hotel finished and it'll be long days. I'm gonna hit the hay." He and Roland picked up everything but the cups and the bowl of eggnog and went off to the kitchen. A few minutes later they popped in to say good night and went upstairs.

"It's been quite a year, hasn't it?" Ellen said when they were gone.

"Quite a year," Kenneth agreed. "I think I might even allow myself to take a break sometime in February, some place warm with lots of sunshine."

"Got anyplace in mind?"

"Simon and I used to fly down to different islands in the Caribbean in January or February. Three weeks or so in the Caribbean might be just the ticket."

"Simon, too?"

"Probably not," Kenneth said. "We have separate lives now."

"Oh, I'm sorry. I – "

"No, it's okay. Still friends, just not together. He still has a financial interest in all this and we still need people to invest. He'll be here on and off but mostly he'll be in New York."

"Is it that easy?"

"Getting investors?"

"No. Separating."

Kenneth shrugged.

"Well, I've not asked but I suspect he and Roland are a couple now."

"And you're okay with that?"

"Oh, sure. It's not about me, anyway. I'm bound by my agreement with the estate to stay here. He needs the city. We're not married, after all, and I've come to enjoy the solitary life in a small town."

"But ten years…"

"That's right. And when something ends there's no reason it can't be okay. We're still close, we're just not partners anymore, at least not that way. That's been clear for a while – before I knew about Roland, actually."

"I thought you loved each other."

"Oh, we still do at some level but it's love without condition, not to say it comes without expectations, but it's always been without conditions."

Ellen sipped her eggnog, fascinated at the simplicity of Kenneth's philosophy. So many of the social mores she'd known in Grants Ferry were confining and judgmental, limiting. And yet, even within those confines, her life had changed dramatically the past year. Kenny's return had inspired her to a new freedom, a future, a world of possibilities and the courage and determination to step away from Archie. Her connection to Grants Ferry was still strong, it would always be home, but she now had an urge to explore, see something new, something exotic, something…

"Archie called," she said.

"This evening?"

"Yes. Just before the service. We've not spoken much at all since Thanksgiving. He's – he says he's ready to end it. Divorce."

"Really?"

"He just wants to buy the house back. That's it."

"I'd have thought he'd try to make a fuss."

"Me, too, which is why I never brought it up. He says he's tired of fighting for everything. Says I'm as good as gone anyway…"

"He's not just setting you up?"

"I can tell when he's working an angle. I'm sure he's serious. He even suggested it could be a Christmas present."

"Did you agree?"

"Not then but I will."

"Well," Kenneth said. "I wish I could say I'm sorry, but – "

"I know." She sipped the eggnog. Having spoken it out loud gave it life and having told Kenneth it removed her fears and doubts. In fact, this could be the opportunity she'd secretly dreamed for the past year. Kenneth was watching.

"So," she said. "The Caribbean?"

"I think so. Someplace along the Antilles chain. I've never been to Jamaica, for instance. I'll spend some time on the Internet, see if I can find a place that will mix up a bit of Caribbean night life and local food with the total peace and quiet of an isolated beach."

"Sounds wonderful," she said, although Grants Ferry would be terribly empty again with Kenneth gone, even for three weeks. She gripped her mug with both hands. Her heart pounded and she struggled to slow her breathing and sipped a bit of the egg nog to relieve the sudden dryness in her mouth.

"Could – would you mind if I come with you?"

*

"The mail's come," Diane said Tuesday morning, "and there's no certificate."

"It shouldn't take two days to get here from Springfield," Kenneth said, "but with Christmas I suppose we should give it another day."

"Just thought you should know."

"Thanks."

Just in case, Kenneth called the State number in Springfield and got a machine that told him the offices were closed for the holiday week and would reopen Jan 2.

The Wednesday and Thursday mail produced no certificate, either.

They went to see Increase.

"We need that last piece to make it official, don't we?" Kenneth asked.

"Technically, yes," Increase said. "I'd accept that he gave you a verbal approval in front of witnesses and we'd be done with it, but I don't want to leave Falwell with even the smallest peg to hang his hat on. Let me see what I can do."

*

"This is going to be some New Year's party," Diane said. "We're about to lose everything and you're going to do it anyway?"

"Of course."

"But the whole last year, I mean, the whole last year, the time, the money…"

"Look," Kenneth said. "Inside I'm frantic and screaming. We had it, right in our hands, and now because of some god damned bureaucrat…" He caught himself, stopped, and took a breath. "Look. This place and all the money I've dumped into it may yet turn into a pumpkin at midnight but I've done everything I can to keep it away from Falwell and his gang of bigots. If I missed anything, I should have followed that little bastard to Springfield and waited while he signed the certificate but none of that has anything to do with all the people who gave up their holidays to help us at the last minute."

He stopped and Diane waited while he calmed down.

"You're not alone in this. Simon has been shitting himself all day. Roland's back at the house right now shoving Imodium into him by the handful and trying to keep him hydrated. In spite of that, you and Simon and I are going to smile and thank these people and show them a great time, even if it's the best and last party we ever throw here. So pull yourself together. It's all theater, after all, and we're going to give them some theater to remember, no matter how it turns out."

Jonathan and his crew began early. They set the dining room up with small tables for four spread through the room, fresh linens, soft lighting. A rented baby grand piano was tuned and polished and waiting in the front corner. A long buffet table ran along the kitchen wall. Jonathan, Edna, and the others had labored through the afternoon. Jimmy Fisher worked feverishly to set the tables, prepare the bud vases, put flower arrangements in the windows, polish the piano, and wipe up any trace of dust he could find. Ten cases of champagne were chilled in the cooler and there was beer and wine and coffee and soft drinks.

Just after six Kenneth called Increase.

"You realize, of course, Increase said, "we're trying to track that guy down after working hours and on New Year's Eve. Not a lot of people answer the phone on New Year's Eve. That doesn't make it any easier. We know he and his family are on a skiing holiday. We think he's up in Stowe."

"Well?" Diane said when he got off the phone."

"Nothing yet."

"Oh, god…"

"Help me with this," Kenneth said.

He'd hand-lettered a piece of builder's Tyvek with felt-tip markers to make a banner that screamed "WE DID IT!" under the theory that if you say something often enough and loud enough it will become true.

Diane was only able to maintain the façade for short periods, though, and frequently retreated to her office to pull herself together again with assistance from vodka and grapefruit juice. Jonathan would see to the logistics of the party, after all. Her single role was to join Kenneth and welcome people as they arrived and if she was numb enough she could do that.

The first of them, Warren and Pearl Thurber came in on the stroke of eight. Others soon followed until the dining room was filled. Simon was at the piano with a pitcher of ice water and a bottle of Gatorade nearby.

The dining room staff, in their white shirts and bow ties, kept the wine glasses filled, circulated with platters of finger food, and left no one wanting for anything. Jimmy Fisher, out of his kitchen jacket and in his starched white shirt and black bow tie, was extremely proud and correct.

Simon worked his way through a collection of the old songs, *Home on the Range*, *Little Annie Rooney, My Sweetheart's the Man in the Moon, Chattanooga Choo-choo, Moon River*, and *Let the Rest of the World Go By*, to name a few. He even included a few show tunes. Some of the older generation sang along or tapped their fingers to the music. Kenneth smiled. This was the vision they'd had and win or lose he would always be proud of the accomplishment. If they lose, he thought, they will have lost big. He'd been broke before but no one ever wants to go there a second time.

Big Frank, settled at a table with Luther and Yvonne, said something that the others found incredibly funny. Earl Stebbins and Clancy leaned toward each other attempting a discussion in a room full of noise. Warren Thurber, at the buffet for the third or fourth time, grabbed yet another beer from the tub of ice. Kenneth moved from table to table to thank everyone personally. Around 10:30 Diane motioned Kenneth to join her. She held onto the door frame.

"How much longer do we have to pretend?"

"Until it's over. Have you seen Increase?"

"He's not here?"

"Haven't seen him. Damned funny, don't you think?"

"I just want to run away."

"I know. It'll all be done by midnight."

"I – I'm going to be sick," she said, and rushed off to the lavatory.

Ellen was with Roland at a table near the piano, enjoying the music, when she saw Diane rush from the room. She excused herself and joined Kenneth.

"What's going on with Diane?"

Kenneth led her to the foyer.

"We may not have won after all."

"What?"

"The state guy, the inspector, never mailed the Certificate of Occupancy. He's on vacation for two weeks and the office is closed. Increase, who isn't even here by the way, said if it were only him he'd accept the verbal okay but with Falwell in the wings we need the certificate signed and on the premises and we haven't got it."

"And you threw the party anyway?"

"Of course. Those people busted their asses for us. They deserve a party."

"Even if you're going to lose everything?"

"My losing has nothing to do with it. They gave, I'm giving back. It's not the party that's going to break us."

"Oh, my god." She stroked his arm. "I'm so sorry."

"Yeah, well…"

The front door burst open. The Houghtons and Irene Bills came in and stood shaking off the cold.

"Ah," Increase said. "Sorry we're so late."

Ellen took their coats and hung them on the long coat rack.

"I confess I was a bit concerned," Kenneth said. "Any news?"

"We're okay," Increase said, "but it's been a long damned time since lunch. Not to worry. We'll get some supper and then I'll tell you about it." He led Judith to the buffet. Irene flashed them the OK sign and followed the Houghtons into the dining room.

"What's going on?" Ellen asked.

"He says we're okay."

Ellen looked at him as if he were out of his mind.

"That's it?"

"Apparently. I'll get a bottle of champagne and join you at the table."

"To celebrate?"

"Whatever it is. Doesn't hurt to be ready."

Kenneth put the champagne on the table and went over to Simon who had been watching.

"What's going on?"

"Increase says we're okay."

"What does that mean?"

"No idea. Just keep playing."

Irene joined Frank and Luther and Yvonne. Increase and Judith joined the Thurbers. Kenneth stared across the room at them, as if willing the food into their mouths but they were not to be hurried. Finally, at 11:45, Increase gave Judith a peck on the cheek, got up, and asked Kenneth to quiet the room. Simon stopped playing and went to sit with Roland and Ellen. Clancy stood in the kitchen door.

"First of all," Increase said, "I think we should all acknowledge the effort that's gone into this fine building." Increase gestured for Kenneth, Simon, and Clancy to join him and the room filled with applause as they made their way to the front. "It's been a long year of struggle and tremendous financial risk for these folks," he said, "along with considerable anxiety caused by the lawsuit. However, when the court order was lifted you folks pitched in to work and meet Kenneth's deadline which is now" – he checked his watch – "about thirteen minutes away.

"As I reflect on what's been achieved here I'm reminded once again that Grants Ferry, at its heart, is a truly good community with good people. Hard work, determination, and a willingness to help a neighbor was all clearly evident these past weeks. Well done, all of you."

Another round of applause. Diane, in her office again, noticed the party noise had died and the music had stopped. She came into the dining room and Increase motioned her to join them by the piano.

"The only missing piece," Increase continued, "the final detail to satisfy the conditions in the will is the Certificate of Occupancy which had been promised this past week and the office in Springfield was closed for the holidays." Grumbling in the hall. Increase held up his hand to quiet them. "So Irene – where's Irene? Irene, you should come up here, too."

Irene's chair scraped as she stood up and then squeezed her way through the tables to join the others. Irene didn't like public acknowledgment. Her face was hot and red.

"Irene, as many of you know, has been an invaluable asset to my law practice. She's put my life in order countless times these many years and I can tell you she's a bulldog when she's given a challenge. So when I asked her to track down this state building inspector she was in her element. Seems the cuss had gone off with his family for a ski holiday up in Stowe. Says he forgot to sign and mail the certificate, even though he understood its importance to Kenneth and Grants Ferry. He and I had quite a discussion earlier this evening, just about the time when I should have been enjoying my supper. He should have been enjoying his, too, but I'm afraid I may have spoiled it for him. I've now made up for my loss, however. It was delicious, by the way. Compliments to the cook and his staff."

A round of applause.

"Now people can take their families on holidays whenever they want and sometimes, as in this case, the holiday might even be arranged at the last minute. And, I suppose, one might be so excited at the prospect that one might forget to sign and mail a certain piece of paper. What is unusual, however, is to have a sudden holiday in the Trapp Family Lodge paid for with a credit card that belongs to people who work for Jerry Falwell and *The Old Time Gospel Hour*."

There was some angry grumbling in the room but Increase held up his hand and it faded away.

"Just to confirm it, Irene also tracked down Jerome Butler, one of the Falwell people who have showed up in town from time to time, and asked him about it. He denied it, of course, so Irene read off the last four digits of the card number and reservation confirmation number to him."

General laughter.

"Given the circumstances," Increase continued, "and the fact that Ed Jenkins, the inspector, had given verbal approval to Kenneth, in front of witnesses, I declare that Kenneth has now met the terms of Fanny's will – in full."

Diane held on to Kenneth's arm to keep her knees from folding under her as people got to their feet and a cheer rose up in the dining room.

Simon jumped up, pulled Roland out of his chair, and kissed him so hard they fell back laughing against the piano.

Clancy grabbed Diane away from Kenneth and bounced up and down like a high school cheerleader. Diane, dealing with the effects of a considerable amount of vodka, was barely able to hang on.

Yvonne cupped her hands and sent a hog call across the room.

Frank pounded his big fists on the table.

Pearl Thurber rocked back and forth. Warren toasted them all with a fresh, sweating glass of beer.

Judith Houghton carefully removed her glasses and blotted tears with her napkin while Irene planted a big kiss on Increase's cheek.

Still laughing, Simon went back to the piano where he banged out *Happy Days Are Here Again*.

Ellen, too relieved to speak, simply came over to stand with and share the moment with Kenneth.

And Kenneth, true to his roots, smiled broadly and silently, the Vermont equivalent of screaming with joyful abandon.

And then it was 2000.

Grants Ferry

*

Epilogue

Town meeting day 2000 was warm and foggy. The remaining snow piles were dirty and melting. Rivulets ran steadily to the street where they eventually found storm drains or gathered in great puddles. Bare ground, where it existed, was soft and quickly turned to a slippery, viscous goo if even slightly disturbed. Mud season. Dirt roads become impassable, streams swell with the run-off and sometimes overflow their banks, everything is wet, and mud tracks in everywhere.

But they still come on town meeting day. A small fire had been built in the stove earlier, but only to chase out the early morning damp. Body heat would soon warm the hall.

Kenneth and Ellen, recently back from three weeks in Jamaica, were tanned and relaxed. Kenneth took their hot dish to the kitchen while Ellen went to find seats.

"Hey, Kenny. How you been?" Warren and Pearl Thurber were already in the kitchen. "What'dja bring? You got something special there? Something from the hotel?"

"No, I made it. Spicy Thai Noodles with chicken and peanut sauce."

"Spicy what?"

"Thai. You know, Thailand."

"Oh, yeah. Right. Tie," Warren nodded. "I just didn't catch the name," he said. He peeled back the aluminum foil on his dish to reveal scalloped potatoes laced with ham and cheese, golden brown on top. "Some of my own pig in there," he said. "Solid food. Sticks with you."

"Great," Kenneth said. "I'll be sure to have some of that."

"You done a great job with the hotel, Kenny. Fine piece of work. I took Pearl there for her birthday last month."

"You did?"

Pearl blushed happily and rocked back and forth.

"Yup. Yup. Never guess she's 48, would you?"

"No, I wouldn't," Kenneth said. "And the meal at the hotel, how was that?"

"You know what we did?" Warren always enjoyed a discussion of meals past. "Young Fisher was waiting table, Jimmy, I think."

"That's right."

"So he brought us some menus but I told him we were looking for something besides just meat and potatoes, you know? I always supposed the kid was a little slow but he asks if we liked seafood. Truth is, we don't know much about it so he made a couple suggestions. The kid's really good. We ordered scallops with garlic and sun-dried tomatoes in a thick buttery sauce, came on top of some kind of macaroni. And we asked this Young Fisher to pick some wine that would go with it. Don't know nothin' about wine, neither. Pretty much put it all in his hands."

"And how'd it work out?"

"Best meal I ever had," Warren said, "and I've had a lot of good meals." He chuckled and patted his stomach. Pearl nodded and beamed and rocked back and forth. "Had some nice warm rolls and butter, a bowl of corn chowder that had a little peppery bite to it to start with. I finished it all off with a killer cheesecake and Pearl had a little chocolate cake that was all hot runny chocolate stuff inside with dark cherries put over it. We had to wait while they made it up to order. Never saw anything like it."

"You had a good time, then?"

"Oh, first class," Warren said. "First class. A little pricey, but for a meal like that… We're already puttin' money aside now so we can do it again one day."

"Really?"

"Yup. Yup. Meal like that's special. Somethin' I'm determined to do once in a while. Nice to have it right here in town. Not somethin' I'd go lookin' for, you know."

"Well, thank you," Kenneth said. "Coming from a man who knows good food that may be the best recommendation we've had so far."

"Any time," Warren said. He gave Kenneth a hearty pat on the back that made his teeth clack together and went in for the meeting.

The room was already too warm. Clyde Putnam, the current town hall custodian, went around with a long pole and pulled the top sash down about six inches in four of the windows. The steamy air escaped and the room cooled as air came in the open front door.

"We just got a five-star rating for the hotel dining room from Warren and Pearl Thurber," Kenneth told Ellen as he sat down.

"You're kidding."

"Blew the egg money for Pearl's birthday. Both of them ordered scallops, something they'd never had before, and Jimmy Fisher suggested a wine to go with it. Said it was the best meal they'd ever had." Kenneth looked over the articles in the warning. "Any surprises this year?"

"I haven't heard of any," Ellen said. "Archie stopped by the store last Friday and seemed to have some concern about the highway contract, but other than that…" Ellen pulled yarn out of her bag and continued to knit. "He says he's moving along with the house purchase. It's funny, but now we've established the new order he stops by to chat now and then, just to talk things over. He seems quite relaxed and okay with the way things turned out. I haven't heard about Rite-Aid in months."

Increase rapped the gavel on the stroke of nine and the meeting began. It was routine business. The housekeeping articles passed smoothly without serious discussion. The school budget went first and even that, which often generated heated discussions over value for money, was passed easily. Mary Louise Turner was up front and ready to defend her request for classroom computers with a hookup to the Internet, but aside from a couple informational questions, her budget passed easily.

"Change is in the air," Ellen said when they broke for lunch.

"You think so?" Kenneth said.

"If there had been a request for computers a year ago it would have been cut out first thing. There's a different mood, a sense of – well, hope, something we've not had here for a long time."

Archie settled down across the table from them.

"How you guys doin'?" he asked but didn't wait for an answer. "Generous mood today, givin' the school computers. Who'da thought that'd ever happen?" A large portion of Warren's scalloped potatoes was on his plate. "You two have a good time while you was gone?"

Kenneth braced himself. This was the sort of setup Archie was famous for. Come in all friendly and then ask a question that would be impossible to answer without being cornered. He and Ellen hadn't announced to anyone they were going away, they'd just gone.

"Very nice," Kenneth said. "After the year I put in and that bitter cold in January, three weeks in Jamaica was just the ticket. It was fun to show Ellen someplace outside Vermont," he added, just to be clear that they had indeed gone away together.

"Well, that's good," Archie said. "I always wanted Ellen to be happy. Don't think I was ever able to deliver on that. She had to put up with a lot."

Kenneth was speechless. He'd actually been given Archie's blessing.

"Few things happened while you was gone," Archie said. He'd picked up some of the Thai noodles. "Warren said you brought this. Thought I'd try it out." He wound up some noodles and Kenneth watched as the pepper crept around his mouth. "Whoa. A little fire in there, ain't there?"

"A bit."

Archie drank his glass of water.

"Dot Brooks sold the diner to Emily Squires and Helen Roberts you hear that?"

"I knew she was thinking about it," Ellen said.

"Ayuh, sold the diner and bought a double-wide down in Florida. No more Vermont winters for Dot."

"Good for her," Kenneth said.

"Oh, and I finally got out of being festival chairman. What a relief that is."

"You're out, then?" Ellen asked.

"Still on the committee, but not in charge of anything. Feels pretty good to tell you the truth"

"Have they found someone else to take it on?"

"They're thinking they might ask Diane," he said.

"Diane?" This was Kenneth.

"They like the way she runs the hotel and they want some new leadership. Tie the Intercourse House to the fair somehow."

The meal over, folks took their seats for the second half of the meeting.

"Archie looks as if he's gotten a little sun," Kenneth said to Ellen as they settled in.

Town business was first up when they reconvened. Before the budget items came up there was the issue of elections to the Board of Selectmen. Archie was up for a three-year term. Dennis Coombs, the undertaker, Grace Boyden, Leonard Harrison, a banker, and Norris Peach were all competing for the three one-year terms. The article was read.

"Mr. Moderator." Warren Thurber was on his feet.

"Mr. Thurber."

"Move for paper ballot."

"Second," someone said.

"Any discussion?" Increase asked.

"Move to question."

There were seldom contests for the various offices and they were usually determined by a voice vote but since there is always a possibility of a request for paper ballots Anna Gardner had them prepared. It took over an hour to hand out ballots as people were checked off the voter list, and then tally the results. Finally, the counting was finished and Increase rapped the meeting back to order.

"Does the clerk have the results of the vote?"

"Yes, sir." Anna said. "For the one-year seats, Dennis Coombs, Grace Boyden, and Norris Peach."

Applause all around.

"For the three-year seat," she continued, "Archie Whitaker, running unopposed, received 97 votes." The house began to applaud but Anna held up her hand. "However, there appears to have been a write-in campaign and after counting this contest twice, I declare that Kenneth Forbes has won this three-year seat with 103 write-in votes."

The applause began and people were on their feet. Kenneth was stunned. Ellen put down her knitting. Warren Thurber pulled Kenneth to his feet and then onto his chair.

Kenneth, dazed, was held steady by Ellen and Warren. As the applause wound down Kenneth's head cleared enough to focus on faces around him. At the front of the room Archie, who had been so jovial during the lunch break, glared at him and absently rubbed his left ear.

"Well, I'm not quite sure what to say," Kenneth began. The room was still. "When I left Grants Ferry," he said finally, " – ran away, actually – I had no intention to ever come back. And yet, when I first drove into town again, it was all familiar – all familiar but thirty years older." A bit of laughter. "The boy who left came back to find everyone had aged but him." Several people cleared their throats while he stopped to gather his thoughts.

"It's been an exciting and risky year. Frankly without the help of the folks who turned up to help us finish the hotel in December it would have been a disaster. There are probably still people who I've yet to thank properly. Simon and I had many things in New York – property, mostly – but with all the people we came to know there we never had the kind of friends who would give so many hours, and at Christmas time, to help someone in trouble. I can never thank you enough.

"I want to say, too, that it's been a privilege to be able to find most of our employees here in the community. Our goal was always to hire local folks and give them training they can take anywhere."

He paused again as images of the past year and years past whirled inside his head.

"The night I graduated from high school down in Springfield, all those years ago, the speaker called on us to contribute, to give back, to build a strong community, better than the one we were born into. I ran away from that challenge in the wee hours of the next morning."

He could easily tell the whole story again but he needed to wrap it up.

"I've only been back a little over a year now, still settling in, really, and what I know is, the Selectboard needs and deserves someone who knows the town, knows the people, and knows the ropes. I'm honored, but it's not me, it's Archie."

Some murmuring began but Kenneth held up his hand.

"In all fairness, if Archie's going to have competition when he runs for public office he deserves to know in advance. For that matter, if I'm going to be elected, so do I." They laughed then and there were nods of agreement. "So thank you all."

Kenneth started to get down from the chair but Warren held him and slowly rotated him full circle while the applause rose up again. At the front of the room, Archie stood, gave Kenneth a thumbs up, and joined in.

His ear didn't tingle at all.

*

Other work by David Chase

A Peasant of West Brattleboro

It's available only in hard copy and can be purchased the old fashioned way. Send your name, address, and $10 to:

David Chase, P of WB, PO Box 914, Keene NH 03431

Postage is free in the United States. If outside the US, write for pricing.

*

As Fair As You Were

David's 3 Act play, premiered in the spring of 2009 at the Eastern Star Grange in Dummerston Center, Vermont.

A free PDF reader copy of ***As Fair As You Were*** can be downloaded at
http://www.plays4theatre.com/bookdetails.php?pr=800

Scripts and world-wide performance licensing are available from:
http://www.plays4theatre.com

About the Author

David Chase is a native of Brattleboro, Vermont. Over the years he has performed in community theater, worked as a carpenter, a truck driver, and a wine sales person, among other things. He served for ten years on the Brattleboro Planning Commission, was a founding member of BCTV Channel 8 in Brattleboro, and he wrote a weekly column for the *Brattleboro Reformer* and the *Keene Sunday Sentinel* for several years. In 1987 he published a collection of pieces from his column in ***A Peasant of West Brattleboro***. He spent a one month residency at The Millay Colony for the Arts in 1989. His three-act play, ***As Fair As You Were***, was produced by Vermont Theatre Company in 2009. In addition to his life in Brattleboro he has lived in Sonoma County, California, and Hannington, Northamptonshire, England. He and his wife Susan now live in Keene, New Hampshire.

Grants Ferry is David's first novel.

Made in the USA
Charleston, SC
15 November 2016